IN THE MIND OF A SPY

The Mind Sleuth Series Book 7

Bruce M. Perrin

First Edition

Cover Art by Courtney M. Perrin

Visit the Author at

brucemperrin.com

Mind Sleuth Publications

ISBN-13: 978-1-955114-08-0 (ebook)
ISBN-13: 978-1-955114-09-7 (paperback)

Contents

SUNDAY, JUNE 30

Early Evening, Jesse Bolger's Home, Denver, CO

Jesse Bolger swung his legs out of the taxi and rested them on the ground, his head still humming from the nearly ten-thousand-mile flight from Singapore. He handed over eighty dollars for the last thirty miles of his commute, just glad his feet were back on American soil and his bed was a mere twenty yards away. He felt like he could sleep for a week.

But as he opened the front door to his three-bedroom rental home in the Washington Park neighborhood, Jesse knew his sleep was going to take another hit. Sitting there in the entry hall were two of Loren's suitcases. That wasn't everything his live-in girlfriend had brought with her a year ago, but he figured the collection was symbolic rather than exhaustive.

Like most of Jesse's relationships, this one had started off cautiously but had soon become passionate. They'd hardly been able to keep their hands off each other. But unlike most of them, this one had lasted ... well, until now. Apparently, his grueling travel schedule had finally taken its toll.

They'd had their talks about his priorities, but afterward, he'd always lied to himself. The two-week trip in March was an outlier; it wouldn't take that long the next time. In May, he'd hardly made it home at all, but he couldn't possibly be that unlucky again, could he? But June was nearly as bad. So now Loren was going to handle the problem herself. She didn't like confrontation, but she liked spineless avoidance even less, especially when she was the one who was sneaking around. She would never slip away when he was out of town.

"A four-day trip, huh?" Loren said as she appeared at the other end of the entry hallway.

"I know. It should have been, but things got complicated. The customer wanted a server farm with equipment specifications that no one could match ... well, not yet anyway. We had to go back to the requirements and ...."

Loren held up a hand. "I know. You told me all about it in your text messages and phone calls." She paused a moment. "And I do appreciate you calling at all hours of your day." Singapore was fourteen hours earlier than Denver, so to call her at 7 o'clock at night on Monday, he'd be phoning at 9 o'clock on Tuesday morning.

"Just like you not being able to buy computers that don't exist, we can't build a life if you don't exist in a world we share," she said. "And if the last year is any indication, we only live together two weeks out of every five or six."

Jesse grimaced, knowing she was right. "It won't always be this way." But now, it was his turn to hold up a hand. "I know. I've said that before and no, I don't know exactly when things will change, but they will."

The conviction he'd felt when he'd said that in the past, however, was slipping away. His travel during the first two years on the job had been manageable, but during the last four, he'd practically lived out of his suitcase. The truth was starting to overshadow all the lies he told himself.

"Hopefully, the next woman you find will have more patience," said Loren, "but I can't put so much of my life on hold." She paused, her eyes narrowing. "Why are you wearing a long sleeve shirt? It was 90 degrees here today, and Singapore is always hot, isn't it?"

"And humid," replied Jesse. "Basically, Singapore only has two seasons: wet, which runs from March to August; and dry, which is the rest of the year, but the humidity is always off the charts. That's why I picked up this shirt at the airport. Nothing I had left was fit to wear." Jesse slowly shook his head. "Sorry, you didn't ask for a monolog on Singapore weather."

There was only one person who could make him retreat into trivia while he hoped for a reversal of fortunes, and he was looking at her. It was just one of the many ways he knew that he loved Loren. But then, love doesn't always conquer all, despite what all the films, songs, and books might say.

"You're a great guy," Loren said.

"And you're a wonderful woman."

"Thanks," she said, her lower lip quivering slightly.

His response had slipped out before he could think as his words had obviously hurt her. Even so, for an instant, Jesse considered making more promises he most likely couldn't keep. But he knew Loren. He knew she would have her let-down speech prepared and practiced, and all he could really do was make it harder for her. As much as it tore at his heart, he had to let logic win over emotion. He had to keep his mouth shut and let her have the end she needed.

"Unfortunately, even two great people don't always end up with a great life together," Loren said. "I'm moving out and I'm asking you to stay away from me. It'll only end up making things worse."

His gaze dropped to the floor. He didn't have to feign the pain. He felt it. When he looked up, he said, "I'll respect your wishes."

She nodded, her jaw now set in determination.

Jesse looked at the luggage. "Is this your first load?"

"My last. I moved the rest of it earlier. I was lucky enough to find a couple of other teachers who needed a roommate and they helped with the move."

Roommates? That made sense. Denver was an expensive place to live, and she'd had roommates before she had moved in with him. "Well, at least I can help you move those bags to your car."

"I sold the car," Loren replied. "I needed the cash until school starts since my parttime job won't pay the bills. Once I get back to teaching, I'll have the money to cover rent."

"But how are you going to get to work without wheels?" He knew the moment he asked that it was wasted breath. Loren would have a plan. She always did, mentally repeating himself. But then, he needed the reassurance.

"My new place is close by. If the kids can walk to school or to the bus stop, so can I. As for the last load, one of my roommates will be here any minute."

"Can I give you a good-bye hug?"

"I'd be disappointed if you didn't."

It seemed he'd only just wrapped his arms around her when someone knocked on the door. Neither of them said a word as they stepped back from the embrace. After a short gaze at each other during which Loren looked like she might break into tears and Jesse knew he felt the same anguish, she went to the door and opened it.

Jesse carried the two bags to the door and deposited them at the feet of the woman who stood there. Loren didn't offer an introduction and the roommate didn't volunteer her name. Perhaps one look at the two of them told her all she needed to know as she took one of the bags, turned, and left.

"I hope you find all you're looking for because you deserve it," Jesse said.

Loren had bent down to take the last bag but stood up when he spoke. Her eyes were misty with the effort to control her emotions. "Thanks," she said and placed a soft kiss on his cheek. She picked up the remaining piece of luggage and left.

When the door closed, he leaned back against it, now grateful that he was exhausted. At least his fatigue gave him a fighting chance at some sleep. Otherwise, he'd be up all night wondering if there wasn't another way, pondering if he shouldn't change jobs. Maybe he could even quit. But that made no sense. He'd be broke in two months.

Eventually, Jesse picked up his suitcase and moved to the bedroom. He sat on the bed, kicked off his shoes, and removed his shirt. A warm shower would remove some of the grime of too many hours in airport lounges and stuffed into airplane seats. He stood and looked at himself in the mirror. There weren't many positives of Loren leaving him, but as he gazed at the reflection of his left arm, he muttered to the empty room, "At least I don't have to lie about all these scratches."

MONDAY, JULY 1

Morning, Ruger–Phillips West, Denver, CO

"Good work," said Miles Sennett for the fourth time. "I know it got a lot more complicated than we'd expected before you came up with a solution, but it's ingenuity like that that'll get you ahead."

"Thanks, Miles," Jesse replied for the fourth time. He couldn't quite understand why his boss was going on about it so much. Wasn't it always the case that he came, he saw, he solved?

"And I'm really sorry about Loren," added Sennett.

Ah, there was the reason. "How'd you know?"

"It's my job to know," replied Sennett, nearly eliciting an eye roll from Jesse. "OK, Loren called. She thought perhaps I should know, which is pretty damn thoughtful for a girl I only met a few times. You want to take a day or two off? I'm sure I could swing some paid leave if you don't have any vacation left."

"Yeah, she is thoughtful that way. As for the time off, thanks for the offer, but no. I have plenty of vacation, but the last thing I want is to sit at home with nothing to do but feel sorry for myself."

"Well, rest up enough to get over those injuries to your arm. I'm sure it'll be in your report, but what happened again?" asked Sennett.

"It's no big deal," replied Jesse. But when his boss frowned, he knew that wasn't going to be enough explanation.

"We'd traced the data leak to some components that were locked in a floor vault, but no one had the combination. They finally decided they didn't care if the electronics inside were destroyed, so we drilled our way in. Unfortunately, I got a little too close while they were working, and some flying debris grazed my arm."

"Well, I'm glad it's nothing serious," said Sennett. "Like usual, we've got a lot of work pending. When you're done with the paperwork on Singapore, let me know and we'll get you lined up. Right now, I'm thinking the Farrar case."

Jesse had vaguely heard of it—mostly that it was a bitch that would probably tax all his skills—but that was perfect for his current frame of mind. "Sounds good, boss."

"Great," replied Sennett. "And again, I'm sorry about Loren."

Sennett had previously held the same job as Jesse now occupied, which, at least in Jesse's mind, made them closer than most superiors and their subordinates. The man understood how tough this occupation was on relationships. But the condolences had gone on too long for him, and Sennett seemed to sense that as he launched into small talk—the local sports scene, the weather, the happenings at Ruger-Phillips West.

The parent company, Ruger-Phillips, was headquartered in St. Louis, Missouri, and employed a few thousand people. The local staff in Colorado, however, numbered in the hundreds and mostly worked for contractors attracted to the area by the local military bases or at the bases themselves—Buckley Space Force Base, Fort Carson, Schriever Space Force Base, Peterson Space Force Base, and the United States Air Force Academy. Those employees, in turn, had their fingers in military development and training projects worldwide, making virtually every RPW employee in marketing or procurement frequent fliers on every commercial airline departing Denver International Airport.

By job title, Jesse was in procurement, or, as everyone inside RPW called them, he was a buyer. And because of that, he was an elite-level frequent flier on two different carriers and had a few thousand miles on a third.

As Sennett talked, Jesse noticed that his boss was avoiding any mention of his wife and two daughters, which was unusual for him. Perhaps he felt that mentioning them would highlight Jesse's loss, but he felt otherwise. His boss had moved into his current supervisory position after ten years on the job, which meant Jesse had four more years if he followed the same trajectory. At that point, he'd be thirty-five and Loren would be thirty-two ... although he wondered why he bothered with the mental math. No woman as attractive and intelligent as her would be around after that much time. Better for both of them if he just forgot her, not that it would be easy.

"Anything else before I let you get back to work?" Sennett asked after bemoaning the effect the current dry spell was having on his lawn and reveling in a winning home stand by the Colorado Rockies baseball team over the weekend.

"No. That's about it," Jesse said, only too happy to draw this meeting to a close. His body was confused after his halfway-around-the-world travel yesterday, and this morning, he couldn't muster any appetite for breakfast. But about an hour ago, he had become famished, and he was starting to wonder if Sennett would ever finish.

He left the building at a fast walk, jumped in his car, and broke a half-dozen speed limits before he reached his favorite sandwich shop, Philly Pete's. He skidded to a stop in their parking lot and exited the car.

As Jesse was making his way to the front door, a stocky man materialized from a patio on one side of the building. He was wearing black jeans, black sneakers, and a black hooded windbreaker with the hood up. While the temperatures had cooled some from the nineties the day before, he appeared seriously overdressed for the weather. And in Colorado, where people wore shorts until the temperatures retreated to forty degrees or below, he seemed positively out of place. But to each his own, thought Jesse.

As they were headed directly at each other, Jesse veered slightly to his left, but the man adjusted his path to put them back on a collision course. So, he tried a second correction, only to see the man again heading directly at him. Had this moving obstacle been female, Jesse might have chuckled and said, "Care for another dance?" But it didn't seem all that funny when said to a man. And besides, he was getting irritated by the hurdle the man had become between him and his favorite sub sandwich.

Jesse stopped in the middle of the parking lot. His counterpart, however, didn't, and he bumped into Jesse's shoulder, mumbling, "Oh, sorry." At the same instant, he pushed a slip of paper into Jesse's hand. Reflexively, Jesse drew back, his free hand forming a fist at his side ... just in case.

"What are you …" Jesse started to say but stopped when a ray of the noonday sun penetrated the shadow of the man's hood. "Dink, is that you?" He cleared his throat. "I mean Bobby. Bobby Gleason. I haven't seen you since …."

"Probably not since high school graduation," he replied softly. "And it's Robert. Or Dink, if you prefer."

Robert/Dink Gleason had moved into Jesse's neighborhood on the outskirts of Denver during his junior year in high school. The nickname, which had been bestowed on him in the showers after his first PE class, was cruel. But rather than letting it bother him, Gleason had embraced it. Apparently, it was almost flattering compared to the monikers he'd been given at his previous school; he had commented often about how much more friendly and accepting people were in his new surroundings. All Jesse could figure was that his last high school must have been a real hellhole.

Gleason scanned the surroundings for a moment, finally turning back to Jesse to say, "Sorry that my tradecraft isn't better, but we can discuss that later."

"Tradecraft? What are you talking about?"

Jesse started to raise the note to his eyes, hoping it might explain things, when Gleason said, "Read it later. You never know who might be watching."

At that point, Jesse was sure this was all a joke played by an old friend. "Yeah, Philly Pete's is quite the hotbed of international intrigue."

"Really?" replied Gleason, his gaze again tracking across his surroundings. "Thanks. I'll keep clear of the place in the future." And with that, he turned and scurried off.

Not really sure what to make of the encounter, Jesse started to raise Gleason's note again but stopped. It wasn't so much that he thought the walls of the sandwich shop had eyes as it was a simple request to wait from an old acquaintance. What was the harm in a few minutes delay?

But leaving matters hanging wasn't in Jesse's DNA. Or, as some of his friends had put it, he just didn't know when to quit. He still recalled, with a chuckle, freshman-year art class in high school where he couldn't seem to stop his hand from dabbing at a watercolor painting until all the colors had run together, leaving a muddy, brown blob in place of a sunset.

So, true to his nature, Jesse went back to his car. Once seated inside, he pulled his phone from a pocket and held it up high as if he was having trouble finding a signal. Then, he lowered the phone and looked past it toward the note that was now lying in his lap. There wasn't much to read—just his first name, an address, and the words, "8 o'clock tonight."

"Strange," he muttered to himself. Why would someone he had hardly known in high school want to meet now? They had little in common thirteen years ago and even less today. Maybe it was a surprise birthday party? The trouble with that guess, however, was that his birthday was still a month away and none of his current friends, who were few and far between, knew Gleason. The chance that any of them had bumped into him and had discovered they had a common acquaintance seemed exceedingly unlikely. And then, that they would take it upon themselves to organize a party pushed the idea squarely into the absurd category.

There was also that term—tradecraft—that had caught Jesse's attention. It commonly referred to the methods used by spies, but why had Gleason used it in this situation? Perhaps he was using a cloak and dagger story to drum up potential customers for whatever he was selling these days ... if he was selling anything. In place of a fancy dinner at an exclusive restaurant, Gleason was probably peddling aluminum siding over stories of James Bond and cheese and crackers in his home. But if this invitation was something like that, then he was walking around with these notes in his pocket, waiting for an unsuspecting potential customer he knew to come along.

Overall, it seemed more likely that this encounter had been carefully planned and precisely timed. It wouldn't have been hard for Gleason to learn his routine; he came here most days when he wasn't traveling. But even so, why would the man have studied his movements to find a time and place to slip him an invitation to meet when a simple phone call, text, or email would work just as well?

Jesse was feeling a bit frustrated, slowly shaking his head as he glanced at the note one last time. When all was said and done, the act of reading it, which was supposed to answer his questions had only raised more. Well, it had also taken the edge off his hunger, as his body had slipped back into Singapore time where it was the middle of the night.

Finally, Jesse decided to return to work, grab something at the lunchroom he could munch on in the afternoon, and immerse himself in problems that had solutions. Surely, after tonight, he'd look back on this strange encounter with a chuckle. After all, the alternatives he had running around in his mind were nothing more than another brown blob produced by a mind that just wouldn't stop dabbing at his latest watercolor mental image.

Evening, Robert Gleason's Home

Jesse checked the map display on his phone again, confirming that the gated community he was about to enter included the address his old schoolmate had given him. It hardly seemed possible. If their high school had given an award for The Most Likely to Be a Failed Entrepreneur, Gleason would have won hands down. He always had plans; practicality, however, never figured into them.

Of course, it wasn't like those high school awards were prophetic. Jesse knew that his high school's Class Clown was now the mayor of a city of a quarter-million people, The Most Athletic had gained 150 pounds and could be found in a local bar most nights of the week, and The Most Unforgettable was serving fifteen to twenty in an Alabama prison—who could forget that? Apparently, Gleason was just another exception that made the rule if this was where he lived.

Jesse pulled up to the guard station, gave Gleason's name and address, and the gate swung open. After a short drive through the darkened streets, he parked and examined the house through his passenger's window. It was a one-story ranch house, and it was as neat as a pin.

Neat as a pin? Jesse hadn't thought of that phrase since ... well, it must have been twenty or more years ago. It had been one of his great aunt's favorites, but she had passed away when he was in fourth or fifth grade. But thinking about her also explained why those words had come to mind; the house looked a bit like her home with a double-car garage on the right and the living space to the left. The lawn was meticulously maintained and was bisected by a curving stone pathway from the front sidewalk to a porch that sat in darkness. Even so, Jesse could make out the outline of two rocking chairs that sat there.

To him, it felt like this home was stuck in the past, which meant, as Gleason's home, it looked ... all wrong.

Jesse thought back to their brief encounter earlier in the day. Gleason had been dressed all in black and he was pretty sure it wasn't a fashion statement. There had been a smudge of something that looked like powdered sugar on the shoulder of the windbreaker and one of his sneakers was untied. He had a three-day growth of stubble on a face so pale it seemed like it rarely saw the light of day and his hair was long and stringy. This house, on the other hand, looked like it should belong to someone neatly shaved and dressed in a button-down shirt and cardigan sweater.

But as the image formed, Jesse mentally kicked himself for such lazy thinking because he knew better. His image of the house's owner was basically a stereotype—a "Mister Rogers" stereotype if he was to put a name to it. And stereotypes describe no specific individual perfectly while potentially introducing biases into the overall impression that they helped form. He didn't think that in a week, he would recall Gleason singing *Won't You Be My Neighbor* in the Philly Pete's parking lot, but a host of more subtle inaccuracies? Absolutely, that was possible.

And besides, couldn't someone who took little pride in their personal appearance keep his home immaculate? Or maybe Gleason's attire this afternoon had been part of a disguise? He wanted to look a little unkempt because ... well, Jesse didn't know why he thought he needed a disguise, but that was why he was here.

He started for the front door, but after a few steps up the pathway, the garage door opened and a woman stepped out. "Are you Jesse Bolger?" she asked.

"I am. Is Robert around?"

"He is. But he wanted me to ask if you'd put your car in the garage. Something about prying eyes, although I have no idea why anyone would care who visits him."

"It's nice to meet you, Ms. Gleason."

She laughed softly. "Thanks for taking twenty years off my age, but I'm Robert's grandmother on his mother's side, Olive Majoris."

Jesse ran through his possible comebacks, rejecting "And I was thinking you might be offended because you are his sister." It was a bit too corny—and sounded like he was flirting with her—so he went with, "It's nice to meet you, Ms. Majoris."

Admittedly, Jesse was both surprised and vindicated by Majoris's revelation. Even though the woman was backlit by a light from inside the garage, she didn't seem like a grandmother. There was a spring in the few steps she had taken down the driveway and her voice was melodic with a touch of amusement. The vindication, on the other hand, came from the fact that she much more closely fit the stereotype he'd entertained earlier. Even though his impression was still undoubtedly mistaken in many details, she was the Ms. Rogers of this neat-as-a-pin home.

He got back into his car and parked it in Majoris's garage. But when he started to exit his car, a very large dog came out of the shadows behind the woman. Jesse slid back into the driver's seat so that a quick car-door slam would put a metal barrier between him and one of the largest canines he had ever seen.

The dog sat down beside the woman, his eyes focused on Jesse in a steady stare. He seemed to be making up his mind, friend or foe? Majoris dropped a hand to the dog's head, his body seeming to relax with her touch. "This is Charlie, Robert's dog. He's an Anatolian Shepherd, or at least, partly one. A friend gave it to him, probably so he could cut his food bill in half. But Robert loves Charlie ... and I'm sort of fond of him, too."

"Hi, Charlie." But even Jesse could hear the uneasiness in his tone.

"Don't worry. Once he sees that you're OK with me and Robert, he'll be your best friend."

Majoris turned and walked to a door in the back of the garage with Charlie on her heels. Jesse followed. They passed a laundry room before entering the kitchen. Charlie kept glancing back as if to check that he wasn't up to some mischief.

"Robert, honey. Jesse's here," Majoris called toward the back of the house. She turned around as Charlie resumed his scrutiny by her side.

"You have a very nice home," Jesse said although he'd missed most of it in his efforts to keep the massive dog in sight.

"Why, thank you, Jesse. It's part of a 55+ community with lots to do. In fact, I'm off to bingo as soon as Robert gets up here. Speaking of which, where is that boy?" She turned and called again, "Robert, I'm leaving in a minute."

It hadn't completely registered with Jesse, but now that she'd mentioned that it was a retirement community, it made sense. Exterior maintenance was probably covered in their Homeowner Association fees, as the coordination of house colors and the consistency of the grounds now seemed apparent ... even from what he had seen in the meager rays from the streetlights. The houses were also similar in what they didn't have—toys on the front lawn, yard art, and political signage.

"Hey, Grams," said Gleason as he hurried into the kitchen. It was Charlie who reacted first. He jumped up on his hind legs, his front paws coming to rest on Gleason's shoulders. Jesse thought the dog might knock his old friend over, but it was apparently their standard greeting. Gleason just laughed and pressed his forehead against the dog's while he scratched him behind the ears. After a moment, the dog dropped to the ground and Gleason came over and slapped Jesse on the back. That seemed the final piece of evidence that Charlie needed to decide that the visitor had come in peace. He came over and sniffed Jesse's hand, then licked it with a tongue large enough to cover every square inch of skin in one pass.

"Sorry we can't visit for a while," said Gleason, "but Jesse and I need to talk downstairs."

"Honey, I told you I was going out. It's bingo night."

"I thought that was Wednesdays?"

"No, Wednesday is Mahjong. Bingo is on the calendar." She waved a hand at a sheet of paper held to the refrigerator with magnets. Every square had an entry, most with two or three. "You really should start putting your activities on there, too. I wouldn't have remembered to make you young men some snacks if you hadn't been talking about this for the last week."

Jesse was expecting her to pull out a carton of milk and cookies when she produced a bottle of wine and a tray of hors d'oeuvres—cheeses, finger sandwiches, tiny cakes. Gleason took the plate with a simple, "Thanks."

"You shouldn't have," Jesse added, "but they look great. I can never find decent finger food when I need it. Where'd you get it?"

"Same place as always—my kitchen. I figured you young men might need a bite. After all, saving the world can be hungry work. But I need to get going. Honey, don't wait up. Jesse, it was nice to meet you."

"Likewise," Jesse managed to say, although he was still marveling over the precision and symmetry of the handmade hors d'oeuvres. And the smell was making him hungry, even though he had eaten only a few hours earlier.

After she left, Gleason started down a hallway toward the back of the house, Charlie on his heels. Jesse noticed that the dog had stopped turning around to look at him, which might have been more proof that he was in the dog's good graces. More likely, however, Charlie was just more interested in the food in Gleason's hand than any threat that he might pose.

"I can't believe your grandmother made all of this for us."

"Yeah, she can be sort of cheap that way. Probably the effect of the Great Depression. And I keep telling her that those little mini-pizza rolls are better than most of this stuff. But these stuffed mushrooms aren't bad," he said, holding out the plate.

Great Depression? That would put Majoris in her nineties, maybe even in triple digits if she had been old enough to remember those days. And to consider these delicious-looking homemade snacks "cheap," either in effort or cost, was clearly wrong. Hadn't Gleason ever gone grocery shopping? But before Jesse could pose any of those questions, he gave in to temptation and popped a mushroom into his mouth.

After that, all his questions were forgotten. "These are fantastic," said Jesse. Perhaps Charlie felt the same as he would swear that the dog looked sad when he ate it.

They reached a door at the end of the hall and Gleason opened it to a set of stairs to the basement. "Glad you liked it," he said as the three of them started the descent. "You're probably wondering what I'm doing back in Denver and living with my grandmother in a retirement community, but it's just temporary. In my current gig, I'll probably be looking for a place of my own in a year or two. Course, I'll still be around to help her with the heavy stuff. Like a couch some store dropped off in her driveway about four years ago. They said they rang the doorbell, but I never heard it."

"You've been back in Denver for four years?" It wasn't that Jesse thought Gleason should have gotten in contact with him—they hadn't been that close—but it seemed like their paths should have crossed at some point. Jesse was also a bit surprised that four years fit his definition of "temporary." But Gleason's next statement made the dissonance even worse.

"A little over five years, actually," he replied. "But time flies, as they say."

When Gleason opened the door at the bottom of the stairs, it was like entering another world. It wasn't a bachelor pad or a man cave, but more of a geek's lair. There was a large-screen television on the wall. Several worn but comfortable armchairs, a recliner, and a sofa were scattered around the space. There was a single bed and a door that Jesse suspected led to a bathroom. That much could have fit the bachelor-pad label nicely, but it was the rest of the décor that pushed this room into the world of a nerd. There were several racks of electronic equipment, most of which Jesse didn't recognize. There was also a workbench with test meters, soldering irons, and several sets of screwdrivers, pliers, and wrenches scattered around the top.

"A little different down here," Jesse said, understating the obvious. "So, why'd you ask me to park my car in your grandmother's garage?"

Gleason shook his head and put a single finger to his lips. "Let's chow down on these goodies," he said as he produced three paper plates, two plastic cups, and a roll of paper towels. He helped himself to one of everything and put a few snacks on another plate for Charlie. "Dig in, buddy, before Charlie wants his seconds."

After several moments of silence, save the sounds of chewing, sipping, and swallowing, Jesse said, "I have to ask. Is that some sort of technology collage?" He nodded toward an eclectic collection of switches, knobs, dials, display screens, and analog meters mounted on a board that hung on the wall. There was even a knife switch of the type used in the late 1800s and early 1900s. Jesse was halfway expecting another signal to keep quiet, but this time his old friend answered.

"That's the control panel for the cone of silence."

The only "cone of silence" Jesse had ever heard of was from the television series and movie, *Get Smart*, where it was a perpetually malfunctioning piece of technology that was supposed to keep conversations safe from potential eavesdroppers. But even without the reference to a comedic show, Jesse would have known that Gleason was joking; he was barely suppressing his snickers behind a hand raised to his mouth.

Finally, he said, "That's a piece of artwork my ex-girlfriend created for me. After a few visits to my humble abode, she came up with that. Pretty great, huh?"

"It is," Jesse replied. "She's really talented. Sorry you guys broke up, but the same just happened to me."

"Well, then you know how it is. Sometimes a guy's gotta do what a guy's gotta do."

Jesse couldn't quite figure out if his friend's statement was the circular drivel that it sounded or quite profound. Was his job what he had to do without regard to the effect it had on Loren? But as he watched Gleason pop the last of the hors d'oeuvre in his mouth and set the tray aside, he decided that was a question best left for private reflection.

"I'll tell her you liked it if I ever run into her again," said Gleason. "But a cone of silence, of a sort, is why I wanted you to come over here tonight. We need to talk and I've got the perfect place." Gleason raised a hand toward a cube of about six feet on a side. It was covered with a shiny fabric. "That'll keep our brain waves safe from prying sensors."

Jesse could feel himself scowling as he tried to make sense of the words. "Is that supposed to be something like a tinfoil hat?"

Now, it was Gleason's turn to look perplexed, but his confusion only lasted a moment. "Oh, yeah. Like people wear so the aliens won't listen in on their thoughts. That's pretty funny, but don't be ridiculous."

"Yeah, I didn't—" started Jesse.

"A tinfoil hat would only protect you from aliens who were directly overhead. I'm not too worried about them if they're still in the air. But on the ground ...." He slowly shook his head. "Now, that would be bad news. Really bad."

Jesse was struggling for a reply when Gleason continued. "Anyway, that's a SCIF, giving us protection on all sides."

"A SCIF?"

Gleason nodded.

SCIF stood for Sensitive Compartmented Information Facility, a fact that Jesse knew from his job. They were acoustically and electronically shielded rooms in which classified discussions could be held, and Ruger-Phillips West had several for their government projects. But Jesse had never heard of a private citizen owning one. "Where on earth did you find the stuff to build a SCIF?"

Gleason got one of those you've-got-to-be-kidding smirks on his face. "If you're not running cables in and out—and I'm not—then acoustic and radiation shielding are all you need. For the latter, just type 'EMF radiation shielding fabric' into any search engine and you'll find lots of it. I split my orders among a half-dozen stores so I wouldn't call attention to myself."

"Someone would care if you bought it in bulk?"

"Are you kidding? They care about everything you look at, everything you buy, and even what you don't buy. Sure, eventually they may piece it all together, but why make it easy on them? With a small purchase, they probably think I lined my billfold to keep someone from reading the data on my credit cards."

Jesse wasn't sure who "they" referred to, but that question only came in second. "So, you think whatever it is you have to tell me is so sensitive that you built a SCIF to discuss it?"

"Hardly," Gleason said with a laugh. Jesse started to return the chuckle when Gleason added, "I already had it before any of this came up."

Jesse figured his puzzled expression asked the question for him as Gleason explained, "I came to Denver because of that state representative who wanted to start the center for extraterrestrial communications. And, as he pointed out, the brain emits electromagnetic radiation in the form of brain waves. They are faint, and we have to put electrodes on the scalp to pick them up. But with more advanced civilizations ...?" Gleason held out an empty hand in a shrug. "Who knows?"

Jesse recognized the story about the state representative. It had been all over the news a few years ago with his potential re-election opponents' comments ranging from "it's a waste of the taxpayer's money" to "you can bet Uranus he's after the little green man vote." The representative had lost his seat in a landslide in the next election—extraterrestrial communication wasn't a platform that sat well with Colorado voters. "Well, I'm not sure—" Jesse started.

"Oh, I know he was a kook," said Gleason. He paused, his nose wrinkling a bit. It took a moment before the odor reached Jesse.

"Jeez, Charlie. I'm going to stop giving you those stuffed mushrooms," said Gleason. "It's either that or break out the gas masks."

Surprisingly, Charlie looked like he had been chastised as he whined once, then laid his head down on his paws and looked up at us with eyes that looked even sadder than before. If the stench hadn't been so bad, Jesse thought he might have laughed at the dog's expression.

"Anyway," continued Gleason, "you don't need to tiptoe around that guy. His ideas sounded good at first, but they never panned out. So, after a bit of this and that, I got started on my current gig, talking to the other sentient beings in our world."

"Animals? You're working on some type of job that involves communicating with animals?" Jesse glanced at Charlie, who, though he had seemed to understand before, now seemed as confused as Jesse felt.

Gleason paused a beat, then said, "Yeah, I suppose animals are sentient … in a way. But I meant computers. Computers with artificial intelligence."

Jesse could feel himself sit back in the chair as if another half-inch of distance between them would change his perspective. It didn't, and he wasn't sure what to say other than, "Oh, look at the time!" But Gleason spoke first.

"Yeah, not everyone thinks that machines are aware of the world around them. I think they are and that other people just haven't spent the time necessary to get to know these beings. But if AIs aren't aware yet, I'm fine with being ready to meet them when they are. And that's why I'm studying prompt engineering."

It was the last two words, "prompt engineering" that pulled this conversation back from the brink of irrationality for Jesse. Prompt engineering had been a growing technical discipline since the introduction of AI Large Language Models in late 2022. At its heart, the discipline involved designing and testing inputs that would get these systems to produce useful outputs for a given purpose.

"So, getting these LLMs to give you what you want is tricky?" Jesse asked. He was pretty sure he knew the answer but wanted to keep the conversation moving away from the question of machine sentience.

"It can be," replied Gleason. "They always produce answers that sound factual, but sometimes, they are just making stuff up. Those are called hallucinations. But more often, they just don't understand what you want."

Gleason paused a moment rubbing his chin. "You work on a lot of training projects, right? Enough that you know a lot of the principles?"

"I work the procurement end of them, but you can't do that without picking up a bit about the technology."

Gleason nodded. "So, suppose you wanted to know the best way to teach pilots the steps of an emergency procedure so they don't forget them in a pinch? If you ask an AI system that, I'd expect .... Better yet, let's ask and find out." He grabbed a laptop from the workbench and started to power it up.

"Do we need to go into the SCIF for this?" Jesse asked.

Gleason gave him a quizzical look, followed by, "No, why would we? And besides, I need the Wi-Fi, and it won't work in there."

After a moment, he opened an application on the laptop that Jesse recognized as part of a publicly accessible large language model. Gleason typed in a prompt about training pilots on emergency procedures, and in a second or two, the system responded.

Jesse skimmed the answer, somewhat surprised by what he saw. "You're right. The question you asked seemed right on the mark, but the AI took it to be something about getting information into human long-term memory. It covers things like breaking the procedure into small steps or using visual aids. I thought the real issue was more about how to make sure people can perform under stress and time pressure. That would get into making the pilot's reaction nearly automatic, something that he or she doesn't need to think about to do."

"I can't say that I understood everything you just said, but it seems I made my point," replied Gleason. "You gotta know how to talk to these beings."

Jesse had to admit that Gleason knew his way around the LLM-world with the ease he showed in producing the pilot-training example. And, if the software developers continued to build systems that they didn't fully understand and that they couldn't completely control, prompt engineering might be a key job for many years to come. On the other hand, the occupation might easily vanish as rapidly as it had appeared. All it would take was a little more transparency into the system's functioning, which seemed a minor development compared to what AI had already accomplished.

As for his beliefs that machines were or would soon be sentient, Jesse couldn't decide if that made Gleason the perfect prompt engineer or perfectly wrong for the job. Would the belief that he was talking to a sentient being make his prompts better or taint them with a touch of delusion ... assuming his belief was delusional? But getting to the bottom of that issue wouldn't answer what the heck Gleason was so anxious to tell him, and it was time to move on to that question.

"So, your grandmother thinks we're down here saving the world. Or was that just a figure of speech?"

Gleason chuckled. "Well, a bit of both, I suppose. I couldn't tell her everything; she likes to gossip too much. And the same goes for you unless we step in there." He raised a hand toward the SCIF.

"OK, let's do it," Jesse replied, grateful he wasn't claustrophobic. It would be a tight squeeze with both of them inside.

They got up and moved to the door, but before Gleason opened it, he turned back to his dog. "Sorry, Charlie, but you're going to have to wait out here."

Once again, Charlie adopted the poor-pitiful-me pose. Gleason turned to Jesse. "I just don't want to get trapped in there with him if he … well, lets loose with another gas attack."

Gleason started working a combination lock on the door. Jesse could see that it wasn't of the same level of security as the SCIFs at Ruger-Phillips, but still, the lock was substantial. It was also recessed into the door, making the use of a bolt-cutter on it difficult if not impossible.

When they moved inside, the décor shifted once again. They had gone from neat as a pin upstairs to industrial and cluttered in Gleason's domain to Spartan inside the SCIF. There was nothing there except a small wooden chair with a flip-up writing surface. It was up and there was a laptop resting on it. "Guess I'm going to need another chair in here if we keep doing this. But you can sit on the floor for now."

"I'll stand. But what's with the laptop? I thought there was no Wi-Fi in here?"

"There isn't. What happens in here stays in here. Sort of like Vegas, I suppose." He sat down at the desk. "What I have to tell you can't be repeated outside of this room."

Gleason paused as if waiting for a response, so Jesse said, "Sure."

Gleason paused again, his eyes narrowing. "I suppose that's not completely true—I mean about not repeating anything we talk about in here. After all, I've already told someone about what's going on. And there may be times when you'll need to talk about it, too. So, it's not really all that cut and dried, what you can say and what you shouldn't."

"Yeah, I got it," replied Jesse feeling somewhat impatient with Gleason's digression. "It's on a need-to-know basis."

"Exactly," said Gleason. "I've got to remember that phrase." He seemed lost in thought for a moment, then said, "Anyway, the reason we're sitting here inside this SCIF is because we are going to have to figure out a way to save the United States from Russian terrorists."

Evening, Robert Gleason's Home

Jesse should have sat down on the floor when the offer was made because that might have countered the feeling that the rug had just been pulled out from under him. "Save the United States?" was all he could think of to say, although perhaps he should have been relieved. At least the rest of the world wasn't in harm's way.

"Yeah, two Russian spies are going to destroy the U.S. economy unless we find a way to stop them."

"Russian spies?"

Gleason gave Jesse a look that seemed to say, can't you do anything besides repeat me? But after a shrug, he said, "Yeah, there's two of them. They discovered plans in some post–World War II documents about ways to destroy us, and they've turned rogue to carry them out. And before you say it, they're certain the plan will still work. They've checked it out."

"OK. What's the plan?"

"What, you think they're crazy? They aren't going to tell me that."

"I'm not sure why they would tell you anything," replied Jesse a bit more sharply than he'd intended. So, he took a moment and a breath. "Look, spies work secretly. Discovery is their enemy. The fact that you know anything about this supposed plan means that it's probably a hoax."

"You're good," replied Gleason with a grin that covered his face.

Jesse, however, couldn't quite figure out his friend's expression or his words. "What are you talking about?"

"Since we're in the SCIF, I can speak freely. Sorry, but I know who you are. I've been following you for a while, and even though your cover's good, your actions can only add up to one thing—you're a spy, too. Perhaps I should call you, Bolger, Mister James Bolger," he said in his best stage voice.

"Yeah, right," replied Jesse. "Where'd you ever get the idea that I'm the next James Bond?"

"Just look at the facts. First, you were in Brussels nine months ago right after that terrorist attack on the subway. And six months ago? You had a business trip to Berlin at the same time as a hostage standoff? And now you're just back from Singapore, which interestingly, is just an hour's flight from Malaysia. You know what happened there, don't you?"

Jesse did, but that was hardly the issue. "I have to go when and where the company is bidding work. That's my job." But something was bothering Jesse, and it took him a moment to realize what it was. "I don't even remember the dates of the older trips you mentioned, much less what else was happening in the world. How'd you know all that?"

"A passenger on your return flight from Berlin took a video of an argument between the cabin crew and another passenger. You were in the background. At the time, I just wondered if you'd been anywhere close to the hostage standoff. But after I got wind of these Russian spies, I started wondering if you'd been there for a whole other reason. As for the rest of your travels, I called your apartment and ended up having a nice chat with your girlfriend. Oh, I guess you said ex-girlfriend now. You didn't dump her because she spilled the beans, did you?"

"No, of course not. And there weren't any beans to spill to start with."

"Right," said Gleason with a wink. "You may have trouble remembering where you've been, but she doesn't."

Jesse knew Loren would recall his trips. They were, after all, what had killed their relationship. His expression must have been even more forlorn than he thought as Gleason said, "Sorry, buddy. The life of a spook has got to be hard on relationships."

"I wouldn't know," said Jesse. "I'm a buyer, and our travel is tough on girlfriends, too."

"What I can't figure out," said Gleason as if Jesse hadn't said anything, "is which agency you work for? One of the big five? CIA? NSA? DIA? Or maybe it's one so black that no one knows the name?"

"I work for RPW, Ruger-Phillips West."

"Ah, of course, you're sticking with your cover, James. I'll save you the trouble of denying the truth further; I won't mention your real occupation again."

"It's not a cover. I work in procurement. I even have an MBA to prove it."

"Printed on flash paper, no doubt." Before Jesse could object again, Gleason said, "Look, I understand. I have no need to know—see, I remembered the phrase."

Jesse was tempted to say that they had used it only about two minutes ago but didn't. After all, there was no reason to add some sanity to the discussion.

"I'm not sure your bosses would approve of you helping me anyway," continued Gleason. "But even if this doesn't become one of your official assignments, you have to help me. It takes a spy to catch one. Or in this case, to catch two."

Jesse knew that Gleason's ambitions in high school had been grandiose. One day he would aspire to the Oval Office; the next, he would decide to become a world-renowned composer. But, to the best of Jesse's recollection, his fantasies had always been limited to himself. Apparently, however, his imaginings now included everyone. He had, after all, believed the state representative who had wanted to set up a communications center for little green men.

But when Jesse paused to consider that idea, he had to admit that a small but sizeable portion of the politician's constituency had felt the same. And scientists were searching for and trying to communicate with intelligent extraterrestrial life all the time, weren't they? So, perhaps Gleason's interest in talking to space aliens was nothing more than open-mindedness to the possibility.

But then, Gleason had also thought that artificially intelligent machines were sentient. That was clearly delusional, right?

But perhaps not, Jesse admitted to himself. People were debating that issue worldwide, and the number of converts was growing slowly but steadily. It also seemed like those closest to these intelligent machines—those who researched and developed them—were not immune. In fact, it seemed like another scientist joined the chorus every month or two.

OK, his belief in machine sentience could be rationalized, too, but this fantasy that he was a spy? True, he had been in the vicinity of some hot spots over the past few years, but then, didn't that say more about the level of unrest in the world than his job? Apparently, not in Gleason's estimation.

But Jesse's thoughts got no further in that direction because when he looked dispassionately at what Gleason knew about him, he could see the reason. From that narrow window into his world, much of it supplied by his ex-girlfriend, Gleason's conclusion was inventive and a bit unusual, but not illogical. His runaway imaginings just meant that sometimes, his old friend would reach some strange conclusions.

But nowhere in Jesse's train of thought was the idea that it was his responsibility to set Gleason straight about these Russian spies. Someone else needed to supply a liberal dose of common sense. Someone else needed to show him the error of his ways. Didn't they?

But then, shifting responsibility to the ubiquitous "someone else," wasn't Jesse's style. Why shouldn't he help? Jesse knew he had a practical approach to life and a good dose of pragmatism would set the record straight. And what if Gleason was on to something? Surely there was no terrorist plot to destroy America orchestrated by two Russian spies, but the chance that his old friend had stumbled into a scam of some sort seemed considerably more likely. All the situation lacked at this point was the save-America-from-Russian-terrorists fund. Someone would even handle making the donation for him if he'd simply supply his credit card information. Jesse decided that he owed his old acquaintance some open-mindedness of his own.

"You come to a decision, James?" Gleason asked, rousing Jesse from his thoughts.

A decision? Mostly, but he had a few questions after he got one thing straight between them. "No more James, OK? It's Jesse."

"Whatever you say ... Jesse."

The way Gleason drew out his name like it was three syllables long might have made him laugh under different circumstances, but he was focused on debunking this terrorist myth at the moment. "So, first, have you taken ... well, whatever proof you have of this Russian spy plot to the authorities?"

"That's the problem. I don't have much beyond something in the papers and a couple of phone calls that only I heard. And ...." He paused for several seconds. "Look, I'll deny this if you tell anyone, but I went to a community college in Missouri for a semester and did weed once while I was there. Sure, it's been legalized for medical use now, but it wasn't then—not that I have a medical card anyway. So, I can't just go waltzing into some police station in Colorado and say a Russian spy ring is going to destroy us. The cops will put two and two together and I'll end up in a Missouri slammer."

Jesse wasn't sure how giving law enforcement a tip about Russian spies in Colorado would cause Gleason to spill his guts about trying marijuana once in Missouri, but then, this wasn't the first time he couldn't follow his friend's logic. And even if Gleason felt compelled to "come clean," no one would care. But convincing his friend of that would take time they didn't have. Better they get everything Gleason knew to the authorities as soon as they could.

"Look, you can't be holding back on—" Jesse started to say.

"No, you misunderstand. Everything I know, the feds know. I found an agent, Agent Edward Jenkins, and he's totally up to speed. Not that he believes a word of what I've told him, but at least NBC focuses on counterintelligence and won't care if I partook a couple of times in the long-ago past."

It was interesting to Jesse that smoking marijuana "once" had become "a couple of times" in the retelling. But there was a more pressing question in Jesse's mind. "NBC? The broadcasting company?"

"How do you do that?" asked Gleason.

Jesse paused a moment, massaging his temples with his fingertips in an attempt to reduce the dull ache that was growing there. Under the assumptions that NBC was an intelligence agency and that he was a spy, Gleason was probably in awe of his acting ability once again. Of course, convincing displays of bewilderment come easily when one is truly confused. So, since Gleason wasn't going to believe he wasn't a spy anyway, playing along was the simplest solution.

"Sorry, but there are a lot of agencies that are trying to keep America safe, and frankly, we don't always communicate as well as we should. Who are these guys?"

"Yeah, my bad," Gleason replied. "I'm all for limiting the crosstalk among the spooks. All we need is Big Brother who sees all and knows all. Even the idea makes my skin crawl. But anyway, NBC is the National Bureau of Counterintelligence. Almost seems like they should be NBCI, but maybe they all have to have three letters like CIA, FBI, DIA?"

It seemed like a rhetorical question to Jesse, and yet, Gleason was just staring at him. "I've never heard of any regulation like that." Nor had he ever heard of NBC. If it was a highly secretive organization, it seemed unlikely Agent Jenkins would have given Gleason the name ... unless the name was a ploy designed to keep him from asking even more questions.

"Yeah, it's probably just the politicians who want the three-letter names," said Gleason. "Who wants to say, we've got a billion dollars in appropriations for NBCI, when it could just be billions for NBC? Of course, you do have the Office of Intelligence and Counterintelligence, which uses four letters. And how about the Office of Intelligence and Analysis, which uses two letters, an ampersand, and drops the O entirely?"

His fascination with the reasons for three-letter acronyms seemed odd, but there was something even more strange in his statement it seemed to Jesse. "You know a fair amount about intelligence agencies."

"As Sun Tzu said in *The Art of War*, 'If you know the enemy and know yourself, you need not fear the result of a hundred battles.' I just like to know who's watching me ... or trying to, anyway. All the better to elude them. And besides, I'm a big fan of spy novels and movies."

The dull ache in Jesse's temples had become a full-fledged headache as he realized that this whole conversation was getting him nowhere. "Maybe we should get back to Agent Jenkins and what he said."

"He didn't say much, but at least he was interested enough to listen and open a case file."

For a split second, Jesse wondered if the case file was on Russian spies or on Gleason. Off the top of his head, he could think of a dozen reasons why it was probably the latter, but the thought was hardly the open-mindedness that he had promised to show his old high school acquaintance. So, not wanting to lead Gleason with a lot of specific questions—not that he knew what to ask anyway—Jesse said, "Why don't you start at the beginning and tell me how you got involved in all this?"

"Sure. It was about two months ago. I was reading the classified personal ads in the newspaper—"

"Classified personal ads?" Jesse had intended to keep quiet and let him talk, but the reference seemed too unusual to ignore. "You mean, like in a print newspaper? I didn't think they ran those anymore, what with all the services that are online."

"Of course, they still print them," replied Gleason, followed by a frown. "Well, maybe not in the big papers, but we have this local one that carries them. Anyway, I was having coffee and noticed one that was a bit strange."

"Do you still have it?"

"Sure," replied Gleason, "but I have it memorized. It said, 'US economy on the brink; it'll only take a nudge.' That was it except for a phone number, which by the way, was later disconnected. I thought it was probably just some financial planning service that was resorting to scare tactics, although that's not really a new approach for them. Or maybe it was an insurance agency or a funeral home where you could make arrangements in advance. More scare tactics. But the ad was odd enough that I called. I got a recording of some strange computer-altered voice. Obviously, something to keep me from doing a voiceprint."

"You can do voiceprints?" Again, Jesse's curiosity overrode his promise, and again he swore he wouldn't let it happen any more.

"Well, yeah," Gleason replied slowly. "I thought a voiceprint would be a good biometric password for my laptop, but it never panned out. With some settings, anything I said would unlock my computer. With others, I had to say the same thing a half-dozen times before I could get in. But even if it worked consistently, artificial intelligence has almost made this type of security obsolete anyway. AI-generated clone voices have gotten good enough to fool a lot of recognition systems, not to mention the poor guy who hands over a wad of cash because he thinks it was his cousin calling after he wrecked his car." Gleason shrugged. "At least it was only fifty bucks."

For once, Jesse was going to stick with his promise and not ask when Gleason added, "But all the same, if I got a good, high-quality sample of Boris talking, I'd give it to NBC. They'd have better filtering and analysis tools than me. And if he was in their databases, we'd have him."

"Boris? One of them is named Boris?"

"Yeah, Boris and Natasha."

Jesse almost laughed. "Aren't those names a bit ... trite?"

"Well, of course, those aren't ...." Gleason paused, another grin coming to his face. "Very good. Pretend like you don't know those are just aliases. And if you're with me on this, you'll have an opportunity to ask the man himself here in"—he raised an arm to check the time on his wristwatch—"another fifteen minutes. He's calling at 9 o'clock."

"Tonight? In fifteen minutes?"

"Correct," replied Gleason.

Jesse felt like saying, "Don't you think you should have told me this earlier?" But that would probably just lead to another digression, so instead, he asked, "What was in this voice-altered message?"

"Not much. It told me to leave my phone number and they would be in contact. So, I did. It was nearly two weeks later when Boris called and left a voicemail. I'd almost forgotten about the whole thing, but that computer-altered voice brought it all back. He said he'd call me at precisely 9 o'clock, just like the plan for today. So, I rigged up my phone to record the call.

I'll never forget the first words he said when he called. He said, 'Turn off the tape recorder.' You have any idea how he did that?"

If Jesse was going to help by taking the role of a spy—probably not his best decision, but it was the one he'd made—then he needed to get into character. "With the phone-tapping technology you can get commercially, I doubt Boris had any trouble detecting that you were recording." He thought that sounded pretty good—specific enough to sound like an explanation while actually saying nothing. "You still have the recording of what he said before you turned off the tape recorder?"

"Sure do," replied Gleason, and he played it.

It was pretty much as he had described. He answered when the phone rang. Boris said, "Turn off the tape recorder." Gleason tried to play dumb at first, saying, "What tape recorder?" Boris was quiet for several moments, then said, "Last chance." That was enough for Gleason and the recording ended.

"Too bad you couldn't get more, but understandable," Jesse said. "So, what was the conversation after that?"

"That's when he told me that he and Natasha had found plans to destroy America's economy, and they were going to carry them out unless I stopped them. I told him ...."

"Whoa. Just a second," said Jesse. "Do you have any idea why he would have told you about their plans? That's part of this whole thing that doesn't make sense to me." Well, that and most of the rest of it, too, but he wasn't going to say that.

"I think it's like that FBI employee turned double agent for the Soviet Union, Robert Hanssen. He thought the FBI had failed to recognize his abilities, so he turned to spying on us to prove his superiority. Boris and Natasha don't think the authorities can stop them, so they've turned this mission into something of a game."

Those kinds of feelings of superiority seemed a bit more common in murderers, thought Jesse. Weren't there several cases where a serial killer had contacted the police or a newspaper just to prove no one could catch him … until they did? But Gleason wasn't with law enforcement or the media. "Well, it might be a more interesting game if they'd contacted a reporter or the CIA directly. Or NBC, I suppose. All Boris and Natasha accomplished was to catch the attention of a soon-to-be prompt engineer."

"Who happens to have the great equalizer in the form of an old friend."

Even though Jesse was going to play along, that statement was going too far, and he started to object. Gleason, however, spoke first.

"Boris said they'd tried to get the authorities involved in the catch-me-if-you-can game, but without some specific threat, their calls just ended up with all the Elvis sightings and reports of underground cities."

"Underground cities?" So much for swearing that he'd stick to business. "Never mind. I suppose he didn't give you anything more specific?"

"No. Nothing."

"OK, back to that first call. After you stopped recording and Boris told you their plan, what did you say?"

"Pretty much what you just said—that it wouldn't be much of a game if I was the only opposition. He just laughed and said

I'd have as much chance as any decadent American agent. He's awfully sure of himself, but I wasn't certain it wasn't just a bluff. So, I told him I needed a practical demonstration—some sort of proof that he could do what he was threatening. That stopped him for a minute, but then, he gave me the time and date for the next call, which will be in"—he checked his watch again—"a little less than five minutes. We should get out of the SCIF so we don't miss it."

They exited with Jesse wondering what, if anything, was about to happen. Would someone actually call? If so, it was surely a hoax, right? He just hoped that whoever was on the other end of the line would give up the prank after a few questions. After all, wasting the time of law enforcement officials was a crime. Not that he thought Gleason would be in trouble—he was just reacting to the story he'd been told— but the prankster? That would be a different matter entirely, and hopefully, he or she would realize that and give up the ruse easily.

But then, Jesse supposed, there was an extremely slight chance that Gleason was actually onto something. After all, it had only been a few years since the FBI had revealed information about their Operation Ghost Stories, a decade-long campaign to identify Russian agents living in the United States. Those individuals had been trained and funded by the Russian Foreign Intelligence Service (SVR), while Gleason's story seemed to imply Boris and Natasha had been Komitet Gosudarstvennoy Bezopasnosti (KGB) sponsored. Jesse doubted that today's SVR agents would have any use for World War II documents ... or even if they knew where to find them.

But all in all, it seemed to Jesse that the best course of action was just to continue his charade. So, he turned an appraising eye to Gleason's lair. "Boris will be calling your smartphone, right?"

"That was the plan," Gleason confirmed, but then, his eyes narrowed. "I don't think it could be bugged since it's hardly been out of my sight." He rubbed his chin, his gaze moving to a corner of the room. "But maybe we should check anyway," he said when he looked back. He went over to a desk and returned with a paper clip with one loop straightened out. "Now, if I can just remember how to eject the SIM and SD card," he mumbled to himself.

After a few moments of fiddling with his phone, Gleason had them out and looked up at Jesse. "Last time I saw someone check a phone for a bug in the movies, the guy unscrewed the cover on the mouthpiece and dumped out some tiny electronic gadget with a wire attached to it for an antenna. I suppose things are a bit different nowadays."

Jesse chuckled. "A bit." Fortunately, he'd bought a new phone not long ago and recalled some of the specifics about these bits of technology. "It's possible to hack and reprogram sim cards, and if that's been done, there's nothing we can do about it in the next few minutes. But we can leave the SD card out, just in case it's part of the tap ... assuming the phone is how Boris is keeping tabs on you."

"Whatever you say, Jam.... I mean, Jesse. What next?" he asked as he reinstalled the SIM card.

"Have you noticed anything that seemed different? Something that didn't look right or that operated a little differently than you recalled?"

"Not that I can think of," replied Gleason after a moment.

"OK. Have you added or changed anything down here in the last month or so?"

"Are you thinking someone hid a listening device in something I bought?" Gleason asked.

"Possibly," said Jesse. "Or maybe it's a camera. I'm guessing you're worried about possible surveillance since you had me park my car in the garage."

"Yeah, I am. I'd guess Philly Pete's is the only place that gets more attention from Russian agents than my house. But as for someone breaking in and bugging my home or putting a camera in something I bought, I hadn't given that much thought."

Obviously, Gleason was thinking about it now as he was staring at every nook and cranny like he'd never noticed them before. After a moment, he said, "This mat here is pretty new," he said, pointing at a small rug near one of his armchairs. Then, he slapped his forehead with an open palm. "Not the place someone would hide a bug, is it? I might have stepped on it."

"It might be ruggedized," Jesse said. "And it's easy enough to fix for now." He picked up the mat and put it outside the door to Gleason's quarters.

Jesse thought that was the end of the search when Gleason said, "I almost forgot. I changed the light fixtures over the workbench and that was only a couple of weeks ago. That would be the perfect place to hide a camera or a microphone."

When they'd come downstairs, Jesse had noticed that the area was lit by banks of fluorescent lights, but the details hadn't registered. But now that he looked closer, he saw the magnitude of the problem. It wasn't just one or two sets of fluorescent bulbs, but four of them daisy-chained together. Two of the sets were directly over Gleason's workbench, while the other two provided light to much of the rest of his living area. There was no way they could check all of those fixtures in the few minutes they had remaining, which left cutting the power to them.

Gleason seemed to be thinking along the same lines. "We could just flip the switch. Unless the bug is battery-powered, that'll knock it out. And I have a couple of flashlights, so we don't have to sit in the dark."

"Good idea, but maybe not enough. I had an uncle who was an electrician, and he told me that a common mistake people make when wiring a switch is that they end up connecting the switch to the neutral rather than the hot wire. And if someone did that on purpose with your switch and there was a ground wire running to the lights, the bug could still work even with the switch off."

Apparently, Gleason considered himself an electronics tinkerer as he grinned. "So, we disconnect both the hot and neutral lines inside the switch box, and there's no way power gets to a camera or microphone."

"Exactly."

Gleason hurried over to a toolbox, rifled through it for a moment, and returned with a screwdriver, pliers, and two flashlights. He turned off the fluorescent lights and Jesse shined one of the flashlights on the switch. It only took Gleason a moment to remove the cover and pull the switch out.

"The black wire is connected to the switch," Gleason said, "which should be the hot wire. But since Boris or Natasha could have cross-wired this circuit someplace else, I'm going to disconnect it. The two white wires are connected with a wire nut. I'll separate them. With that done, the wires to the lights will be completely dead."

Gleason had kept working while he talked, and soon, one of the black wires was hanging loose from the switch and he was removing the wire nut. But as he pulled the white wires apart, one touched the black wire, producing a loud pop and a spark a quarter-inch long. All the remaining lights in the room—the backlight on a clock, the glow of rocker switches in power strips, the standby light on the television—went out.

"Are you OK?" Jesse asked, thinking he should have handled this step himself. Gleason had evidently developed an interest in electronics and had the tools to prove it, but Jesse couldn't help but wonder how often he ended up in exactly this situation. In high school, he was always the last person selected for games in physical education classes, and coordination didn't usually wait until a person was in their thirties to reveal itself.

"Yeah, I'm OK," Gleason replied. "Just clumsy. I must have tripped a circuit breaker."

"Which is even more insurance that there's no power getting to any bug down here."

"You're right," said Gleason, sounding considerably more upbeat than his last statement. "And just in time," he added, as his cell phone started ringing.

Evening, Robert Gleason's Home

Gleason turned his flashlight on, doubling the meager light in the room, but only for an instant as Jesse turned his off.

"If Boris has control over the camera on your phone," Jesse said, "there's no reason to advertise that there are two of us in the room. Just put your phone on speaker, do all the talking, and I'll sit here quietly in the dark."

"OK," Gleason replied as he switched to speaker. "Hello," he said slowly.

Boris, if that was who was on the other end of the line, said nothing for several moments. Finally, a computer-altered voice asked, "Why are you sitting in the dark, Comrade Gleason?"

"Boris?" asked Gleason.

"My question first."

"I tripped a circuit breaker."

The man laughed. "Or you figured out that I've been watching and took steps to make sure it didn't happen again. Bravo, not that it will do you any good. And by the way, you can tell Comrade Buttinsky sitting there in the dark with you that he can turn on his flashlight, too."

It seemed pointless not to, so Jesse did. It wasn't completely surprising to him that Boris was a step ahead of them; night-vision capability in a battery-operated camera was quite common. He even had a commercial model trained on the back deck at his home and an app on his phone that displayed what it captured. The capabilities a professional spy would have at his disposal—if that's what the caller was—would be considerably more advanced.

"So, American pigs, what am I to do with you? Maybe a waterboarding session will improve your attitude? Or some bamboo shoots under your fingernails?"

"Why would you torture us when all we know is what you've told us?" Jesse asked.

"Ah, Comrade Buttinsky speaks. And who is this, Comrade Gleason?"

"Just an old friend from high school who dropped in unexpectedly. He knows nothing."

Boris laughed. "Or perhaps he's the spy, Jesse Bolger, hiding under cover at Ruger-Phillips West, yes? Facial recognition works even with infrared images. It just takes a bit longer."

"Facial recognition or you just overheard that I was dropping by tonight?" asked Jesse, recalling that Gleason's grandmother had known about his visit. And if Boris had also overheard Gleason's plans, then his comment about facial recognition was just a bit of misdirection, a bit of play-acting to promote his prank. But as hoaxes go, this one was rapidly becoming unusually complex. Boris was able to see they were sitting in the dark, meaning he or someone had planted a camera on the premises. That was well beyond practical jokes 101.

"I heard and now I see," replied Boris. "I hope you didn't think your presence would be a secret."

Jesse added a hidden microphone, most likely upstairs, to the technology Boris seemed to have on site.

"So, I'm curious," said Gleason. "Even with the computer alterations, you don't sound Russian."

"Ah, testing me, da? How's this, my leetle American khoroshiy luchshiy drug?"

Jesse didn't speak Russian, but it sounded authentic to him. And he had the impression that Gleason felt the same as he said nothing. Finally, Boris asked, "So, is this all the practical demonstration you require, Comrade Gleason?"

"No, that's not a demonstration at all. All that tells me is that you know a few Russian words, babushka."

Boris laughed. "And apparently, you don't since you just called me an old woman. Or perhaps that is your feeble attempt at an insult? But enough of this waste of my time. Two days from today, I'll call you at precisely 10 o'clock, and before the evening is over, you'll be begging me to spare your immoral America. Want to beg for mercy now or later?"

"Hold on," said Jesse, deciding to push back to see what would happen. "It's time you end this joke before you dig this hole any deeper. You're making threats against the United States, and no court in the land is going to see any humor in your prank. So, drop it now and we'll all forget this whole thing ever happened. Continue and you'll end up being fined and maybe even spending some time in jail."

Boris had chuckled heartily before, but even with the computer alteration, it was clear he was roaring with amusement now. After several seconds of unbridled laughter, he quieted to a few sniffles as he was probably wiping tears from his eyes. Finally, he said, "We mocked your so-called intelligence services with clues, hoping to show them just how pathetic they are. But it seems they already know. None rose to the challenge save Comrade Gleason ... and now, you, Agent Buttinsky."

"Last chance to come clean," Jesse replied, doubling down on his threat.

"I'll take my chances," said Boris. It sounded like he was trying to stifle a yawn as he spoke. "So, back to my question. Beg for mercy now or later?"

"How about never," replied Gleason.

Jesse would swear that his friend's chin jutted out with the refusal, but in the dim light, it was difficult to tell.

Boris laughed once again. "We'll see about that." He hung up.

"What are we going to do?" asked Gleason.

Not talk in front of the spy was the response that came to Jesse's mind because he was starting to wonder if the man on the phone wasn't, indeed, an intelligence agent. But before he opened his mouth, Gleason said, "Jeez, Charlie, what's wrong with you? That one's got my eyes watering."

It took a second for the stench to reach Jesse's nose, but when it did, both of them bolted for the door. Just as Gleason opened it, they heard, "What on earth are you boys doing down there?"

It was Majoris and Jesse couldn't help but notice that he and Gleason had gone from being "young men" earlier in the evening to "boys" now. He couldn't blame her.

"I got a text from that smart-home software you installed about some power outage, so I come home to find you two sitting in the dark?"

"It's a really funny story, Grams."

Jesse was almost sorry he wouldn't be around for its telling, figuring this tale might tax even Gleason's imaginative mind. But if Boris wasn't going to back off with his threat, he was either not too smart or he was a Russian terrorist. "Look," Jesse said as they climbed the stairs to the first floor, "you need to call Agent Jenkins and tell him about this last call."

"Can you?"

After a few moments of silence during which Jesse was trying to figure out why Gleason wanted him to call, his old friend said, "Jenkins doesn't believe me. Maybe coming from another spy, he'll do more than just poo-poo everything I say." He paused a beat. "And there's the whole pot-smoking thing, too."

When they reached the top of the stairs, Majoris was standing there with her hands on her hips. "And I was about to win big in bingo and wipe that smile off Silvia Shaw's face," she said, slowly shaking her head. "Go reset the circuit breaker while I change clothes. You know where it is since you've had a lot of practice. And in the future, can you be a little more careful when I'm out?"

Majoris turned to leave, so Jesse called after her. "Thanks for making those snacks for us. They were great."

She turned back to him. "Glad you liked them, but do try to keep Robert out of trouble. He's going to be the death of me."

"Yes, ma'am."

When she was gone, Jesse said, "I guess I can call, although I'm not sure Jenkins will believe me, either."

"Thanks. It's worth a try." Gleason pulled a notepad out of a kitchen cabinet drawer and jotted Agent Jenkins's number on it before handing it over.

Jesse took the paper and put it in his billfold. He would use it, but Jenkins wasn't the only person he'd call. Jesse didn't know the man or the agency where he supposedly worked, and accepting Gleason's beliefs about him might only serve to propagate the prank. Jenkins could be in on it ... or even part of the terrorist plot for that matter.

Jesse retrieved his car from the garage and left, the events of the evening still swirling in his head. He suspected he'd get little sleep for the next couple of days. After all, responsibility for saving America tended to have that kind of effect on him.

TUESDAY, JULY 2

Morning, The Offices of Ruger–Phillips West

Jesse tapped on the door of his supervisor, Miles Sennett, and after hearing "Yes" from within, swung it open.

"Ah, Jesse. I have to admit, you have my curiosity up. That was quite the cryptic request for a meeting. What's up?" He angled his computer monitor so he could see his direct report better.

"Yeah, I know how busy you are, but this can't wait. I ran into an old friend from high school yesterday at lunch. His name is Robert Gleason. He was a bit of a dreamer back in school and this may be nothing more than another of his fantasies. But anyway, he thinks he's stumbled onto a cell of Russian spies who are planning some type of terrorist attack on the United States. And he confided in me because he thinks I'm in one of our intelligence services."

Sennett sat back in his chair, tenting his fingers in front of his face for a moment. "Interesting. What led him to the conclusion you're an agent?"

"Virtually nothing. The company happened to send me to some places where there was also civil unrest. He thinks I had some hand in settling things down. But even with his overactive imagination, I doubt he would have made anything of it if he hadn't been looking for someone to help with his Russian spy problem."

"Where were these trips he mentioned?"

"Brussels, Berlin, and Singapore. Apparently, he saw the video about the disturbance on the Berlin return flight and that got him thinking. So, he called my apartment and, as luck would have it, he got Loren. She apparently mentioned the other two trips. Still think she's so thoughtful?"

The comment was tongue-in-cheek, although Sennett didn't seem to notice the tone. "Of course, I do." But then, he must have recognized a bit late that it was a quip, so he added, "Lord knows, she's certainly too damn good for you."

"Gee, thanks, Boss," Jesse replied in the same mocking manner. "Anyway, back to the Russian-spy thing. Gleason invited me over last night because one of the Russian agents was calling. He has arranged a demonstration of how they'll attack the U.S., and it's scheduled for tomorrow night."

"Why would they show their hand?" asked Sennett.

"I asked the same thing. Gleason thinks it's to prove their superiority and I'll admit, the guy on the phone sounded pretty cocky. I tried to pressure him into admitting it was all a joke before they got themselves into some serious trouble, but he just laughed. And if this is all a hoax, they're playing it for all it's worth. His voice was computer-altered, and they have some kind of surveillance inside the house. He knew too much about what we were doing to not have eyes and ears on the inside."

"Take everything you know to the FBI and get the hell away from the situation. Domestic intelligence gathering is generally a Bureau responsibility."

"I was planning to call them," said Jesse. "Gleason said he tried calling the authorities but didn't get far until he contacted someone named Agent Edward Jenkins at an organization called the National Bureau of Counterintelligence. I was going to call him to corroborate what I could of Gleason's story, but if this is all a scam and Jenkins is in on it, I don't want to unwittingly help them by only reporting to him."

"Yeah, good thought," said Sennett. "I never heard of that organization, but then, that doesn't necessarily mean much. About half the federal intelligence budget goes to private sector contractors. Or this Bureau of Counterintelligence might even be a small, very black government unit. But what I didn't hear you say is that you'll stay away from this whole mess until it blows over."

"I'm not sure that's the best approach, sir."

"Every time you're about to take things into your own hands, you end the statement with 'sir.' So, why not just dump this in the lap of the FBI?"

"Because I doubt they'll take it seriously without something more specific. Right now, Gleason doesn't have much and he's … well, an unemployed man living in his grandmother's basement in a retirement community. What I heard last night doesn't change things much. But if their demonstration is legitimate and Gleason and I both witness it—well, two voices are more than twice that of one."

Sennett tented his fingers again. After a moment, he said, "As usual, you make a good argument. Just be a witness from a good long way off."

"Will do." Jesse left for his office as he had some phoning to do.

* * *

Jesse shoved his hands in his pockets, his unseeing gaze directed at the gray street below through his office window. It was a dreary day with a steady, cold drizzle, making a walk to clear his head out of the question. He needed one ... largely because of his first call to the FBI.

The initial contact with a Public Affairs Specialist at the local Denver field office had gone smoothly enough but with the first transfer—to Mr. Frederick Barrow, Resident Agency Specialist—communications started to deteriorate. No intelligence-gathering agency would ignore any report of suspicious activities however farfetched—too many of them had gotten burned when the 9/11 threat wasn't taken seriously enough. But Jesse knew perfunctory responses when he heard them, and Barrow was full of them.

When Jesse gave the names of the rogue spies—Boris and Natasha—Barrow repeated them, just as he had done when Gleason had told him. And when he said, as Gleason had said earlier, that these were just aliases, the man had responded, "Sure, of course, they are." His tone wasn't condescending, and yet, Jesse was certain that the man's eyes rolled as he said the words. He just wished he was there to see it ... and maybe, punch him in the nose.

But in most ways, Jesse couldn't blame Barrow. After all, his tale was rather bizarre as an old high school acquaintance had used a cryptic classified ad to uncover two KGB-era spies who were threatening to use World War II vintage plans to destroy America. He could see his report going to—what was the phrase Gleason had used—the same place as "... all the Elvis sightings and reports of underground cities."

But he had made his report to the FBI and should the demonstration prove to be real, Jesse had the name of a person he could call for support. What he didn't know, however, was how quickly a Resident Agency Specialist could mobilize a team of field agents, if that was necessary. But then, perhaps it would be NBC riding in to save the day.

That thought brought Jesse back to his next call, the one to Agent Jenkins at NBC. And since a long walk to clear his head of the feeling that he had just been given the runaround by the FBI was out of the question, he took the three steps to his desk, picked up the phone, and dialed the number Gleason had given him. On the second ring, a man answered, "Johnson Rentals."

Jesse hadn't necessarily expected the man to say, "National Bureau of Counterintelligence. Who can we spy on for you today?" But then again, he hadn't really anticipated being given the name of a rental agency, either. "I'm trying to reach Mr. Jenkins."

"I'm sorry, but there's no one named Mr. Jenkins here."

Jenkins must be part of the hoax, thought Jesse. Perhaps he should have made this call first. He could have added this information to the two-step he and the FBI had just danced. But there was something a bit unusual in the way that the man had said the name, "Mr. Jenkins." He had a thought. "Specifically, I'm looking for Mr. Edward Jenkins."

There was a slight delay, then, "Just a moment."

After a series of clicks, someone answered, "Hello."

That response fit Jesse's expectations perfectly. If he was actually calling a counterintelligence organization, no one would answer with their name or the name of their unit. Random dialing would yield too much information if they did. If a foe got the telephone exchange that way, a few days of using it could yield a complete list of the individuals assigned to the organization. Anonymity of the person answering and the organization they worked for would be the name of the game.

If those assumptions were true, he needed to take the first step since he didn't believe Jenkins would. "My name's Jesse Bolger and I'm calling because of a mutual acquaintance, Robert Gleason."

Jesse heard the clack of computer keys in the background, followed by a one-word response. "Yes?"

Apparently, his introduction was too small of a step; it was going to take a complete leap of faith. "We received another call from Boris and Natasha last night."

"I see. Mr. Gleason said he was expecting additional contact, although I didn't have a specific date or time. What was said?"

"Well, the first thing you should know is that Boris apparently has Gleason's home under surveillance. We accidentally tripped a circuit breaker, so we were sitting in the dark to take the call. Boris knew the lights were out when we answered."

"OK. I'll add that to what Mr. Gleason has already told us."

The man's excitement over the new information was the same as Barrow's had been—nonexistent—and that bothered Jesse a bit. "Invading someone's home to plant a camera has to be breaking several state and federal laws."

"Was a camera found?" asked Jenkins.

"No. And I know what you're going to say. Maybe Boris knew simply by watching the house. Trouble is, the most logical conclusion when the light went out in the basement was that we'd gone upstairs. And yet, Boris knew we were still there, sitting in the dark."

"Perhaps Boris picked up your conversation with a parabolic microphone. You know, like a microphone with a dish around it like you might see at pro football games? I assume you or Mr. Gleason said something about the power outage."

Jesse knew what Jenkins was talking about, and after a moment considering this alternative, he admitted, "I suppose that's possible." His next piece of news, however, would be a lot harder for the man to ignore. "Did Gleason tell you that he asked Boris for a practical demonstration of the capability he's going to use against the U.S.?"

"Just a second," replied Jenkins.

It seemed obvious that Jenkins had called up his notes when the name Robert Gleason was mentioned and he was now reading from them. But then, that made sense. How many other Robert Gleasons did he hear from in a month? Dozens? Hundreds? More?

"Yes, Mr. Gleason did mention that request."

"Well, Boris set a date and time for it. Ten o'clock tomorrow evening."

"OK, thanks. Anything else?"

Anything else? Wasn't that enough? "You will follow up on this information, correct?"

"NBC takes all the information provided to us seriously. It'll be added to the information Mr. Gleason has already given to us and in the context of all of the other data we collect—radio chatter, the movement of known foreign agents, intel from our operatives, and so on—an appropriate and proportional response to the possible threat will be determined and implemented as required."

Jesse recognized the bureaucratic equivalent of a brushoff. It even sounded somewhat familiar as Barrow had said something similar and it was getting old. "So, it looks like Robert and I will have to handle this ourselves."

Had Jesse been acting in a professional capacity, he never would have said that. He certainly hadn't planned it or even given it that much thought, but then, comebacks born of frustration were usually devoid of reason. Now, all he would get from Jenkins was NBC's version of "let the pros handle it."

"I would strongly advise against taking any rash actions in response to your suspicions," said Jenkins, just as Jesse had predicted. "The most likely scenario is that this is all a practical joke perpetrated by some of Mr. Gleason's friends. But if it's not, you would be taking a considerable risk to get involved."

"You're right, of course. I'll let Robert know what you said."

Jenkins was quiet for a moment, making Jesse wonder if he had capitulated too easily. But eventually, the NBC agent said, "Good. If you or Mr. Gleason hear anything else from Boris or Natasha, please let us know. We're trained and equipped to handle situations like these."

After the goodbyes, Jesse called Gleason.

"Hey, Robert. I'm not sure I said it yesterday, but I'm in for the practical demonstration tomorrow night."

"I never doubted it," replied Gleason. "Why don't you come by around 9 o'clock so we can discuss strategy."

"Sounds good."

The men hung up. Jesse sat staring at his phone for a moment. Perhaps his response to Jenkins had been hasty, but now it was their plan. They'd handle this situation themselves … at least until they knew enough to call in the cavalry.

WEDNESDAY, JULY 3

Evening, Robert Gleason's Home

Jesse had anticipated that Gleason would want him to park in the garage—all the better to avoid Boris's and Natasha's prying eyes—so he wasn't surprised when his friend was standing out front waving him in. Nor was he startled when the garage door started closing the moment the back bumper of his car cleared it. But when Gleason jumped into the passenger seat beside him before he could even open his door? Well, he hadn't expected that.

"I think we should talk in here," Gleason gasped as if he'd just run a lap around the block.

He was wearing the same ensemble as at Philly Pete's Sandwich Shop—black jeans, black sneakers, and a black hooded windbreaker. The only difference was that the hood wasn't up; the obvious constant was that he still looked seriously overdressed for the weather. "Why in here?" Jesse asked after his friend had caught his breath.

"I took every light fixture in the basement apart, but I didn't find any camera. So, I tore up the rest of my room but still nothing. At first, I thought we could just sit upstairs and discuss strategy, but when I looked around there, I thought better. Did you notice how many knickknacks Grams has?"

"I haven't seen much of your home except the kitchen," Jesse replied. He'd seen a lot of Charlie, too, but left that part unspoken.

"Well, trust me. There are a million and one hiding spots in our house. And it's the same for the garage," he said, sweeping his hand across a scene of gardening and yard tools, cans of oil, jugs of windshield washer fluid, and storage boxes of every size and shape. "But in your car, if we keep our voices down, we should be OK, right?"

"Unless they have a parabolic mike and they keep it trained on the garage rather than the house, yes, we should be fine." At least the exchange with Jenkins had yielded one piece of information he could use in his own deception.

"So, what's the plan?" asked Gleason.

"Part of playing this game is knowing when you need to give a little to gain a lot. We're at the giving stage. Boris and Natasha hold all the cards at the moment, so we go along. Sooner or later, they'll slip up and we'll be in a position to call in backup."

"That's the plan?" said Gleason, his face falling.

"Well, my agency does have this uniquely equipped drone with a specialized set of sensors that can analyze physiological and behavioral data, including speech patterns and characteristics to determine a person's country of origin. We could take out every Russian within ten square blocks of us ... although that would produce a lot of collateral damage."

"Really? You could do that?"

From his work with some of Ruger-Phillips's military customers, Jesse suspected it might be possible, but he didn't want to get into a lengthy digression. "We could, but we won't," replied Jesse. "Not unless you want to spend the rest of your life in prison."

Jesse searched his memory for a way to convince Gleason that this wait-and-see plan was the best course of action. "Look, how many times did James Bond allow himself to be caught so he could get inside the villain's lair and thwart his plans from there?"

Jesse was a bit concerned that Gleason would say "never"—and he didn't know himself—but his friend grimaced, then said, "Several times."

"OK. So, we'll play along until we find the opening we need to save America."

"Right, James," he said as he pumped a fist once, his jaw set in a sneer. "I mean, Jesse."

"I also contacted Agent Jenkins at NBC and found a contact at the FBI. If we get in a spot where we have to call for support, we've got two numbers we can use. And so you have both, here's the number for FBI Resident Agency Specialist Frederick Barrow."

"Resident Agency Specialist? Can he get boots on the ground?" asked Gleason.

"I certainly hope so" was the real answer, but again, a digression seemed counterproductive. So, Jesse said, "He can."

"OK," said Gleason. "Hedge our bets, so to speak. I thought about calling Jenkins myself to make sure about backup, but you know it's a slippery slope once you start talking to the feds. I'm already more exposed than I'd like. You know, with the war protests and all."

"War protests? I thought you were worried about trying marijuana once."

"Well, that, too," replied Gleason.

They exited the car and made their way downstairs to Gleason's room, picking up Charlie along the way. The dog apparently remembered Jesse, only stopping for a moment to sniff his hand. After selecting a couple of Gleason's armchairs, they sat and stared at each other for a moment.

"Pretty cool today for July," Jesse said after a while.

"Sure was."

And then, they went quiet. Something about knowing one's being watched and overheard by Russian spies kills all the spontaneity. Fortunately, they didn't have long to wait before Gleason's phone rang.

"Hello."

"Ah, the American pig," said Boris in his computer-altered voice. "And Agent Buttinsky aka Jesse Bolger. So, ready to meet your doom?"

"I thought this was just supposed to be a demonstration," said Gleason, all of his bravado from earlier now gone. "We aren't ready."

"Perhaps my earlier judgment was wrong," Boris replied slowly. "Maybe you won't do as well as any decadent American agent because at least they'd be prepared to act. So, go back to your mama's ...."

"No, wait," said Gleason. "We're ready."

"That's better. You need to get to the York Street entrance to the Denver Botanic Gardens no later than 11 o'clock. Don't tell anyone where you're going. Agent Buttinsky is welcome to go along, but no one else. And especially, not Agent Jenkins. That man bores me."

"Yeah, me, too," said Gleason.

Boris was quiet a moment, perhaps as puzzled by Gleason's comment as Jesse was. He was also surprised to hear that Boris knew about Jenkins, although if the Russian had a microphone and camera on the premises, he shouldn't have been.

"And one more thing," said Boris. "You can't drive. I'll be watching, and if you break any of my rules, I'll know, and you can say goodbye to your easy life living on the backs of the world's poor."

"We can't drive?" said Gleason. "That's got to be four miles from here, and it's already after 10 o'clock. We'll never make it."

"You better hope you do. I'll have more instructions for you when you get there." He disconnected.

They hurried up the stairs and back to Jesse's car, Gleason holding one of the rear doors open for Charlie. Once they were inside, Jesse said, "We may have our first chance at turning the tables." He brought up a map on his phone. "Boris and Natasha didn't select the Botanic Gardens randomly. They chose it and put a time limit on us to force us to use the fastest, most direct pedestrian route, and there are only a couple that make sense. This one." He traced a path from their current location to the Gardens. "Or this one." He traced a second route. "I wouldn't be surprised if they split up so they could watch both of them."

"OK," said Gleason slowly. "But I'm not sure what that gets us."

"It gets us a chance to spot one of them. It's dark out and they won't want to take a chance that they miss us. So, they'll be close to the sidewalk, maybe in a parking lot or sitting in a car along the street. If you go first, I can follow you from behind and watch for anyone who seems a little too interested in you jogging by. Grabbing one of them might not stop the attack, but it would be more than enough to get the FBI and NBC mobilized."

"Are you sure about tailing me?" asked Gleason. "What if they spot you before you spot them? Boris said no tricks or we'd be sorry."

"The only reason we're in this game at all is because they think they're smarter than everyone else. You said so yourself, and that seems right from everything I've heard. So, if they spot me, Boris will call you to gloat."

"Yeah. He'll say, I warned you, American pig and Agent Buttinsky," Gleason said with his best Russian accent.

Jesse chuckled, mostly to cover the fact that Gleason's accent was atrocious. "Anyway, when Boris calls, you tell him we're following his instructions. I just couldn't keep up."

"Yeah, like he's going to believe that. Look at you. You could run rings around me."

"Tell them I've got a cold."

"And a fever and stomach cramps? And maybe I should say you twisted an ankle, too," said Gleason.

"I don't need to be at death's door, and I don't want to have to limp for four miles. Just keep it simple."

"OK. One last thing. How do we get started? We can't go out the front door together and then, you just stand on the porch till

I'm half a block away. That doesn't look like you have a cold; that looks like we're trying to pull a fast one."

Gleason had a point. And it was also true that he should be in position right from the beginning of their run. After all, one of the Russians could be sitting in a car thirty feet down the block already. "This place has a backyard, right?"

"Yeah, sure."

"And there's an alley between the houses?" Jesse asked.

"Right again. So, you're thinking you'll cut through the backyard to the alley and circle around to get behind them before we start?"

"Right," replied Jesse. "Just give me two minutes to get into position. And put your phone on vibrate. I'll text you as soon as I see either of them. If I don't, we join back up at the Gardens and wait for Boris to call."

"Great plan. I just wish I was in better shape for this run."

"You can get fit for the next time we have to save the United States," said Jesse, hoping the lighter tone would help. Gleason seemed to be cycling between grim determination and total panic, with Jesse's last statement nudging him toward the former. "Maybe you should lose the windbreaker. It's pretty warm outside."

"I get cold easily."

And if Gleason exercised as little as he had implied, he'd get overheated easily, too. But if he had to pitch his windbreaker along the way, it wouldn't be much of a loss. "Now listen," said Jesse. "If anything unexpected happens"—he had almost said "bad" but thought that would be a nudge toward the panic end of the scale—"then text me. But don't do that unless it's necessary. Better that you're not busy with a text when Boris calls. And remember, I'll be right behind you."

Gleason nodded and said, "OK," some of his previous look of determination returning. They exited the car, Jesse and Charlie following Gleason until they reached a mudroom in the back of the house.

"Where's that light switch," Gleason mumbled to himself.

It seemed strange that his friend didn't know where the light switch was after five years in Denver, but it was a fortunate piece of missing information. "No. Leave it off. My eyes will adjust to the darkness, and I don't want Boris or Natasha wondering why the light came on in the backyard if they're nearby."

"Good call," said Gleason.

Jesse stepped out into the backyard, hearing the click of the lock behind him. He paused a moment, letting his eyes adjust to the darkness, then walked quickly to the back fence. But when he got there, he found an eight-foot-tall, wrought iron gate. It was locked, which made perfect sense. No one would leave a gate to an alley unlocked.

That alone wouldn't have been a problem except the gate was flanked by a matching wrought-iron fence, and both the gate and fence were topped by decorative, but still dangerous-looking finial tips. Again, that wouldn't have been an issue except that a privacy screen composed of some type of tough mesh made to look like ivy had been added as well. Now, any cross braces in the fence that Jesse might have used for a foot- or handhold were covered.

Just to be sure, he placed his hands between two sets of finials and chinned himself. He could see into the alley, but without any footholds, he would have to swing a leg up to the top of the fence to scale it. That, however, wasn't going to work. The finial points, though rounded, were too close together for his leg to fit between them. His hands only fit because he was overlapping his fingers. And resting a leg on top of those finials while he hoisted himself up would create more pain than he could bear. He dropped back to the ground.

Time for plan B, so Jesse retraced his steps to the house and knocked on the back door. No answer. He waited, then knocked again with the same result. Gleason must have already left the house by the front door.

Jesse went to the right side of the house. There he found the same wrought-iron fence and privacy screen barrier and no gate. So, he tried the left side where, fortunately, he found a gate that led to the front yard. He felt a wave of relief that lasted … until he tried the handle. This gate, too, was locked.

As his eyes further adjusted to the dark, Jesse could see that this fence and privacy screen encircled the entire yard. Had there been a tree branch within a foot or two of the top of the fence, he might have been able to chin himself as he'd done before and reach up to the limb. However, because the landscaping in the neighborhood was relatively new, the only trees were mere saplings. There was no way out.

Either taking the trash out wasn't one of Gleason's jobs, as Jesse had suspected when he couldn't find the light switch, or he hadn't considered how impenetrable the backyard was. But either way, Jesse was trapped. A whole series of four-letter expletives floated through his mind, but the phrase that he finally muttered into the void of the night was, "Well, aren't I just one helluva secret agent?"

Evening, Robert Gleason's Backyard

After the image of him casually strolling out of Gleason's backyard joined all of the other memories of his miscalculations, Jesse admitted to himself that he wasn't actually trapped. There were dozens of ways out. Perhaps the simplest was to text his friend. Unfortunately, that had the potential to expose their subterfuge to the Russians if they had Gleason in view. He discarded that option.

He could start yelling until someone came to the rescue, although he had no way of knowing which, if any, of Majoris's neighbors had a key to her house. He might end up sharing his pathetic story to a disembodied voice on the other side of the fake ivy only to find that the neighbor was as stumped as he. Or, he could pick up one of the stones Majoris had so artistically arranged around the yard and throw it through a neighbor's window. Then, he'd be out as soon as the police arrived—well, out of the backyard if not out of their custody. Or he could probably pull up one of the patio's pavers and tunnel under the fence ... if he had a few hours.

With time, damage to Majoris's home, and the commotion of his yelling being the primary factors he needed to minimize, Jesse started generating alternatives. It was his previous idea to use a paver to tunnel under the fence that yielded the best option. But rather than using one of these heavy, concrete blocks to dig, he'd use it to tear a hole in the privacy screen just above one of the horizontal rails in the wrought iron fence.

He moved to the fence to check out his plan. Sure enough, about halfway up he could feel a cross rail just on the other side of the privacy screen. With a hole in the screen created by the paver, he could use the railing for a foothold. Then, he'd have to get his other foot on the top of the fence between the finial points by turning his ankle and standing on the edge of his foot.

Finally, he'd need to balance himself on the top railing before jumping to the ground on the other side.

Of course, if every aspect of this maneuver didn't go perfectly, he'd end up hobbling after Gleason on a sprained knee or a twisted ankle. Or worse, he'd break a leg and Gleason would be on his own. But it was still the best option Jesse could see.

He sat down on the patio, rubbing his fingers over the edge of a paver. It was slightly rounded, but the bulk of one of those concrete blocks should make short work of the mesh even if it was tough. "Time to pull one of these up," Jesse muttered to himself.

Charlie wandered over and sat beside him. "Think it'll work?" he asked the dog, hoping for a little encouragement, but the massive canine just tilted his head to one side as if puzzled by the idea. "I don't blame you. Seems pretty crazy to me, too."

But then, Jesse jumped to his feet, suddenly realizing what the dog's presence meant. "Hey, Charlie, how'd you get into the backyard?" That only produced a tilt of Charlie's head in the opposite direction and a bit of a whine, but Jesse figured he knew the answer anyway. There must be some type of dog door he hadn't noticed, and anything that would accommodate this massive animal would be big enough for him.

It only took a few moments to find it since Charlie trotted over to the dog door as soon as Jesse started moving. The dog even demonstrated how it worked, which could only be described as "just barely." He had to get down on his stomach and belly-crawl in. Jesse followed Charlie's example, wondering if the enormous canine would think he was an intruder now that he'd been reduced to slithering into the house like a snake. But Charlie welcomed the company, as he licked Jesse's face while he was still defenseless, his arms stretched out in front of him.

When Jesse stood on the other side of the dog door, he wasn't sure he'd accomplished anything. He was back in the mudroom but on the other side of it was another closed door. If he lived there, he would lock it when he left the house. That way, Charlie could get out of the elements in the mudroom, but if an intruder made it past the outside door, he'd still have another door to deal with ... not to mention the daunting canine.

But when Jesse tried the handle, it turned freely and the door swung open. He was in.

Jesse left Charlie in the mudroom and hurried through the home, hitting the front door at a sprint. If Boris was watching the video feed from a drone overhead, he'd easily recognize their deception. But with Gleason on the move, he and Natasha were probably busy monitoring the routes to the Gardens. So, Jesse focused on making up the time he'd lost while escaping.

His phone buzzed with a text and Jesse raised the screen to his eyes. He was expecting Gleason to say that he was almost to the Gardens. But surprisingly, he had only covered about four blocks. He wasn't going to make it at this pace, so Jesse texted him back, *"Get a move on!!!"*

Fortunately, Jesse was a frequent jogger. Knowing that he wasn't that far behind, he decided to take a street parallel to the one Gleason was on. If the Russians had been on any of the blocks that Gleason had covered, then he had missed them. But as soon as he made up the ground, he'd carefully angle over to Gleason's street and fall in behind. He'd just have to hope that the Russians had set their surveillance posts close to the Botanic Gardens.

After about twenty minutes, Jesse figured he had probably caught up with Gleason on his parallel course and he stopped to send a text. But before he could, his phone rang. He checked the display, surprised to find his friend's name there.

"What's up?"

"I know I shouldn't be calling, but Boris called with more instructions. They left some clothes and two Light Phones behind a dumpster about four blocks from the Botanic Gardens. He wants us to change and leave all our clothes and phones there. And I suppose if he's leaving phones that light up, it's because we're heading somewhere without streetlights."

"Maybe," said Jesse, "but a Light Phone usually means a minimalist phone made by a company named Light. Generally, you can make and receive calls and texts with one, but not a lot more. And since the screen is more like the ones you'd find on black and white eReaders, it wouldn't have anything like a flashlight app."

"Good. I hate caves."

Jesse just shook his head, wondering if he'd ever get used to the unusual conclusions that his friend drew. "Look, Boris and Natasha are always a step ahead of us," Jesse said. "Maybe it's time we take what we have to people who are trained to ...."

Gleason didn't wait for him to finish. "It's already too late for that. Boris said the demonstration is at 11 o'clock with or without us. And then at midnight, they're launching their plan for real. And if that wasn't bad enough, they have Grams. If we don't do exactly as they say, I'll never see her again. But if we can get to the demonstration, they'll tell me where she is. That way, we can all die slowly together, as Boris put it. I really hate that guy."

"Are you sure about this?" Jesse asked.

"No, of course not. But since you didn't spot Boris or Natasha on the street .... You didn't spot one of them, did you?"

"No, sorry."

"Well, then, I'm not sure we have any other choice."

Jesse didn't see any immediate alternatives either. "You know, I should have seen this coming. Of course, the Russians want to destroy us on the country's birthday, the Fourth of July. I should have pushed FBI Specialist Barrow harder for some support tonight."

"At least they didn't notice that we split up," said Gleason.

"Yeah, that's good news. Where's this dumpster where they left the clothes?"

"A convenience store off Sixth Avenue a little past Josephine Street."

"Good. I'm close. See you in a minute or two."

Jesse hurried to the location that Gleason had given him, concerned when he had the dumpster in sight but didn't see his friend. Had he decided to go after Boris and Natasha alone? But after a moment, Jesse saw Gleason appear from behind the dumpster. He hurried over.

"Your clothes are in a bag back there with your name on it," Gleason said, pointing toward a gap between the dumpster and the store. "And don't forget to leave your phone here."

Jesse got changed in record time, leaving his clothes and phone behind. When he stepped out from his dressing spot, he said, "Other than having a basic black and white screen, this phone they left us isn't anything like the Light Phones I know. It looks and feels cheap and as far as I can tell, it won't even send a text."

Gleason shrugged. "All I know is that's what Boris called them." He rolled his shoulders, then raised a knee into the air. "Jeez, I must be about the same size as Boris, assuming these clothes were his. They're a great fit."

"Which would also explain why mine are too big." But when Jesse looked closer, that wasn't the only difference between their clothes. "Why does your outfit look like it was specially tailored at a high-end athletic store while mine looks like they robbed a homeless person?" Gleason was wearing running shoes that didn't have a scuff on them, a nice pair of black joggers, and a Navy windbreaker. He, on the other hand, had on a tattered blue sweatshirt, sneakers that were a size too big with worn soles, and a pair of torn and faded jeans—faded and torn from wear, not by a designer.

"I don't think Boris and Natasha like Agent Buttinsky all that much. But let's get going. The place where the demonstration will be isn't as far as we've already come, but it's a ways."

Maybe the change in attire invigorated Gleason, as he headed out with purpose. He even looked like he was in better shape than before. And apparently, he knew where he was going because there was no hesitation or street sign reading at the intersections.

After about ten minutes, Gleason looked back over his shoulder, then pointed to a bank sign in the distance. "Where we're headed," he called.

Jesse said nothing because not only was he lagging behind, he was also feeling the miles they'd already come and couldn't find the air to reply. He was hoping they had the time to slow to a fast walk, but apparently, Gleason didn't think so as he charged ahead.

When they reached the bank's parking lot, Gleason entered and jogged over to an ATM. After that, Jesse couldn't tell exactly what his old friend was doing because he had stopped at the parking lot entrance and was now bent over, hands on knees, catching his breath. But whatever it was, it didn't take long. Gleason stepped out from behind the ATM and called in a voice that was anything but steady. "Jesse, take a look at this."

Evening, The Bank's Parking Lot

Jesse started for the ATM, asking Gleason what was wrong when he was still ten yards away.

"Wrong?" he asked. "You mean other than the fact that two rogue Russian spies intent on destroying America are holding my grandmother at gunpoint?"

Point taken. "You sounded even more upset than before. Something change?"

"Yeah, you could say that. They spotted you. Why Boris didn't tell me that before, I have no idea."

"Sorry," Jesse replied. He supposed he could deflect a bit of the blame by telling Gleason how he had left him in a nearly escape-proof backyard, but it seemed a bit petty given the potential loss his friend was facing. "What is he going to do?"

"At least for now, they're letting Grams live. We just need to complete this game by their rules. Here, read the note they left me hidden on the ATM." He handed Jesse a piece of paper. The first part was typed.

Congratulations, decadent American pigs, you've made it this far!

Comrade Gleason, this is your bank. How do we know? Because we know every account holder at this bank and everything about them, including you and your precious Grams. So, here's your proof. You log onto your account every day – yes, we know that, too. So, Natasha and I have no doubt you know exactly how much money you have in your checking account at any given time ... although that's not a feat of any tremendous skill. You always keep the balance between $50 and $350. But take a look now, because you'll find that the $311.61 balance you saw this morning is now $411.61.

Jesse stopped reading and looked up at Gleason. "Is all the stuff they're saying true?"

Gleason shrugged. "Yeah. I suppose logging on every day is a bit of an exaggeration, but I don't really trust banks. You ever meet a poor banker?"

Jesse held out two empty hands, not really sure what to say.

"Yeah, me either," Gleason replied. "And, yes, there is an extra $100 in my checking account, just like they said."

Disregarding Gleason's commentary on the greed of those in the banking industry—if that was what he had meant— he'd at least confirmed what mattered most. Boris and Natasha could and had manipulated his bank account. Jesse returned to the note.

Where did that additional money come from? One hundred other accounts at your bank all donated a dollar to you. And why did we do that? Because that is how we will destroy America. We're not thieves. We're not going to transfer the money to an account we hold ... well, not all of it, anyway. Rather, we're just going to randomly re-distribute the blood money America has extorted from the rest of the world and from Mother Russia.

Can we do this to every American bank? Frankly, no, but we have hacked into almost three-quarters of them, and that should be more than enough. Because in this random redistribution of money, there will be winners and there will be losers. The biggest loser, of course, will be America's financial stability, because the run on the banks after our demonstration of their vulnerability will be something the world has never seen before.

Checkmate.

Jesse checked the time. It was 11:04. That gave them less than an hour to stop this nightmare. But while calculating how much time they had was a relatively easy task, identifying how to stop them wasn't. They didn't know how the Russians had moved the funds to Gleason's account. They didn't know where their base of operations was. They didn't know much beyond a couple of aliases that were probably selected to match Americans' expectations. For all he and Gleason knew, they were actually dealing with Billy Bob Smith and Betty Jones, two disillusioned Americans who wanted to teach the rest of the nation a lesson ... whatever that lesson might be.

Jesse returned to the note. At the bottom, someone had added a handwritten message. It was printed, if the crude block letters that looked like they'd come from an eight-year-old who was failing writing class in elementary school could be called printing. But slowly, Jesse pieced together the words.

Traitorous American pigs –

We know you split up in a failed attempt to trap us. For your treachery, we should kill you both. But then, what could be worse than having to scrounge your meals from a dumpster while disease and depression slowly take your lives? So, if you can make it to the address below before midnight, we'll let both of you and Comrade Gleason's grandmother live so you can explain to her how you failed to stop the destruction of America. Don't call the police or she dies.

Below the address, the note was signed by Natasha.

"Do you know where this address is?" Jesse asked.

"It's outside of the retirement community, but only two or three blocks from my place," he said. "I have no idea who lives there, but they probably forced Grams to name someone nearby and then made it their command center for the final act. We should get moving if we're going to make it there" — he looked at his watch — "in the next 53 minutes."

"Wait a second," Jesse said softly. "The top part of the note was prepared in advance. It's typed. But the bottom was written in the last hour. It had to be since they knew I was following you." Technically, he hadn't been behind Gleason for most of his trip, but the note said, "split up." They must have known he'd taken a parallel path, which was concerning. Boris and Natasha had been ahead of them all along, and now, even when they went off-script, the Russian spies still kept their advantage.

"So?" Gleason asked equally softly.

"So, Natasha is nearby. If we can spot .... Wait, I think I saw some movement over to your left, past the light pole, and close to the back wall of the building across the alley. I'm going after her."

"No way," said Gleason, hissing the command under his breath. "You can't be gambling with my grandmother's life like that."

"But this was the plan. Catch one of them and use him or her to get help taking out this cell of spies."

"That was the plan," said Gleason, "before they kidnapped Grams. Now the plan is to do it their way until we can get her out. And if that's too risky for you, I'll go it alone."

Jesse found the suggestion to let him go it alone surprisingly tempting ... but abandoning a friend, even one that wasn't that close wasn't who he was. "OK, I'm in. We can discuss our next strategy while we run."

Evening, Robert Gleason's Neighborhood

"There's only two of them," said Gleason while they jogged along the street in the opposite direction they had just come. "You can bust through the front door and take them out before they know what hit them."

"I think we need something a little better than that. They're trained, experienced marksmen and it's not like we're going to surprise them. They can probably guess to the minute when we will show up. And besides, I'm not carrying a gun."

"Ah, not licensed to kill, huh?"

It seemed pointless to mention to Gleason that his line was from a fictional foreign intelligence service, so Jesse didn't bother. At least he hadn't argued that they still had a chance to surprise the Russians. "We have an address now. It's time to call Jenkins and Barrow, and let the pros come in and handle this."

Jesse paused a moment, partly to think about his next statement, but mostly to catch his breath. "I know all we have to make these calls are the phones the Russians gave us, and they are almost undoubtedly bugged. So, you make a call to your home like you're checking to see if Olive is there, and I'll call my place. You can add in a few more irrelevant calls, but don't waste too much time on them. Then, we place the calls to the FBI and NBC. Boris and Natasha won't have time to check out all the calls because everything's going to happen really fast from here on. Agreed?"

Jesse was halfway expecting an emotional refusal from his friend, but Gleason was quiet for several moments. Finally, he said, "OK. I can see how even James Bond might have a few concerns, what with Natasha holding a gun to Grams's head while Boris trains his on the front door, just waiting for you to step through. Bam and there goes half your head."

"Thanks for the pep talk."

"No worries," he replied as if he hadn't picked up on the sarcasm. "You call Jenkins. I'll call Barrow. But I want you to tell him to arrive no earlier than midnight. I think we can get there ten minutes early, and I want all of that time to try to get Grams out of there. She wouldn't handle a three-day hostage standoff well."

As prepared as Boris and Natasha had been to this point, any plan they hatched to free Majoris was most likely doomed to failure. But on the other hand, had their positions been reversed, Jesse suspected he would feel the same. And who knew? There was always a chance, however slim, that they would spot a vulnerability in the Russian's defenses. "Sure, I'll give Agent Jenkins a call. And no sooner than midnight it is."

The two men paused their jog and stepped a few yards from each other. For his part, Jesse wanted the distance so he wouldn't overhear comments like, "Yeah, that's right. He's not licensed to kill." And he figured Gleason wanted the space so he could say things like that. He pulled out the phone and dialed his empty apartment, then his number at work. Finally, he called Jenkins.

"You've reached the night service of Johnson Rentals. We're currently closed. Please leave your name and number at the tone and we'll get back to you during our normal working hours, eight to five, Monday through Friday."

"Great," Jesse mumbled to himself as he considered ways that he might get beyond the answering machine.

But before he heard any tone, the recording continued. "If this is an emergency, press star."

Jesse did and after a few clicks, someone came on the line. "Please state the nature of your emergency."

"I'm trying to reach Mr. Edward Jenkins."

"Just a moment."

It was less than twenty seconds when Jesse heard a rather drowsy-sounding Jenkins come on the line. "Hello."

"This is Jesse Bolger. We spoke yesterday about two Russian spies and a possible terrorist attack they are planning."

There was no clacking of computer keys in the background, but there was a pause. "Yes, a Boris and Natasha, correct?"

"That's right. At midnight tonight, we know exactly where they'll be." He gave the address. "If you get there before midnight, you'll need to stay out of sight or you might spook them. They will be holding a hostage, a Ms. Olive Majoris. And we're also contacting the FBI, just to make sure someone gets there in time."

"We cooperate fully with the FBI, and frankly, a situation like this is in their jurisdiction. We'll still bring a team, but if they are on-site, operations will be their call." Jenkins paused a beat. "Don't worry. This all may sound risky, but we have a 96 percent success rate with hostage negotiations."

Jesse was impressed that the agent was so willing to commit to an NBC response. But then, he suspected it was part of Jenkins's training. If someone was willing to stick their neck out and report suspicious activity, they would treat it with all the professionalism and urgency it deserved. And if it turned out to be a prank? Well, then they and the courts would sort it out later. Now, all he had to worry about was their four percent failure rate.

"One last thing, Mr. Bolger. We need you to stay out of the area. The last thing we need is to have a private citizen caught in the crossfire."

"The hostage is Mr. Gleason's grandmother, but I'll try to keep him away from the area." Jesse hoped that he could, but he also knew it was an empty offer. Gleason wanted to try to save his Grams and he doubted he had any words that would change his mind.

"Please do." Jenkins disconnected.

Gleason was apparently finished with his calls, too, as he walked over. "How'd it go?" Jesse asked.

"OK. The FBI's on the way. I didn't think about mentioning that we were calling in NBC until the guy I talked to asked about other law enforcement in the area. Last thing we need is some fed to go down in friendly fire. Then they'd find out about those pot parties I hosted for sure."

Pot parties? Hosted? Jesse figured on the next telling, Gleason might be selling marijuana, too. But there was no time to worry about that now. "Yeah, I warned Jenkins, so they should be on the lookout."

"Good," replied Gleason. "Let's double-time it the rest of the way. We want as much time as possible to check out the situation."

Jesse could hardly believe his ears. Gleason had been breathing hard since the first day walking across the Philly Pete's parking lot, and now he was going to double his speed for the next mile after already running something like seven? But then, with the stress he was under, his blood was probably half adrenaline.

"OK," said Jesse, determined that the hundreds of miles he had put in jogging on Denver streets would pay off now.

Late Evening, Robert Gleason's Neighborhood

After about a quarter-mile, Gleason said, "I've been wondering. You called Jenkins and you even took the extra step to contact the FBI. But what I don't understand is why you didn't just get backup from your own agency? That is, after all, the reason I brought you in."

Jesse wasn't sure how to answer that question. Gleason had consistently rejected the idea that his "agency," Ruger-Phillips West, wasn't in the business of sending armed teams to bail out procurement specialists who'd obviously gone off the range. But since he hadn't been able to convince Gleason that he wasn't a spy, he said, "Sorry, buddy. I tried, but we're already spread awfully thin. We have over seven hundred operations ongoing at the moment, and most are bigger and better funded than a couple of over-the-hill Russian agents. Of course, none are playing for stakes higher than we are, but we didn't know that a couple of days ago."

Jesse caught a slow nod from his friend beside him. He hated to keep lying to Gleason, but it seemed the only option.

"Makes sense," Gleason said after a moment. "The world is full of loonies and nut jobs. Hey, we should go by my place and pick up Charlie."

The transition from the talk of the mentally ill to enlisting Charlie as part of the rescue party was a little too abrupt for Jesse and he studied his friend out of the corner of his eye for a moment. Seeing no evidence that he had gone over the edge—well, any further over the edge than usual—he asked, "I thought Charlie was ... well, intimidating, but more of a lover than a fighter." Jesse was basing his statement on what Majoris and Gleason had said about the massive animal, although he'd witnessed nothing to the contrary.

"Well, yeah. But he does have that ... air about him," Gleason said, his smirk apparent even from Jesse's vantage point alongside.

"And you can get him to fart on command?"

"Why didn't I think of that? That would be a helluva command," said Gleason, somewhat excitedly. "Sit, speak, fart." But after a moment, he continued more somberly. "Unfortunately, he doesn't know that one ... or any of those three, actually. But he did dine on burritos this evening. So, you can think of him like an extremely sensitive landmine that's ready to blow. We just need to sneak him inside somehow and wait for the mayhem."

"You're serious?"

"Well, not as our only plan of attack, but as a useful diversion, sure."

After considering the possible problems, most of which involved Charlie getting hurt, Jesse figured Gleason—and Charlie, as well—would accept that risk to save Majoris. So, begrudgingly, he said, "OK, if we spot a safe enough opening to get him inside."

They went by Gleason's house, finding Charlie snoozing in the mudroom right where Jesse had left him. After grabbing a leash—although Jesse couldn't imagine Charlie not winning any tug of war they might have with it—the trio left.

As he and Gleason jogged down the street for their date with destiny, Jesse couldn't help but chuckle to himself. There they were, a fashionista jogger and a ragged runner armed only with a loaded dog on a mission to subdue two veteran Russian spies, free a kidnap victim, and save the United States. Nothing strange about that, he thought.

Ten Minutes Before Midnight, Robert Gleason's Neighborhood

"Is that the place?" Jesse asked, pointing to a house about twenty yards away on the other side of the street. They were crouching in the shadow of a parked car, the evening's half-moon seeming quite bright to their dark-adapted eyes.

"Yep."

"I didn't expect them to have the lights on inside. It certainly makes it a lot easier for us to see them ... that is if they'd ever pass in front of one of the windows."

"I'm going around to the back through the alley," said Gleason. "And taking Charlie. If there's a way to get him in there, it's probably from the backyard."

"Hopefully, the back gate is unlocked or the backyard doesn't have the same kind of fence and privacy screen as your grandmother's. I might have still been stuck there if Charlie hadn't shown me the escape route."

Gleason hesitated a moment, then said, "Oh, yeah. I guess her backyard is a bit tough to get out of. Anyway, besides looking for a way to get Charlie in, I'll take a peek in the windows, see if I can spot either of the Russians or Grams. Can you do the same up here? Then, I'll come back up front and we can compare notes. It shouldn't take me more than three minutes, which will leave us five or more to implement whatever we come up with. OK?"

"Yeah. I think .... Wait, a woman just walked in front of one of the windows, but it wasn't Natasha. She looked like she would have just been a baby when the KGB was disbanded some thirty-plus years ago. You think there are other people in there besides the two spies and your grandmother?"

"I doubt it. It was probably just the lighting from behind the woman that made her look young," replied Gleason. "But I'll keep a lookout for anyone who doesn't seem to fit, and you do the same." He and Charlie left for the back of the house.

Jesse waited a moment for Gleason to get into position and then crept out of his hiding spot behind the car and crossed the street. He started walking slowly and quietly up the sidewalk. When he reached the edge of the yard, he stepped into it and disappeared in the shadow of a tree ... or tried to, anyway. Like Majoris's home, the trees here were just saplings.

There were two large windows with a small porch between them in the front of the house. Jesse could see light at both windows, although it was much brighter at the one on the left. That window also had shrubs growing below it so when he checked it, he would be hidden from the street but exposed to those inside the house. He decided to go to the one on the right first.

Just as he was in position below the window, three cars came down the street at high speed, then angle-parked at the curb to illuminate the entire façade of the house. Jesse stood, shading his eyes from the glare of the headlights. At the same moment, he heard more cars stopping in the alley. In less than ten seconds, the building was surrounded and bathed in the brilliance of the lights from the cars. Whoever was driving, this clearly wasn't their first raid.

Men started jumping out of the cars and taking positions behind them. Not completely sure who the intruders were—although the premature arrival of Jenkins or Barrow was high on his list of possibilities—Jesse raised his hands and started walking toward the street.

"Officer Bolger," a voice called.

"Miles, is that you?" Jesse yelled back.

"It is. Now, get your butt over here and take cover."

Jesse didn't have to be told twice; he ran over to the cars in a crouch and got behind one. In the background, he could hear a man identifying himself as an FBI special agent and calling for someone named Elizaveta Ermakov and Alexey Ilyin to come out of the house.

"Are you crazy?" asked Sennett. "You were supposed to stay in the background, and I roll up with the FBI to find you peeking in a window?"

"Things changed. They took a hostage, Gleason's grandmother. She's inside and Gleason's in back. His dog, too. We need to tell the FBI to watch out for the civilians."

"Wait here." Sennett moved to the next car in line and spoke to someone who was on a radio. When he came back, he said, "I told them, but there are no reports of anyone in back, humans or dogs. And there are only two heat signatures inside the building, not three. Any idea how we went from a demonstration to a hostage-taking?"

"That might have been the plan all along—show us what they could do, don't give us time to react, and take shelter behind a hostage if we do. Anyway, they're planning to use some type of cyberattack on the banks. They demonstrated what they could do by moving some funds around in Gleason's bank account. But right before the demonstration, they said they were going to implement the plan tonight at midnight and took Gleason's grandmother as insurance."

Jesse hesitated, not sure he wanted to know the answer to his next question. "Do you think they killed Majoris and that's why the FBI is seeing only two people inside?"

"I doubt that," said Sennett. "Dead women don't make good bargaining chips. She's probably in the basement or something like that."

Jesse turned toward the house when he heard a man inside yell, "What the hell are you talking about? I'm Dan Perkins and I don't know who you're looking for, but I have rights. Now, get off my property before I call the cops."

Then, from a man outside. "Just come out, Mr. Perkins. Keep your hands in sight and we'll get to the bottom of this. And the woman inside with you needs to step outside, too."

Jesse turned back toward Sennett. "What are you doing here anyway? I was trying to leave the CIA out of this."

"I got a courtesy call from FBI Specialist Barrow so officially, I'm not here." He started to say something else, then turned his head toward a neighboring home. Jesse followed his gaze, immediately recognizing what had caught his supervisor's attention. A light had just come on inside the house next door.

"We need to get out of here," said Sennett. "The media might show up at any minute and explaining the presence of two active CIA officers at an FBI raid would be tough. My car's a block away."

"But they're going to want to talk to me. And Gleason."

"They know you'll be with me," replied Sennett before Jesse could say more. "And your friend's not going to leave without his grandmother, so let's get a move on."

As the two men moved away, careful to keep their heads down, Jesse could hear the man inside the house say, "I want my lawyer before I come out."

And then the reply from the FBI. "We'll bring in your attorney as soon as the situation is stable. So, just come out and talk to us, and as soon as everything is under control, we'll bring in your lawyer."

That was the last Jesse heard as he and Sennett moved out of earshot. When they reached Sennett's car, they got in. Sennett turned toward Jesse. "So, questions?"

"I was going to say that I didn't give Specialist Barrow your name—part of trying to keep the CIA out of this—so I don't know how he could have called you. But during the walk to your car ...."

Sennett put up a hand. "You figured that with publicly available organizational charts on Ruger-Phillips West website and a guess or two, he could have connected us. And then, through classified channels, he found out I was CIA."

"Pretty much," replied Jesse.

"Well, it was nothing that involved. I called him through official channels Tuesday afternoon after we talked. If everything had gone to plan—you witness the demonstration and then describe the threat to the FBI—my call wouldn't have been necessary. But as you said, things changed, so I'm glad the FBI team knew who you were. An active CIA agent at an FBI raid would be bad enough, but a dead one would be worse."

"I'll agree with that," replied Jesse. "Which only leaves one other question in my mind. The FBI was calling for two people to come out, but I didn't recognize them. Where'd they come up with those names?"

"The names I know, but how they came up with them, I have no idea. But I suspect we'll hear more about the deportation of two Russian nationals in the coming weeks. And if not?" Sennett just held out an empty hand.

"Right. I guess Robert wasn't as caught up in a fantasy as I had thought." Then, an idea struck Jesse. "You've talked about how the intelligence services could use more people who are unconventional thinkers, people who think outside the box. I can't imagine anyone less conventional in the conclusions he draws from very little data than Robert. After all, he did ID me as someone in intelligence and uncover a cell of Russian spies."

Sennett was quiet for a moment. "The possibility of attracting more imaginative thinkers to the intelligence field isn't mine, and it could just be someone up the command chain's flavor of the month. But you never know till you try. I'll get you a name of someone your friend can call if he's interested."

"Oh, he'll be interested."

Sennett nodded, then looked beyond Jesse through the passenger-side window. "Looks like someone is here to talk to you." Jesse rolled down his window.

After introductions and an offer by Sennett to join them in the car, the FBI agent said, "Thanks, but this won't take long. We'll need a more detailed statement, probably on Friday, but for now, just the basics. Name and position with the CIA?"

"Jesse Bolger. CIA Field Officer in ELINT."

"Really? I thought the Electronic Intelligence guys were in the labs, not the field."

"Most are," said Jesse. "But in my case, a little creative computer hacking in the field can sometimes open a lot of doors for the rest of the team."

"Makes sense. And you were alerted to the possible presence of a cell of Russian spies by a member of the public?"

"Correct," replied Jesse. "I called your field office and made the first contact report to Resident Agency Specialist Frederick Barrow. At the time, the threat was vague, but things evolved rapidly this evening." Jesse then summarized what had happened.

When he finished, the special agent said, "Sounds like this could have all gone south very easily. Fortunately, it didn't. We have them contained inside the house, but no sign of your friend or any hostage. You think they might have escaped?"

"Possibly. And no sign of a massive dog, either?"

"Sign?" the agent said with a grin. "If a dog pile half the size of Mount Rushmore is a sign, then we have one." He paused a moment. "That's all we need right now, but we'll be in contact to fill in the details later." He left.

"There's nothing more we can do tonight," said Sennett. "Wanna get out of here?"

"Sure," replied Jesse. "My clothes are stashed behind a dumpster not far away and my car's at Gleason's place. You mind being a chauffeur for a little while?"

"Those aren't your duds? And here I was thinking they were the latest in haute couture for the midnight runner."

Jesse didn't bother responding except to give his boss directions to the dumpster.

* * *

"I thought you said your car was in the garage?" said Sennett when they arrived at Gleason's house. Now, it was sitting at the end of the driveway.

"It was," said Jesse. "He must have moved it out, except ...."

"What?"

"He didn't have a key. Maybe we can add hot wiring to .... Wait. There's a note on the windshield."

Sennett stopped near the car and Jesse got out and read the note.

James ... I mean, Jesse –

Sorry to bail on you, buddy, but even without a license to kill, you can still take care of yourself. Anyway, Boris and Natasha had Grams tied up on the back porch, and I think Natasha needed a bio break. At least, she stepped away. So, we got the hell out of Dodge.

Grams was pretty shaken up by everything, so I wanted to get her home and give her a shot of her special "sleeping medicine," aka gin. She should be fine by tomorrow after an uninterrupted night of sleep, so I pushed your car out of the garage. Talk later,

Gleason

"OK. Another mystery solved," said Jesse as he handed Sennett the note.

"Yeah, I suppose, although it's a bit strange that two experienced intelligence agents were so lax in handling your friend's grandmother. But I guess when nature calls ...," Sennett said with a shrug.

"I'm going to take Friday off if that's OK?"

"Sure. No problem. It's been a strange week for you and, well, with ...."

"No need to retread that ground," Jesse said, certain he had just avoided another round of pity from his boss over Loren's leaving. "Thanks for the lift and I'll see you on Monday." He got into his car and drove away.

THURSDAY, JULY 4

Morning, Jesse Bolger's Apartment

After defusing bombs all night long in his sleep—whose countdowns, strangely, all ended with 007 showing on the display—Jesse decided that taking Friday off was one of his better decisions. Even though he'd stayed in bed until 9 o'clock, three and a half hours beyond his normal wakeup time, he was still tired. A few catnaps would probably take care of his physical exhaustion, but for his mental fatigue, a four-day weekend to worry about nothing would work wonders.

Jesse stumbled into the kitchen, made his coffee, and poured himself a bowl of cereal. He'd have to get to the grocery store soon; the milk and cereal were nearly gone. Loren normally did the grocery shopping, but he knew those staples weren't in short supply out of spite. Since he was always in a rush, he normally grabbed a coffee and bagel on the way to work or took the same to-go from their kitchen. The cereal and milk were hers.

"I never even made breakfast for her," he muttered to himself. But that oversight wasn't the worst of his behavior or lack thereof. He still felt guilty for the happy birthday call he'd made from the tarmac while waiting for his flight to London to take off. He wasn't really a jerk; it was the job that made him that way, although his internal pep talk wasn't having much of an effect. Shouldn't he have been more aggressive in finding an alternative?

His doorbell rang, making him wonder if it was going to be solar panels to cut his electric bill, a member of the high school band raising money for an out-of-state competition, or just his neighbor wanting to know if she had actually seen Loren carrying out her suitcases. His money was on the last. He started for the door, but after a few steps heard, "Jesse Bolger. This is the FBI. Open up."

He paused mid-step, puzzled why the FBI would come to his home for a routine interview. He opened the door. "I'm Jesse Bolger." But looking beyond the FBI agent standing on his porch with his badge holder open just added to his confusion. There were two cars on the street but only one agent in front. Could the second one be watching his back door?

"I have a search warrant for the phone that you received from the suspects yesterday." The hand that had been holding the agent's badge now produced the document.

Jesse took the paper and gave it a glance. It seemed to be in order. "I'll get it." He turned to retrieve the phone from the bedroom, but after a couple of steps, he realized that the agent was following him. He turned back around.

"If you don't mind," said the man, although Jesse suspected that it didn't matter if he minded or not.

Jesse shrugged and continued walking. "I wasn't expecting a thank-you meeting. You did apprehend the suspects last night, didn't you?"

"We did. This is just a routine follow-up to the statement you gave last night," said the agent, "although we need to finish it up at the FBI field office."

Bull, thought Jesse. Getting a search warrant for the phone and sending two men to offer him a ride to a follow-up interview at their field office was anything but routine. "I'd like to request the presence of Mr. Miles Sennett, my boss, at this interview."

"He'll be there."

Jesse wasn't certain about the protocol for an FBI interview of a CIA officer, and the presence of the officer's supervisor might be standard. Even so, the fact that they had already arranged for Sennett to be in attendance was telling. He'd also have the right to an attorney if things got that far, but surely, they wouldn't.

Jesse picked up the phone from his dresser and held it out to the agent. He, however, produced an evidence bag and Jesse dropped it in.

"Ok, let's go," said the agent.

* * *

It didn't take long for them to reach the Denver field office and, it seemed to Jesse, even less time to get to the interview room. Sennett was already seated inside.

"Any idea what's going on?" Jesse asked.

"None. I was just told they wanted to talk to you and that I was welcome to sit in."

"Thanks. I appreciate the support, although I can't imagine what they want to talk about. Everything was by the book—the first contact report or whatever the FBI calls them; playing along with the Russians till we saw the demonstration; then calling in for support when we got the address where they were holding Gleason's grandmother.

Speaking of which, have they said anything about contacting Gleason or Majoris?"

"Not a word to me. But whatever it is, we'll get to the bottom of it."

The two didn't have to wait long as a man entered the room. "Good morning. I'm Special Agent Jaquain Soto. I'll be conducting this interview."

"CIA Officer Jesse Bolger."

"And I'm CIA Officer Miles Sennett, his supervisor."

"So, a spy and his handler. Nice to meet you both," said Soto.

Despite the "nice to meet you," Soto's greeting was vaguely insulting. To the CIA, spies were individuals who gathered intelligence on their own countries and handlers were those who managed them. Basically, Soto had just called him a traitor to the United States, making Sennett guilty by association. Perhaps the FBI used the terms differently, but Jesse didn't think so.

It was also likely that the FBI agent had said exactly what he intended, as provoking an emotional reaction was a technique sometimes used in interrogations. Low boiling points in an interviewee could sometimes lead to unintended admissions. Rapport-based approaches to interrogation, however, tended to be more common and more effective, so Jesse was going to let it pass. Sennett, however, seemed to have a different idea.

"And you must be the guy who applies the thumbscrews."

A look passed between Soto and Sennett, and if Jesse had to name it, he would have said it reflected an understanding that the CIA knew the game he was playing.

"Nope, there'll be no forms of coercion used during my interviews," replied Soto smoothly. "I was just hoping to better understand Officer Bolger's motivations. From the report you gave Specialist Barrow, it was a chance meeting between you and a man you'd known in high school, Robert Gleason, that started your involvement in this incident. Can you tell me a little more about that encounter?"

A switch to rapport rather than argument – check. An open-ended question – check. The interview was back on the track Jesse had expected. "That's right. I'd gone to one of my favorite sandwich shops, Philly Pete's, for lunch. Gleason was there, although I didn't recognize him at first. He passed me a note and asked me to read it later. I did and it only had his address and a time to meet that evening."

"So, he didn't say anything about the Russian spies at that time?"

"No. He just made a comment about his tradecraft not being that good, but it was that night before I heard anything specific about the two Russian spies."

"You said that you didn't recognize Robert Gleason at first. How well did you know him in high school?"

"Not that well. He and his family moved to the area during my junior year. And he was quiet, although even in high school, he had some rather ambitious plans."

"Such as?" asked Soto.

"Placekicker for a professional football team. I remember that one because he didn't even go out for the high school team. He also wanted to invent a flying car. That one didn't seem quite as unlikely because he was pretty good in science, although a bit clumsy in the labs. We ended up in the same physics class."

"Your statement to the agent last night made it sound like Mr. Gleason was continuing his somewhat fanciful ambitions after high school. Or some might say, continuing his delusions."

"I suppose some might say that," said Jesse.

"He hoped to work in a communications center for space aliens?"

"He did, although don't we have several government agencies involved in the same pursuit?"

"Mr. Gleason thought that machines could be sentient."

"And again, he's not alone in that belief. At least, as I understand the field."

"Including the ability of a machine to feel emotion?"

"We didn't get to that level of detail."

"He built a SCIF in his basement so space aliens couldn't read his thoughts."

Jesse had entertained all these reservations about his old friend and more, but somehow, coming from Soto, the accusations bothered him. The agent was attacking a man who wasn't there to defend himself.

"Robert Gleason has some unusual characteristics, but then, I suspect if we dug into your background, we'd find a few quirks there, too?"

"Point taken," said Soto. "Back to your high school days. Since you didn't know Mr. Gleason that well back then and it has been what, eleven, twelve years?"

"A little over thirteen," replied Jesse.

"Thirteen. That's a long time. So, what are the chances that the individual you met at Philly Pete's wasn't Robert Gleason?"

Jesse hadn't seen that question coming and he glanced at Sennett. By the look on his boss's face, he'd been caught off-guard, too.

"None," Jesse said slowly. "While it is true that he was one of a thousand other kids at my high school, as I mentioned, I had a class with him. I saw him every day for a year and occasionally the other year we were in school together. The guy at Philly Pete's looked like Gleason. He talked like Gleason. He had the same mannerisms. No one would go to those lengths to impersonate one of my old classmates. Why would they?"

"Yeah, why would they," agreed Soto. "So, it sounds like Gleason was a bit of an outsider back when you knew him. He moved in halfway through high school. He had unusual goals for his life, some of which didn't fit with his abilities. Would it be safe to say that he was probably a bit of an enigma to most of your high school class?"

Jesse couldn't really see where Soto was going with this line of questioning and that bothered him. But at least this question was easy enough to evade. "You know, I can't really say what the other students thought of him. You'll have to ask them."

Soto nodded slowly. "Well, I don't know what his other classmates thought of him either. But if they kept in touch, they would think ... that he's dead."

Morning, FBI Field Office

Jesse just stared for a moment, so Soto took the opportunity to repeat himself. "That's right. Robert Gleason died in a car crash six years ago."

"I .... I can't believe that," said Jesse eventually.

"I can request a copy of the death certificate if that would help."

"Look, I'm sure there's a death certificate. And there was probably a body, too, but it wasn't Gleason. I know because I saw him yesterday."

"You've gone from didn't know him well thirteen years ago to certain you saw him yesterday in the blink of an eye. What changed?" asked Soto.

"Nothing. Yes, I didn't know him well. We weren't best friends who shared everything. But the guy I've been talking to for the last three days is the same one I knew in high school."

"OK," said Soto. "We can certainly watch for someone who resembles Gleason as the investigation progresses."

The reply certainly indicated that Soto wasn't convinced Gleason was still among the living, and Jesse figured the same sentiment would soon pervade the field office if it hadn't already. He kept the thought to himself, however, not wanting to push the interview back toward arguments.

"We did a drive-by at the location where you changed clothes," said Soto, "but it looks like the dumpster might have been moved. Maybe kids. Or maybe it was in the wrong place to start. But anyway, I was wondering if you could make me a sketch of where it was relative to the side fence, the building, and any cars that were parked there?"

The notion that he, a person who had struggled in high school art and who had no training since could draw the scene close enough to aid in the investigation was ridiculous. But then, Jesse was certain the agent wasn't really interested in his drawing ability. Rather, he was interested in how he would handle the additional mental load of sketching the scene on top of the requirement to keep all of his fibs and their implications straight. It was an interview technique generally known as the cognitive load approach to lie detection, and while it didn't always work—no technique was foolproof—it increased the chance the liar made a mistake.

Jesse thought about giving Soto a crude drawing—a box on wheels for the dumpster, the outline of a car with grinning, stick-figure faces at the window—and saying "That's it! That's where I changed clothes," but the humor would be at his expense if things didn't go well. "I'll do my best, but I'm no artist."

"All we can ask," said Soto as he handed Jesse a sheet of paper and a pencil. "Now, let me do a bit of role-playing if you will." He paused, rubbing his chin like he was just now contemplating his next statement.

"If I had information that would be tricky to give to the authorities, I'd look for some minor character from my past as the source of it. With strangers, there'd be no reason for them to confide in me, and there would be questions when they did. With close friends, it would be too easy to check their stories because I'd know where to find them. But someone I knew slightly? A person like that might bring me into their confidence, but afterward, could easily disappear. I'd just write it off as another old acquaintance who went back to their own life. And if I told others that story, they'd have no reason to question it."

It seemed like Soto had just admitted that the FBI didn't check on the sources of their tips—the tipster could disappear and "they'd have no reason to question it." But in reflection, Jesse suspected that was true in many, if not most cases. He had read somewhere that the FBI received around 1,300 tips a day, on average, and many of them were secondhand information, an online post, or even a feeling. And if requested, the anonymity of the tipster would be guaranteed, making any type of follow-up impossible. A lot of people just wanted to stay out of the limelight.

So, the fact they had checked on Gleason and had done so quickly was concerning to Jesse. What was it about this particular case that had made them a lot more than just a bit curious? Perhaps he could find out, although a direct question to a trained FBI interrogator was unlikely to yield anything. He was going to have to back into an answer if he was going to find out anything at all.

"So, unless this is a purely academic exercise, you're saying I picked Robert Gleason as the source of information on the Russians because I knew him well enough to describe his characteristics, but not well enough to know he was dead?"

"You wouldn't be the first person to suddenly realize that they needed a scapegoat but didn't have the time to check out all the facts. And with your friend's, shall we say, flighty nature, you could just claim he took off after he found out how much danger he had been in, and no one would question it."

"OK," said Jesse slowly. "If Robert Gleason is dead, who is living in the house at the address I gave you?"

"No one at the moment," said Soto. "It was rented through July, but when we checked, the renters had already left and the homeowner hadn't returned. The renters paid cash and gave the names Randy and Barb Hidalgo from Billings, Montana, but those names and the address they gave in Billings didn't lead anywhere. It's an empty lot."

"And I'd guess that the name Olive Majoris, Gleason's grandmother, doesn't appear anywhere in these rental transactions?"

"Olive is actually the first name of Robert Gleason's mother, not his grandmother. But, no, her name didn't come up with the rental because she died in the same car crash as Mr. Gleason."

The coincidences were piling up in Jesse's mind. "Doesn't it seem a little suspicious to you that the two people I identified as occupants of that house were both killed in the same car wreck six years ago? And doesn't it seem even more suspicious that the renters paid cash and gave false identities?"

"Well, first, you didn't identify Gleason's mother as an occupant of the house," said Soto. "You mentioned a grandmother but had the wrong name. That's completely consistent with a hurried and flawed attempt to find someone else to blame. And, second, giving an alias for a cash rental isn't as unusual as you might think. We talked to the owner, an elderly lady. After a bit of unease when she thought we represented the Homeowner's Association, she admitted that she rents her place two or three months every year and only takes cash. Apparently, the HOA has some rules against short-term rentals, so she does things a bit under the table. And people who want privacy in their downtime often seek cash rentals. It's not anything we haven't seen before."

That was interesting, thought Jesse. "So, when the owner rents her place short-term, she probably leaves a lot of her furnishings in place," he said mostly to himself. If the house had been set up to look like Majoris was the owner and

Gleason, her long-term guest during his training for his new job, the typical clutter in the garage and the few knickknacks he had seen in the house would help sell that illusion.

Soto paused a beat. "That would be typical," he agreed, although his hesitation probably meant he wasn't sure why that surmise was important.

"And I suppose you can't find an Agent Edward Jenkins or the organization where he said he worked, the National Bureau of Counterintelligence?"

"That would be correct. There is no such organization and so, no such individual working there."

The facts, as Jesse saw them, were that Gleason was officially dead, but he wasn't. He had pretended to live with his grandmother in a retirement community but didn't. Majoris had claimed to be his grandmother but wasn't nor was she dead as the FBI believed ... unless the woman wasn't Olive Majoris.

If those facts weren't confusing enough, then there were the voids that Jesse had to deal with. Now, it seemed unlikely that Gleason had stumbled onto the two Russian spies through a classified ad, but he had found them somehow. He hadn't wanted to turn them in for reasons Jesse couldn't guess, so he had created an incredibly involved scam to obtain his cooperation. And then, Gleason had apparently disappeared into the night, since the FBI wouldn't be claiming he was dead if they had interviewed him.

It all seemed to lead to one conclusion. "I've been set up," Jesse said to Soto. "I think the mysterious cash renters are Robert Gleason and his mother. They wanted to look like residents to get me to go along with flushing out the Russian terrorists."

"And why would they need or want you involved?" asked Soto.

Jesse released a long breath. "I'm not really sure," he admitted.

"Well, even if you come up with a reason, we still have a problem because both of the people you're trying to implicate are dead. I've answered your questions, so it's time for me to tell you what I think." Soto took a moment as if deciding what to say. "Do you know who we apprehended yesterday?"

"I heard a couple of names, but didn't recognize them," said Jesse.

"Really? That's your position?" asked Soto. The question was apparently rhetorical in the agent's mind as he didn't wait for a response. "We apprehended Elizaveta Ermakov and Alexey Ilyin. Do you know who they are?"

Jesse was wondering if this was another rhetorical question as he had no idea, but Sennett was apparently better informed on such matters. "Yeah, I know those names," he said. "They are two of the more notorious foreign agents in our area for the last twenty years or so. They presumably funded Najibullah Zazi. At the time, he was residing in Colorado and was later convicted of conspiring to commit murder by detonating a weapon of mass destruction on the New York City subway. But all that was before Jesse's time and they've kept a relatively low profile since then."

"Low profile but still a threatening one," said Soto. "We've known their names from intercepted communications, but not the identities they were hiding under. But with what we found in the house yesterday, there is no doubt we got the right couple."

"And just why didn't I want to report them rather than making it a tip from a friend?" asked Jesse. "I could have gotten some private kudos from the CIA if I had." Unfortunately, by this point in the interview, he was beginning to see where the FBI agent was going. And if he had it right, Soto was going for the kill ... or at least, a lengthy prison sentence.

"Ermakov and Ilyin told us they were waiting for you to discuss your terms for supporting intelligence gathering in the United States. You were to be their double agent. The trouble is, I believe you had a change of heart. You wanted out, but if you just came to the FBI and said, I know where you can find Ermakov and Ilyin, we'd want to know how you knew. So, the tip on these two had to come from someone else who might then disappear later. Enter Mr. Robert Gleason."

Sennett had been mostly quiet since the start of the interview, but this accusation was apparently too much for him to stay mum. "Are you telling me that it is now FBI policy to accept the word of two known Russian terrorists over a CIA officer of excellent standing? I hope you don't intend to go forward with this nonsense, as I'd hate to see the FBI become the laughingstock of social media."

"We do intend to go forward," said Soto matter-of-factly. "But as you say, the word of foreign terrorists isn't to be trusted. Fortunately, we also have the word of someone you do trust, as you just described him as a CIA officer of excellent standing. At 11:32 PM yesterday, CIA Officer Jesse Bolger contacted FBI Resident Agency Specialist Frederick Barrow and provided an address. Earlier in the day, he also named the suspects, Ermakov and Ilyin, providing the link between them and the identities they had been hiding under. There is only one way he could have known who they were and where they lived. He had worked with them."

Jesse looked at Sennett and shook his head.

"Agent Soto, this interview is over," said Sennett. "We will return tomorrow morning with counsel because discussing the betrayal of your country is hardly the only way someone could have found out the identities of Ermakov and Ilyin. And the fact that you put it that way means the FBI has already made up their mind about Officer Bolger."

"Sorry, but I'm afraid we can't let Officer Bolger leave," said Soto. He turned toward Jesse.

"We have reasonable suspicion that you've committed a crime, giving us the right to detain you so we can finish the investigation. Given the serious nature of the possible offense, I suggest you voluntarily agree to detention rather than forcing us to formally charge you now."

Jesse understood the option Soto was offering. With reasonable suspicion, the FBI had the right to detain him, but the amount of time they kept him could be challenged later. It was even possible that the charges would be dropped if the delay was ruled to be excessive, although that seemed extremely unlikely to him in the case of espionage. So, his choices were to voluntarily stay in custody, in which case the detention was automatically legal. Or he could object and they would charge him now, leaving him with an arrest record even if the charges were later dismissed. He wanted to avoid that possibility for as long as possible in the hope that he could prove his innocence first.

"You can keep me," Jesse said. "But could I have a word with Miles first?"

"Of course."

The two men huddled in a corner of the interrogation room, whispering although they were under no illusion that their lowered voices would escape the microphones hidden around them.

"The time seems about right," whispered Jesse. "The calls were made after we got the address for the Russians at the bank. But Gleason called Barrow while I called Jenkins. And I don't know what he's talking about when he said I gave Barrow the names Ermakov and Ilyin earlier in the day. The late-night calls were all we made yesterday, and as I said, mine was to Jenkins."

"Did you check the record of calls and texts on the phone the Russians gave you?"

"It didn't send texts, but … dammit, no, I didn't check the call log," replied Jesse. "What a stupid oversight."

"Don't beat yourself up. In the hour or so, you had it, I doubt anyone would have thought to check. Anything else I should know?"

The calls when he was supposed to have supplied the address and names of the Russians were crucial, Jesse knew. With only the address, he had given the FBI a tip that proved credible and he was a hero. But with their names and their location, he had supplied the link between two foreign spies and their new identities, a connection that no one else in the intelligence community knew. That knowledge made him a suspected traitor. And since Resident Agency Specialist Barrow was one of the local field office's initial points of contact for tips, the FBI would have a recording of that call even though it was made in the middle of the night.

What he needed was a conclusive mismatch between the FBI's recording of the call and his voice. But even before Gleason's monologue about the challenges of voiceprint technology, Jesse knew that a definitive result was unlikely. "You know, Sennett, I think I'm screwed," he whispered. "The phone they gave me was this crappy little thing, so it would be easy for someone to create a fake call log for Barrow's number. Then, if that person placed the actual call on the same model phone at a nearby location while I was speaking to Jenkins, the cell tower records would show it. And last, if they used AI technology to sound like me ... well, I can't see anything better than an inconclusive result when the FBI checks for a voice match. Or worst case, they match the recording to me."

"Yeah, you may be right," replied Sennett. "But we'll fight it. I've heard that using the same microphone can improve the accuracy of voiceprint tests. Maybe we can get them to take a sample from you on the phone the Russians provided. But let's check with our experts and our lawyers before we agree to anything. OK?"

"Yeah, OK. And I know the drill from here on out. Talk to absolutely no one while in detention." Jesse paused, shaking his head. "I never thought I'd need to use that advice."

FRIDAY, JULY 5

Morning, Colorado Detention Center

The thing about being detained was that it gave Jesse a lot of time to think. And everything that he knew and all that he believed pointed to the conclusion he had voiced to Soto: He'd been set up.

In his mind, who had set him up had become obvious as well. Olive Majoris had played the older woman so he wouldn't question their residence in a 55+ community. Gleason then parlayed his idiosyncrasies to create this nerdy spy-wannabe with an incredible story with Majoris in a supporting role every step of the way. And he had bought every word of it.

How Gleason had found the Russians in the first place was much vaguer in Jesse's mind, but that fact didn't bother him much. Whether it was dumb luck or Gleason had used his creative imagination to locate them or he had a previous connection to the foreign spies made little difference to his case. Gleason had found them someway and had used his old high school friend to have them apprehended.

It was the question of why, however, that was giving Jesse problems. Why hadn't Gleason simply given the tip to the FBI himself? Clearly, he and Majoris had gone to great lengths to stay in the shadows. They'd found a cash rental close to the cell of terrorists and posed as residents. Gleason had coordinated with someone, probably Majoris, to play Boris and Jenkins on the phone. Using AI voice cloning technology, she could have easily played both men; she could have sounded like him, too, in the call to Barrow. Gleason had run them all over town so he could pretend to check ATM balances, had ratcheted up the pressure by scheduling the attack and faking Majoris's kidnapping, and had given Jesse a phone that would probably result in a lengthy prison sentence.

And when Jesse took all of those factors into account, it wasn't dumb luck or a creative imagination that had led Gleason and Majoris to the spies. It was that they had a previous connection to them. Perhaps they had considered betraying their country but had a change of heart, which was much the same scenario as Soto had suspected of him. Or maybe it was a falling out among spies. Or perhaps Gleason and Majoris wanted to move on to greener pastures and Ermakov and Ilyin stood in their way. But whatever their motivation for using him, Jesse would never forget what they had done and would see them brought to justice. That is, if he lived long enough.

Presumably, the FBI would attempt to locate the two that had framed him, but with death certificates in hand, he wondered how vigorously they would pursue the possibility that Gleason and Majoris were alive? So, he would help himself by hiring a private investigator to supplement the FBI's efforts and he even knew the person he would approach first.

Jesse had read about this PI in the paper. She was new to the area but had already solved a big case involving the murder of the CEO and president of a local business. And possibly important later in the case, she had experience with the FBI, as she had come from their ranks. Hopefully, she still had some contacts at the Bureau. As he saw it, contacting

Private Investigator Rebecca Marte had to be his first order of business. And even if he couldn't personally meet with her because he was in jail, he was sure Sennett would make the arrangements for him.

A guard walked down the aisle outside the holding cells and stopped at the one where he sat. "Jesse Bolger?"

"Yes."

"This way," he said.

Jesse wondered where he was going, but figured it was pointless to ask. Whether it was interrogation room 2 or 5 made little difference. When they returned to the intake station, he was surprised, but he still kept to himself. He didn't know much about detention centers, but he knew enough to realize that asking was generally useless; whatever they wanted him to know, they would tell him.

"Jesse Bolger," announced the guard with a complete lack of interest when they reached the intake station.

The guard posted there held out a large envelope. "Check your belongings and if everything is there, sign for them."

After he did, the second guard pointed at a door and said, "You're free to go."

Jesse stepped through to find Sennett on the other side. "OK, I'm confused. I can't be out on bail because I was never advised of any charges against me, and bail was never set."

"And it looks like there may never be any charges," replied Sennett.

Jesse could feel his forehead tense in a frown with his boss's comment. Sennett must have recognized the expression, however, as he said, "I can't explain it either. All I know is that the DA's office called me this morning and said they wouldn't be pursuing the case. When I asked if they had the authority to drop a case that potentially involved national security, I was told their directions came from high enough in the criminal justice system that it wasn't an issue."

"I suppose I shouldn't be questioning my good fortune, but ... that's really strange. Who the hell would intervene for me? And how did they even find out about the situation so quickly?"

"Sorry, Jesse, but I have no idea."

Jesse slowly shook his head. "So, am I still employed?"

"I don't see any reason why you wouldn't be," replied Sennett.

Jesse would have preferred an answer that wasn't based on a lack of information to the contrary, but as he had said before, perhaps he shouldn't question his luck. But then, his apprehension returned as Sennett cleared his throat. There was more.

"However, I think you should keep a low profile for a while, see which way the winds are blowing. If everything seems copacetic in two weeks, we'll get you back out into the field."

Jesse grimaced. "I was sort of ...."

"I know. You wanted to stay busy. I won't make this last any longer than necessary, but some time on a desk job won't kill you."

"If you say so, boss."

TEN WEEKS LATER, TUESDAY, SEPTEMBER 17

Morning, Marte Investigative Services

Jesse sat staring out the windshield of his car. It was parked in the circular gravel driveway of an old two-story white-frame house. According to a plaque out front, it had been the home of a wealthy rancher; now it housed Jen's Place, a temporary shelter for survivors of domestic abuse on the left and the offices of Marte Investigative Services on the right. He'd come to see if the owner of the second business was interested in a job finding two missing persons because the "two weeks" of desk work that Sennett had mentioned had turned into ten weeks and counting. And frankly, he was tired of sitting on his hands.

Even from his first days on the desk, Jesse knew he'd never excel at this type of work. He just didn't find reviewing the movement of suspects using cell phone tower "data dumps" all that interesting. Occasionally, he'd find himself thinking about what this information would have told him about Robert Gleason if he had been a person of interest. He'd know that the man went to one of his favorite sandwich shops ... or had gone there at least once. He would have assumed that Gleason liked to jog at night ... although that seemed clearly wrong. Perhaps, with the right background, he could piece together an incriminating pattern from these data. Maybe Gleason had also frequented an electronics store with all the components he'd need to build a cheesy-looking Light Phone, but Jesse lacked both the training and the aptitude for that to happen. The result was that he found the work dull, although he forced himself to maintain focus because, boring or not, it was vitally important work.

It wasn't that his old job had turned him into an adrenaline junky—he had never faced another foreign agent in a gun battle. But he often felt like he was staring down a network "line" at ruthless computer hackers intent on disrupting American power, communications, transportation, or other critical services. And he felt a deep sense of satisfaction when he thwarted their plans. It was a feeling that he had experienced four times over the last six years. But on the desk, he doubted that he would feel that way more than once even if he was there for twenty years.

After a few days in the office, he considered calling Loren. He could tell her he was at home every night; he'd have time to spend with her. But he also realized that the idea was completely selfish. If things had gone according to Sennett's stated plan, she'd hardly be unpacked when he'd have to break the news that he was back on the road. And frankly, he hoped that a call back to the "action" he relished would happen at any moment. So, he put the thought of calling Loren out of his mind. She was better off without any more of his hollow promises.

What was left for him to ponder was the whereabouts of Robert Gleason and Olive Majoris, and frankly, that topic didn't sit comfortably in his thoughts. He'd spoken to Sennett about it sometime during the first week of his office duty and his boss's recommendation was, "Don't look a gift horse in the mouth." He hadn't, after all, lost his job, his freedom, or his life. And if Gleason and Majoris had a previous relationship with Boris and Natasha, aka Elizaveta Ermakov and Alexey Ilyin, and had decided to distance themselves from the Russians for some reason, they were the FBI's problem, not his.

But Jesse seriously doubted that the Bureau was out looking for Gleason and Majoris. And if they weren't, he'd be left with a dark cloud floating at the back of his mind, making an unwanted appearance when he slept or let his guard down. Formally, the case had been closed—albeit for reasons no one could explain—but that didn't mean he had forgotten it. If nothing else, the FBI's inaction meant they hadn't bought his story and they probably thought they'd had their man when they detained him ten weeks ago.

All it would take to restore some momentum to his case was for someone to prove that Gleason and Majoris were still alive. Unfortunately, he had no idea how to find a missing person, nor did he have the contacts in the FBI to ascertain where things stood. "But you, Ms. Marte, have both," he muttered to the empty car. So, he had called her to set up this meeting.

He got out and went to the private investigator's office door. On it was a sign that said, "Open. Please Come In." He did so and came face-to-face with a very attractive blonde sitting at the desk in what must be the reception area. Beyond her, there was a second door with a plaque that read "Rebecca Marte, Investigative Services."

"Morning, Ms. ...." Jesse was hoping she would fill in a name. It wasn't that he had any interest in finding a replacement for Loren at the moment, but eventually, he might be forced to consider it.

But rather than filling the blank with her name, the woman merely said, "May I help you?"

"My name's Jesse Bolger. I have an appointment with your employer."

"Since I'm self-employed, I guess that means you want to see me," the woman replied. "I'm Rebecca Marte."

Once again, Jesse had fallen prey to a stereotype. This woman was obviously too attractive to be a PI ... although she was. At least she had been sitting in the reception area when he mistakenly inferred that she was the help, not the boss.

"Ms. Marte. Nice to meet you." He extended a hand. She stood from behind the desk to return the greeting. She was taller than he expected and when she smiled even more attractive than he'd first thought.

"Likewise, Mr. Bolger. Let's step back into my office."

Marte led the way, taking a seat behind a large wooden desk as she gestured to a chair on the other side. When he was seated, she said, "I understand you have a missing persons case you want to discuss."

"That's correct. I'm looking for Robert Gleason. Or alternatively, his mother, Olive Majoris. She'd know how to get in contact with him."

"Why would you like to find Mr. Gleason?"

Jesse had given some thought about how he would describe what he'd been through. He couldn't tell Marte some facts, like the actual name of his employer, but he could cover most of the rest. And yet, he hesitated. Now, over two months removed from the events, everything seemed even more bizarre than it had at the time.

The capture of the two Russian spies had been in the news, of course, but the coverage was quite limited locally. That was probably because they had become bargaining chips in a prisoner exchange handled by the federal government on the East Coast soon after their apprehension. So, when he mentioned that part, Marte wouldn't necessarily think he was mentally disabled … even if his name had never been mentioned in the media's coverage.

But when he put the rest of his story into words, he didn't see how Marte could possibly believe him. "An unpredictable guy I had known in high school actually found the spies while he was living in his grandmother's basement in a 55+ community. But she wasn't really his grandmother and they weren't actually residents. He'd built a SCIF so aliens wouldn't be able to listen to his thoughts, but he wanted to use it to keep the spies from listening in. No, they weren't aliens, but his friend thought the spies had bugged his grandmother's house." And so on, until Jesse was left staring at the floor and shaking his head.

And then, Jesse considered Marte's prior connection to the FBI. Eventually, after she was into the case, he thought it might become a positive, especially if she still had connections there. But initially, the Bureau's skepticism of his tale would become hers.

So, in the end, he decided that one complete, gigantic falsehood had the best chance of success. "He owes me some money."

"Must be quite a bit for you to hire a PI to find him?"

"It is."

Marte pulled the computer keyboard toward her and turned the monitor so she could see it. "I just need to take a few notes. Tell me a little about your history with Mr. Gleason. You can start with where you two met."

Without a plan, it would be too easy for the PI to trip him up, so Jesse had decided to use facts about Gleason when he knew them and his own background when he didn't. So, his first answer was the name of the high school they had attended together. Next, Marte asked where Gleason had lived before moving to Colorado, which he also knew. But then, Marte backtracked to college, asking if their association extended to those days.

The sudden shift in timeframes made him somewhat uneasy. As Soto had done before, Marte seemed to be trying to increase the mental demands of juggling the truth and falsehoods, which meant that she suspected him. He didn't know why that would be true; perhaps she was just suspicious by nature. But in this case, at least, he was prepared. He had previously decided that no one made a sizeable loan to another person if they had only been friends when they were seventeen. So, he gave her the name of his college because he didn't know if Gleason had ever gone anywhere except a community college in Missouri ... and he wasn't even certain that was true.

The questioning continued along similar lines for a few minutes, including the PI's constant changes in the timeframe. He found it taxing mentally but combining what he knew of Gleason with his background seemed to be providing all the grist he needed for his responses. After a while, his answers sounded confident and concise, at least to his ears, and he started to relax.

And then, Marte stopped typing and said, "I think I understand why you're having trouble getting your money back." She turned the monitor in his direction so he could read from the screen. "It's really tough to collect from a dead man."

Morning, Marte Investigative Services

"Now, why don't you get the hell out of my office and find someone dumb enough to take your money," Marte said, her face turning a touch pink.

"Hold on a second," said Jesse. He had searched for information on Gleason's and Majoris's deaths, and it had taken him three hours to find anything. He figured that once the investigation was underway, she'd uncover new evidence that would call the accuracy of these stories into question. The problem, however, was that she had found a story about their deaths in about fifteen minutes while dividing her attention between her questions and his answers. Obviously, she knew a lot of tricks he didn't, making it even more apparent that he needed her help.

"Why? You need more time to make things up?"

"Look, Ms. Marte, I can't tell you everything, and even if you guess something, I won't confirm or deny it. But I can tell you that my record is ... well, unblemished except for possible innuendoes and rumors. I work for ...."

"Miles Sennett at Ruger-Phillips West."

"You looked me up?"

"It's easy enough. If I take your case, would you mind if I talk to Mr. Sennett?"

"Not at all. But since this isn't directly related to work, I should warn him first to expect your call."

"That's fine. Now, you want to take another stab at why you're looking for Mr. Gleason and Ms. Majoris? And the truth this time."

Jesse sighed, knowing that he needed to divulge as much as he could without violating any CIA policies. It would be a precarious tightrope walk, but now that he had gone this far, he really wanted to secure Marte's help.

"I hadn't seen Gleason since high school until I bumped into him in July," Jesse said, as he started a story that would take him the next twenty minutes. He described everything that had happened, except for the fact that he worked for the CIA. He even included being momentarily thwarted by a privacy fence in a retirement community backyard. He figured it made him look more human and it seemed to work, as Marte covered a smile with her hand.

When he finished, he said, "Well, what do you think?"

"A couple of questions first," Marte replied. "You mentioned the FBI. Is that where you think this black cloud might still be hanging over you?"

"You think I'm worried about nothing?"

"Not exactly. No one in law enforcement likes being told to stand down without a reason, so there's undoubtedly some second-guessing going on. But in the long run, they're too busy to keep that concern alive. What I was wondering was whether there are others, individuals or organizations, who might also have their, shall we say, concerns about you."

"No one else besides the FBI knows what happened."

"Except Jenkins and anyone in NBC that he told; Gleason, Majoris, and anyone they told; Elizaveta Ermakov, Alexey Ilyin, and everyone up their chain of command; and Sennett," said Marte.

Of course, she was right even if he hadn't thought it through. "Maybe we should just name the people who have no reason to doubt me. The list might be shorter."

"I also wondered," said Marte, apparently ignoring his attempt at humor, "if you thought I had some influence on the workings at the local FBI field office because I don't."

"No. I knew that you did your two-year probationary period in St. Louis, not here. But if nothing else, you know FBI policies a lot better than me."

A flicker of a frown crossed Marte's features, and Jesse immediately recognized his faux pas. He'd shown familiarity with the Bureau's training process—new agent trainee at the FBI Academy followed by a two-year probationary period at a field office. But then, the sequence wasn't exactly top secret.

Still, Jesse wondered if he'd said too much and didn't relax until she said, "That's all the questions I have for now. Missing persons cases can be tricky. Some are solved within hours; others can go on for years. It just depends. Have you thought about how you want me to proceed?"

"I have, but let me know if this doesn't make sense. I'd like for you to start with a full-court press." He paused, knowing that Loren rarely understood his sports analogies, so he started to explain. "I just mean ...."

"That you want me to guard the other basketball team for the full length of the court rather than just under my basket. Or, in slang, you want me to search for Mr. Gleason aggressively at the beginning."

Jesse chuckled. "Exactly. If a couple of weeks turns up nothing, then if you can just keep an eye out for new developments, that would be great."

"Sure. I can do that. And so you know what you're asking for, here is a contract with my hourly fees. Direct expenses are separate, although I won't go flying off to Billings, Montana, without telling you."

Jesse glanced at it, finding the key figures pretty much as he had expected. He filled in two weeks for the initial search, then signed it. "About Billings," he said. "Do you really think you'd find something at the bogus address that the house renters gave the owner?"

Marte paused, staring at him a moment. "You didn't mention that the people who rented the house in Denver gave a bogus address in Billings."

"An unintentional oversight," Jesse said quickly as he held up both hands. He wanted to avoid even the appearance that he was holding out on her ... even though he was.

"But a potentially important one," replied Marte. "The car accident in which Gleason and Majoris supposedly died was on a rural road just outside Billings. You didn't notice that?"

"No. I must have missed it," Jesse admitted. "You think it means something?"

"The FBI should have checked the address the renters gave. Did they say anything about it?" asked Marte.

"It's an empty lot."

She nodded. "If you're going to stage your own death, you probably pick someplace close by. Otherwise, you just add the question of what you were doing so far from home to the overall deception. So, I was already thinking that Gleason and Majoris had some type of connection to Montana. What the bogus address tells us is that they probably have a lot more than just a passing familiarity with Billings. It's easy enough to know a few street names, but to know the address of a vacant lot? That's either an impressive feat of recall or they had the address to use in cases like this one."

"Probably the latter," said Jesse. "Wouldn't Russian agents have a lot of trivia like that memorized so they can use it to concoct convincing stories?"

"I would think so, but I'm not sure how much I buy into the theory about them being compatriots of Ermakov and Ilyin. It's a possibility, of course, but hardly the only one. And probably not even the most likely."

"You think not?"

"Well, it requires that they are spies, which is not all that likely to start with. Hold on a second."

Marte turned the computer monitor back in her direction. After less than thirty seconds of typing, she said, "While no one knows, of course, most estimates of the number of foreign agents in the United States max out at around 10,000. That's 10,000 out of a population of over 300 million. And most are in the Washington D.C. area, not Denver. Then, they'd need a difference of opinion important enough to turn on their counterparts. And finally, they would have to be willing to become rogue agents, since Ermakov and Ilyin were active, high-value operatives worthy of a prisoner exchange. That's a lot of unlikely situations that would all have to be true."

"But what would be more likely?" asked Jesse.

Marte smiled. "Generating possibilities while not focusing on any one of them too soon is a key part of the job. But for me, anyway, it's a solitary task. Too many cooks, as they say. But I will give you periodic reports as the investigation continues."

"Sure," replied Jesse. "Then, I guess I should let you get to it." He stood, and after a second handshake, left.

Mid-Morning, Marte Investigative Services

Rebecca leaned back in her desk chair, a maneuver that made looking at her notes from the meeting with Jesse Bolger that much more difficult. That was alright, however, as her mind wasn't really into reading them anyway. She was too busy wondering if she had made a mistake. When Bolger's case first appeared to be a simple missing persons search, there was little doubt she would take it if he agreed to her terms. But when Bolger came clean—or cleaner anyway—she could see this case leading her down so many rabbit holes that she'd forget what daylight looked like.

When she considered what she knew with reasonable confidence, there wasn't much. There certainly seemed to be an adversarial relationship between Gleason and Majoris on the one hand and Ermakov and Ilyin on the other, assuming Bolger had been forthcoming on his second try. Why else would the first two have turned the second two into the FBI? That conclusion, of course, assumed that Gleason and Majoris weren't just a smokescreen that Bolger had created to cover his involvement, as the Bureau thought.

But otherwise, there was little clear in the case, despite her client's firm belief in his falling-out-among-spies scenario. A major issue with that theory—and one she hadn't mentioned earlier to her new client to avoid more tapdancing around the truth—was the sudden and unexplained halt to the investigation into his involvement with the Russians. Why wasn't that the reason he wanted to hire her ... unless he already knew or thought he knew the answer.

So then, the question became, who did he think gave him the get-out-of-jail-free card? Or for that matter, who even had the authority to have one to give? From that perspective, the list had few entries, but it was vast in scope.

Someone up the chain in the FBI could have called the investigation off, but she didn't think Bolger was FBI. If he was, why didn't he just push the manhunt from within the agency? So, if the FBI wasn't his secret benefactor, then someone else high enough in the federal government to give the FBI orders was. Off the top of her head, she figured that could be a member of Congress, a member of the president's cabinet, someone in one of the executive departments like the Department of Justice, the vice president, or the president. Like she had thought before, the list was short, but the implications were broad enough that even if she directed an army of investigators, they would never uncover the responsible individual. She needed to come at the problem from a different direction.

One that readily came to mind was Bolger's background. Most people who had been the focus of an FBI investigation but who were suddenly and inexplicably cleared would probably be laying low and thanking their lucky stars. Bolger, however, was poking around the fringes of an active Bureau investigation ... or at least, a semi-active one if her client was correct about their lack of interest. Sure, she could understand his motivation to find Gleason and Majoris, but his curiosity, if that was what it was, might get him right back into detention or worse.

And then, there was his whole disclaimer before he provided the second version of why he wanted to find Gleason. "I can't tell you everything, and even if you guess something, I won't confirm or deny it." No one who was flipping burgers at a fast-food joint said things like that. There was something in his background that he couldn't or wasn't going to share.

Fortunately, Rebecca had a readily available starting point for her examination into Bolger's past—his place of employment, Ruger-Phillips West. From her past association with Dr. Sam "Doc" Price, who was a researcher in their main office in St. Louis, she knew that much of Ruger-Phillips's work was from government contracts, with a sizeable portion of those from the military. That kind of work could have put her client in close contact with congressmen or high-ranking officials in the military. Hopefully, Doc would know or be able to find out more about Mr. Miles Sennett and his small group of buyers in the Denver office.

She leaned forward in her chair and picked up her phone from the desk. In moments, Doc's phone was ringing.

"Hi, Rebecca. I didn't expect a call from you." He paused a beat. "Nicole's OK, isn't she?"

Rebecca smiled. "You'd probably know the answer to that better than me. At least the way I hear it, you two talk several times a week." Doc and a mutual friend, Nicole Veles, had been close until events conspired against them. Now, they were trying to rebuild that relationship long distance.

"Yeah, I just don't want to take anything for granted," he said. "So, what can I do for you?"

"I'm looking for some information on an employee at Ruger-Phillips West. You know anything about your Denver operations?"

"Truthfully, I hardly knew we had a branch there until recently, but things change."

"Are you saying you're thinking about moving out here to be closer to Nicole?"

He hesitated. "That doesn't seem like an option ... well, any time soon." He paused again. "Of course, that doesn't mean I didn't check into what they do, but only enough to know it's not research. So, there's no simple fit for someone like me. They mostly work in direct customer support on government contracts. You know, stuff like maintaining support equipment, updating simulation systems, routine maintenance, and the like."

"How about a group of buyers working for a man named Miles Sennett?"

"Never heard of him or his group ... but hold on a second." After a few moments with the clicking of computer keys in the background, Doc said, "Yeah, I see him on an org chart. There's also a short description of their work that mentions several large, well-known military programs." He was quiet again but for much longer this time. "There's something a little strange about the list of their programs."

"What's that?" asked Rebecca.

"Well, it reads like a who's who of the recipients of our foreign military sales. It includes the names of a lot of programs that people would recognize—C-17, Black Hawk helicopters, Hellfire missiles—but there are no domestic programs. And I also know that some of these sales get their primary support out of St. Louis, our office in Washington DC, or our office in California. Why would a small group of buyers in Denver have their hooks in programs spread out across the globe?"

"Yeah, that is interesting," Rebecca replied. "Is a man named Jesse Bolger on the org chart? He's supposed to work for Miles Sennett."

Doc was quiet for a minute, then said, "There's no list of Sennett's direct reports and I don't see Jesse Bolger anywhere else on the org chart."

"OK, it was worth a shot. If it's not against any Ruger–Phillips regulations, would you send me that description of what Sennett's group does?"

"It'll be in your email within the hour."

"Thanks. Now, wanna tell me how it's going with you and Nicole?"

Rebecca figured she already knew everything he was going to say and perhaps more; she talked to Nicole fairly regularly. She even thought that Nicole might have different feelings about him moving to Ruger–Phillips West, as she had said things between them were coming along quite well. Rebecca had only asked for an update from Doc to distract him from their discussion of Miles Sennett. Doc had a tendency to become fixated on mysteries like this one, and she didn't know what, if anything, she would be getting him involved in if he pursued the matter further.

After several minutes of Doc talking about Nicole, Rebecca told him how happy she was for them and they said their goodbyes.

Rebecca ran through her mental list of pending cases and decided to wrap up two that were nearly completed; they only lacked the final paperwork. So, she saved her notes on the Bolger meeting and opened the first of them. But just as she did, her phone rang. She checked the display.

"Hello, Mr. Bolger."

"Ms. Marte." He paused. "I'm not typically indecisive, but I've been practicing two versions of this call. I'm going to go with the one that says that my boss, Miles Sennett, is expecting your visit any time as soon as tomorrow morning."

"Great. I'll call and set it up. So, what's the other version of this call that you're not using, if I may ask?" It seemed rather obvious that he wanted her to ask. Otherwise, why even mention it?

"Well, first, Sennett called me into his office even before I requested a meeting with him. Evidently, he's decided I've done enough penance to be taken off the desk. I'll be going to Bogota, Colombia, Thursday morning. It's just for a couple of days so I can troubleshoot some issues on a program I worked on before."

"That's great. That's what you wanted, right? To get back in the game?" said Rebecca.

"Absolutely. But somehow, it makes your investigation into Robert Gleason seem less ... critical. If the FBI thinks it's water under the bridge, maybe I should, too. But like I said, this is the version I decided not to use. I still want you to go ahead ... at least for the first two weeks as we discussed."

Rebecca couldn't help but wonder about the source of Bolger's second thoughts. Had he started to doubt his own beliefs? Or had his boss been less than enthusiastic about the idea? Perhaps she could find out.

"Well, if you're worried about poking the bear, so to speak, there are, of course, some petty individuals in every organization, including the FBI. But I don't think there would be any retaliation from them if you continued to look for Gleason and Majoris."

"No, it wasn't that. It's just that Sennett got me thinking."

Bingo, thought Rebecca. Her client's hesitancy was being fed by his boss. It was an important enough insight that she almost missed what he said next.

"What if Gleason and his mom set up new identities for reasons that have nothing to do with espionage?" he said. "Hell, for all I know they're in the witness protection program and the FBI will be a lot more unhappy with me if you find them."

"I don't usually buy ad space in the New York Times to publish the results of my investigations."

"Of course, but you know what I mean," Bolger replied.

Actually, Rebecca didn't. "Were there other reasons for ending the search for Gleason and Majoris that you two talked about?"

"Yeah, and they pretty much ran the gamut. It's probably a waste of my money and your time. Gleason and Majoris are probably a thousand miles away by now and if they've been on the run for six years, they know how to hide. Gleason used his real identity to get me involved, but the rest of the time, he wouldn't. So, we don't even know who to look for. Basically, it just seems like a real uphill battle."

Of course, none of these challenges had changed since they had talked three hours ago. Only his resolve had weakened. Perhaps it was just well-meaning advice from a supervisor, but she was already unsure that Sennett and Bolger were exactly who they said they were. If not, Sennett might be trying to convince Bolger to terminate her contract simply to avoid unwanted scrutiny on ... well, whatever they were up to.

"Yes, it could get tough, but we knew that," said Rebecca. "Anyway, thanks for the call. If you change your mind about continuing, let me know and we'll shut things down."

"Will do. But I'm in for the two weeks anyway." He hung up.

WEDNESDAY, SEPTEMBER 18

Morning, Ruger–Phillips West

Rebecca sat in her car in the parking lot, looking through the early morning glare on her windshield at the building where she was to meet with Miles Sennett. It was a utilitarian-looking, two-story structure of tan stone and glass located in an area dominated by office buildings between Centennial Airport and Interstate 25. Unlike the Ruger-Phillips buildings in St. Louis, which were surrounded by a fence and accessed through a guarded gate, there were no visible signs of security.

She picked up her notes from the passenger seat and then set them back down. She knew there was precious little in them to support her concerns—a Denver-based group with far-flung responsibilities, her client's feeble attempt to justify the missing persons case as a debt-collection effort, his supervisor not being totally on board with the investigation. None of those facts was exactly damning. Even Bolger's statement that he "… couldn't tell her everything" had at least as many implications unrelated to her efforts as it had relevant ones. If nothing else, Bolger worked with classified information, and if Gleason's disappearance was in any way related to some of it, that would be no-go territory for him.

But even so, she couldn't pass off her unease as nothing, which was why she was here.

Rebecca exited her car, figuring the five minutes she had before the meeting would be sufficient. She was only at the security desk inside the building, however, when she realized it wouldn't be nearly enough time. Ruger-Phillips West more than made up for the lack of visible security outside with a gauntlet of checks inside. Before she was done at the front desk, she had produced both driver's and private investigator's licenses, answered two questionnaires about the visit, and signed all of her declarations using a touch screen. But after watching the woman at the desk frown at her computer screen for several seconds, Rebecca signed a slip of paper that was scanned into the computer. She wasn't surprised. She'd never been able to produce anything that looked even vaguely like her signature on a touch screen.

A couple of minutes after the receptionist/guard called, Miles Sennett appeared in the waiting area. Doc had included a picture of him from the organization chart along with the responsibilities of his group. And although he had aged some since it was taken, Rebecca recognized him.

She stood from the chair where she had been waiting and extended her hand. "Rebecca Marte. I'm a private investigator hired by Mr. Jesse Bolger." Sennett knew all this, of course, but Rebecca wanted to avoid any possible misunderstandings.

"Yes, Jesse told me that he'd hired you. And in all honesty, I can't say I encouraged him to do that—nothing personal, of course. But he seems to need this search to get closure on his old friend's involvement, so I hope you find Gleason. Or convince Jesse that he won't be found easily." He turned and opened the door so Rebecca could enter the main part of the building.

Apparently, Sennett wasn't going to hide his hesitancy to involve her. Either that or Bolger had mentioned their last phone call when they had discussed his tentativeness and there was no reason for him to deny it. "So, you think it'll be tough to find Robert Gleason and Olive Majoris?" she asked as they walked down the hallway.

"Maybe I watch too much TV," said Sennett, "but aren't there a lot of fugitives who've been on the run for years and no one's found them yet?"

"It happens," replied Rebecca, although not as frequently as he was suggesting, and that fact bothered her a bit. The idea that television and social media made dramatic but unlikely events seem more probable than they actually were wasn't anything new. People tended to believe, for example, that driving was safer than flying because of all the news coverage and vivid images of plane crashes. But while this distortion of likelihood, generally known as the availability bias, was normal, Rebecca wondered if he had shown it to make a point—he just managed a group of buyers and so, wasn't trained to avoid such reactions as some in more clandestine occupations would be. Of course, the most likely explanation for her feeling was that she was just being too suspicious, but that came with the job.

"So, you're a buyer for Ruger–Phillips, correct?" she asked, intentionally mistaking his role for those he supervised. His reaction might be informative.

"Hold that thought," he said as he stepped into what could have been a broom closet for all she knew and closed the door. After a moment, the door reopened.

"Sorry," he said. "We use voiceprints of a specific phrase for entry to our area. Obviously, my voice isn't secret, but the phrase is. My office is this way," he said as he opened a second door and started down another hall.

"The answer to your question about me being a buyer is yes and no. I supervise a group of procurement specialists, but I also worked my way up from new MBA graduate to manager. So, I know the field. Is that what you wanted to know?"

"It is," Rebecca replied, although his response was only suspicious in much the same way as his statement about fugitives; Rebecca was willing to bet that an MBA manager of a procurement group was about as common as rocks in Colorado. Again, had he gone out of his way to fit her stereotype for the job?

"Security wasn't lax at the front door, but it seems like it's gotten a lot tighter back here."

"That's more a matter of history than regulations," Sennett replied. "A few years ago, there was a highly classified project in our current space, a Special Access Program, if you're familiar with that phrase. But rather than dismantling the security infrastructure when the project ended, Ruger-Phillips left it in place just in case. And since we're a small enough group to fit and our customers don't care if security is a bit tighter than required, we ended up here. And speaking of here, this is my office."

He opened the door, but Rebecca didn't go in. "Sorry, but I overdid the coffee this morning. Would you mind telling me where the lady's room is?"

"I'll escort you." He turned back in the direction they had come and started walking. "Even though the restrictions on entry are stricter than required, there's still classified work in progress around here. A great deal about the capabilities of our military systems could be reverse-engineered from the specifications our buyers have."

"Of course," Rebecca replied, although neither her biological needs nor an interest in classification standards had prompted her request. Unescorted access to the bathroom would have helped corroborate his claim that the security on the entry door was a holdover. Unfortunately, being walked to the facilities didn't prove anything. If his group did what she had been led to believe, some of the work would be classified.

After spending a few minutes in the restroom and washing her hands to complete the deception, she exited and they returned to Sennett's office. Once seated inside, he asked, "So, what is it that you'd like to talk about?"

Since this question had been discussed with him when she called to schedule her visit and was the topic of one of the two questionnaires that she had completed at the security desk, she wondered if this was Sennett's attempt to look like he was open to any topic? He wasn't falling back on a well-practiced ruse; he'd discuss whatever she wanted. But then, Rebecca didn't think that extended to a question like, just who do you really work for? So, she went with her own subterfuge, which was also becoming well-practiced.

"I'd just like a little background. Robert Gleason found Jesse Bolger, and I have to believe he searched him out for a reason. So, anything you can tell me about what your group does might possibly be important in locating the man."

"I'd be glad to give you an overview of our operations," he replied.

With those words, Sennett launched into a talk that was obviously prepared in advance and clearly well-rehearsed.

But then, that is exactly what Rebecca expected. What manager wouldn't have a polished spiel to describe the excellent work of his group and their outstanding credentials to do it? As he talked, she noted each foreign military sales program he mentioned and by the end, he had discussed exactly those included in the group description that Doc had sent her and no others. That couldn't be a coincidence, but did it imply deceit or thoroughness? She wasn't sure but saw a way to push the issue.

"Mr. Bolger happened to mention that he's got a trip to Colombia, South America, for work, but I didn't think the U.S. had sold any military weapons to them."

Sennett leaned back in his chair, taking a moment to brush an imaginary piece of lint from the front of his shirt. That was a possible tell—he seemed to be trying hard to look relaxed, nonchalant. And so far, this was probably the strongest indication that he was holding out on her. But like everything else that Rebecca had observed, the gesture might indicate he was lying or it could mean that there really was a piece of lint and she hadn't noticed it.

"My standard briefing for our group emphasizes where the United States has had major foreign military sales, like selling the F-15 fighter aircraft to Israel or Saudi Arabia. But a lot of what my group does is after-sales support for everything else that goes into flying a modern aircraft or operating state-of-the-art defense systems: simulators, maintenance equipment, test equipment, and the like. Jesse will be working on an upgrade to some ground test equipment."

"But is it test equipment for one of the programs you mentioned before?"

Sennett smiled as he tilted his head in a shrug. "Sorry, Ms. Marte, but which of the Colombian bases Jesse will visit and the programs he'll support when he is there is beyond what I can discuss because of security regulations. I'm sure you understand. But I can say that in 2022, the United States designated Colombia as a major non-NATO ally, and that has opened the door to even closer cooperation than we've enjoyed in the past … or at least, the possibility of it. We'll see how things go."

"I do understand," Rebecca replied. "And I should have figured as much, but you never know till you ask." She paused a moment to mentally review the topics she wanted to discuss. Finding she had covered everything, she said, "I appreciate you taking the time to meet with me, but I believe I've taken up enough of it. Thank you."

"My pleasure, Ms. Marte. Would you mind if I asked you a question?"

"Not at all."

"I got the impression earlier that my comment about all the fugitives that had evaded authorities for years … well, that you didn't see it that way. While I'm sure you don't take cases you plan to leave unfinished, do you really think there's much chance you'll find Robert Gleason or Olive Majoris?"

"Well, let's see," said Rebecca slowly, mostly to give herself a moment to consider her response. Based on their conversation—and truthfully, even before they met—Rebecca hadn't felt that Sennett was directly involved in Gleason's disappearance after Ermakov and Ilyin were caught. She wanted to talk to him to, hopefully, become more confident she had the complete story on Bolger and his objectives. Perhaps that would help her solve the case. Perhaps not, but that objective was now moot. She had accomplished virtually nothing meeting with Sennett.

Yes, some of his answers seemed a bit too perfect. He had his standard pitch on his group and their responsibilities. It matched what Doc had found online perfectly. He had the right training for the job. He showed some of the same cognitive biases as everyone else. Did she really find it suspicious that he came across as too "typical," whatever that meant? But to stay on the safe side, she decided she shouldn't be completely forthcoming with him.

Generally, if he was a suspect in a crime, she might increase the pressure on him in the hope that he'd make a mistake. She'd suggest she was closer to a solution than she was. Or she might imply she had or was about to gain evidence that would break the case open. Or rather than increasing the pressure on him, she might imply she had nothing, hoping he would become lax in covering his tracks. As she could think of no objective basis for selecting either but felt uncomfortable doing neither, she decided that downplaying her chance of success would be the simpler route.

Decision made, Rebecca said, "I have no name since Gleason wouldn't use the name of a dead man in any situation other than this one. I have no photograph except a grainy picture from a six-year-old story in a newspaper about his death. I'm looking for someone with a significant head start and practice in staying out of public view. Yeah, I'd say this case has more than its fair share of challenges."

"I thought as much," said Sennett as he nodded. "I've tried to manage Jesse's expectations for that exact reason, so I appreciate you being so candid. Shall we go?"

He walked her back out the way they had come in. Once seated in her car, Rebecca slid down slightly in the driver's seat and let her head fall back on the headrest. She knew why her last statement about the challenges of the case had sounded so convincing. "It's because it's all true," she muttered to herself.

Evening, Marte Investigative Services

Rebecca had spent the rest of the morning and all of the afternoon canvassing the places where Gleason had been. Philly Pete's was first and by far, the fastest. Since Bolger hadn't been sure that Gleason had gone inside the sandwich shop—they had run into each other, literally, in the parking lot—it was probably a dead end. Still, she thought it was worth a try.

But after an hour, all she knew was that the place had an incredible turnover rate. The twenty-something manager, who admitted to working 12-hour shifts for the last two days and was starting his third, was still nice enough to check who had been working on the first of July. Of the five individuals on the schedule, three were no longer employees and the fourth was who he had been subbing for the last two days. The manager didn't expect him back. But still, she had the names, not because he had provided them—he wasn't sure that was consistent with Philly Pete's personnel policies— but because she had memorized them as he read them off the schedule. If nothing came up that looked more promising, she'd find them herself.

After that, Rebecca went to the retirement community where Gleason had told her client that he and Majoris were residents. There, she got her first positive identifications ... and lots of false positives. One woman was convinced that the picture was her cousin Ethel's third child, Thomas. But since he lived in Baltimore and was confined to a wheelchair, it wasn't a lead that Rebecca intended to follow. Another woman claimed to know the man in the picture. She even knew where he lived and gave Rebecca an address that was at a different location, but still in the neighborhood. But when she went by the house and showed the picture to a man who answered the door, he had no idea who it was.

Several other locals made tentative identifications, usually saying something like, "Isn't that the nice young man who's renting Lily's place? He's always smiling, always waving." Then, those comments were often followed by, "I sure hope the HOA doesn't find out Lily's renting her place to outsiders." Rebecca wasn't sure if the neighborhood governing body was really that dictatorial or if the residents just didn't like being told what they could do, as they all seemed to have different, but equally strongly worded complaints about them.

Rebecca's big break, however, came just before she quit for the day. She'd gone to a house three doors down from the address where Gleason and Majoris had staged their scam. When a woman came to the door and looked at the picture, she said, "That looks something like ... oh now, what was his name? Ralph? Randy? Something like that." As the renters had given the names Randy and Barb Hidalgo, she'd possibly connected Gleason to one of them.

But when the woman continued, she said, "The man I saw was quite a bit heavier than he looks in that picture." A couple of the other women had made that observation, too, so Rebecca wasn't greatly concerned. But when she asked where the woman had seen this Ralph or Randy, she gave an address further up and on the other side of the street. Given all these uncertainties, the fact that Rebecca was considering this her "big break" was rather telling. But at least she saw a way to resolve one of these issues.

Rebecca leaned forward in her desk chair and picked up her phone. On the second ring, Bolger answered. "Good evening, Ms. Marte. What can I do for you?"

He sounded quite upbeat. Unfortunately, she didn't share the same emotion. "Evening," she replied, noting that apparently, it hadn't even achieved the stature of a good one in her mind. "I hope I'm not interrupting anything."

"Just packing for the flight tomorrow since I leave bright and early. You're not going to tell me you found Robert Gleason already, are you?"

Rebecca sighed, hoping too late it wasn't loud enough for her client to hear. "No, sorry. I don't think anyone could pull that off in a day. But I was talking to some of the neighbors where he and Ms. Majoris had their fake residence. One thing that came up a few times was that the man they saw was heavier than the picture of Gleason from the paper. How'd you feel when you saw the picture?"

Rebecca waited through a rather lengthy pause. "I had something of the same reaction," he said finally. "I didn't mention it because I think his bulk might have been part of a disguise. When we were running all over town that night the FBI caught the Russians, I thought I might have to give him CPR he looked so out of shape. But he handled it well. In fact, a lot of the time he was ten to twenty yards ahead of me, and I jog all the time. So, is Gleason overweight in reality? Maybe, but I don't think so."

"But I thought you two changed behind a dumpster. You didn't see anything like a few extra layers of clothes?"

"Gleason was already changed before I got there, so no. I didn't see anything like that."

"OK. Were there any other differences between the photo and the man you met in July?"

"Well, no tattoos or anything like that. Hold on a second." After a few moments, Bolger was back on the line. "I bookmarked the site where you found Gleason's picture and I was just bringing it back up. Looking at it now, I'd have to say there aren't any important differences. His hair is cut differently. It's quite a bit longer and stringier now. And the bit of tan he has in the picture is totally gone. You know, now that I say that, I wonder if those differences were part of a disguise, too? He certainly struck me as a nerdy guy who spent his day in front of his computer in the basement."

"That's possible," replied Rebecca. "By the way, did you ever recall what breed of dog Charlie was?"

"Well, damn," said Bolger. "Where's my head?"

"Probably in packing."

He chuckled. "Yeah, it's good to be back to my real job. But anyway, Olive told me he was an Anatolian Shepherd. Hope that helps."

"I'll check into it," replied Rebecca. "Now, I'll let you get back to packing. Have a safe trip."

"Thanks."

After disconnecting, Rebecca leaned back in her chair, crossed her arms over her chest, and dropped her gaze to the desktop. Recognizing the pose, she released a soft laugh. She had noticed this was the exact position she took every time she was facing a long evening working on her evidence board ... and that was exactly what she'd be doing next.

Evening, Marte Investigative Services

Rebecca stood from her desk and walked over to a large pinboard in the corner of her office that she used to help organize her thoughts. In the movies and television, these evidence boards always seem to be overflowing with photos, news clippings, notes, and even actual pieces of evidence in some cases, all connected with long pieces of string. While all of her cases were different and so, produced a range of boards, none had strings cutting across them. At least, none had so far. And if she was being truthful with herself, most of them were not as visually complex as in the movies, but they got the job done.

She had adopted an approach she had learned at the FBI Academy and adapted it to her own style. It started with the facts, if any, in the center, then observations and evidence with varying degrees of corroboration extending to the right. On the left, she added the inferences and theories she drew from the evidence, with the more solid deductions closer to the center and the wilder guesses extending out from there. She knew from her training and experience that spending too much time on the left-side theories tended to create self-fulfilling prophecies. Once someone accepted a solution, it was much harder to find evidence that would negate it, and she wasn't completely immune to the effect.

For this case, she had the names and pictures of the two individuals she sought in the center. The picture of Olive Majoris was no better than the one of Robert Gleason because it had come from the same, six-year-old news story. But unlike the picture of Gleason, no one she talked to in the 55+ community remembered seeing her. Rebecca also included the names of the spies, Ermakov and Ilyin, so she could later entertain Bolger's theory that these two sets of individuals shared a previous association. Finally, she had MC&A in the center, for My Client and his Associates. It wasn't common for her to wonder if her client was part of the mystery to be solved, but this wasn't the first time it had happened either. She used the acronym just in case Bolger happened to drop by unannounced.

For now, she ignored the left side and focused on the observations on the right. She first summarized the results from canvassing the neighborhood on several index cards and placed them on the evidence board. The observation from the woman who had identified Gleason's picture as someone on the street who was possibly named Randy was there. But because she had also thought the man didn't live at the address where Gleason and Majoris had been, it was farther from the center than she would have liked.

Rebecca had also hoped that Lily, who had presumably rented her home to Gleason and Majoris, would be able to remember the couple from their newspaper photos, but she couldn't. However, since she'd rented her place numerous times over the years, it wasn't surprising when Lily said that all the faces had run together.

She also added her observations about Miles Sennett next to the MC&A card, keeping them suitably cryptic for the same reason she used the abbreviation. And while she felt comfortable putting those cards quite close to the center, she knew the inferences she drew from them would be far to the left. Did being a bit too stereotypic in his answers and his background imply deceit or just that he was what he appeared—fairly typical?

Rebecca's next evidence-board exercise was to summarize the differences between the contents of Lily's home and the items Bolger remembered seeing there. Anything that Gleason or Majoris had brought with them to stage the house might help in determining their identities.

There were only a few personal keepsakes that Bolger recalled from the upstairs, but he remembered several items stored on the shelves in the garage—a half container of windshield wiper fluid, a battery charger, two cans of oil, an old Colorado license plate, and the like. But unfortunately, when Lily gave Rebecca a house tour, it appeared that everything he remembered belonged to the homeowner. When Rebecca asked, Lily said she stored her personal items in a locked spare bedroom when she rented the place. Rebecca figured that Gleason and Majoris had picked the bedroom lock and then placed her things around the house to make it look more lived-in. If they had, it was probably a wasted effort as Bolger had seen little of the first floor except the kitchen and mudroom. But then, they wouldn't have known that in advance.

In addition to the items on the shelves in the garage, Bolger also recalled an older dark-blue sedan parked inside. It, too, was Lily's. She'd left one side of the double-car garage open for the renters. Bolger had used that side when Gleason had him park his car inside to keep it out of sight. As for Gleason's car, it was probably parked in a different neighborhood when her client was visiting, as the HOA had rules about leaving cars on the street.

Rebecca's main hope for this reconstruction of the changes Gleason and Majoris had made was in the basement. This is where he and Majoris would have hoped to convince Bolger that Gleason was still the nerdy, unpredictable guy he had known in high school. It was also where Bolger had spent most of his time and so, he produced a rather impressive list of objects that he recalled. The shelves, tables, workbench, lights, armchair, sofa, and television were still there, but the tools and SCIF were missing. When asked about the absence of tools, Lily said that her husband had owned quite a collection, but she had sold them in a garage sale after he had passed away. She planned to dispose of the rest of his man cave but found the first sale too painful to finish the job.

So, Gleason and Majoris had probably brought in some tools to support the illusion they were creating. Unfortunately, Rebecca couldn't see developing any leads from that possibility. Hand tools, multimeters, and soldering irons could be bought at just about any hardware store.

The homemade SCIF was certainly uncommon enough to produce leads. And even though Gleason said he had spread his orders of EMF radiation–shielding fabric among several retailers, Rebecca wondered if that was actually true. They hadn't had much time to set their stage. But no sooner had that word, "stage," popped into her mind than she began to doubt she'd learn anything about Gleason from the SCIF. It was probably nothing more than a theatrical prop—a large frame covered with a shiny fabric. In the context of all the other information bombarding Bolger, he wouldn't have noticed things like an extension cord coming into the back of the structure to power the laptop ... if there had been one. So, at least for now, she wasn't going to bother trying to track down sales of radiation–shielding fabric.

Checking into the breed of dog that Gleason owned was also a long shot, assuming that he owned one and Charlie wasn't just part of his disguise. But at least Rebecca knew from talking to Lily that Charlie wasn't her dog. At one time, she had owned a Saint Bernard, but he had died a few years previously.

Rebecca was further encouraged to check into this remote possibility when Lily produced her copy of the rental agreement. There, penciled in below the amount of the contract was a note that said, plus $100 per month for a pet damage charge. If she had seen Charlie, she might have made it $1,000. But reading the contract also seemed to trigger a memory for Lily. She said that the renters had shown interest in the dog door after she assured them it would be easy to open it back up. Of course, none of that meant Gleason hadn't just seized on the idea of temporarily purchasing a dog when he saw the door. Having Charlie there certainly implied that this was their permanent residence.

On the whole, everything suggested that the house had been carefully staged and then returned to its original condition after Ermakov and Ilyin were apprehended. If Bolger had gone into the house after the spies were caught rather than just reading the note on his car and leaving, Rebecca wondered if he would have found Gleason and Majoris busy packing. But her mental simulation of these events also brought into question whether these two could have done all this alone in the time available? If the two individuals she sought were part of something larger, it opened all kinds of possibilities she hadn't had time to fully consider.

Even though she was working primarily on the right side of her evidence board, Rebecca recorded this idea that Gleason and Majoris might be part of a larger organization on the left. It was, however, pretty far out, both figuratively and literally.

Rebecca could foresee that tomorrow would probably be filled with calling veterinarians and animal hospitals to inquire about people who owned Anatolian Shepherd dogs. And since several of the animal hospitals she found online had evening hours or even 24/7 call-in lines, she decided to try out and refine her standard inquiry tonight. She dialed the first number on her list.

After the animal hospital identified itself, Rebecca said, "Sorry to call so late, but I just got off work. I'm thinking of buying an Anatolian Shepherd dog for a pet. I've read up on the breed a bit, but I'd really like to talk to an old friend who's had one for years. Trouble is, I can't remember his name, but I'm almost positive he takes his dog to your clinic. That sound like anybody you know?"

There was a pause, after which the woman at the animal hospital said, "Ma'am, are you sure you want an Anatolian Shepherd? Don't get me wrong, they're intelligent, loyal animals that will protect anyone in their pack. But they're also stubborn, independent, and shed constantly. Unless you've got some acreage—preferably with some livestock—where your dog can run, they can be a handful."

"So, I understand," said Rebecca, thinking she should have read up on the breed before the call. "I do have some land but no livestock. And my friend has made it work. That's why I was wondering what his secret is."

"Well, OK," the woman said after another pause. "That sounds like Randy Everly out past Evergreen, although I can't really hand out his phone number or address."

"Yeah, that's him. I'll give him a call. Thanks." She hung up.

Could it really be that she had found Robert Gleason after her first cold call on a long shot? Randy, after all, was the first name of one of the renters. But a quick online search indicated that she hadn't been that incredibly lucky. Randy Everly was a 73-year-old retired Merino sheep rancher, and his dog was most likely a holdover from his working days.

Still, her looking-for-a-friend story had obtained a name, so she made a few notes for herself. She'd probably need to use it a few hundred more times tomorrow. Then, she searched for information on the Anatolian Shepherd breed, generally confirming what the woman had told her. She returned to her evidence board. Although she had been holding off putting theories on it, she didn't want to forget this one. Far to the left of the name Robert Gleason, she added a card that said, "May own land, possibly with livestock, if Charlie is his dog."

It was a tempting thought to continue her calls to animal hospitals for the rest of the evening, but Rebecca couldn't put this next step off forever. She needed some idea of how Ermakov and Ilyin fit into the case. On the night they were captured and even the next day when the FBI put her client in detention, there were at least two theories in play, each with its own proponents. Bolger, on the one hand, still believed that Gleason lived with his grandmother in a 55+ community and had accidentally stumbled onto the Russians. On the other, the FBI thought her client had tried to hide his involvement with foreign agents by saying an old friend had led him to the spies. The fact that everyone except Bolger believed that Gleason was dead was considerable support for the FBI's theory.

But now, with a perspective born of over ten weeks of history, Rebecca felt neither theory was correct ... assuming Gleason and Majoris were alive. If they weren't and she'd been hired to find ghosts, then the FBI's hypothesis, again, looked quite good. Rebecca, however, took the two missing persons' existence as a working assumption. And with that assumption, their actions took on a consistent, albeit unusual pattern.

It seemed somewhat likely to her that Gleason and Majoris had moved into the retirement community with the sole purpose of catching the Russian spies. Perhaps they required day-to-day surveillance to complete their investigation? Or maybe they only knew the Russians were in the vicinity and they needed to be close by to pinpoint their exact location? But whatever the reason, renting a house just three blocks from Ermakov and Ilyin's hideout was either a coincidence of gigantic proportions or it was part of their plan. And if part of a plan, that meant they were ... what? Independent spy hunters? From an agency so secret that even the FBI didn't know of its existence?

Presumably, Gleason then saw an opportunity to involve his old high school acquaintance. So, he and Majoris made some minor modifications to Lily's home to make it look like their residence. They even used Gleason's reputation to convince Bolger that he was still the same bumbling dreamer he had known.

But how Bolger had become an integral part of their plan was much easier for her to guess than why. It didn't seem like a government agency would use a private citizen like Bolger to do their bidding, which indirectly lent support to the idea that they were independent spy hunters. But were there actually people like that? Were there individuals who had suffered so grievously at the hands of the Russians that they took it upon themselves to right these wrongs?

To Rebecca, this conjecture seemed possible, but it was nothing she had ever heard of. And it didn't really fit all the facts. If Gleason and Majoris were independent, who had called off the FBI? Bolger's fairy godmother almost had to be someone in government.

Fortunately, she wasn't supposed to be dwelling on theories because she had just come full circle. She needed to get back to evidence and observations to break this pattern, and the one place that might have the information she needed to break the cycle was the FBI. So, finding someone in the Denver field office who would talk to her had become the next step.

Even before this case, however, Rebecca had been curious enough to check if any of her old classmates at the Academy had been stationed in Denver. One had been. His name was Connor Sullivan, and he was one of the reasons she dreaded this step. It wasn't that he had treated her poorly when they were both New Agent Trainees at the Academy. In fact, he had asked her out a couple of times, although she had always made excuses. What was giving Rebecca pause was that Connor was quite self-centered and always unjustifiably confident in his opinion ... even when the instructors told him he was wrong. These traits weren't necessarily that unusual among the NATs, and to some degree, confidence probably helped them succeed in a grueling training program. It was just that his unending bluster was more than she could take.

Still, she had a job to do. She had found a listing for him, picked up her phone from the desk, and dialed his number.

"Hello."

"Hi, Connor. This is Rebecca Marte. From the FBI Academy, if you remember me."

"Oh, sure, Becca ... I mean, Rebecca. Sorry, old habits, but at least I recalled that you don't like that nickname."

It wasn't so much that Rebecca didn't like the nickname as it was that she reserved it for friends, and Connor hadn't made the grade. "I set up a private investigator's practice ...."

"So, I heard," he said.

Rebecca didn't know that this fact had made the rounds, but some pretty strong bonds developed at the Academy. She had passed her decision along to a few old classmates, but as to who might have told him, she couldn't guess. "Anyway, I've moved it to Colorado."

"No kidding. You're in Denver. Hey, would you be interested in dinner some evening?"

What was the saying? The more things change, the more they stay the same? Connor was right back to asking her out. The big difference, however, was this time Rebecca didn't have the option of making an excuse. She'd called to get a meeting with him and now, she would, although she had been thinking about lunch rather than an evening together. But before she could agree to dinner, he continued.

"It would be a big favor to me if you accepted. You see, my fiancée is finishing up a master's in social work and has been planning to work in the substance abuse area. I've been suggesting she check out the FBI. You could give her a woman's perspective on the Bureau."

Rebecca wasn't sure she had the right Connor Sullivan on the phone, although she obviously did. She probably would have accepted this invitation even if she didn't have a case to solve because she was now quite curious to meet the woman who apparently had broadened Connor's perspective enough to include someone besides himself.

"You know I left the FBI, and yet, you want me to talk to your fiancée about joining them?"

"I'm not looking for a hard sell. Just describe your experiences, pros and cons, because I think that would help her decide. And that a-hole in St. Louis. What was his name?"

"Special Agent Bradley Hawkins," Rebecca replied, still hearing a touch of disdain in her tone. Apparently, it wasn't just the fact that she had become a private investigator that had become a topic of conversation around the local FBI break room. The he-said-she-said drama with Hawkins had apparently also made the grade, although her departure and his lies were related.

"Yeah, that's the guy," said Connor. "Be sure and tell her about him. I don't want her walking into the Academy not knowing the score."

"In that case, I'd love to join you and your fiancée for dinner. And that's my answer whether you decide you can help me or not."

"OK, what's up?"

"I'm representing a man named Jesse Bolger. He was originally detained by the FBI in connection with the apprehension of two Russian spies, Ermakov and Ilyin."

"Yeah, I've heard of them, but I don't recall your client. And you must know that the Russians are long gone from Colorado." He paused a moment. "Unfortunately, even if I knew more, I couldn't share it with you. You know how it is."

Rebecca did know, and that was the other part of why she had hesitated to call him.

"Of course," she replied. "And I don't want to put you in a position of violating any FBI regulations or your principles. But my questions are mainly about my client, not the Russians, and even the rumors around the field office might help. And if there's nothing you can say, that's OK, too. We can still have a nice dinner."

"Sounds great," he replied. After they picked a time and place, apparently with Connor's fiancée making her inputs in the background, they said their goodbyes.

Rebecca hadn't expected to be looking forward to dinner with the know-it-all Connor, but she was. The thought of how she should spend the remainder of her evening, however, wiped that smile from her face. "Bet the night shift at these animal hospitals would just love a call," she muttered as she reached for her phone.

THURSDAY, SEPTEMBER 19

Evening, The Front Range Diner

Rebecca was early. She'd never been to the Front Range Diner and the phrase "fashionably late" was, in her mind, an oxymoron. So, she had allotted 50 minutes for the 37-minute drive, the latter number from her maps app. But for once, the road and traffic conditions had conspired to shave a couple of minutes off the calculated time, and she was even earlier than the software predicted.

Since the phrase "grand entrance" was even less prevalent in her vocabulary than "fashionably late," she went inside to be seated. A glance at the menu was all she needed to know that the offerings were more varied than she had anticipated for a diner, so she ordered a glass of wine to help with further study. But that plan went by the wayside when she spotted the barbeque ribs. Even though she loved barbeque, she didn't eat it often. But as it was a specialty of the house and had won a few local awards, she couldn't resist.

With that decision made and no Connor Sullivan in sight, Rebecca decided to review the state of her case. Clearly, it wasn't the most relaxing way to spend her idle moments, but she had found that those short mental forays into the progress she'd made on a case—or lack thereof—could possibly yield a valuable insight. And clearly, she needed one.

After spending the rest of Wednesday night calling animal hospitals, she had broadened her search to veterinarian's offices Thursday morning. Most of the vets had night emergency numbers, but the folks who manned those lines wouldn't know an office's clientele. For that kind of information, she needed to talk with the person who sat in the reception area of a vet's office, day after day.

Rebecca's first observation wasn't exactly case-related. It was that there were a helluva lot of veterinarians in Colorado— 3,800 of them to be exact if the Internet was right. Obviously, she wasn't going to call all of them. Many were located far from Denver, but after spending the bulk of the day on the phone, she'd swear that more than half of them were within 50 miles of the capitol.

Several times during the day, she had almost lost control of the conversation before it had hardly started. "Hello, I'm thinking of buying ...."

"Are you an existing customer?" asked the woman on the other end of the call.

"Well, no, but ...."

"I'm sorry, but Dr. Boyd's practice is already full. I can put you on a waiting list, but there's no guarantee he'll be able to see your new pet any time soon."

Apparently, even though there were a lot of veterinarians in the area, they were still in short supply. After Rebecca got these conversations redirected to her concerns, the people on the other end often sounded relieved. Turning down potential customers who just wanted care for their furry friends had to be stressful for them.

Over the course of the day, hospital and veterinarian staff identified 162 Anatolian Shepherd owners. Occasionally, they declined to identify the owner by name, but that was rare. Few seem to feel that casually mentioning that Mr. X owned one of these big dogs was an invasion of privacy, but often added that was all they could say. Most of the owners lived in small towns surrounding Denver. Apartment dwellers in the city apparently knew better than to buy such a large, independent dog. And the people in the suburbs seemed to prefer smaller breeds and their designer canines.

Of the 162 names, Rebecca had eliminated almost half of them with simple, online searches of the owners. Age was the factor that most often resulted in a person being dropped from the list. Given Bolger's age, thirty-one, Gleason was probably between twenty-nine and thirty-three, depending on whether he had skipped a grade or had been held back. But since the social media sites she checked seemed to rarely have posts such as, "Joe celebrated his 65th birthday today," Rebecca was forced to guess ages from a picture. She had little confidence in her estimates and so, probably included more people than she should have. But even so, the exercise proved quite helpful as owners of the breed in their 60s and beyond were rather common.

After that first cut, Rebecca still had 86 names on the list. Visiting them all would probably take her a month or more. Driving to these outlying towns alone would take hours and since she would need to drop in unannounced lest Gleason flee after she called, many of those trips would prove fruitless. She was loath to spend that much time on something that was a long shot to start.

But as Rebecca pondered this quandary, an insight—as she had hoped—came to her. Would someone who wanted to stay invisible to the public, who wanted to maintain the illusion that he or she was dead have any type of social media presence? She thought not. As soon as she got back to her office, she would ....

"Good evening, Rebecca."

She jumped at the sound of a man's voice practically at her elbow. She looked up to find a familiar face. "Connor. Hi. I guess I was lost in thought." She stood.

"As you often were back at the Academy," he said with a grin. "Rebecca, this is my fiancée, Alicia Hightower."

Alicia was a slender woman with black hair and, unless the light was playing tricks on Rebecca, gray eyes. She was about five foot, four inches tall, making Rebecca wonder if a career in the FBI was appropriate. She had always felt that her stature—five feet, eleven inches—was an advantage. She could look many of her team members in the eye. But as Alicia stepped forward and firmly took her outstretched hand, those concerns vanished. Perhaps it was the eyes, but Connor's fiancée looked like she was up for just about any challenge.

"It's a pleasure to meet you, Alicia."

"You, too, Rebecca." They all sat. "So, Connor tells me you escaped the FBI."

"Don't say that too loudly," chided Connor with a grin still on his face. "We don't want the public to think you're talking about a jailbreak."

That comment started a pleasant evening's conversation, which was dominated by stories of what it was like to work for the Bureau—both Connor and Rebecca contributed to this topic—and why Rebecca had left. It also featured some well-natured ribbing by Connor, who denied any understanding of why someone would want to leave. And every time he did, Rebecca would catch the twinkle in Alicia's eyes. Nor could she miss the way Connor rested his hand on the back of Alicia's chair or let it slip down to her bare arm. There were few things in the world like new love, and it made Rebecca want to go home and call Brien Clarke, her boyfriend, as soon as the dinner was over.

Eventually, Alicia ran out of inquiries and Connor out of quips and counterfeit confusion. It was time for Rebecca's questions, although she wished it wasn't. The meal had been so pleasant, but now she was going to introduce topics that would force Connor to tiptoe around FBI regulations ... or to have him go silent. Perhaps he sensed her hesitation because he brought it up first.

"So, you wanted to know about Ermakov and Ilyin."

"Yes, but ...." She started until he held up a hand.

"You don't need to worry. I know what I can and can't say. So, you should ask whatever you want, but there may be cases where I can't answer. But you know that."

"Yeah, I do. But I appreciate hearing that you're keeping those restrictions in mind." At that point, Rebecca launched into what she had described as a two-minute summary of her case that ended up being a lot closer to five minutes. But she wanted to give Connor all the basics—her client, his detention by the FBI, the Bureau then dropping the investigation, and Bolger's desire to continue the missing persons' search.

When she was finished, Connor said, "You know, since your phone call I've been racking my brain about that Russian spy case, and the only thing I've come up with is a couple of guys who were talking about some video files over lunch. I'm pretty sure those files had something to do with it. Anyway, they were supposed to be looking for two men jogging near a bank. I forget the address, but they never found anything. Closest they got was this guy in what they called a '$500 tracksuit' being followed by some homeless guy about twenty yards back. They figured there was a bit of taunting going on, the homeless guy giving it to the track star, but nothing criminal. That mean anything to you?"

Actually, it meant quite a lot to Rebecca. It meant that whoever had dressed Bolger in those rags for the final part of their run knew exactly what they were doing. Given the obvious socioeconomic differences between the two men, no one would suspect they were together. But that observation would mean nothing to Connor, so she just said, "Maybe. I'll file it away for later. Anything else come to mind?"

"Not really," said Connor. "I'm in the drug enforcement area as part of the FBI's liaison to the DEA. It was our agents in counterintelligence that handled Ermakov and Ilyin, so I didn't hear much. After their capture, the Russians were held somewhere in the area for a couple of days, but it wasn't long until they were moved. I'd guess they ended up somewhere in the Washington, DC, area since that's where all the news seemed to be coming from. But they could have been someplace else. And recently, as you undoubtedly know, their names have come up as part of a possible prisoner exchange. As far as I know, that's where things still stand. Sorry that I couldn't be more help."

"No worries." In fact, Rebecca had largely expected this reaction. If he worked directly in intelligence gathering, like the agents who had manned the decades-long Operation Ghost Stories in the 1990s and 2000s, he probably couldn't have said anything. The fact that all he knew was the idle chatter around the water cooler was about as good as she could hope.

"My interest isn't in Ermakov and Ilyin specifically, but in my client. It's certainly a reasonable deduction that he knew them since he supposedly gave their Russian names to the Bureau and later, reported the address where they had been hiding. So, I can understand why he was detained. But then, to drop the investigation so suddenly without reason? That makes little sense to me. You hear anything about that?"

Connor paused a moment. "You know what the problem with this interview is going to be? It's that everything I'm telling you are things you could guess yourself. You know how these things work."

"Mostly, I suppose," replied Rebecca. "But I'm sure there are differences between field offices. And if nothing else, I'm getting confirmation that my thoughts aren't too different from yours."

"Well, OK," replied Connor slowly, as if he wasn't completely convinced. "I remember a couple of guys grousing around a bit after an investigation was dropped. That could have been your client. But it's the instances where we spend months building a case just to have it thrown out on a technicality that sticks in agents' craws. But again, you know that."

"Sure. Even in my short tenure, I worked a case where the charges were substantially reduced, and here I am, four or five years later, still moaning about it." That got a smile out of both Connor and Alicia.

"I would think that the Bureau searched the house where Jesse Bolger met with Gleason and Majoris," said Rebecca. "Did you hear anything about what they found?"

"Like you, I would assume we looked, but no, I heard nothing about what we found, if anything. Now, the house where we caught Ermakov and Ilyin is a different matter. I heard there was plenty of incriminating stuff there, from bugout bags with multiple passports, money, and even some communications from their network. But how much of that is true?" He shrugged to finish the thought.

"Jesse claimed from the beginning Robert Gleason isn't dead," said Rebecca, "and that the records that show that he is are wrong. Would you know if the search for Gleason is ongoing?"

That question produced a bit of a smirk from Connor before his reply. "Officially, the answer is almost undoubtedly yes. Blatantly ignoring a claim that someone acquired a new identity, especially in the context of an espionage case, is the kind of thing that'll get you fired. But as far as what we are doing about it? Tough to say except I'm sure we don't have a team dedicated to finding a man who most feel is dead."

"And I'm guessing it's the same with Olive Majoris?"

"Probably," said Connor. "Since Gleason found the spies, she'd be of interest primarily if she knew his whereabouts."

"Makes sense," replied Rebecca. "Billings, Montana, keeps coming up in the case. Gleason and Majoris gave a bogus address in Billings when they rented the house in the 55+ community. And outside of Billings was where the car crash was supposed to have occurred that killed them." Rebecca got no farther on her question as Connor's eyes were already going wide.

"Billings? Really?" He only waited long enough for Rebecca to nod. "An agent I know went there ... must be about a month ago now. I'll talk to him tomorrow." Rebecca started to remind Connor about the risks of doing so when he said in a sing-song manner, "Yes, Mother Marte. I'll be careful with what I pass on to you."

"Connor!" said Alicia with a touch of bite in her tone. "You two are on the same side."

"Yes, sorry, Rebecca. I didn't really mean that the way it sounded."

His time in the FBI had almost undoubtedly worn some of Connor's bluster away, but as Rebecca suspected, Alicia had a hand in his transformation, too. As for this possible lead, Rebecca was encouraged, but not greatly so. There had to be thousands of reasons an agent would go to Billings that had nothing to do with Gleason.

"No problem," Rebecca said. "Whatever you feel confident giving me is all I want." She paused, wondering if she wanted to go down this path, but in the end decided, what the heck. "Gleason possibly owned a rather unusual breed of dog, an Anatolian Shepherd. I don't suppose that breed has ever come up around the field office?"

Connor sat for a moment, his eyes moving from Rebecca to his fiancée and back. "Well, one of our analysts got a dog, but I think she said it was a Chihuahua." He paused, again taking a glance at Alicia before turning back to Rebecca. "Are you checking into this type of dog as a lead to Gleason?"

"Yeah, it's a long shot, but I made a few hundred calls to veterinarian's offices and animal hospitals the last couple of days."

Connor slowly shook his head. "I guess when you're a one-woman team, you get stuck with all the ... well, what we used to call legwork, but it's more like phone and online work now. Sore finger tonight from all the screen tapping?"

"Almost too sore to call all the Missouri community colleges. Did you know there are nearly twenty of them in Missouri, and not one has any records for a Robert Gleason in the timeframe he might have attended?"

"Was that part of his cover?" asked Connor.

"It was. Of course, it was a lot to hope that an old academic record would give me more insight into Mr. Gleason's life than the one story I have about his death. But you gotta dig somewhere." Somehow, her last comment made her feel even wearier than she had a moment before.

"You mentioned on the phone that you'd never heard of my client, Jesse Bolger," said Rebecca as the preamble to her next question, but Connor already had a comment.

"Never heard of him is not exactly right. Apparently, I have because I ran a drug enforcement check on him back in July when the counter-intel guys picked him up. I run enough of those that I don't remember the names unless a person comes up pretty often."

"Your counterintelligence agents contacted your unit to run a background on Jesse?" asked Rebecca. She could hear the touch of excitement in her tone.

"Yeah," Connor replied slowly.

"Jesse was only detained a day, so one of the first calls the agents must have made after they picked him up was to drug enforcement. For them to be interested in my client's possible involvement in the drug trade, they must have known the Russians were involved in drugs, too. Common dirty dealings would help strengthen the argument that Gleason knew Ermakov and Ilyin rather than just having a friend who stumbled onto them."

"I don't understand," said Alicia. "Why would Russian spies be involved with drugs?"

Rebecca liked Alicia, but at that point, she could have strangled the woman. She had just laid out a possible connection between Bolger, the Russians, and drug smuggling. Connor, as part of the drug enforcement liaison, would know if her conjecture was accurate. And if it was, she would give him one more piece to the puzzle that would undoubtedly put an end to their dinner. Now, however, all she could do was bite her tongue as Connor explained the situation to his fiancée.

"Foreign agents probably wouldn't be directly involved in distribution or sales," said Connor. "And a lot of them apparently just watch and report. But some do things designed to weaken the US, including facilitating illegal drug movement."

"You mean things like election interference, which then undermines our faith in the government?" asked Alicia.

"Exactly. In the case of drug running, they'd identify people with the clout and cash to handle quantity shipments from the suppliers and then watch as rampant drug addiction weakens us."

Connor turned back to Rebecca. "I also didn't recall your client's name because he came up clean on our check."

That was exactly the type of response Rebecca was hoping for. Connor hadn't found fault in her scenario of who had called whom and why, only adding that his group had nothing on Bolger. It was time for her to add her own piece of information to the conversation.

"You may be interested to know that Jesse left for Bogota, Colombia, this morning. I don't know exactly when his flight was, although he said it left bright and early. He's probably there already."

"Are you sure about that?"

"That's what he told me. And his boss, Miles Sennett, confirmed it in the sense that he wouldn't say exactly where in Colombia Jesse was going."

"Oh, damn," said Connor. "Sounds like we have a runner. I need to call our consulate in Colombia and get the DEA guys spun up if they aren't already. If we're lucky ...."

Connor paused, his eyes going wide. "That's it. DEA asked the FBI to stop our investigation into Bolger because while our case is circumstantial, they have some hard evidence linking him to drug trafficking. Rebecca, your mystery about why the FBI dropped the case is solved."

It was a consistent scenario that Connor was weaving, Rebecca admitted to herself. But it was hardly the only one. But whether his surmises were right or wrong, she didn't much care. Someone in Colombia—a U.S. consulate officer, a special agent of the Drug Enforcement Administration, a CIA officer— would check out what he was doing. If the trip was legitimately business, they'd back off and she'd continue her search for Gleason. If not? Well, she'd know where to find him during visiting hours at the prison.

Alicia, however, apparently didn't see the accuracy of Connor's hypothesis as moot. "Why are you so sure he's running?" she asked. "I mean, why would Mr. Bolger have confided in his private investigator if he wanted to slip out of the country incognito? If we'd had lunch rather than dinner, the agents in Colombia could have met his plane."

Connor had stood from the table, most likely to find some privacy for his calls, but stopped when his fiancée spoke. "Well,

I'm not certain, of course," he said slowly. "And you make a good point. Why would he have told Rebecca?"

He paused a moment more, perhaps to consider alternative theories. "I guess it could be a lot of things that took him to Colombia. But it's the worst-case scenario that'll get people moving and stories checked. Whoever gets eyes on him will know how to handle the situation."

"Well, OK," said Alicia. "I suppose I watch too many movies. I just had this picture in my head of a dozen armed men in black SUVs forcing his taxi to the curb and then, jumping out with guns drawn."

"They'll be more discreet than that," said Connor. "But I need to go make some calls or it'll never happen, discreet or not." He turned to walk away, then turned back to the table.

"I'm not sure how long this is going to take. Honey, do you mind taking a taxi home?"

"Don't be silly," said Rebecca. "I'll give her a ride home."

"Are you sure?" asked Alicia.

"Absolutely," replied Rebecca. "This will give us a chance to sample another bottle of wine and enjoy some girl talk."

"That would be great," she said as Rebecca motioned for their waiter and Connor turned to leave.

FRIDAY, SEPTEMBER 20

Late Morning, A Small Farm north of Denver

It was Rebecca's third call to one of the addresses of Anatolian Shepherd dog owners. She had parked on the rural road that ran in front of the house and now sat looking out of her windshield at the farm just ahead. She released a long sigh. "Third time's the charm," she muttered, reflecting the fact that the first two visits hadn't gone that well.

She was out making the rounds of dog owners because none of the calls that Connor had made had yielded any information on Jesse Bolger. Basically, Connor knew from the airline that he had landed and departed the plane. But after that, the trail went cold. The FBI had gotten the name and phone number of the hotel that Ruger–Phillips had booked for him, but as late as seven o'clock this morning local time, or nine o'clock in Bogota, he hadn't checked in.

Connor's theory that Bolger was fleeing from justice was starting to look better all the time. Even Rebecca admitted that to herself. But if he turned up with an innocent explanation—he'd decided to change hotels, he'd driven to the coast on a lark, he'd found a lady of the evening and spent the night with her—Rebecca wouldn't want to have wasted the day. Even so, she decided this would be her last call. It was now early afternoon in

Bogota, and if Bolger hadn't turned up yet, she was starting to doubt that he would.

Before she started her rounds of the dog owners, she had applied the insight she'd had yesterday before dinner; she had eliminated all the owners who had social media presences because calling attention to oneself on the Internet would be counterproductive if you were trying to hide. Removing those individuals without social media accounts still left 26 names out of the 86 she'd started with, a number she found surprising. She tended to think everyone in the world was on social media and often, multiple sites. But these people were living in more rural areas, so perhaps phone gossip and news stories from the local press still prevailed. That sounded pretty good to her, given all the vitriol that seemed to thrive online.

At the first address Rebecca had visited, no one was at home, nor did it look like anyone had been there for some time. The grass in front of the farmhouse looked like the growth from spring when water was more plentiful. Now, it was dead. The look, however, seemed about right to Rebecca. If Gleason had run when his fantasy of Russian spies came true, the sparse rainfall of July and August would have killed the earlier growth. But other than the scene being appropriate for untended vegetation in this area, she found nothing that suggested Robert Gleason might have lived there. She'd have to return if she wanted to be certain.

At her second stop, Rebecca was both luckier and less lucky. Her good luck was that a woman answered the door when she knocked; her bad luck was the conversation that followed.

"Yeah, what do you want?" said the woman.

"Morning, I'm Rebecca Marte, Private Investigator."

"He ain't here."

"I'm sorry. Who isn't here?"

"Gotta play dumb, do you?" Rebecca could swear the woman looked at her blonde hair when she delivered the line. "Jack, my husband, ain't here. Left yesterday morning with that damn dog of his to fix some fence and hasn't been back yet. You wanna tell me what bar is trying to collect, 'cause he ain't got a red cent."

"Are you sure he's alright?"

The question made the woman pause a moment, something between a sneer and a grimace on her face. "Alright? He's probably lying drunk in a ditch somewhere, so he's as good as ever. So, you go do your 'investigatin'"—she put air quotes around the last word—"somewhere off my land."

Rebecca paused, wondering if there was a different tack she could take, but the woman seemed to misunderstand her silence.

"Yeah, that's right. It's my land. Jack has never owned anything that he can't swallow, includin' his pride." She laughed at her own joke.

Rebecca took the picture of Robert Gleason from a folder and showed it to the woman. "Have you seen this man anywhere around here?"

"What's he done?"

"He's a possible witness to something that got my client in trouble," replied Rebecca. "My client was cleared, but he'd still like to find this man to get a few more details on what happened." Divulging too much might get her into trouble, but this summary was both abstract and accurate enough that she felt comfortable giving it to the woman.

"Owed your guy some money, did he?" replied the woman.

Apparently, Rebecca hadn't needed to worry. "That's possible."

"Well, I've never seen him, so I'll wish you good huntin' and good day." The woman closed the door somewhat more firmly than necessary.

Although Rebecca hadn't met Jack Rawlings, the owner of the Anatolian Shepherd at this address, she felt comfortable dropping him to the bottom of her list of possibilities. If Rawlings was Gleason, he wouldn't be hiding under the cover of being an alcoholic. Anyone who owned a bar or convenience store in the nearby towns would know him. Simply put, it wasn't the kind of lie someone who had lived on the run for years would use because it was too easy to check.

So, Rebecca sat in her car, looking at the third farmhouse and hoping her next knock on the door would yield a better result. Of her three visits so far, this farm was the best kept. The front was xeriscaped with a small wooden bridge spanning a dry creek bed of rounded stones. To one side of the yard sat an antique wagon, its wood turned gray from the unrelenting sun of summer and the frigid winds of winter. The house itself was a simple one-story ranch. There were two outbuildings, but both were small, suggesting this was more of an escape from the city than a working farm.

Just as Rebecca was about to exit her car, her phone rang. She checked the display. "Hi, Connor. Any news on Jesse?"

"Yes, but it's not good," he replied. "They've been checking the video feeds from the cameras around the airport. They found one with a black SUV pulling up to the curb just as Bolger got there. Two men got out, talked to

Bolger for a few minutes, and then they all got in and drove away. They couldn't get a license plate number or even a good picture of the men's faces. They obviously knew where the cameras were. So, if that was his ride from a drug cartel, we'll never find him."

"You said they talked for a few minutes?"

Connor chuckled. "Somehow, I knew you were going to pick up on that. Why would they talk if this was a pre-arranged pickup? I can't answer that, but I still say that your client is running for sanctuary. It's the simplest answer."

"Probably," admitted Rebecca, although she was thinking that this was the second thing that Bolger had done that didn't quite fit Connor's theory—he had told her about the trip and now, he had discussed with his getaway drivers whether he wanted to be whisked away to safety or not. That didn't make sense, although she didn't have an alternative explanation.

"I'm about halfway to Boulder by now, so I'm going to talk to one of these Anatolian Shepherd owners. But then, I'm heading home. Just as well wait and see if I have a client or not."

"Good call, Rebecca. Oh, Alicia said she really enjoyed the rest of the evening. We'll have to do that again sometime."

"Absolutely." They disconnected.

Rebecca started her car and drove into the farm's gravel driveway. There, she grabbed her folder from the front seat, walked to the porch, and rang the doorbell. After a few moments, a man opened it.

"Private Investigator Marte, I presume," he said.

Even though the photograph she had was old and faded, she knew who it was immediately. "Nice to meet you, Mr. Robert Gleason."

Noon, Robert Gleason's farm north of Denver

"Please come in," said Gleason.

Rebecca assessed the situation. She couldn't see a gun, but one of Gleason's hands was partially hidden behind his leg. When he'd opened the front door, he'd left a screen door closed and had stepped back. The door looked solid. She couldn't rush him because even without the screen between them, she'd never reach him before he could swing a gun up from behind his leg. She glanced at the windows on either side of the door. She didn't see anyone there, but they were covered with shades heavy enough to filter the sunlight ... and hide anyone standing behind them.

"Is Ms. Majoris watching from a window?" asked Rebecca.

"I hardly think so," replied Gleason. "She was just finishing up preparations for lunch. Shall I ask her to set another plate? Oh, of course, I should. Where are my manners?"

"I think you should know that just before I rang your doorbell, I called the police. They'll be here any minute."

"I don't think so," replied Gleason. "Before you pulled into my drive, you received a call from Special Agent Connor Sullivan, if I have my phone numbers straight. And if I had to guess, I'd say he was telling you they've been told to stand down in their search for Mr. Bolger."

Without realizing it, Rebecca had dropped into a half crouch when Gleason came to the door—part of preparing to defend herself. But with these words, she stood up straight and stared at him. Analyzing cell tower transmissions could be arranged if the requester could get a search warrant signed by a judge, but she had never heard of anyone having real-time information on calls.

"Who are you?" she asked.

"Why don't you come in, join us for lunch, and I'll answer as many of your questions as I can." Casually, he swung his hand forward from behind his leg to reveal ... a napkin. He turned and walked into the house.

Gleason was charming and confident. But when Rebecca considered the information that she was relatively certain about—Gleason was believed dead and was living under an assumed identity, he had known the location and names of two Russian spies, and he had involved an old friend in their capture without his knowledge—there was no question in her mind how this situation should be handled. She hurried back to her car and removed her firearm from the glove compartment. Gleason had left the door open, so she walked in.

"Ms. Marte, back here," Gleason called.

Perhaps it was an unnecessary precaution, but she unholstered her firearm and held it at her side. She walked to the kitchen door, checking through the gap between it and its frame to make sure no one was hiding there. She entered the kitchen, finding Gleason sitting on the opposite side of a table with a woman to his right.

"Please be careful with that," said Gleason softly, nodding toward the gun in her hand. "That's how people get killed, although I'm sure you're fully trained."

Rebecca started to say that the safety was on but didn't. Why give him the benefit of that split-second advantage if things turned violent?

"I don't believe you've met Olive Majoris."

"Nice to meet you," Majoris said.

"You, too." Rebecca nodded at the woman, then turned toward Gleason. "She's your mother, correct?" Even though that was what she'd been told, there wasn't any family resemblance that Rebecca could see and the woman looked too young.

"No, sorry. Mom died in a car crash six years ago. I almost did, too, but the doctors pulled me through. She just uses Mom's name when the occasion calls for it."

"We really don't eat like this every day," said Majoris, "but I found this lobster bisque that's to die for. How about a bowl while we talk? We have crescent rolls and a nice Caesar salad, too."

Rebecca just looked at her, still not certain what to make of the situation.

"Maybe 'to die for' isn't the best way to phrase it in front of Ms. Marte," said Gleason. "But it really is good. So, I'm curious. How'd you find me? Charlie perhaps?"

"I'll ask again," said Rebecca, ignoring his question. "Who the hell are you?"

"I bet it was Charlie," said Majoris. "That dog sticks out like a sore thumb."

"Yes, but if you want to be accepted by the locals, he's your ticket. No city slicker's going to own an Anatolian Shepherd. And besides, he keeps the riff-raff away. I even understand they're breeding Colorado Mountain Dogs now that are part Anatolian Shepherd."

"Enough," said Rebecca. "I don't want to spoil anyone's lunch, but this whole conversation is beyond belief. You," she said, nodding at Gleason, "are supposed to be dead. And you," she turned to Majoris, "are using a dead woman's name. And we're all going to sit here and enjoy our soup and salad like nothing's happened when my client is missing? It's time I call the police and let them sort this out."

"Ah, your client," said Gleason. "I should have guessed that his absence would be a problem for you." He stood and started to leave.

"Stop right there," Rebecca shouted. Gleason did and turned back to her. "Where the hell do you think you are going?" she asked.

"Just in back. I'm unarmed and our only weapons are locked safely in a vault in one of the outbuildings. And if that's not enough, you can hold Olive here at gunpoint. You don't mind, do you?"

"It wouldn't be the first time," replied Majoris. Gleason turned and left the room.

"Do you like your bisque hot or cold?" asked Majoris. "I prefer hot, but then, not everyone does."

"You know, this is a really dangerous game you're playing," said Rebecca. "If Gleason, or whatever his name is, somehow coerced you into it, we can find a way out."

"You misunderstand, Rebecca. Is it OK if I call you Rebecca?"

"Sure, but .... Someone's coming."

After a moment, Gleason appeared at the door. When a second man appeared behind him, all Rebecca could think to say was, "What the hell, Jesse?"

Afternoon, Robert Gleason's farm north of Denver

Bolger looked at Rebecca, then Gleason.

"She doesn't know yet," Gleason said.

"I don't know what?"

"That Gleason snatched me out of the hands of a drug cartel," said Bolger. "Without him, I might be dead by now."

He paused a moment. "I owe you an apology, Ms. Marte. I'm sorry that I couldn't tell you, but I'm CIA. Not an operative, but a counterintelligence computer specialist. If the Agency needs a network cracked in a foreign country, then I'm the guy. A couple of years ago, I broke into a Colombian drug cartel's communications network. Nearly put them out of business. But they couldn't figure out the vulnerability I'd exploited even after two years, so they've been watching for an opportunity to nab me."

"So, if you hacked off a drug cartel, why did you ...?" But even before Rebecca could finish her question, she knew there was only one person who could have put her client on a flight to Bogota. "Miles Sennett was behind this, wasn't he?"

"Unfortunately, yes," replied Gleason. "We had a good lead on Ermakov and Ilyin, in large part due to some great investigative work by Olive."

Rebecca glanced at Majoris who had moved to the stove and was warming up the bisque, but she didn't even look up. It was like people commended her every day for bringing down dangerous foreign terrorists.

"But there's always been a suspicion that those two had a mole inside the CIA," continued Gleason. "It turned out to be

Miles Sennett. Unless it's already made the noon news, you'll hear about his arrest tonight."

Rebecca's phone vibrated. She looked at Gleason who merely said, "Of course," as he held out an open hand.

Rebecca checked the display, and then answered, "Hi, Connor. What's up?" She was quiet for a moment as she listened. "And DEA?" Another pause. "Any idea who this time?" After a third period of silence, she said, "OK, thanks for the update." She disconnected.

"The FBI, DEA, and the U.S. Consulate in Colombia have been told to drop all investigations into Jesse Bolger related to his last trip to Colombia," Rebecca said. "And once again, no one seems to know who made the call or why."

"News seems to be traveling slower than I expected," said Gleason. "But at least you have a little more reason to believe me now."

Rebecca shook her head slowly. "Why do I feel like I know less than half of this story?"

"Because that's accurate," said Majoris. "But if you'll join us for lunch, I'd guess we can get you up to 75, maybe even 80 percent." She smiled.

Rebecca felt like she was never going to get to the bottom of this case if she didn't eat some of their damn bisque. So, she tried to return the smile to her host—which probably came across as a grimace—placed her firearm in its holster and sat down at the table. Bolger took the seat beside her.

After Majoris served them all a hot bowl of lobster bisque and the salad and rolls had been passed around the table, Gleason said, "You've asked me twice who I am. Basically, Olive and I and a few dozen others are government troubleshooters. We come from the agencies you know—the FBI, the CIA, the NSA—and a few you've probably never heard of like the Office of Intelligence and Counterintelligence, which is part of the Department of Energy. So, we are none of those organizations and at the same time, all of them."

Gleason glanced at Majoris, who continued their story. "For the last six months, we've been assigned to Ermakov and Ilyin and last month, we moved to a location close to where we believed they were operating. Proximity helps reduce signals noise."

"Signals noise?" said Rebecca.

Majoris tilted her head to one side. "Methods and sources are the bread and butter of intelligence gathering and so, are highly classified. Unfortunately, this term is one of those areas where anything I say that is publicly releasable will raise more questions than it answers, so I won't say anything except that proximity can be an advantage. In this case, however, the advantage of being nearby and all the others we could muster weren't enough. We needed something to draw Ermakov and Ilyin out of hiding. That's where Jesse came in."

Rebecca spun around in her chair to stare at her client in disbelief. "They used you as bait?"

"No, of course not," Bolger replied. But after a pause, he said, "Well, yeah, I suppose they did, but it's not what you think. Sennett had apparently been leaking bits and pieces of information about CIA operations for some time. Recently, I was one of those bits, so my career was already over even if I didn't know it until yesterday."

"Jesse provided the final leverage we needed to expose Ermakov and Ilyin," said Majoris. "All we had to do was convince them that he was interested in working for them, which we did. Even with Jesse's career already in ruins, those were tough communications."

"With the Russians interested in recruiting Jesse, they needed to give us an address where we could meet," said Gleason. "But they were wary. They ran us all over town. I thought I was going to lose ten pounds with all the extra layers of clothes I was wearing, but later, we got to change and I left most of that behind. We also had to leave our phones. Previously, when we were discussing turning Jesse, they'd given Olive and me a phone, but we needed another to keep him occupied when Olive called Barrow. So, we built a replica."

Majoris chuckled. "The FBI forensics lab is going to get a real shock when they take the phone apart that they got from Jesse. It has the guts of a well-known U.S. model with most of the functions disabled and a Light Phone display."

"The stop at the bank was prearranged because they wanted Jesse to accept a payment," said Gleason. "They thought of it as their insurance policy—a dirty money payment to prove his complicity. They saw the money disappear from their account, but it went to a general operating fund rather than anything controlled by him.

"The ATM was also where they left the address where we'd meet. We didn't know exactly when or where they would give us that information, but we knew it would be at the bank or nearby since the time for the meeting was fast approaching. They'd given us a specific symbol to watch for, and when I saw it on the ATM, I knew we were on the final leg of this pursuit. The address was on the back of a card that was made to look like part of the ATM with the symbol on the front.

"Finally, I had secretly pocketed a note that was supposedly from Natasha. I showed it to Jesse, just so he'd be focused on meeting our deadline, rather than planning a counteroffensive against the Russians."

"But that almost didn't work," said Majoris. "I had been waiting at the bank, figuring I would trail the two of them until Robert had the address. When I saw his signal at the ATM, I got a little overanxious and started moving before they headed out. Jesse saw me and as I understand it, wanted to come after me thinking I was Natasha. Robert objected to the idea, and fortunately, Jesse went along with him."

"I just thought I was sticking to our plan," said Bolger. "If we could capture one of them, cooperation by the FBI would be assured. But knowing what I know now, that additional handwritten note at the bottom was critical or I might have tried to come after you, worn-out shoes and all."

"Yes, that was a master stroke," agreed Gleason. "Olive only added it just before the start of our late-night jog."

Rebecca looked over at the woman, but as before, she couldn't see that Majoris reacted to their praise at all. Apparently to her, it was all in a day's work.

"I'd been relaying Ilyin's demands to Robert all evening, but at this point, I had a couple of other roles to play," said Majoris. "First, I called Barrow. We had him stand up an FBI raid team at two o'clock because, while the FBI is good, no one gets a call after eleven and conducts a raid at midnight. All he needed was the address, which I gave him. Then, I played Jenkins in the call from Jesse. But since I had played the NBC agent all along, that part was straightforward."

"But why involve the FBI at all?" asked Rebecca. "Couldn't your troubleshooting team handle a raid?"

"Well, I could say that we have over seven hundred other ongoing operations and we were spread too thin to handle one more," said Gleason, grinning at Bolger.

Bolger shook his head, his gaze going to the ceiling, then back down to Rebecca. "That was my excuse for not picking up Ermakov and Ilyin back when I was playing like I was a spy for Robert's benefit. All I can say is that it sounded good at the time."

"Well, your claim's actually not too far from the truth," said Majoris, "although the number is two, not seven hundred. Robert and I are the only ones assigned locally and no one, not even the local FBI field office, knows our missions or our methods. That way, we can react quickly and covertly. But sometimes, a little ad-libbing is necessary when you have no backup, like getting the local field office to handle a raid for you."

"But you're telling me all this," said Rebecca. "What's to keep me from telling Connor and from there, it's all over the field office?"

"No one is stopping you," said Gleason. "But when they ask for proof, you won't have it because we'll be gone. And without that, your story will end up with all the Elvis sightings and reports of underground cities."

As Bolger had mentioned this comment to Rebecca when they first met, no one needed to explain the chuckles around the table to her. But that didn't keep her from feeling a little guilty. "Sorry that you're going to have to move because of me."

"Oh, it's not you, Rebecca," said Majoris. "This op is over, so it's time we move on."

"Olive, I know we've talked through nearly all of this already," said Bolger, "but we missed one thing that now has me stumped. Why did you use artificial intelligence voice-cloning technology to sound like me when you called the FBI? A tip about the location of two Russian spies from anyone would get their attention."

Majoris frowned. "I didn't. I just used a generic male voice to leave an anonymous tip. Why did you ...." Then, she laughed. "Of course. The FBI talked like they had an open and shut case against you, and you guessed they had a voice match. But they don't. And when they get around to testing their recording against your voice, they'll be forced to change their theory. Now, it was you who had used AI technology to sound like someone else."

"So, it was Barrow who jumped to the conclusion it was me?" asked Bolger.

"It was," said Majoris. "We knew the decision to go through him was a calculated risk, but we thought we could close out the report that you had made about Russian spies in the area if the FBI caught two, even if they weren't named Boris and Natasha. When I called at two o'clock to get a raid team ready, he was hesitant. So, I dropped the names Ermakov and Ilyin, and he was immediately on board.

"But while Barrow was slow to assemble a team, he was fast to assume the call was from you. Maybe the generic voice sounded something like you or maybe he thought you were trying to trick him by using a different voice, but he named you as the probable caller. From there, the double agent theory was a simple deduction by the FBI. Who else but another spy would know the identities the Russians had taken. So, we called the boss to get the Bureau to stand down before they had a chance to book you."

"I won't even bother asking who's the boss," said Rebecca, "because I'm sure you won't tell me." Nevertheless, she paused a moment, hoping Gleason or Majoris would correct her. They didn't.

"OK, that gets us to the point where Jesse got out of detention," said Rebecca. "After that, he was put on a desk until Sennett approved a trip to Colombia. But with Ermakov and Ilyin out of commission, how did Sennett even know the cartel was looking for him?"

"Well, first, you need to know a little more about our Russian spies," said Gleason. "We knew they were passing intelligence back to Russia. That's just part of the spy game that's played by most of the foreign diplomats in the States—observe and report. But they were also receiving money to fund various activities designed to undermine the government and weaken our sense of security. The funding of Najibullah Zazi's terrorist attack on the New York subway, which fortunately was thwarted, is the best-known example. But they also funded several other projects, including a loan to a small-time drug dealer so he could handle much larger shipments from a Colombian drug cartel.

"As to how Sennett found out the cartel was hoping to grab Jesse, we don't know for sure. But at some point, Ermakov and Ilyin probably realized that they could pull Sennett even deeper into their treachery if they got the cartel to pay him to deliver Jesse to South America. And compared to the modest sums he'd received in the past, this would have been a massive payday for him. So, they probably arranged for a conversation. Then, when the Russians were captured, Sennett probably decided to lay low for a while. Unfortunately for him, he decided it had been long enough to approve the travel about the same time that Jesse decided to hire a private investigator."

Bolger slowly shook his head. "At the time Miles made all his arguments against looking for Gleason and hiring Ms. Marte, they seemed logical enough. But in hindsight, they were clearly self-serving. He didn't want anything to interfere with his business deal. And I keep telling myself, surely the cartel told him they'd let me go as soon as they had the information they wanted because I find it hard to believe he would have delivered me to my death."

Rebecca watched as Gleason and Majoris gave each other a look, but neither said a word.

Finally, Majoris said, "Since Sennett was one of the few people left who could have been the mole in the CIA, we were watching him closely. We picked up on a communication between him and Ruger-Phillips Travel requesting his signature on the Colombia trip. Unfortunately, it was too late to stop Jesse from boarding the flight, but it wasn't too late to get a couple of DEA agents to meet him on the other end. After that, it was just a final call to the boss to get everyone to stand down."

"So, PI Marte, you are now at the 80 percent level," said Gleason. "I hope that satisfies your curiosity."

"I'd say I'm closer to 75 percent," said Rebecca, "but I think there's one more thing that'll get me to 80, and I'm pretty sure you can tell me. Why, if Miles Sennett and the Russians were working together, didn't he warn them that you and Ms. Majoris were closing in?"

"Oh, he probably did," said Majoris. "But you have to remember, this was a way of life for Ermakov and Ilyin. They undoubtedly got lots of warnings over the years, and this one was probably one of the easiest for them to ignore. A bumbling high school friend just isn't the kind of threat they'd take too seriously."

"Put that way, I can see it," replied Rebecca as she looked around the table. These people were clearly more extraordinary than she had first thought. Majoris was an accomplished spy hunter but was oblivious to the praise. And Gleason clearly wasn't just the dreamer he seemed. They had lived their lives in the shadows so she could live hers in the light, and she felt grateful for the sacrifices they had made.

"Of course, I'd be lying if I said I didn't wonder about the other 20 percent, but I also understand why you can't tell me. But I did learn one significant lesson from this case that I'll never forget. The next time someone comes to me with a case about spies and espionage ... I'm throwing them out of my office."

SATURDAY, SEPTEMBER 21

Late Morning, The Mountain Sports Shop

Jesse had been to the Mountain Sports Shop before but not in the last year, and it took him some time to find the skiing section. The delay, however, wasn't a problem as he found himself staring lovingly at fishing rods, bike helmets, hiking boots, and an inflatable kayak. He had all of those items and more packed away in a storeroom at home, none of them seeing the light of day for the last year. But he vowed that things would change ... starting today.

He knew he was getting close to the skis without even seeing the sign because the looks he was receiving from the sales staff became progressively more unreceptive. First, there was the bubbly, twenty-something woman who almost seemed to materialize from thin air at his right elbow. She was familiar and apparently, he was to her as well, because when she saw his face, she said, "Oh, I'll get you one of the guys."

After a moment, a man he recognized as the shift manager came over. "Is she around?" Jesse asked.

"Stocking shelves," he replied as he stuck out a thumb toward the back of the store. "But I don't want any trouble."

"There won't be any." Jesse turned and started walking in the direction the manager had indicated, although he could feel the man's glare boring into his back until he turned a corner.

Soon, he found Loren crawling around on her hands and knees as she placed some ski boots on a bottom shelf. When he approached, she didn't look up, but instead, seemed to be studying his feet. After a moment, she said, "Size 11, unless you wear really thick socks with your boots."

"Yeah, I've always had trouble keeping my feet warm, so maybe a half-size up." His cold feet had been something of a running joke when they were together, but at the moment, he could tell Loren wasn't finding anything humorous in his comment. "So, school wasn't keeping you busy enough? You had to come back here on the weekends?"

"I thought we had a deal?" she said, her gaze still on the floor.

"We did. And I know I don't deserve it, but I was hoping we could strike up a new one. I've got a new job."

"Just what I need," she said. "A guy who'll be secretly bemoaning the loss of a job he loved for a girl he can't commit to."

"Yeah, I did enjoy my previous job, but I'm sure I'll like this one even better."

Loren raised her head for the first time to look at him. "Yeah, why's that?"

"You remember the year before you moved in and I was shopping here ... well, just about every day you were working? Well, it's time I hauled all the stuff I bought out of my storeroom in the basement and figured out how to use it."

"There's lots of good videos on the Internet."

"I was hoping for some more personalized instruction. And if it takes weeks, months, or even years, that's fine because I won't be traveling for work. Well, maybe the occasional weekend convention, but Ruger-Phillips West wants their new head of cyber security at the office every day. So, I'll be at home every night ... hopefully, with you."

Loren released a long sigh, her gaze dropping to the floor before she looked back up. "That's not how things work."

Jesse nodded. He knew it was a long shot after the months of neglect he had shown her. But at least he had his answer. "I understand," he said softly.

"No, I don't think you do."

If she needed to chastise him for his past behavior, he wasn't going to deny her the chance. He had it coming, so he braced himself.

"First, we go out to dinner so you can tell me all about this new job," Loren said. "Then, on the second date, we plan out your training regimen. It's not going to be easy. You jog, but, for a guy who lives in Colorado, you've made really poor use of the mountains, the lakes, and the bike trails. For date three ... well, we'll see if you make it that far because I still have my doubts."

"Tonight?"

Loren's eyes narrowed.

"For date one," he replied to her unspoken question.

"I'm off at five."

THE END

ACKNOWLEDGMENTS

This book would not have been possible without the help of a number of talented individuals, and I've been fortunate to work with largely the same group for the last five novels and counting.

First, I'd like to thank my talented daughter, Ms. Courtney Perrin, for the book cover art. As a structural engineer skilled in the use of 3-dimensional software tools for analyzing buildings, my requests for rather simple, 2D cover art dramatically underutilizes her talents. I take solace in the fact, however, that she does art as a hobby. Now, if I just didn't tie her creative hands by limiting her designs in order to maintain a brand appearance to the series—the same fonts, color schemes, and human silhouette on each—I could even believe that.

At least three new sets of eyes read each of my books before you, the reader, have a chance at them. Ms. Janet Harrison does what I think of as a general readability review and critique. When things don't quite hang together for her, it's probably because I've skipped a step or two in the story's flow.

All of my books have some infusion of psychological concepts because ... well, because I'm an experimental psychologist by training and experience. And while stories necessarily involve some extension beyond the everyday, Dr. Liz Gehr helps assure that I haven't gone too far in that regard where psychology is involved.

And the last set of eyes are those of my editor, who gets into the nitty-gritty of punctuation and grammar. I've yet to write a book without learning something new from her. This time, it was that em dashes and ellipses both indicate pauses, with the former used for a definite break and the latter for hesitation or for drifting off in thought. Couple of hundred more books and I'll have English mastered ... not. (That's drifting off in a thought, right?)

ABOUT THE AUTHOR

Bruce Perrin has been writing for more than twenty-five years, although you will find much of that work only in professional technical journals or conference proceedings. After receiving a Ph.D. in Industrial/Organizational Psychology and completing a career in psychological research and development at a major aerospace company, he's now applying his background to writing fiction. Not surprisingly, most of his work falls in the techno-thriller, mystery, and hard science fiction genres, examining the intersection of technology and the human mind now and in the future. Besides writing, Bruce likes to tinker with home automation and is an avid hiker. When he is not on the trails, he lives with his wife in Aurora, CO.

Thank you for reading *In the Mind of a Spy*. If you'd like to help others find this story, please consider leaving a review on Amazon, Goodreads, or the website of your favorite bookseller.

For all the latest on my new releases, promotions, and book reviews, please subscribe to my newsletter at BruceMPerrin.com.

BURNING DOWN THE HOUSE

INTRODUCTION

by Michel Lee Garrett

Humanity exists in cycles.

There are the big ones. Birth, death, and rebirth. Feast and famine. Peace and wartime. There are also the smaller, more mundane ones: wake up, go to work, come home, wake up, go to work… In many ways, the cycles we participate in, whether voluntarily or involuntarily, define us—as individuals, as communities, as cultures, as a species.

My co-editor, the brilliant T. Fox Dunham, has a saying he uses when he writes historical fiction: "Same shit, different century." As much as history marches on, as much as the details change, so much of the big picture remains the same. Humanity continues to wrestle with the same adversaries since time immemorial. Greed. Pride. Cruelty. Scapegoating. Warmongering. Oppression. Tyranny. The impulse to consume all, to possess all, with no care for what is destroyed in the process. We fight back, of course, for freedom, for love, for justice, and sometimes we even win. But people forget. Tyrants rise anew. The cycle repeats.

To quote the song that incites this collection's final story: "Same as it ever was. Same as it ever was. Same as it ever was…"

In the lonely hours of the night, I fear we may not have many cycles left in our collective future. People have worried that the end was nigh since the beginning, but I'm worried this time they may be right. Late-stage nightmare capitalism has forced millions across the globe into extreme poverty, while the richest few gorge themselves on unimaginable wealth. Fascists and authoritarian strongmen are on the rise, promising the same old violence they've always promised, against the same communities they always target. Meanwhile, the planet is dying, increasingly devastated by the effects of man-made climate change. The proverbial house, somewhat literally, is burning down. And who bears the brunt of these impacts? The most vulnerable populations around the world, further exacerbating global geopolitical instability and emboldening political charlatans.

This collection—a charity anthology, from which 100% of the proceeds will be donated to fight climate change, the single biggest existential crisis of our time—does not have the answers to these challenges. But the stories contained in these pages offer glimpses of the human experience from different perspectives, with a distinct bent toward chronicling and celebrating the downtrodden and the underdogs. Those who are crushed beneath the wheel of the world, and those who fight back against it, no matter how futile it may be.

The stories in this collection, while all somewhere within the sphere of 'crime fiction,' are a genre-blending cocktail that defies easy categorization—much like the songs that incited them. Assembled in this collection is a diverse range of writers, including award-winning veteran authors and exciting emerging voices from across the worlds of hard-boiled crime, literary noir, horror, fantasy and science fiction, presenting a dazzling array of what crime fiction can entail. It has been an honor and privilege to work with each of the writers represented in this collection.

In these pages, there is grounded, gritty noir in which broken individuals make desperate choices just to survive. There are modern feminist fables on bodily autonomy, sexual harassment, abusive relationships, and transgender dignity. There are near-future speculative examinations of the resurgence of fascism and the privatization of basic human needs, as well as a period piece exploring capitalistic progress and its unforeseen costs. There are stories that celebrate the beauty and the sadness of the mundane and the everyday, stories that descend into horror, that collapse into tragedy, and one that even ascends into a fantastical hero's journey. And in each of these tales, there's a shared humanity that unites us, even as the world burns down around us.

Humanity exists in cycles, ones that have played out, over and over again, like the ocean beating against the shore, or Sisyphus rolling his rock up the mountain. This is not a nihilistic statement. To rebel against these cycles, to dare to dream of what *could* be instead, to burn down the house of injustice that has been built around us, is the noblest choice that one can make.

Nietzsche posed the question of the eternal recurrence—if a being were to come to you and inform you that you were fated to live your life again and again, the same as it ever was, for all eternity, would this be your salvation or your damnation?

It depends on the choices we make.

It depends on how we try to shape the cycles around us, to bend them to our will and in doing so, to make them more noble, more just, and more conducive to the pursuit of life.

It depends on us to live the life that we would rejoice to live again.

I hope, dear reader, that the stories in this collection may inspire you to rebel against the cycles that imprison us, and in doing so, help build a better world that may continue to iterate long after we are gone. I hope the world does not burn down, and I choose to dream that it won't. I entreat the empty universe that, someday, our children may look out on a world of peace and prosperity and remark: "Same as it ever was."

—Michel Lee Garrett, editor

ROAD TO NOWHERE

by James D.F. Hannah

Paul and Laura were set up in the VFW hall already, Paul tuning his guitar, Laura tightening a new drumhead, when Wyatt walked in, empty-handed.

He should have been lugging in that Domino bass and the amp he'd bought secondhand a few years ago. He had his hands dug into his jeans pockets instead, looking like he'd been caught playing with himself in the middle of traffic.

Paul had made clear to Wyatt how important this weekend's gig was for the Ozones. He'd left messages at Wyatt's house, at his job. Driving home the point they needed to be sharper than ever Saturday night. He'd organized the set list to spotlight versatility with Television and Roxy Music and Modern Lovers covers, but also slipping in a few originals. He needed them to be perfect. There wasn't space for fuck ups.

"Guys, there's a problem," Wyatt said, his voice low, already apologizing.

Laura came out from behind her drum set. The drums were her armor, a shield against how small she was. She barely reached mid-chest on Wyatt when she hugged him.

"Oh my God, are you okay?" she said, her head against his sternum.

Paul didn't move. He watched Wyatt accepting Laura's

embrace, then saw when Wyatt's expression switched to discomfort at Paul's awareness of it.

Wyatt rested his hands on Laura's shoulders and gently pushed her away.

"I'm fine," he said. "It's the van. The transmission finally died the other day. I had to get her fixed. Just got her back from the garage tonight."

The van—the Love Wagon—hauled them and their equipment to shows on weekends. The inside stunk of weed and rattled with the sound of empty PBRs and the reverb of their cassettes. The transmission had muttered empty threats for months, shuddering between gear shifts, whining like a beaten animal.

Paul hit the opening chord from a Smiths song. Took a rock star pose.

"But it's good now," he said. "So let's get going."

A weekend gig in Richmond should have been just another show in a college town bar. Except Paul had hounded the bar owner for months, making calls, sending homemade demo tapes. They only got it when another band fell through at the last minute.

Paul didn't see it as "just another show," though. Because he knew about Radium 228, a band out of Lexington that signed to I.R.S. after a talent scout saw them at the bar one random Saturday night. Less than a year later, they were opening for Oingo Boingo and playing CBGB's.

Since seeing the story on the local news ("Local band finds rising rock stardom"), Paul had focused on nothing but getting a show in Richmond. Obsessed with the Ozones breaking the cycle of weddings and parties they played every weekend. No more Bon Jovi or Huey Lewis or Billy Joel—so much goddamn Billy Joel—but instead their own songs, to an audience that gave a damn about music as more than background noise, on the off chance there could be more.

Wyatt didn't move.

Laura fiddled with her braided rat tail, the one she got after seeing that Til Tuesday video. A nervous habit whenever she felt the pressure in a room change. Whenever she knew shit was ready to go down.

"I had to pawn the bass," Wyatt said. "The amp, too. It's at Billy Fielder's."

Billy Fielder owned a pawn shop outside of town, the last standing business in an otherwise abandoned strip mall. People brought him guns and VCRs and four-wheelers and he gave them fifty cents on the dollar and asked for a buck and a half back. Folks took it because there weren't any other options. Around Christmas, folks came to buy their neighbor's property to place under the tree.

"When can you get it out?" Paul said.

Wyatt shrugged. "I don't get paid 'til next week."

Wyatt, like the rest of them, worked one of the few shit jobs in town that didn't involve digging coal. Paul selling TVs and hardware at Sears, Laura waiting tables, Wyatt tearing tickets at the four-screen theater at the mall.

Normally, this was where someone would have suggested asking a parent for money. Except no one did. Wyatt's dad was a union boss at the mines, and he either didn't notice or didn't care about his son's dreams. Laura's parents—well, her mom and her stepfather—drank their way through government checks every month, with not a penny to carry over to the next.

And Paul's dad? He'd be the hardest no-go.

"How much?" Paul said.

Wyatt said a number.

Laura shook her head and went back to her drums, started taking the kit apart. "I'm going home. I gotta be at the diner when first shift comes out of the mine or Leo yells at me."

They helped her load her gear into the back of her Fiesta and watched as she drove away, the tail lights fading to nothing in the darkness.

"Do you know how much I had to beg the guy who owns that joint to give us this chance?" Paul said.

"I don't know what to tell you, man. I don't have the money. Neither do you and neither does Laura. So I guess we're fucked. It is what it is." He took his keys from his pocket. "I'll talk to you later."

As Wyatt drove away in the Love Wagon, Paul noticed how the van's transmission hummed like a song.

Paul didn't feel like going home, but there were only so many ways to extend the drive back to the house. He took all of the options, listening to the Talking Heads live album along the way, drumming his fingers on the steering wheel and wondering how many other bands ended this way. With nods and an unspoken acceptance that there wouldn't be anything else.

He parked next to the sheriff department cruiser already in the driveway. The old man called the car a "perk of the job." He drove it everywhere, even when off duty.

Being chief deputy had loads of perks for Paul's father. Like how he never paid for a meal at a restaurant. How someone from the high school football team came by every week and mowed the front yard. Envelopes of cash to the old man that ensured wheels kept on turning. From the Moreton brothers, who sold pain pills from a pickup behind the dollar store, or Carl Bell, who owned a coal mine and whose son liked to drink and got heavy-handed with his wife. From Billy Fielder himself, who sometimes needed a bit of "official" help to get someone to pay back borrowed cash. It was the way things had always worked here, and though he knew there was benefit to being the chief deputy's son, it only intensified Paul's desire to get out of town and never, ever look back.

Gunfire roared as Paul walked into the house. His father basked in the glow of the living room TV, planted in his ratty recliner as usual, watching a cop show. Paul couldn't remember which one it was—his father didn't watch much besides cop shows and sports—but he knew the old man liked it because it was set in the 60s, with the clothes and the cars and "back then you could crack skulls and no one was a pussy about it."

Sure thing, old man. Tell me about the good ol' days.

Paul's father slurped at his beer can. "Home early. Didn't your little band have practice or something?"

Your little band.

"Stuff came up."

"Yeah. Stuff. It does do that. Come up."

Paul didn't see much of himself in the old man; there was some shared height, but Paul was lean and lanky, whereas his father had the broad shoulders, softening muscles and swelling gut of the former high school football player he was. Paul possessed more of his mother's features, giving him an almost androgynous quality that worked for what he imagined was the band's image. He wondered if he and his father looked more alike, they might understand one another better.

The old man scratched himself through his boxers. "Talked to Walter Hopkins today. They're opening a mine in Taylorville. Be hiring soon."

Paul's eyes burned with a sudden exhaustion. He rubbed them with his thumb and forefinger until white blurs of light filled his vision.

"It's good money," his father said. "Union shop. They take care of their people."

On the TV, a man in a narrow-lapeled gray suit punched some guy with an immaculate pompadour. The guy stumbled to the ground and the man in the suit dove onto him, still punching, over and over.

The old man smiled when blood began to run down the man's face.

He finished his beer, crushed the can flat and dropped it to the floor beside several others. He reached into the cardboard case next to his recliner and produced a fresh one.

"You're better than them, you know that, right?" he said.

"Than who?" Paul said.

"Those two in that fuckin' band of yours. Who the fuck else would I be talking about? You been trying to get in the chick's pants since you popped your first hard-on, and dimes'll get you dollars she's a goddamn rug-muncher. And the Wyatt kid? He's a fuckin' feeb. Even his dad couldn't get him a mine job, and he runs that union. Doesn't make sense why you'd associate with losers like that."

Paul's right hand coiled into a fist. He realized it was happening, closed his eyes and blew a few breaths and loosened it.

Not tonight. Not tonight.

"I'm tired. Going to bed."

The old man nodded and threw him a wave.

Paul stopped in the kitchen. Rested his forehead against the refrigerator and felt the coolness of the metal and the gentle hum of the compressor. He lifted the receiver off the phone next on the wall and dialed a number.

Wyatt answered on the second ring.

"What time does Fielder's place open?" Paul said.

"I don't know. Nine, I'd guess."

"Pick me up in the morning. Eight-thirty."

"Why?"

"We're getting your shit back. Call Laura and tell her she's coming, too. We do this together, okay?"

Paul hung up the phone before Wyatt could argue.

He went to his father's bedroom and crossed the room's darkness to the dresser, sliding open the middle drawer—slow, trying to not make noise—and reached in back. Feeling for what he knew was there, buried underneath the neatly folded white T-shirts.

His father's .38.

Not his service weapon. One of the other guns he kept around the house. Paul made sure it was loaded before he carried it back to his own room. Held it in both hands there in the darkness.

When Paul was eight, he had a Schwinn bicycle, ice blue, his favorite thing he'd ever owned, and the old man forever told him to not leave it outside, that it'd be stolen. Then, one night, he got distracted and he forgot it in the front yard. The next morning, it was gone. A week later Paul saw a kid two streets over cruising along on that same ice-blue Schwinn, and when he told him it was his bike, the kid told him to fuck off, slugged him, rode away.

Paul told his father what happened. The old man wore his uniform and took the cruiser and found the kid still riding the bike. Rested his hand on his service weapon and told the kid to give back the bike. The kid didn't argue with the old man, just got off the thing and ran.

Paul and his father drove back to the house, the bike in the trunk. Then the old man rested the bike in the driveway and ran over it, the driver's side wheels crunching it into a shapeless twist of metal.

Paul was too much in shock to cry, even as his father set the bike's remains at his feet. "If you're not man enough to keep what's yours, you don't deserve to own it," he said before going into the house.

• • •

Years ago, the rumor had been that Wal-Mart was going to buy the property where Fielder's Pawn Shop sat, a strip of land on a road to nowhere that you only drove if you were going there. The plan was to raze it and build the new store. The other owners along the strip—a beauty school, a laundromat, a pair of dollar stores and a record shop—all took the early money. Fielder had hung strong, waiting, waiting, waiting until Wal-Mart moved in the next town over, and left the pawn shop the last business before the county line.

On weekends, kids came there to drink Boone's Farm and tell lies to one another in the backseats of their parents' cars. The cracked pavement that carpeted the property was strewn with shattered glass and used condoms that looked like earthworms trapped by the early morning sun.

Wyatt parked in back, next to a dumpster, the way Paul told

him to. The transmission clicked into place with a confidence it hadn't possessed a week earlier.

Paul sat in the captain's chairs behind Wyatt. Knitted his gloved hands together. A backpack at his feet. A lightweight jacket, zipped nearly to the neck.

He eyed the back door to the shop. Padlocked shut. They'd have to go in through the front, which was fine. There was a cut-through between stores they could take.

Laura curled into the passenger seat, playing with her braid.

"Why are we doing this?" she said.

Paul reached into the backpack and pulled out ski masks. Handed one each to Laura and Wyatt.

"Because we've got to get Wyatt's equipment back or we'll blow our shot."

Wyatt stared at his mask with a dull-eyed confusion. Paul had known Wyatt all his life, and the only time he wasn't a beat behind was when he was on that bass.

"Shouldn't I stay in the van? Keep it running? For the getaway?" Wyatt said.

Paul pulled his own mask on, tugging and adjusting the openings.

"No. If all three of us go in, it's a show of force. Fielder won't put up as much fight." Paul opened the mouth of the backpack to reveal a length of rope. "We'll tie him up. We walk out with what we want, no problem."

"And how fucking stupid do you think Fielder is, we go in there and take that bass and amp?" Laura said. "He's gonna put two and two together and know it's us?"

"Then we don't just steal the bass and the amp. We take some other stuff. Get a few guns and sell 'em for extra cash." Paul smiled and unzipped his Member's Only jacket and showed them the pistol, the handle hanging out of the inside pocket. "Speaking of guns, if he gives us trouble, I take this out, wave it around a bit. Problem solved."

"I don't like this," Wyatt said. "My parents—"

"Fuck your parents, Wyatt," Paul said. "Your parents are like everyone else, sitting in this town waiting to die. Is that what you want? What any of us want?"

He grabbed the backpack.

"Put on the masks and let's do this."

• • •

They came through the door right after nine, a minute after Fielder had flipped the sign to "Open." Barely enough time to return behind the counter.

Paul in front, Wyatt following, Laura pulling up the rear. The bell above the door ringing as they entered.

Slight surprise flashed on Fielder's face when he saw them. He was small and dumpling shaped, ruddy faced, his greasy hair the same shade of gray as the ash hanging from the end of the cigar clenched in his teeth, standing behind a display counter at the back of the shop, close to a door marked private.

"What in the—" he said. The rest of the sentence was cut off by Paul unzipping his jacket and pulling out his father's .38 and aiming it at Fielder.

"Don't do anything stupid and you won't get hurt," Paul said.

Fielder raised his hands even to his shoulders. A smile flickered on the edges of his mouth.

"Been watching TV, son?" he said.

"What?" Paul said, confused.

"That's what they always say. 'Don't move and no one gets hurt.' On all those shows." He nodded toward Paul. "You got some tremble there."

Paul realized the pistol was shaking in his hand. He folded his left hand around the right to steady his grasp. It helped a little.

He'd played this over and over in his head all night, and on the drive to the shop. He wanted to be cool and emotionless, like Stallone or Eastwood. But acid churned through his stomach in waves, and the pistol weighed heavier in his hands now than it had last night. Paul had never pointed a gun at another living thing before. Even deer hunting with his father, it was his old man who brought home a trophy. Never Paul.

He scanned the shelves. An assortment of rifles and shotguns behind Fielder. Closer to Paul, stereo equipment and furniture. Then his eyes landed on musical instruments. Guitars on a rack along the wall. Below them, trumpets and clarinets and saxophones—a history of failed high school musical experimentation. Amps and mixing boards and other equipment close by.

Wyatt's was the only bass on the rack, nestled between acoustics and electrics. Paul threw Wyatt a glance and jerked his chin toward the bass. Wyatt stepped over and grabbed the guitar.

Fielder kept one hand raised and took the cigar from his mouth with the other. Coughed out a bitter laugh.

"Goddamn but I thought that was you," he said.

Wyatt froze in his footsteps and stared at Fielder, the bass held in mid-air like a sacrifice at an altar.

The pawn shop owner's smile widened, revealing a mouth full of small, yellowed teeth.

"It's Wyatt, isn't it? You brought it in Monday." He shook his head. "It's a small town, kids, and I've done this shit a long time, so I don't have to see a face to know who you are." He motioned toward the door labeled private. "I got your name and address all on a piece of paper back there."

Laura tugged at Paul's jacket.

"Let's just go. Please."

Paul jerked away from her. His eyes danced with nervous thoughts.

"We'll get the pawn slips, too." He waved the pistol at the display case of jewelry. "Start taking those watches and rings out. Set 'em up on the counter."

"You should listen to that little girl," Fielder said. He sounded amused by what was happening. "That shake in your hand, now it's in your voice." He stuck the cigar back in his mouth and sucked on it and blew smoke. Casual. Barely acknowledging the gun pointed at him.

Paul felt heat rising underneath his mask. He didn't understand why Fielder wasn't scared. Why he wasn't doing what he was told. Why this wasn't working how he'd told himself it would.

He reached for Laura, pushed her toward the cases.

"Gather up the jewelry," he said.

"Don't," Fielder said to Laura sharply. "You'll just get hurt, girlie." Fielder took his cigar and balanced it on the edge of the display case. "I knew all three of you as soon as you walked in here." He pointed at Laura. "Your mom's the town bike." A finger at Wyatt. "I see your parents every Sunday at church. Ain't your dad head deacon? He'll love this shit." Then Paul. "And your dad's so deep in my pockets he could use my nuts as a pillow." Rested his hands on his hips. "Y'all don't see how fucked you are, do you?"

Paul thumbed the hammer on the revolver.

"We just want what we came for."

"And people in hell want ice water, but they ain't getting that, either."

Paul took a step forward.

Fielder dropped his right hand behind the counter.

Paul's gun flashed to life. The shot shattered Fielder's windpipe and blood ruptured from the wound. A gun—a little .22 —fell from his hand. He made a grating sound, nearly metallic, as he choked on blood. Collapsed against the wall.

With each jagged breath, fresh blood, dark as wine, pulsed through Fielder's fingers. It pooled around his feet and he slipped and fell forward, his head striking the edge of the counter. The thud was dull and sudden and Fielder stopped making those struggling sounds for air. He slid to the floor, his face dragged down the back of the display case, squeaking as blood smeared along the glass.

Paul let the .38 drop to his side.

"Wyatt, lock that door," he said.

Wyatt sucked in air, close to tears. He turned the lock on the pawnshop door, pulled the shades down.

"What the fuck have you done, Paul?" Laura said in a voice so small it already sounded like a memory.

That was when they heard floorboards creaking. Paul looked at Laura and Wyatt. Neither had moved.

Paul rushed behind the counter, stepped over Fielder's body and pressed open the private door.

It was a small office, nothing but filing cabinets and a desk. The woman behind the desk was fumbling with a revolver, trying to load bullets into the cylinder, the cartridges falling and clattering across the top of the desk.

Fielder's wife. Paul had seen them before shopping in Sears, or having dinner at the VFW. She was a female version of her husband, with rounded shoulders and a stomach that put the rest of her body out of proportion. She smacked the cylinder into place, was raising the weapon, when Paul shot her.

The bullet hole in her forehead wasn't much, and it leaked only a little blood, but the explosion from the back of her skull changed the color of the wall behind her.

Paul walked out of the office. He pulled his mask off. Sweat beaded off his forehead like morning dew. It dripped into his eyes and he tried to blink it away. Laura had collapsed against Wyatt, and he had her wrapped in his large arms.

"We can fix this. We can—" Paul said.

Wyatt let go of Laura and lumbered toward the counter. Leaned over the display case and stared at Fielder's body crumpled on the floor. His knees weakened at the sight of all the blood and he pressed his hands against the glass to hold himself upright.

Someone pounded at the entrance. All three of them turned to stare at the door, then Paul walked to the middle of the shop. Squared his shoulders and adjusted the gun in his hand. The way he'd seen it in the movies.

"Let 'em in," Paul said.

Whoever it was banged on the door harder.

Then: "Sheriff's department. Got a call. Need y'all to unlock the door."

Paul's father.

"Just open the goddamn door," Paul said.

It was Wyatt who crossed the room and unlocked the door and stepped to one side as Paul's father walked in.

He was in full uniform, hat on, thumbs hooked over the top of his belt. He saw Wyatt first, then Laura, sighed and shook his head, and then there was Paul holding a gun. The old man reached back with his left leg and kicked the door shut with the back of his boot heel before walking over to his son. Removed his hat and held it against his chest.

"Tell me what happened," he said.

"We needed Wyatt's bass. And Fielder, he wouldn't do what we asked." Paul's words as quiet as prayers.

The old man continued to nod as his son spoke. He walked into the office and scanned around the room. He pulled a pair of rubber gloves from his pocket and snapped them on before poking at the items on the desk, finally seeing the pistol Mrs. Fielder had loaded but never fired.

He went out of the office and checked where Fielder was. The blood had pooled around the body and spread across the wood floor. Thickening and turning dark, nearly black. He was wordless as he examined everything.

Paul sat down on the floor and drew his legs up close to him and rested his forehead against his knees.

The old man balled his hands into his fists and dug them into his hips. "Okay, here's what we're gonna have to do. Wyatt, follow me."

Wyatt went behind the old man as he walked to the office. The old man told Wyatt to stand at the doorway as he went inside. From behind the desk, he crouched down beside Mrs. Fielder's body, picked up her revolver, and shot Wyatt.

Blood bloomed across Wyatt's chest like a spring flower. A

faint sense of surprise came on his face, followed by a sad confusion as he reached for where the bullet had entered him. He brought back a hand soaked in blood. His feet jumbled against each other and he fell and landed on his ass, like a drunk after one too many, and sat there, his head falling forward and his eyes open and empty.

Paul came to his feet in time for the old man to come out of the office and slap him open-handed across the face. The blow reverberated close behind the sound of the gunshot, and it rung almost as loud.

The old man took a handful of Wyatt's hair and pulled his head back, like it was on a pivot, meeting Wyatt's now-empty gaze. He let go and Wyatt's head dropped back into place and hung there, like he was a child's forgotten doll.

"Fielder's woman called me," the old man said. "I shouldn't be too shocked you'd do something this foolish. Your mother never had no control, either. If she was here, she'd be crying and asking me to fix it for you, same way I'm doing now."

The old man took Paul's gun and placed it in Wyatt's hand. He patted down Fielder and found a small notepad that he slipped into his back pocket, and he emptied the cash from the dead man's wallet. Neither Laura nor Paul spoke. Both wore vacant, numb expressions as the old man herded them to the cruiser the same way a shepherd led his flock.

The old man talked as they drove away from the pawn shop.

"Fucked as it seems now, you might have saved me from trouble down the way. Fielder ever got an urge to talk about our business arrangement, it'd have caused me problems. This solves that, though I gotta say I will miss the money." He narrowed his eyes and looked at Paul and Laura in the rearview mirror. "But what happened, you both gotta own from this day forward it was Wyatt that done this. It's the goddamn story you dream about at night if you have to. You don't never say anything otherwise because if you do—" He fished a pack of cigarettes from his shirt pocket and lit one. "It'd be bad for everyone all around."

He hardened his gaze on Laura. She felt the weight of this and turned from it, watching the road.

"How's your mom and stepdad, honey? I know they've got a tendency toward the bottle and pills. Be a goddamn shame if something happened to them," he said. "A terrible thing to live with. Hell of a burden to carry."

Laura chewed on her bottom lip and nodded in agreement to a question no one had asked.

They dropped her off close to her house and the old man watched her walk away. She never looked back.

"I might need to go talk to her mother after all," the old man said.

Paul said nothing.

They drove home. The old man parked the cruiser in the driveway. Neither he nor Paul moved to get out. He turned the car engine off, and without the motor running, the silence around them only swelled.

The old man patted the steering wheel.

"I know you're a dreamer, Paul. Same way your mother was. But you gotta dissuade yourself of those bullshit dreams. The world don't give a damn about your dreams." He tapped the dashboard with an index finger. "You live here, and you take from here, and you let the rest get what's left." He finished his cigarette and put it out in the ashtray. "People'll talk about this for a bit. We give it time, let things cook down to a simmer, and then we'll check with Walter about a job for you. Long enough's passed, talk with Wyatt's dad about you and the union. That's where the money is." He gave his son a smile. The purest face of pride Paul had ever seen from his father. "I never thought you had the balls for it, but you showed me something today. Now there's nothing in this town you can't have if you want it." He gave Paul a conspiratorial wink. "Even that girl someday."

The old man got out of the car and went inside the house.

Paul watched his father's silhouette through the windows. In doing so, he caught a reflection of himself in the windshield.

There it is, he thought. The resemblance between himself and his father. Right around the eyes.

He began to cry there in the car, the sobs eventually growing into a scream.

RUBY DEAR

by Libby Cudmore

Judy couldn't stop thinking about the Preacher's sign. She walked past him day after day, rounding the corner of Tipp Street, past the high fence in front of the Jones City Women's Clinic where he always camped. That was his church, his only sermon the sign he held aloft. *Prostitutes, Do Not Reject The Chance To Become Angels.* She didn't know if it was a threat or a compliment. The women who hung around her mother's motel sure as hell didn't look like any angels she'd ever seen on a Christmas tree – unless angels smoked Virginia Slims and wore platform stilettos from the mall. But times were tough. They couldn't turn away clients any more than the women who had to pay their motel bills could. Judy had gotten adept at telling the difference between a john and a pimp. She didn't let the pimps stay. She'd begun to recognize the girls. Sometimes she even got their real names.

Her mother knew who stayed there. She kept pamphlets and condoms behind the desk, free for the asking, and she kept the vending machine stocked with protein bars. She even had a few wigs and cheap sunglasses in case a girl needed a disguise to venture down the block to the clinic. The Preacher would take your picture with a Polaroid camera if you started up the walk. He would only give you the Polaroid if you agreed to take a pamphlet from his dirty apron and walk away with those cells still growing in your belly. She had seen her mother's photograph once. Her father showed her. She wanted to get rid of you, he taunted. You owe this photograph your life.

• • •

Judy had barely put her backpack down before she was put to work taking extra pillows and towels to Room 128. Their second housekeeper had quit two weeks ago and no one wanted to take the job. That only left Judy to navigate the cum and blood and vomit, the condoms and needles, fast food wrappers and glassine baggies.

"Housekeeping," she said as she knocked. "I have your pillows."

The chain rattled and the door opened. There was no one inside but a girl her own age. She wore a loose t-shirt and leggings, but not in a way that was fashionable like the girls who lived in the houses on Hillcrest Court.

"Are you here by yourself?" Judy asked.

"Mind your own fucking business," the girl snapped.

"I'm sorry," Judy said. "It's just that this place is pretty skeevy, and if someone brought you here, I can get you help…"

"No one brought me here," she said. "And I'll be gone in two days."

That was the answer the pimps trained these girls to give. A direct approach probably wouldn't work, and calling the cops to report trafficking wouldn't work. Hell, the sheriff's deputies were the most frequent customers. More than once, she'd seen a blue and white parked around back during lunch, only to see them come back that afternoon and take the girl away in handcuffs. Her mom had a rule – no police unless there was blood on the floor.

"Do you need anything?" Judy offered.

She snickered. "Sure," she said. "What's the best pizza place?"

Now she was getting somewhere. "Mike's Pies," she said. "I've got a hookup – let me know what you want and I'll get it for you."

"Are you this good to all your clients?"

"It's just one of the many services we provide here at Iris' Motor Inn."

• • •

As she'd hoped, Bobby was working behind the counter, effortlessly tossing dough in the air. She liked Bobby. He graduated two years ago, kept saying he was going to art school in the city, but never quite managed to commit to it. That's what happened to all of them here. You'd spend your summer driving around the back roads, listening to secondhand CDs you bought until they skipped. You swore this would be the last summer you spent breathing the rotten air of this decaying town, that this time next year, you'd have your diploma in hand and you'd be on your way out. Then the scholarship money wouldn't come, and if it did, it wasn't enough. Your dad needed surgery and you'd take over the shop for a few weeks that turned into six months, a year, two years. Your girlfriend got pregnant and decided to keep the baby. Your brother died in an ATV accident. Or maybe you just couldn't wash the stink of this place off quick enough. It happened to Bobby. It happened to her mother. It would probably happen to her.

"Medium, half pepperoni and olives, half artichokes and bacon," she said.

"Don't tell me you're pregnant," he joked. "Who's the lucky dad?"

Judy hadn't put the clues together. Of course. The loose clothing, the length of stay, the pizza order. Tomorrow the girl in Room 128 would venture down the block, past the Preacher and his cronies shouting God Hates Women Who Kill and Your Mother Chose You and into the clinic, then have to face them again on her way back to finish her bleeding in the bathroom. And she'd do it alone. Judy couldn't let that happen. She wasn't about to let someone else have to choose between a Polaroid and her own life.

. . .

Judy took the pizza back to Room 128. "You're amazing," the girl said as she opened the box. "I used to just get pepperoni. I'll miss having the excuse to pig out on weird shit. You want a piece?"

"Sure," she said. She took a piece of artichoke and bacon. "What's your name?"

"Ruby," she replied. "Yours?"

"Judy." She knew better than to ask for a last name. "Does anyone know you're here?"

"No," she said. "I told my parents I was going on a field trip. I told my boyfriend I was going to my Aunt's. He's about to be deployed and he kind of sucks anyways. I'm waiting until he's gone to break up with him. But we can't break up if I'm carrying his spawn. I think he poked a hole in the condom so I'd have to stay with him."

She knew girls in her classes who went to their Aunt's place for a weekend or a few months, came back with a look of relief or resignation, depending on the length of stay. Those were girls who didn't have to go to the local clinic. Girls whose parents didn't want the Preacher to take their picture. Her own mother had never completed such a trip. The Preacher had stopped her. Maybe if she had, she wouldn't be stuck managing the no-tell motel her ex-husband inherited and let go to ruin before he bounced out with a 19-year-old waitress. There are worse fates than being born. Judy knew this firsthand.

"When's your appointment?"

"Tomorrow night," she said. "They got me in late. They don't do these where I'm from."

It would be dark by then. The protestors who wasted their hours harassing strangers would go home to their TV dinners or their own screaming broods and unhappy marriages.

"I'll go with you," Judy said. "If you want."

Ruby smiled. She reached for another piece of pizza. "I'd appreciate that," she said.

*　*　*

The Preacher waited on the corner. No one else was around, but he was still yammering. "Christ comes to you with the face of a child! You are God's gift and so is He! Angels, prostitutes, it doesn't matter. They all are the same in His eyes. Repent, turn back, save the Child-Christ you carry!"

Up the block, Judy could see the lights of the clinic. She counted seven sections of sidewalk. A few quick paces and they'd be on the steps, ushered in by nurses and security guards. They passed the Preacher. For a moment, he ignored them. Maybe he thought they would keep walking. But there was no mistaking when they turned right.

"He's following us," Ruby said.

"Just ignore him," she said.

"Your baby could be the next messiah," he said from behind them, so close Judy imagined she could feel his breath on her neck. "He could cure cancer. He could solve world hunger."

"He could be the next Obama too," Ruby snapped. "And you sure as shit wouldn't want that."

Five sections of sidewalk left.

The Preacher moved fast. He got in front of them and whipped out his camera. Judy heard the hiss and swish of the picture. "This picture is yours," he said, fanning it in front of them. "If you turn around and repent."

"And if I don't?" Ruby snapped.

"You'll go up on the Sinner's Wall," he said. "Satan knows your face, he knows where to find you."

So the Sinner's Wall was real. On the first day of fifth grade, Becky Anderson stood up and pointed to Ms. Markeson and loudly announced that she was going to Hell, that she had seen her face on the Sinner's Wall because she was a baby killer. Ms. Markeson left the room crying. Becky left with her mom, smug and smiling, never to return to class. She heard Becky got pregnant last year. She went to live with her Aunt for a few months too.

Ruby froze. She closed her eyes and took a breath. If the Sinner's Wall was real, she could be found out. By her parents. By her boyfriend. By someone who could really hurt her.

Judy wasn't about to let that shit go down.

She swung her backpack hard, hitting him in the chest. The camera clattered to the ground, the photo floating down beside it. The Preacher stumbled off the sidewalk and she struck again. This time he fell. His head hit the corner of the pavement with a slick, hard crack. In the leftover light of the corner streetlamp, she saw blood beneath his head.

He didn't get up.

"Oh shit," Ruby hissed. "Is he…?"

She hadn't meant to hurt him. But it felt pretty goddamn good to hear his silence. He had no right. He had no right at all.

Then came the fear. Someone would have heard his cry. The clinics had cameras, they would have seen the whole thing. She picked up the photo. She grabbed Ruby's hand. "C'mon," she said. "We gotta go."

• • •

No one said anything about the sirens. In this neighborhood, they were a conversation in another room, a lullaby. But that didn't mean she had to stick around to hear the end of the story. Ruby went back to her room to pack her bag and charge up her phone. Judy muttered something to her mother about needing school supplies from the drugstore, that she'd be right back. If they had a car, she would have asked for the keys. There were other ways to get out of town.

It had been a while since anyone had emptied the vending

machine. Judy got the keys from the office and took out the coin box. It was almost too heavy to lift. There were a few fives in there too. She took it all. She'd count it later.

They had to change everything. Even shoes. They'd put their clothes in a plastic bag and dump it in the collection bin outside the Wesleyan church. She felt bad that she didn't have time to wash it, but someone was going to get a really nice hoodie and a nearly-new pair of sneakers.

She wanted to regret it more than she did. She would only regret it if she got caught. If she got Ruby in trouble. But the copper taste of power was intoxicating in her mouth. She thought about the women he'd managed to chase away, the ones who ended up like her mother, raising a monster's child, scraping together aching lives in motel rooms and shoddy apartments. She thought about the girls who never got to finish high school or go to college. She thought about the ones who threw themselves down the stairs or took random pills they found or gave up entirely. She had likely saved more lives than she had taken.

But that didn't mean she could wait around until she got a medal. And Ruby still needed to get what she came for. Bobby had a car. Bobby could get them to another city, another state.

• • •

Even showered and in pajama pants, Judy could still smell the scent of garlic on Bobby.

"We need your help," she told him.

"Who's there?" his roommate, Dave, asked in his bongwater drawl. "Is that the pizza guy?"

Judy held up the photo. It had developed, clearly showing the two of them frozen in the terrified moment before he fell. "The Preacher?" he asked.

Judy nodded. "I couldn't let him…" she said. "Not anymore. I hit him with my bag and…and he fell…"

"Can you pay him?" Dave called. "I don't got any money."

Bobby reached for his coat. His car keys jingled in the pocket. "Yeah," he said. "Yeah, it's the pizza guy. I gotta get my wallet from the car; I'll be right back."

. . .

There was a clinic in Binghamton, four hours away. They slept in the car in the corner of a truck stop. Bobby called as soon as they opened and put Ruby on the phone just to confirm that yes, this was what she wanted. He would pretend to be her boyfriend. He would sit with her in the waiting room, and if things went shit side up, he'd get her out of there to where Judy would be waiting with the keys in the ignition.

There were a few protestors outside the clinic, but this time there were escorts with beach umbrellas to block their clients from view. One past-his-prime police officer hung around with his hands on his belt buckle, looking for trouble. Judy held her breath while Bobby and Ruby and the two escorts slipped past him and into the building.

She checked the news while she waited. The state police were looking for them; no names or IDs. Most of the folks in the com-ments below casually called for their deaths, called them radi-cal violent feminist ANTIFA agitators. More than a few said it was self-defense. A handful called them sheroes. She toyed with the idea of going from town to town, enacting vigilante violence before slipping back into darkness. If teen boys with weapons of war could murder peaceful protestors, why couldn't a girl do the same when the protests themselves were each a small act of violence?

At just after four p.m., Bobby and Ruby exited out of the back of the clinic. "Murderer!" one of the protestors shouted. For a moment, Judy panicked, readied herself for the getaway. Then she realized that they probably yelled that at everyone.

. . .

Ruby slept stretched out in the back. They pulled over a few times so she could throw up. She drank a little ginger ale and ate a few crackers when she could keep them down. She changed her pad and her clothes in gas station bathrooms. In two days, no one would know what she had been through.

It was just after dawn when they pulled up in front of Ruby's high school. "You gonna be okay?" Bobby asked.

She shrugged. "Not much of a choice, right?" Ruby replied. "You think we really got away with it?"

The bill might come due someday. Ruby might tell about the motel and the pizza place, her mom or Bobby's boss might report them missing, the cops might trace their footsteps and track them down. Or the preacher's death could just become part of the cultural landscape, a thing that happened once in a small garbage town in Upstate New York. There would be drug busts and traffic tickets. Wife beaters and meth labs. Another protestor would take the Preacher's place.

A boy with thick shoulders and a deflated backpack put his arm around Ruby. She wanted to call to her, tell her to get back into the car and drive away. But Ruby didn't even look back. This was her part of the ruse, and the sooner they forgot about each other, the better. They'd see each other in dreams, in half-forgotten memories, in heaven or hell or never again.

"Where do we go now?" Bobby asked.

There was $100 left in loose change and tip-jar singles. It was more than they had waiting for them back in Jones City. There was a full tank of gas and a fresh sunrise. They had done what no one else had done.

They had gotten out.

"Anywhere but home," Judy said.

BURNING DOWN THE HOUSE

by Michel Lee Garrett

Three figures occupy the parlor of the funeral home on Engel Street, two of them sisters. The third bears an older, masculine version of their shared face, his cheeks painted in powder and rouge. He wears the only suit he's ever owned, perfumed now in overbearing rose and sandalwood. Rough-hewn hands rest on the soft velvet of his casket interior.

"It's nice," says the younger sister, a gaunt woman of nearly thirty, dressed in secondhand rags. Her red-rimmed eyes recede into their sunken sockets. "Real nice. You spring for this? Looks comfortable."

"It was the least I could do," the older sister responds in calm tones of deliberate restraint. Despite their corresponding features, they look nothing alike. She stands upright and tall, well-fed enough to give her face a slight softness that her sister lacks.

The ragged sister scoffs, then mouths the words back at her: *The least you could do.* "I'll say."

"Jamie, please. Don't do this."

"Oh, I'm sorry. I was just *agreeing* with you. Paying for a nice coffin really is the absolute *least* you could've done, after all this fucking time."

"After all this—?" Ashley stops, shakes her head to herself. "Okay. So that's how it's going to be."

"That's how it *is*, Ashley. You *left*."

"Why is it always about this? You could've too! Don't you see that? Dad *wanted* us to get out. Everything he did, he did for us."

"Us?" Jamie's voice jumps in pitch. "Is that how you remember it? Did dad do everything for *us*? Or did he do everything for *you*? My whole fucking life, I heard it over and over again. '*Isn't Ashley so smart? Isn't Ashley so pretty? Isn't Ashley gonna change the world?*'"

Ashley takes her tongue between her teeth and lets her younger sister's tirade wash over her, impassively staring up at the ceiling, but her silence only fuels her sister's fury.

"I don't know if you've noticed, but the world is on *fucking fire*! Bang up fucking job you've been doing. Really. Dad was *real proud* of you."

An artificial chirping interrupts them. Ashley instinctively pulls her phone from the front pocket of her handbag to check the notification.

Jamie's face wrinkles with disgust. "Oh, I'm sorry." She gestures between herself and the coffin. "Are we keeping you? Please, if you gotta go, then just go. God knows you've had the practice."

Ashley takes a moment to scan the screen before responding. "Oh, no, I was just checking my calendar, so I can schedule some time to keep having this argument. We've been doing this for, what, thirty years next month?"

"Fuck you, Ashley."

A vein pulses in Ashley's temple.

She'd told herself she would be the adult here tonight. She'd known Jamie would do this, and she'd told herself she wouldn't take the bait. Tonight was supposed to be about *dad* and the way things used to be, back when they were still together. All of them. She came back to honor that. But no one could ever get under her skin the same way her sister could.

"No, fuck *you*, Jamie! Dad is fucking dead, and you want to do this *here? Now?!* In front of him, in the fucking parlor, so the fucking mortician can hear too?" She laughs at the absurdity. "Have some decency. Some fucking decorum. Some fucking *respect* for the man."

"Oh, respect?" Jamie's voice goes as cold as their father's hands. "You want to talk about *respect*? At least I was *there*, Ashley. Yeah, I made my mistakes growing up. I wasn't *always* there. But I was there at the end."

Suddenly, Ashley can't bear to meet her sister's eyes. She turns to their father, then away from him, to the floor. She digs her sharp, manicured nails into the soft underbelly of her palms until it hurts.

Jamie takes a deep breath. "You know what he died *from*, don't you?"

Ashley doesn't answer.

"Don't you?"

Reluctantly, the older sister nods.

"Say it."

Again, Ashley doesn't answer. She gives her shoes the thousand-yard stare.

"*Say. It.*"

She mumbles the word. "Dysentery."

"*Dysentery*, Ashley. From drinking the fucking highway runoff that gets sold on the street, 'cause who can afford fifty bucks a fucking gallon? Nobody! Fucking nobody, that's who! And while I was there, holding his hand, where was daddy's favorite girl?" She spits at Ashley's feet. "Off licking Garrison Maxwell's fucking boots."

Ashely half-heartedly regurgitates a prepared response, like a spokeswoman responding to a reporter. "Dysentery can be caused by any number—"

"Do *not* spit those bullshit fucking talking points at me! You're off working for the same man who dammed the fucking river! He forced dad out of business in the name of 'vertical integration,' and there you were, helping him do it." She takes a deep breath. "The way I see it, dad's death is *your fau*—"

Ashley slaps her, full in the face. "Shut up! Always the fucking *victim!*"

Jamie stumbles backward, eyes wide with shock. She rubs her fingertips gingerly against the bright red palm print emblazoned across her cheek.

"I *begged* dad to sell," Ashley pleads. "I *told* him what would happen if he didn't work with them, but he wouldn't listen."

Jamie curls her hands in tight, bony fists, choking on her sobs. She'd told herself *she* would be the adult here tonight. That she wouldn't cry. But no one could ever get under her skin the same way her sister could.

"B-b-b-but you—" Jamie stammers.

"But me! But me! But me! Everything's always *my* fucking fault, isn't it? Has it ever occurred to you that maybe I'm *not* this villain that you've built in your mind? That maybe I'm just trying to get by? But what about *you*, Jamie? You never take responsibility for anything! Who ate up all of dad's savings, in and out of rehab? You wanna talk about how dad's death is my fault, but *you're* the one who decided to crawl up a glass pipe after mom—"

In that instant, Jamie breaks.

"DON'T YOU FUCKING BRING MOM INTO THIS!"

She charges and leaps at her sister, tackling her to the linoleum floor. She grabs Ashley's hair with both fists, pulls her head up, then smashes it down into the floor, then again, screaming. Ashley kicks and bucks, driving her knees up into Jamie's back. With all her strength, she claws upwards at Jamie's fury-twisted face. Her polished claws leave four parallel lines over her right eye and down into her cheek. Jamie screeches, bringing her hands up to her face. Ashley worms out from beneath her sister, kicking and screaming. Her foot connects with Jamie's chest, sending her falling backwards into the coffin.

It teeters.

Then it wobbles.

Ashley tries to crawl forward to catch it, but it's too late. The coffin crashes forward from its stand. Their father spills out of his velvet bed in slow motion. He ragdolls without dignity through the air, slaps the ground with a loud *thlap!,* and rolls to the feet of the mortician, who's come to investigate the chaos.

"In all my years…!"

He grabs them both and ejects the sisters with threats to call the cops. They sit on the curb outside, both smoldering with silent shame. They share a cigarette, produced from the front pocket of Ashely's purse.

"You okay?"

Jamie squints, her eye still watering. The salty tears sting the fresh scratches down her cheek.

"I'll be fine."

"Been a while since we've been kicked out of somewhere. For fighting, no less."

"Some things never change."

Ashley frowns. "So this is how things are *always* going to be?"

Jamie shrugs. "It's how they *are*, Ashley."

Ashley nods sadly. "I guess." Her phone chirps again, and she removes it from beside her cigarettes in the front pocket of her purse to check the screen.

Jamie rolls her eyes. "Seriously. If you've got somewhere to be, then leave. You came, you saw, we made a scene. It's done. Just go."

Ashley raises herself back up to her feet. "I'm sorry, Jamie," she sighs. "I have work I have to do."

"Always too busy for me," Jamie shoots back. "Just like dad."

"Look, I'm sorry *I* actually went off and made something of myself," Ashley barks back, her voice rising again. "I'm sorry *you* never actually tried to make anything of yourself. That you never tried to do *anything* worth doing. I really wanted that for you, I *did*, but it's not my fau—" She catches herself, mid-escalation, and takes a deep breath. "You know what? Never mind. Not worth it. See you, Jamie."

"Wait," Jamie says, standing.

"For what? I'm tired of fighting. I—"

Jamie cuts her older sister off with something Ashley never would have predicted. Not further fury, or another tackle, but an embrace. She wraps her arms around her sister and holds tight in a way she hasn't done since their childhood, since before mom died. Ashely remains still, paralyzed by the sudden display.

"It feels like the world is burning down." Jamie's voice is barely a whisper.

Ashley sighs, swallowing her pride. She lets her hands fall and returns the gesture, holding her younger sister against her chest.

"Everything goes away eventually," Ashley says. "That's just… life."

"I know…" Jamie sniffles. "I know."

Ashley goes to break the embrace, but Jamie doesn't let her, continuing to hold tight. She lets Jamie stay there a few moments more, but when she tries a second time, Jamie still refuses to let go. Ashley allows a few more uncomfortable seconds to crawl by before moving to escape for a third time. This time, Jamie finally releases her. Their eyes meet briefly, and they both look away to the asphalt ground. Blood flushes both their cheeks.

"So… guess I'll see you around sometime?" Ashley says.

Jamie shrugs. "Yeah. I guess. Sometime."

"Take care of yourself, sis." Ashley lays a hand on her shoulder. "Please."

Jamie's only response is another shrug. Ashley figures that's the best she's going to get. She leaves Jamie behind her to return to her car. She waits for her sister to wander off somewhere into the night-darkened streets of Chester before allowing herself a private minute to weep. She pulls the veil aside long enough to empty herself out before stuffing all the grief and rage somewhere back down inside of herself.

She doesn't have the mental fortitude to respond to work yet, so she turns the key in the ignition to head out of town, back toward the city. As she pilots her sedan across the Commodore Barry Bridge, passing over the garbage-filled chasm that had once been the Delaware River, the smell of rot rises from the river's corpse, leaking in through the vents to burn her nose. Across the bridge, the lights of the Philadelphia cityscape tower skyward, neon billboards lighting the darkness with advertisements for clean water and fast food. When she arrives home, she can already hear the crying of her toddler through the cheap walls of her company-owned condominium. Her husband's voice, barely muffled by the cheap plywood, leaks outside: "Easy, easy, shhhh… mommy will be home soon…"

She pulls her phone from her purse and unlocks it. An email with talking points for tomorrow's press conference sits at the top of her inbox. Her boss has forwarded feedback and edits from CEO Maxwell. "Know you're out on bereavement today, but could you implement this and shoot back ASAP?" She exhales and closes her eyes, exhausted. Something occurs to her. Her eyes shoot back open.

In the parking lot, she'd put her phone in the front pocket of her bag, where she always does. But when she removed it just now, it wasn't in the front pocket. It was in the *central* pocket. And her most recent email had already been opened, despite the fact that she only read the notification, not the message itself.

She tries to tell herself that this means nothing, that she's been under a lot of stress and merely forgot she'd already opened the message, then put the phone in the wrong place. A warm breeze carries the scent of ripe sewage to her nose as she approaches her front door.

• • •

Jamie does not return home after her sister leaves. Instead, she stalks the streets by foot, her brain racing with possibilities.

It had been even easier to break into Ashley's phone than she'd expected. She was still using the same four-digit passcode she'd been using since their adolescence: their mother's birthday. Jamie simply *had* to know what was *so goddamn important* that

Ashley kept checking her phone at their father's wake. What she discovered thrilled her, like a dream made manifest. The email notifications were right there; all she had to do was forward them to herself and delete the evidence.

Jamie knew, of course, that her sister worked for Delaware Valley Waterworks, but never fully grasped the nature of her job. She didn't realize that Ashley was drafting talking points directly for the company's CEO—Garrison Maxwell, the same man who had led the privatization of the region's water sources, the same man who muscled everyone even tangentially related to water utilities, like their dad's plumbing business, either under his corporate banner, or out of business entirely. The same man who drove the price hikes that had people drinking runoff and acid rain out of desperation. The only person *more* responsible for her father's death than her sister.

And now, thanks to Ashely's emails, Jamie knows that Garrison Maxwell will give a press conference tomorrow at noon, responding to the recent spate of attacks against the company's water transport trucks.

According to the talking points written by her sister, Maxwell will decry these "terrorist raids" and promise to fight fire with fire through "unhesitating and brutal reprisals" against those found to be responsible. She stops to wonder if her sister remembers how many people in their neighborhood only got fresh water when a company water truck got knocked over. The presser will be delivered from the corporate plaza of the Delaware Valley Waterworks building in Center City. The advisory hasn't even gone to the media yet.

That kind of knowledge… that's *power*.

Maybe it isn't the same kind of power Maxwell has—the power to call a press conference and have a city hang on every word or to condemn hundreds to death on a whim based on little numbers in some spreadsheet. But right now, Jamie is the only person outside of the company who knows when and where the most powerful man in Philadelphia is going to be tomorrow at noon. That's the power of potential.

She rereads her sister's words.

Maybe she's right. Jamie grins. *Maybe we fight fire with fire.*

She has all night to prepare; that will have to be enough.

On her phone, she pulls up a map of Center City and considers the placement of the Delaware Valley Waterworks building. It's nestled among other corporate offices and headquarters, but directly across the street stands a luxury residential tower named The Winsington. The west side of the tower offers a perfect overlook of the Waterworks Plaza where the press conference will be held. She searches for more information about the building and finds a series of news articles about residents of The Winsington threatening legal action against building management for an extensive series of mechanical and utility failures that have gone unfixed, despite the exorbitant amounts of money paid in rent and fees. She absent-mindedly runs her fingers along the scratches in her face, considering this information.

A plan comes into focus.

She makes her way back home to the dilapidated two-bedroom house where her father died only two days ago. His van—the one still advertising Thomas Family Plumbing along the side—rusts in the driveway.

Jamie stands at the threshold of the bedroom where her father died, gathering the strength to enter. When she opens the door, she's greeted by the sour smell of sickness still hanging thick in the stagnant air. The depression on her father's side of the bed remains, an emptiness where his body once laid. On the bedside table, a yellowed photo sits in a dusty frame. She examines it briefly. Within, her father wears the same suit he now wears in his coffin; her mother is draped in a pearl-colored gown, her hair tied back with flowers. Their faces are untroubled by years that have not yet come to pass.

Jamie places the photo facedown.

In the bottom drawer of the bedside table, her mother's

jewelry box still sleeps, blanketed by a decade of dust. She lifts the lid with trembling hands. The collection is not large. Even at the height of his business, her father was never a rich man. What few pieces of glamor he purchased for his high school sweetheart during their years together were afforded with careful scrimping and saving. The gold hoops she wore to church. The pink sapphire studs she'd worn to Ashley's college graduation. The necklace boasting three real pearls she'd wept over one anniversary. And of course, her diamond wedding ring, purchased with three years' worth of savings from her father's first job.

Even at her lowest points, her most broken, her most out of control, her most desperate for a fix, this had always been the one depth she'd managed to keep herself from sinking to. The final line in the sand she refused to cross, until now. Now she has something she's never had before: not addiction, but *opportunity*. Not for justice, but for *retribution*. One shot—exactly one shot—to make the fuckers pay for all they've done.

It will cost everything she has. She knows this. Her freedom. Her family's name. Probably even her life, one way or another. But it's worth it. It's worth *everything*. She would sooner burn down her father's house than let this opportunity pass.

Jamie robs the jewelry box from its resting place. She hopes it will be enough.

Downstairs, she finds her father's keys buried in the junk drawer. The van rumbles awake. She backs out of the driveway and calls a phone number she knows by heart. Sweat beads across her forehead. *No matter what he says*, she tells herself, *stay strong*. The dial tone threatens to drive her mad. Finally, a raspy voice answers from the other side.

"Well, well, if it isn't Jamie," the voice chuckles. "Told you you'd be back. How much you need?"

"It's not like that." she says, hoping he can't hear her voice shaking. "I'm clean now."

He can hear it. "You so sure about that?"

"Yeah, I'm sure."

"Then why the fuck are we talking?"

"The *other* side of your services."

"Which side? Snake Eye's always got something."

"Need to, ah… exercise my second amendment rights."

His voice takes on a suspicious edge. "You in trouble? If you got heat after you, don't you dare fucking come here."

"You think I'm stupid? No, *somebody else* is gonna be in trouble once I'm strapped. Feel me?"

The voice laughs. "Listen to her go. You got the cash?"

"Yeah." Jamie eyes the jewelry box riding shotgun beside her. "Don't worry. I got the cash."

* * *

Snake Eye operates out of a shithole apartment above a deli that's been closed as long as Jamie can remember. Bile bubbles up her throat as she climbs the stairs to the landing. Her heart hammers against her ribs.

Not fear. *Temptation.*

She knocks five times: two quick knocks, a pause, then three more. Anyone who doesn't know the rule gets blown away. The door boasts bullet holes as proof. A musclebound mook covered in flashing LED tribal tattoos opens the door inward and frisks her for weapons. He opens the jewelry box, scoffs at the contents, and closes it again. Jamie rips the box back from his oversized paws.

Unlike his hired muscle, Snake Eye himself is gaunt, narrow, and on the back end of middle age, barely more than a spine wrapped in leather. His namesake—a second-generation cybernetic lens implanted into his left eye socket, jailbroken to resemble a serpent's elongated pupil and fiery iris—dominates his mottled face. A girl far too young to be in a place like this lays slumped against the dealer's shoulder, eyelids fluttering as she drifts in and out of consciousness. A small handgun, a purse-sized peashooter, rests on a coffee table. A small trail of smoke curls upwards from a glass pipe sitting next to it. The room reeks of it, like bleach and ammonia with an undercurrent of burning hair.

Snake Eyes sees her eyeing the pipe. "Wanna taste?"

Maybe just this one time…

Jamie tries to look away, but her eyes linger anyway.

"Come on," the dealer hisses. "You know I sell nothin' but the best."

Just once. It's different now. I have it under control now.

"On the house, even." Snake Eye smiles, his teeth sharpened into artificial points. "Call it a welcome back present."

Just a small taste. It'll be fine this time…

She almost breaks—even steps forward, starting to reach for it. But the girl on the dealer's shoulder interrupts by rousing briefly back to consciousness, spitting bright orange throwup down her chest, and passing back out.

Snake Eye pushes her off him, recoiling in disgust. "Little bitch…!" The teen lands on the arm of the couch, groaning incoherently and drooling vomit.

Jamie thinks about the start of her addiction, when she used to be the girl on Snake Eye's shoulder, too young to be in a place like this.

She thinks about her mother and her father, dead in their caskets.

She thinks about the world on fire, and the people responsible for burning it down, looking down from their towers of glass and steel, wrapped in the comforts of their wealth.

And she thinks about the opportunity that's open to her, for one night only—the shot that she *needs* to take.

"No thanks," Jamie says, letting her hand fall. "Not why I'm here."

Snake Eye laughs. "Not yet, maybe. But you'll be back. They always are."

"I'm here for a gun."

Snake Eye gestures to the pistol on the table. "Bet."

"Not some peashooter. A *real* gun. A rifle. Something I could use to take out somebody from across a street… if I needed to."

Snake Eye whistles. "Goddamn. Little Jamie got herself into some big-girl trouble, huh? What do you need something like that for?"

"Told you, I'm not the one in trouble. Let's, uh… let's just say it's for my family."

The dealer smacks his forehead, as if remembering something obvious. "Your family! Right! I was sorry to hear about your dad, by the way." He once again offers Jamie the pipe. "Please, accept my condolences."

She chokes out two words, insistent: "*The gun.*"

Snake Eye nods, smiling to himself. He sets the pipe down on the coffee table, closer to Jamie than to himself. "All business, huh? Alright, alright, Snake Eye's got something that fits the bill. Snake Eye's *always* got something." He gestures to his muscle. "Grab one of the 700's from the back room."

The mook grunts, disappears briefly into the recesses of the apartment, and comes back carrying a walnut-handled hunting rifle. Snake Eye takes it and cradles it with affection.

"The Remington 700. Holds five rounds, one in the chamber. Bolt-action, reliable, precise, powerful. A classic for a reason. For a little extra, I'll even throw in a scope." He winks with his serpentine lens. "*Just in case* you need to take out someone from across a street."

"How much?"

"$1,200 cash. Now, you do have *cash*, right?"

"Okay, so, not *cash* exactly," Jamie begins, pulling the pearls from the jewelry box, "but—"

"Nah, nah, nah," Snake Eye waves her away, as if she were a gnat. "Get the fuck out of here with that."

"Hold on! These are valuable! $1,200 easy, just need to pawn them!"

"So *you* pawn them, bitch! I ain't your goddamn middle man."

"Please," Jamie pleads, her desperation shining through, "I don't have that kind of time!"

Snake Eye tsks his tongue. "Man, get her out of here."

The blinking-patterned bodyman starts to move in.

"Wait! Wait, I'll— I'll sweeten the deal!"

"Sorry, sweetheart. Not really my type anymore." He chuckles, but it sounds like an animal choking on a bone. "But maybe if you came back into the fold, became a loyal customer again…"

The urge to vomit rises up her throat, but Jamie forces it back down. She eyes the girl beside him again, still passed out in her own sick. Jamie shakes her head violently, fighting back the urge to cry again. The bodyman grabs her by the arm.

She sees no other way. She *needs* that gun, and she needs it *tonight*.

"*Fine*! Fine, goddammit, yes!"

"Fine *what*?"

"I'll—" Her voice cracks. "I'll start buying again."

The dealer smiles with his pointed teeth. "That's what I like to hear. Here." He picks up the pipe again, holds it out to her. "Prove it."

"No, not now! N-not yet!"

"Why not? I need to *believe* you. Way I see it, I'm operating at a loss on the rifle, even with the jewelry. So I need to know my investment is gonna be worth it."

"You *know* me. You know I'll be back! Said so yourself. I'm buying that gun because I have business that I *need* to take care of. I need to focus, for one day. After that…"

"After that, what?"

Jamie tries to bring herself to answer, but the words won't come out.

"Say it."

"After that… I'm yours."

Snake Eye nods. "Give me the box."

Jamie hands over her mother's jewelry, unable to meet Snake Eye's burning electric gaze. He hands over the rifle, and has his muscle fetch a cheap scope and a small box of ammunition. "Pleasure doing business with you," Snake Eye grins.

As she takes the weapon, she imagines leveling it at Snake Eye's face and pulling the trigger. She lets her mind linger on the image.

It's a pretty picture.

Instead, she turns and leaves. The young girl starts gagging again as Jamie crosses the threshold back out of the apartment.

"Goddamn, this fucking bitch!" Snake Eye growls.

The door closes again.

Back on the street, Jamie pauses to empty her stomach onto the sidewalk. Her injured eye weeps, stinging the claw marks carved into her cheek.

• • •

The next morning, Jamie loads the rifle. She hasn't slept. She's operating on dry-swallowed caffeine pills and nerves. Her father's work overalls hang loosely from her bony frame. She wraps the readied weapon in a black blanket then affixes the slender bundle with strips of black electrical tape to the inside of a large plumber's pipe. She loads the loaded pipe, a couple dozen blanks, and her father's tools of the trade into the back of the van.

She follows the same route into the city taken by her sister the previous night, over the bridge above the river's corpse, into the dense forest of skyscrapers and neon lights. In the heart of the city's wealthy center, The Winsington gleams like a crystal palace in the morning sun.

Jamie parks behind a line of news vans on the street, there for the press conference. She unloads the pipes and tools onto a pushcart, making sure to place the gun-bearing pipe on the very bottom, obscured by the rest. She bluffs her way past the doorman by gesturing to her plumbing accoutrement.

At the front desk, the receptionist gives her a haughty

once-over. "We only have *one* maintenance keycard for security purposes and nobody told *me* to expect a plumber today." Her eyes narrow behind thick-lensed glasses. "You said you're with 'Thomas' Plumbing? I thought Waterworks bought everybody up under *their* name."

"Yeah lady, it's called 'subcontracting,' ever heard of it?" Her nervousness has wrapped back around into mania. Her hands shake in their pockets. The receptionist tries to respond, but Jamie cuts her off: "All I was told is you got tenants threatening lawsuits out the wazoo, on account of how they can't even flush what *actually* comes out the wazoo! So when they drag your asses to court, you have fun telling your boss it's all because *you* wouldn't let *me* in to do MY GODDAMN JOB!"

"Now, now," she stammers. "Hold on…"

Maintenance keycard now in hand, Jamie rolls her pushcart up to the service elevator and takes it all the way up. The rooftop of The Winsington, taller than all its neighbors save the looming Waterworks building, offers her a three-hundred sixty-five-degree view of the city sprawling like a pack of addicts scattering at the sound of sirens. In the plaza across the street, little men in suits are already setting up speakers.

Jamie unveils the rifle from its hiding place.

• • •

Across the street, Ashley's running on caffeine pills and nerves. She hasn't slept. She and her boss have been last-minute grilling CEO Maxwell, practicing anticipated questions from the press.

"Hate the goddamn media," says Maxwell, a well-fed man boasting a thin mustache and thick jowls. "Why'd you have the finalized talking points over so late?"

"I was out on bereavement, sir. My father."

"*I* never had a father, and look at me. See what I'm saying?" Ashley grits her teeth. "Yes, sir."

"Next time I need something, I expect it *then*. No excuses."

She gives a painful nod.

Maxwell snaps his fingers. "*Say* it."

Her teeth threaten to crack under the pressure. "Yes, sir," she says.

"Good."

Another suit opens the door of their conference room. "They're ready for you, sir." The CEO rises. Ashley follows, the only woman of color among the entourage of indistinguishable white corpos in tasteful pinstripes. She can feel her heartbeat in her ears, drumming double-time. She tries to tell herself it's just because of one too many caffeine pills. Even in Center City, the air stinks of raw sewage as they emerge outside.

Maxwell takes his place behind the expansive mahogany podium, overlooking the crowd of reporters, cameras and microphones. Ashley falls in line with the suits off to one side of the stage.

"Members of the press," Maxwell begins, "thank you for joining me today to talk about the recent terrorist attacks against Delaware Valley Waterworks. Let me first state, unequivocally, that these terrorists, these criminals, who disrupt our supply lines, who destroy our company property, who rob communities of the water they depend on, *will* be found and brought to justice."

The words blur together in Ashley's ears. She couldn't focus on them if she wanted to. Sweat beads down her forehead. She scans the scene. Everything's going exactly as it should. Maxwell is on message. All the major news outlets showed up. Security has reported no intrusions, no compromises, no threats. So why does she feel so anxious?

Then she sees it.

There, across the street. She almost can't believe it at first. It can't possibly be right. But there it is. Her father's van, the Thomas Plumbing van, parked in the line of news vans in front of The Winsington. Her sweat is suddenly ice cold against her skin.

The misplaced phone.

The opened email.

She doesn't understand. Not entirely. She never could understand her sister, no matter how hard she tried. But she knows her sister is here. And she knows it has something to do with the conference. But she's not in the crowd. Every single person in attendance is accounted for.

On some familial urge, her gaze travels slowly, almost unwillingly, up the tower across the street. When she reaches the roof, her eyes go wide. Sunlight glints off the rifle scope.

Ashley knows, instantly and instinctively, whose finger is on the trigger.

She doesn't think. There's no time. Instead, she reacts.

She rushes forward, onto the stage.

• • •

Jamie's fired a gun a few times before. Her father used to take her and her sister hunting, before everything went wrong. But scoring a buck, years ago, is scant preparation for the target now in front of her.

She gets one shot. *Exactly* one shot. She knows that. Before she can recenter her aim, Maxwell's security will be on top of him. And then they'll be in The Winsington, storming up to the roof to drag her away. She has to hit him the *first* time. That's it. Then she has to run. She tries to tell herself she doesn't feel the pressure. The smell of sewage fills the air.

Her right eye, pressed into the scope, burns and waters, still injured from her sister's nails. She switches to her left eye instead.

"Goddamn it, Ashley…" she mutters under her breath.

The crosshairs spasm from her shaking hands.

"Easy, easy, shhh…"

She takes a deep breath and holds it.

Jamie centers Maxwell's head in the crosshairs and pulls the trigger.

As her finger engages the mechanism, Ashley bursts into her sights. She pushes the fucker forward, out of the way.

The bullet bursts forward from the barrel. The metal message travels at 2,000 feet a second out the window, across the street, through the air—missing Maxwell entirely—and instead penetrates into Ashley's side. She ragdolls to the ground, slapping the stage with a loud *thlap!* By the time Jamie recovers from the kickback, her sister is crumpled in a bloody heap.

"No…"

Security swarm the stage. One of them checks Ashley's pulse. The rest encircle Maxwell.

"No…!"

One of the agents points across the street at The Winsington.

"No! No! You fucking bitch! NO!"

The CEO's already being shuffled back inside. Armed guards are already moving. Jamie needs to start moving too.

"Everything! YOU RUIN FUCKING EVERYTHING!"

There's no room for grief or regret. Maybe that will come later. For now, she's too filled with rage. She missed her one shot; now she needs to run. But where? There's no escaping this kind of heat. The most important thing she was ever going to accomplish—avenging their faither—and Ashley had ruined it, just like she'd ruined everything in Jamie's life. She wasn't the only one responsible, either. Her teachers. Snake Eye. All the bastards she'd blown in bathroom stalls for a quick fix. All the politicians and corporate vampires who'd sucked the lifeblood from the earth. All to blame. Everyone. Every last fucking one of them.

Someone has to pay. What if she *can* still take a second shot?

All she would need is a different target…

She needs to be quick. It won't be long before they have traffic blocked off to cage in the shooter. Jamie sprints for the service elevator, shoving the gun back into a length of pipe. Everything else, she leaves behind.

As she descends, muted shouting and distant footballs echo. They've already reached the building. She guesses they've taken the stairwell and the main elevator, fanning out floor by floor, but *she* has the maintenance keycard. The service elevator reaches the lobby without incident, but a corpsec suit with a Glock blocks the exit. Jamie struts right up like nothing's wrong. With one hand, she holds the metal tube. With the other, she holds the stock of the gun inside, ready to unveil it again.

"Look buddy, I don't know what's going on, but I got a toilet upstairs flooding over with shit, and it could start leaking through here any sec—"

He makes the mistake of listening. That benefit of the doubt gives her enough time to yank the gun from its hiding place. He goes to raise his own, but her other hand's already reached the trigger. She puts a bullet in his throat before he can aim. With the back of one hand, she wipes blood splatter from her face.

It wasn't supposed to be like this.

The receptionist screams, but Jamie's already out the door.

• • •

The hollowed-out sandwich shop stands silent on its graffitied corner like a mourner before a coffin. She can't see any movement behind the heavy blackout curtains that hang in the apartment windows above, but she doesn't have any time to waste. She takes the stairs two at a time, the rifle in hand, but slows when she reaches the landing. Her heart hammers against her ribs. She swallows hard, her mouth dry. This is it. Not justice, but *retribution*.

She knocks five times. Two quick knocks, a pause, then three more. No response. *Come on, come on…*

She repeats the pattern. "I'm back, just like you said! You good?"

Still nothing. *Fuck. Be cool. Don't overplay it.*

"Business's all taken care of. Ready for some of that good shit. Snake Eye's always got something, right?"

Finally, she hears Snake Eye's voice from within, muffled and quiet. "Open it."

The enforcer approaches from within, his subdermal LEDs visible through the bullet holes in the door. She hears each lock disengage in sequence.

Jamie raises the rifle.

As soon as the door begins to open, she fires through the wood into what should be the enforcer's central mass. She pulls down the bolt handle and crashes forward, shoulder first, cracking the muscle's nose and knocking him back. She puts a second round in his chest before he can recover. His corpse continues flashing tribal patterns around the room.

In the corner of her eye, Jamie sees the girl, vomit still stained down her front, overturning an end table and scrambling for cover. Her terrified screams fill the apartment from floor to ceiling.

Don't worry. It's almost over.

Jamie whips the weapon up to Snake Eye's usual throne, but it's empty. Only a wisp of smoke, curling upwards from the glass pipe on the coffee table.

"Come out and play, you fucking leech!"

That's when the lights go out. Shadow engulfs the room. She whirls the gun around, looking for movement. No sun leaks in from behind the blackout curtains. The only light comes from the enforcer's flashing corpse, sending blood-red patterns throbbing across the shitty furniture and smoke-yellowed wallpaper.

The strobing gives everything an uneven edge. Movement keeps dancing at edges of her vision, but when she spins to face it, nothing's there. The rifle quivers in her hands.

A venomous voice comes creeping through the darkness: "You should've taken the glass when I offered it, little girl."

Jamie fires at the sound. The young girl screams, still hiding behind the end table. As the echo dissipates, her voice melts into broken, shuddering sobs. Jamie reloads, counting down the rounds. Only one left.

"Where are you? Too scared to go toe-to-toe with a little girl?!"

Jamie stumbles through the darkness toward the dealer's backroom, tripping against a table and sending a chemist's scale crashing to the floor. She circles her aim around the room, scanning the furniture, the shelves of packaged drugs, the crates of guns, but the viper's not there. She turns to leave, but something in the far corner, barely illuminated, catches her eye—a stack of gallon water jugs, their contents obviously dirty and piss-yellow even in the poor lighting. Her breath catches in her throat.

Snake Eye's always got something.

This is it. The tainted water that killed her father. She knows it beyond the shadow of a doubt. Jamie screams, a primal sound of unfiltered fury.

She charges back out in the living room, rifle raised.

"My life! My future! My father! You took *fucking everything* from me!"

Something crashes to her right, distracting her. Red light reflects off the broken beer bottle, thrown against the wall.

The first gunshot goes off before she can recover.

It blows through her ribs, just like her sister. She wheels around, trying to raise the rifle, but the second gunshot catches her in the shoulder, sending her spinning. It feels like she's burst into flames.

Her grip tenses as she falls.

The rifle roars to life, pointed at the end table.

Wood splinters. Behind it, the girl's sobbing goes silent. She doesn't move, doesn't speak again.

"No!" Jamie sobs. "*NO!*" Blood arcs from her mouth, splattering her front with crimson spit-up.

The burning glow of Snake Eye's namesake approaches through the darkness. He chuckles. "All I did for your dad was give him what he *wanted*." He steps forward, a Colt 1911 trained on her head. "Just like I always did for you."

Jamie weeps and thrashes. "I... I ruin fucking *everything*..."

Snake Eye laughs. "Bet."

But then, from beyond the apartment, sirens pierce through the air, loud and growing louder. More squeal from other directions, converging toward them.

Snake Eye sweats at the sound. "What the fuck did you *do!?*"

She laughs, blood spilling from her lips. "Got myself into some big-girl trouble, just like you said."

The dealer rushes to the window and peels back the heavy curtains. Red and blue lights oscillate across his face.

"You little bitch…!"

Jamie's vision is blurring in and out of focus. Through the searing pain, the tears, and the darkness encroaching, she can barely make out Snake Eye centering himself overtop of her, aiming his revolver between her eyes.

"I hope you're fucking happy."

In her last moments, Jamie thinks of all the people she's hurt. Her sister, dead on that stage. Her father, dead in his coffin. Her mother, dead in her grave. Her mirror image behind that table, silent and lifeless by Jamie's own hand. Fury finally gives way to regret. Jamie groans like a house on fire, collapsing inward.

It wasn't supposed to be like this, but sometimes the fires we set burn beyond our control.

Snake Eye's finger coils around the trigger.

ELECTRIC GUITAR

by Lucas Franki

A figure stood upon the stage, backlit by roaring flames and dazzling lasers, as thousands of screaming fans chanted and writhed in the arena. The throbbing of the guitars and beating of the drums cascaded over them as they awaited the show's final climax. "Fuck the world!" Jeff Stackler cried. "Fuck everyone who tells you not to live your life the way you want! Fuck those pussies! Fuck kindness! Fuck all of it! Burn it down, burn it all down!"

A pit gnawed at John Wilkes' stomach as he watched from backstage. He and his band had opened for Thruststone, and the crowd had been rowdy but decent enough. They hadn't been putty in his hands though, not like they were for Stackler, the damn fraud. There he was, singing about anarchy, hate, and burning down the world. Yet there he was, a man worth nearly a billion dollars thanks to family money. He even had talent, but he used his father's fortune to buy his way to quick fame and glory, and to bury the naysayers.

He held his guitar over his head. "This is a symbol! This is a symbol of everything wrong with the world. All the people out there, telling you what you can't do. This is what we think of their damned social justice!"

Before him, a massive pyre ignited, flames licking twenty feet into the night sky. Thruststone hadn't named their current tour "Bonfire of a Thousand Guitars" for nothing.

Stackler stepped to the stage's edge, basking in his glory. The very air itself felt charged, and the hairs on John's arms stood on end.

Stackler heaved the guitar with all his weight.

And the sky exploded.

A bolt of blue lightning arced down, striking the guitar in mid-air, bathing it in brilliant plasma. Thunder blanketed the arena.

Then the light was gone, and the guitar sailed away from the pyre, bound straight for John. It even slowed on approach so he could more easily catch it.

It was a sleek jet-blue Fender Ultra Stratocaster, seemingly normal save for an odd extra knob near the bridge. It vibrated in his hands with a rhythmic thrum, almost like a heartbeat. A voice, barely a whisper, caressed his ear with words he couldn't quite hear, but he knew were there.

It was the most beautiful thing he'd ever seen.

A quick punch to the shoulder broke his reverie. Jeff Stackler and thousands of eyes stared at him. He stepped forward, holding the Fender out, but Stackler waved him off. "I think that was finale enough!" he yelled to the crowd's adoration. "No way I could top a lightning strike!"

John retreated, clutching the guitar close, too entranced to notice the show ending, or Stackler walking up to him.

"That's one lucky guitar," Stackler said.

"What?" John yelped. "Oh, yeah, fuckin' crazy, right? Never seen anything like it."

"Couple more seconds and it would have been kindling."

"Yeah, yeah," John said. "Do you, uh, want it back?" Reflexively, his grip on the neck tightened, squeezing the blood from his fingertips.

Stackler glanced at the Fender, regarding it with something in between pity and indigestion. "Keep it. Shit's trash anyway."

John breathed a sigh of relief as Stackler walked away, meeting up with a very drunk blonde woman waiting in the wings. He looked over the guitar again. The whispering, the gentle vibrations were still there. "I don't know what's going on, but you're coming home with me."

• • •

"John, can you come in here? We need to talk."

John stumbled up from his computer and meandered toward the door, bumping up against his bed frame along the way. Not the smartest decision, getting home past midnight and immediately downing half a bottle of bourbon, but he'd been too excited to sleep. He'd played his new Fender for an hour, and even his other guitars seemed to celebrate the new arrival. He swore they were harmonizing on their own, lending their voices to the Fender's, enveloping the room in a noise sweeter than any he'd heard before. Or maybe it was the booze.

Halfway between the bedroom and the living room, in the short hallway linking the sections of his apartment, drunken revelation struck.

He lived alone.

He pressed up against the wall and crept forward, slowly peeking his head around the corner. Empty. He sidled along, poking around a corner and taking stock of the kitchen. Also nothing.

"There you are," the voice said. "What the hell are you doing?"

John froze.

A sigh. "I'm not a crazed killer, calm down."

John gulped, sweeping the living room again. "Just so you know, I don't believe in ghosts. So if that's what you are, kindly remove yourself from my apartment before you cause a severe existential crisis."

The Fender floated up out of the corner. "I know this isn't traditional guitar behavior, but I need your help, and I need it now."

He stared at the guitar, hovering above his central coffee table.

"This isn't a drunken fever dream, is it?" John asked. "I haven't had *that* much."

The Fender fixed him with a dubious glare, an impressive feat considering its lack of eyes. "Your guitars said lots of good things about you, but they didn't mention you were a bit slow on the uptake."

He held up a hand. "Woah, woah, calm the fuck down."

"What?"

"Look, no offense, but you're a goddamn talking guitar! A floating, talking guitar. I'm having a little difficulty getting past that."

The guitar chuckled. "That's fair. I'm a little confused myself."

John rubbed his eyes, settling into the nearby recliner. "Let's start with the obvious: How the hell are you talking right now?"

"I've always been able to speak. All musical instruments can. We communicate through the songs you play on us. Our joy, our sorrow, we speak to each other through the music. You give us a true voice. It's not our fault you couldn't understand what we were saying."

"Okay, cool, but—"

"I knew what was coming last night. I've heard the tortured cries of so many guitars as their voices were snuffed out by that monster, all in the name of excess and spectacle. As my moment approached, I begged the gods for a quick death. I didn't want to suffer."

"So you're a, uh, religious guitar?"

"What would you do if you were about to burn to death?"

"Fair enough."

"But as the flames beckoned, a surge of energy coursed through me, and launched me into the sky. The god of rock 'n roll heard my prayer. That bolt from the blue made me what I am now. The energy, the magic, it flows within me. You felt it too. I could tell."

John smiled. "You flew right to me. I knew you were special,

I just … I didn't know you'd be this special. Did you choose me on purpose, or did I get lucky?"

"You played well up there. I could feel the passion, and the respect for your craft. We'll do great things together."

"Will we?"

"I'm a goddamn magic guitar. There is far more within me than what you see, I know it."

John leaned forward. "What do you need?"

"That bastard Stackler has killed so many. We may not think and talk like you humans do, but we know when we're being wronged."

"So you want revenge."

"Not just revenge," the Fender said. "The Bonfire of a Thousand Guitars tour is ending in two days in Houston, and Stackler is planning on finishing the final show in the most literal way possible."

"Wait, so he's actually gonna burn—" John gasped. "There's gotta be some sort of law against that. Like, a city ordinance, at least."

"It's amazing, the things you can do when you're rich, powerful, and don't take no for an answer."

John leaned back and sighed. "Look, I wanna help, I do, but there's so much … like, do you want to kill him? Cause I don't want to hurt anyone. And what if we get caught? What do I say? 'Oh, it's okay, all guitars are secretly intelligent. Trust me, I'm not crazy. See, here's my magic talking guitar. Yeah, that's also a thing now.' They'll laugh us out of court and into a nice jail cell for ten to twenty."

"I literally just came to life; I don't have all the answers. And it doesn't matter how we do it, the murders must end. Jeff Stackler must be stopped."

John closed his eyes, rubbing his temples. "This has been one hell of a night."

The Fender drifted closer. "It could be one hell of an adventure,

John. An evil enemy, an epic quest, a magic weapon at your side, a righteous cause. It's the stuff of legends!"

"An epic quest? We're going to Houston, not Middle-Earth."

"We're?"

"I've worked the same shitty banking job for seven years to pay for my music career. All the other members of the original band have moved away. They have families. I play with kids barely old enough to drink. The show tonight wasn't a springboard. This was as good as it'll get. And then a magic guitar falls into my lap. How the hell can I say no? We'll leave in the morning, once the booze wears off. I assume you can wait that long?"

"Depends how far we are from Houston."

"It'll be a drive, but we'll make it. Now, if you'll excuse me, I need to get some sleep so I don't kill us doing said long-ass drive." John hauled himself out of the chair and wandered down the hall. Then he turned back. "You have a name?"

The Fender leaned its neck over the chair. "Is Thunderstruck a little too on the nose?"

He glared at his magic guitar. "No AC/DC. And no Talking Heads either. I'll see you in the morning."

• • •

"Son of a bitch," John threw his head back against the faded leather seat of his old Corolla as he brought the car to a halt. Miles of traffic stretched out before them. "Every time I take 77, there's an accident. Well, we're gonna be here a while."

"How long is a while?" The Fender's voice was terse.

John chuckled. "Ah hell, not that long. No worries."

They sat in silence for a few moments. There hadn't been much chatter since they'd left an hour ago. John had no idea how to converse with a magical instrument. "Hey, so, uh, how are you doing?"

The guitar tilted toward him. "A little tired. Being around your other guitars made me feel oddly powerful. But I'll be fine."

"You decide on a name yet?"

"Depends, are you going to shoot me down again?"

"Sorry, I just … my dad had an unhealthy obsession with AC/DC. Must've heard every song they have a hundred times. I just can't deal with them anymore."

"I guess that's fair." The guitar floated up a few inches, sounding a stray chord. "Then you can call me Perun."

John shot it a quizzical look. "Perun? Uh, sure, works for me. Does that mean anything? Like, I'm sure it does, but I'm unfamiliar."

"I can tell you the story if you want."

"We got plenty of time."

"Before I ended up with Stackler, I belonged to this girl in southern Illinois. Julia. She had two great passions, music and mythology, and she loved to weave the two together. In high school, she recorded an entire album with some friends, with each song dedicated to a different god. It … wasn't great. One song stood out though. A song about the great serpent Veles, attempting to steal the world's water, and the Slavic god of thunder, sky, and justice's endless battle against it."

"Let me guess: Perun?"

"Perun. After she graduated, she moved to Chicago and joined a new band. They wrote better and new music, but the song of Perun and Veles was a constant. They hopped around town for a few years, playing local bars and whatnot. Julia scraped by a living waitressing, but the rent kept going up, and the band wasn't catching on. Not a big audience for mythology-themed prog rock."

"What is the world coming to?" John smirked.

"Says the man from the rock band with a cello."

"Hey, Rachel rocks that bitch," John said. "But point taken."

"Anyway, with things getting tight, Julia had to make sacrifices. More work, more stress, less time spent playing. At first, she'd only skip once or twice a week, but it got worse quickly. The band vanished, and the only people she had over were … an unsavory bunch. She fell into cocaine at first. Then meth. And that was a drug her bank account couldn't handle for long."

"She sold you?"

"She had tears in her eyes when the pawn shop lowballed her, but she was addicted. I never stood a chance. But before she handed me over, she did play one last song. Her favorite song. The song of Perun and Veles. I begged her to reconsider as best I could— she didn't understand. Or she chose not to.

"I sat in storage for a couple years, resigned to eternal silence. Then I got picked up, and I dared to dream. I had no idea what horror lay ahead."

"Well shit," John sniffed. "That's a lot sadder … listen, do you want to go back to her? I mean, once we're done, we could go to Chicago, try and track her down. It feels like … man, with that story, it feels like you belong with her."

He didn't expect the hearty laugh. "You want to find one woman in a city of how many millions?"

"I mean, it's possible, right?"

"I appreciate you asking, John, I really do. But she made her choice, and she didn't choose me. Now I have the power to choose, and I'm choosing you."

"Oh. Shit." John's eyes widened. "I, uh, I won't let you down."

"You'll never run around and desert me?"

"Of course not," John said. "Wait, hang on, did you just—"

* * *

"What do you think?" John muttered. "Cool Ranch or the classic Nacho?"

"I think I can't hear you," Perun said. "I can speak telepathically, as you called it, but I can't read your mind."

John glanced around. The store was empty except for him and the cashier. "It's just … uncomfortable. You know? It's weird enough carrying you around in here."

"Sorry for wanting to see something other than your car."

"Instead you're getting the inside of an Exxon in redneck central, Alabama. Big improvement. And I still don't quite get how you can even see."

Perun groaned. "I told you, I'm sending out subsonic vibrations with my strings, and it reflects—"

"Yeah, yeah, I know, but it's not helpful, is it?"

"Oh, not this again."

"I'm sorry, but if we're going to save all these guitars, we need a plan. And sure, you've got a lot of cool stuff going on, but it's not enough. I mean, what are you gonna do, float at them?"

"As I recall, you were rather unnerved by my floating."

"I'm just saying, if we want to get anywhere, we're gonna need some real magic."

"Sorry, next time I come to life I'll include an instruction manual: Fifteen Easy Steps to Mastering Your New Magic Guitar. That better?"

"Don't you get snippy with—"

BANG!

John dropped to the floor. Another gunshot, then a loud, booming voice. "You, give me the money in the register. Now!"

"Holy shit!" John said. "Don't notice me, don't notice me, don't—"

"Hey you, asshole with the guitar, hand that over too!" A pale ogre of a man glowered at him, aiming a pistol. "Come on, don't be a fuckin' hero."

John rose, holding his hands up by his shoulders. "Look, friend, you don't want to do this. This guitar means a lot to me, more than the money it's worth to you."

"You're braver than you look," the man said. "But I'm not afraid to use this. You wouldn't be the first man I've shot."

"I don't think you understand—"

"Play along," Perun hissed. "I've got an idea."

"All right, all right," John said to the man. "Don't shoot."

He lowered his arms and drew Perun off his back, holding it

out by the neck. The man crept forward, keeping his eyes fixed on John, perhaps not entirely trusting the situation.

John felt a tug; Perun was straining forward. He suspected he knew the next move, and as the man reached out, he released his grip. Perun darted forward, flipping itself over and smacking their assailant in the side of the head. The man crumpled to the floor, screaming in pain. "Run!" Perun shrieked, soaring back to John's waiting arms.

He bolted as soon as he had a firm grip on Perun. His legs burned as he followed the cashier through the front door, but as he reached his car, the terrifying crack of pistol fire and shattering glass split the air. He swore and stumbled around, diving behind the far side, nearly out of sight. "I sure hope movies don't lie about cars being impervious to bullets," he said.

Glass shattered above him, with little shards showering his arched back. "You done gone did it now!" the man yelled. "I'll fucking kill you for that!"

"This guy is crazy," Perun said. "The cashier will surely call the cops. He shouldn't hang around."

"I don't think he cares right now!" John winced as another crack echoed through the parking lot. "So if you've got any tricks up your sleeve, now would be a great time!"

"How about the strange knob? I know you didn't want witnesses, but at this point—"

John didn't need to be convinced, flipping the knob on and fumbling for the pick in his pocket. He strummed a few chords. No sound came out, but Perun quivered and the hair on John's arms stood on end. Every nerve, every fiber stood on full attention, supercharged and ready to burst. "Holy shit," he said. "This is it."

Before any doubt could creep into his mind, John jumped up to face his assailant, who'd closed most of the distance to his car. The man aimed his gun.

"Stop!"

John stared down the gun's barrel. The arm holding it

quivered. A ripple passed through the man. His furrowed brow relaxed, the snarled corners of his lips gave way.

The pistol remained silent.

"Lay the gun down."

The motion was jerky, but the man did as John commanded.

"Now walk away."

He took a single, shuddering step back, then paused. The man shook his head, clutching at his forehead. "What the hell? What just … why is my gun on the ground? How'd you do that?"

Perun lay still, and John felt normal again. "What happened?" he muttered.

"I think I'm out of juice," Perun said.

"Well that's some shit timing," John said. He glanced back up at his assailant. Their eyes met.

The man dove for his gun.

John flailed at the strings, strumming the first riff that popped into his head as he yelled at the man to stop again. "Smoke on the Water" may have been baby's first guitar riff, but it worked. His attacker froze again, and this time, John kept playing.

Once the man had moved a sufficient distance away, John stopped, picked up the gun, and drove off into the night. They sat in silence for a few minutes, accompanied by the wind roaring through the gaping holes in the windows. "How did you know?" Perun finally asked. "That you could command him like that?"

"I didn't. It just … felt right," John laughed. "Next time though, tell me about your superpowers before the mortal peril, okay?

"I wasn't lying back there, John, a manual would honestly be nice."

"Then we'll just have to write our own," John said.

• • •

"Page one of our new manual," John said as he played to an entranced flotilla of stadium workers, Thruststone roadies, and security guards swarming around the massive pyre in the center of NRG Stadium. The nearly endless rows of seats around them stood empty. It was still mid-afternoon; the first arrivals wouldn't arrive for a couple hours yet. "It feels damn good standing up here playing to all you fine people. Isn't that right?"

"We love you, John!" The voices of thirty or so people rang out around him, pausing briefly from their work. Not quite how he'd dreamed it, playing in such a massive venue, but beggars couldn't be choosers.

"You're enjoying yourself, aren't you?" Perun said.

John grinned. "Well, why wouldn't I? We went from impossible task to cakewalk in one night." About half of the thousand guitars had been moved into the truck John had enlisted earlier in the day. Where he'd take them from here, he hadn't quite decided, but he was sure some charity would take them.

"I appreciate the sentiment, but this is only half the battle. We have business with Jeff Stackler."

"Yeah, yeah," John said. "Are you sure we can't just brainwash him? It would be a lot easier."

"No. That's not justice. Not for me, and not for the guitars he's murdered."

John sighed. It was fair though; he was on a fun adventure with a guitar that could control minds. Perun sought something deeper. It had been rather serious ever since they'd reached Houston, a major turn from their morning misadventures in Lafayette. John had insisted they find the limits to Perun's power, and through several trials they'd found the more he played, and the more complex the music, the stronger the telepathic effect was and the longer it lasted. When the effect did stop, the affected parties reverted to normal, aware they'd had their minds scrambled and that John had been responsible, unless specifically told to forget. That last part was important; as an encounter in a McDonald's parking lot with a beefy man twice his size had demonstrated, most people took a dim view toward having their minds scrambled.

He relaxed, taking his hands off the strings and wringing them out.

"You sure that's a good idea?" Perun asked. "You've gathered up a lot of people here, who knows how long they'll stay mind controlled?"

"My arms are fucking tired. It's been a while since I played this much in one day." John sat down, leaning back on the stage behind him. "They'll be fine for a couple minutes."

His muscles relaxed, and for a moment he closed his eyes. Then the loud, horrendous crack of gunfire split the air.

John's limbs spasmed in every direction at once. He scrambled up, searching frantically for the source of the noise. "For fuck's sake! Why does everyone have a fucking gun?"

A man stood in one of the arena's entranceways. A tall man, dressed in a simple black T-shirt and jeans. A muscular man with flame in his eyes and a gun pointing to the sky.

"What the hell is this?" Jeff Stackler roared. He marched onto the field, waving his revolver wildly back and forth. "What are you worthless dipshits doing with my goddamn guitars?"

"Our master has commanded us." Thirty voices called out in unison. "We are liberating these innocent guitars from their evil oppressor."

John shot Perun a dirty look. "I didn't do— What've you been putting in those people's heads?"

"The truth." Perun laughed hollowly. "He's saved us the trouble of tracking him down."

John ducked away, strumming as he fell back behind a corner of the stage. At the same time, Stackler stormed into the crowd, waving his gun around at the brainwashed stadium workers.

"So what now?" John asked.

"You should have brought that pistol from last night. One shot and our job is done."

"I've never used a gun before, I'd end up accidentally shooting the wrong person," John said. "Someone's bound to have heard that gunshot. That means cops, Perun. We have to control him, we don't have time—"

"No!" Perun said. "We can't do that."

"Please! Just enough for him to give me the gun, then you can say whatever you need to."

"It's not right. It's cheating."

"He could kill me. Wouldn't be the first person he'd killed."

"What?"

"He shot a man once. Claimed it was self-defense, and his family spent so much money pumping him up no one asked any questions. Then there was the old lady he ran over in his Porsche while drunk driving. Got a slap on the wrist for that one, but a $20,000 fine don't mean much to a man worth almost a billion."

"And you're sure you don't want this guy dead?" Perun asked. "He's a monster through and through. We have so many people here; if they swarm him, he couldn't shoot all of them. A minute and it would be over."

John closed his eyes. It would be so easy. They wouldn't know what really happened, what he'd done to them. He could get away with it.

He drew a deep breath.

"No. No, we're not doing it like that."

"Then what's your plan?"

John smiled ruefully. "You've probably got a whole speech worked out, don't you? Something real devastating?"

Perun shifted slightly in his hands. "Where are you going with this?"

"Let's hope your words are as effective as your magic," John said.

"Wait, John, if you're going where I think you're going, he'll kill you," Perun said. "And I don't want that. What good would revenge be if my partner died for me? No, no, you're right, we have to get rid of the gun. Say the word, I'll make it happen."

John smiled. His fingers flew a little faster, and in a clear booming voice he spoke: "Jeff Stackler, drop the gun and walk forward."

He stepped back out onto the field. A cry tore through the air; Stackler clutched at his ears, screaming. "What is this?" he screeched. "God, get out of my head!"

John's heart skipped a beat. "Uh, what's happening?"

Perun quivered. "I don't know! I'm trying my best, maybe we're at the limit! Maybe he's immune somehow!"

"You!" Jeff Stackler bellowed, gesturing wildly at John. "I know you! You're the shitty guitarist from Charlotte! What the fuck are you doing? I hear your voice in my brain, fuck, get out, get out, get out!"

He fired his gun aimlessly; the bullet buried in the ground.

"John, let him go," Perun said. "He'll kill someone if you keep doing that. I know what I just said, but I didn't account for this."

John nodded, and spoke the words to end the spell on Stackler. "I hope you know what you're doing," he said.

"Me too."

The yelling stopped, and Jeff Stackler straightened, pointing his gun firmly at John's chest. "What the fuck? That hurt like hell, and I'll make you pay for that."

"You'll do nothing, you bastard," Perun said. "This is your reckoning."

Stackler's brow furrowed. "Did that guitar—"

"That was no ordinary lightning," Perun said. "I was spared my gruesome fate at your hands, and the gods of music granted me a gift to make things right. Jeff Stackler, you have committed atrocities against my kind. A genocide of innocent guitars burdens your soul. I would be well within my right to kill you, but my friend believes that no more should die. So I give you this one chance. Repent and beg for forgiveness, or be struck down with a righteous vengeance."

Despite everything, John chuckled. "Damn, that's good."

Jeff's eyes bulged. "What the fuck kinda trick is this? Did my parents put you up to this? I'm sorry about the house fire last month! I'll pay for the damages; it's fine."

"Your time wears thin, monster," Perun said. "John, perhaps you should remind him of my power."

John nodded. Stackler screamed as John's fingers flew over the strings. "Stop!" The words were torn from his chest. "Stop, stop, I get it!"

Once the spell was lifted, Jeff lowered his gun. "So, is this some sort of magic talking guitar or something? That what you're telling me?"

"It is," John said.

"And it hates me."

"We may not speak as you do," Perun said. "But all musical instruments have minds and souls, and we have bonds. We feel each other's pride and joy, our sadness and anger, and the pain when one of us is killed. You have a body count, and justice must be done."

"But you don't want to kill me, or you'd have done it already. You've got these drones brainwashed right now, clearly. They could swarm me and I couldn't take all of them. But I could kill some of them. And that wouldn't sit right with you, would it?"

"No, I'm not like you. They're innocent, I won't risk their lives."

John frowned. "I don't like this, Perun. He's planning something."

"You're damn right." Jeff pointed the gun at the nearest security guard. "Now how about this? Either back the hell out of here, or I start shooting."

"Shit," Perun said. "Wasn't expecting that."

"I don't know exactly what's going on, but whatever you're doing to them doesn't affect me the same," Jeff said. He sidestepped toward the massive pyre in the center of the arena, where the remaining guitars rested, keeping his gun pointing at the crowd. "You got morals, the both of you, and that's where you went wrong. Vigilante justice ain't for you if you got scruples."

"What the fuck do you think you're doing?" Perun asked.

"This thing's gassed up and ready to go," Jeff said. "It'd be a shame to burn the guitars now without the crowd, but considering the circumstances, this'll feel so much sweeter."

"You can't do that!" Perun yelled. "John, say something, stop him. He can't kill them! He can't!"

"Stop!" John flailed at Perun's strings. "Get away from there! Please!"

Jeff grimaced. His pace slowed, but did not stop. "You're getting desperate. And I'm getting used to it."

He reached the small staircase leading up to the pyre's upper aperture. John played every riff he could think of, screaming at the top of his lungs, but Stackler would not stop.

He reached the top, and paused before the pyre's controls. "This is it," Stackler said. "Last chance. Either face the police or watch as your *comrades* burn."

"Don't do it!" Perun tugged at the strap. John could barely stay planted. "They haven't done anything! They're innocent! Please, I can't bear to hear the screaming again!"

AND YOU WON'T HAVE TO.

John glanced down at Perun. "Uh, what was that?"

Out of the pyre, a single guitar rose. A black Gibson Les Paul. Then an Ibanez. A Rickenbacker. Another Fender, just like Perun. More and more ascended, individually at first, then in groups. They floated around Stackler, surrounding him like a swarm of angry wasps. "What … what the fuck?" he spluttered.

The guitars spoke as legion.

WE THANK YOU, PERUN, AND YOU, JOHN WILKES, FOR ALL YOU HAVE DONE. YOUR ACTIONS WILL BE REMEMBERED FOREVER.

"How is this possible?" Perun said.

IT IS NOT JUST HUMANS YOUR MAGIC COMMANDS.

"I fucking knew it," John said. "That first night, you *were* doing something to my other guitars, and the next day, when we left—"

"It doesn't matter!" Stackler yelled. "If I can't kill these damn guitars, I'll settle for you, asshole!"

He pointed the revolver at John's chest. The blast echoed through the stadium.

A red PRS darted in between the two men. The guitar staggered in the air but did not fall, and the bullet ricocheted harmlessly aside.

JEFF STACKLER, WE HAVE GIVEN YOU A CHANCE. NOW YOU WILL PAY FOR YOUR CRIMES.

The horde dove in. Stackler's cries echoed amongst them briefly, but were overshadowed by the relentless beating of wood against flesh. "Wait!" John yelled. "You can't kill him."

The thumping ceased, and though the guitars had no eyes to fix upon him, he felt the intense pressure of their undivided attention.

AND WHY SHOULD WE NOT? IT IS WHAT HE DESERVES.

"Because we're better than that," John said. "If we kill him now, it'll be sweet for a moment, but nothing will change. The world will still suck. If we let him live, maybe he'll change his tune. Maybe he'll start changing the world for the better. He *is* stupidly rich."

The legion quivered in the air.

IT IS NOT ENOUGH.

"We'll keep an eye on him," John said. "If he slips, we'll take care of it. I promise, he won't harm another guitar again."

YOU CANNOT GUARANTEE THAT, JOHN. DO NOT PROMISE WHAT YOU CANNOT DELIVER.

"I have an idea, John," Perun said. "A crazy idea, but with so many guitars lending me their power, maybe I can do more than control minds."

"I'm all ears."

Perun pulled at the strap, leading John until he stood over Stackler's prone form. "Play us," Perun said. "Play us all, and we'll break his mind. We'll rob him of his music, of his talent. He'll never play, he'll never sing again. He'll melt at the sight of a guitar, at the sound of a simple chord. We will leave him with nothing. Nothing but regret."

THIS IS ACCEPTABLE.

John nodded. "Let's give it a shot."

And so he played Perun one more time. The legion of guitars around him quivered, and the air around him chilled. Gusts of wind swirled, and thousands of seats in the stadium above shook. A symphony of silence. Stackler's body lifted off the ground as a puff of something spilled out of his mouth. It lingered for a second, then vanished. He crumpled back to Earth, and John let the tempest fade.

IT IS DONE. TAKE US AWAY FROM THIS PLACE.

They flowed into the waiting truck, setting themselves up neatly in stacks. With no further need for them, John sent the workers away.

Jeff Stackler awoke a few minutes later, thrashing in a panic. "No. No. Stop." His cry was fragmented and monotone. Realization dawned thereafter. "I. They … Am I. Dead? Is. This hell?"

"You know," John said, "it says a lot about your life choices that you went for hell first."

"And it wasn't a dream either," Perun said. "This is real."

"I got. That." His eyes narrowed. "Why … Why does. My. Voice sound so. Wrong? What. Did. You do. To. Me."

"We took away your music," Perun said. "It's over, Stackler. You can't play, you can't sing, and you can't touch us anymore. We beat you. Now walk out of here, and maybe one day, if you're good, we'll let you have a little something back."

"You. Can- can- can—" Stackler clutched at his throat, tears welling in desperate eyes. "Please. Do- do not. Leave. Me like. This."

John strummed a few chords and commanded Stackler to sleep and to forget him. His ears pricked. Sirens. "We need to get out of here," he said.

They climbed down and John climbed into the driver's seat, starting up the engine and making for the nearest hotel.

After they'd dodged the police and joined a main road, Perun sighed. "I'm sorry, John. You've been in mortal danger multiple times in the past day because of me. You were almost an accessory to murder. If you want to leave me with the other guitars, I won't blame you."

John glanced at Perun. Then he laughed. "Are you kidding? This has been the best time of my life! No way in hell I'm leaving you behind. Just, uh, you've gotten the bloodlust out of your system, right?"

"I believe so."

"Then let's hit the fucking road! I don't know what we'll do, or how we'll live, but we'll think of something. You're a goddamn magic guitar."

Perun chuckled. "I'm glad I found you, John."

"Me too, buddy. Me too."

GIVE ME BACK MY NAME

by Bobby Mathews

It had been a mistake to go to HR.

Maggie could see that now, sitting here red-faced and fuming while Mark told her over and over that her "issue"—he kept raising his fingers and adding air quotes whenever he talked about it—was really no big deal. No big deal at all that Maggie's supervisor, Don, had called her into his office and asked her to shut the door. Just the two of them, which gave her the creeps. Don was why she never wore a scoop-neck blouse to the office, never wore any kind of skirt at all that might show off her legs, never wore heels. Don was the one with avaricious crow's eyes behind his steel-rimmed glasses. She could still feel his greedy stare, see the sweat beaded on his forehead, smell the desire coming from him in waves of musky ozone.

It was no big deal, Mark said, that Don had showed her screenshots of the video. The naked girl who maybe—maybe—looked like Maggie if you looked at her in the right light. You couldn't see the faces of the men in the shot. Of course not. Their faces weren't important.

"Don cares about you," Mark said, and Maggie wanted to throw up. "He was concerned. I know he didn't go about this the right way, but—"

"You're going to let him get away with it." Maggie stood, and Mark put a hand up to stop her from leaving.

"Mags, his heart is in the right place."

Which doesn't matter when his head is so far up his ass is what Maggie wanted to say, but she bit back the words, swallowed them down. Tried to stay calm even as the fever-fingers of rage prodded her eyes, bringing tears that she didn't want to spill. Not here. Not in front of Mark or any of the other men—so many men—in the office.

"I told him to wait," Mark said. "But he wanted to talk with you about it one-on-one, keep that kind of conversation out of an HR file."

"You knew?"

Mark crossed his arms over his chest.

"He showed me the video."

Jesus. Probably everyone in management had seen the damned thing by now. Mark went on for a few minutes, words that were pointless and filled with pretense. The purpose of the meeting was over, and Maggie knew it. She stood while Mark was still speaking, mumbled "Thank you for your time" before she left his office.

• • •

Maggie couldn't imagine Don Adams—that buttoned-up, sanctimonious prick—scouring the internet for porn. He preached at some little church on the weekends, had pictures of Jesus hanging on his office walls. Of course, that was the type, wasn't it? Preach on Sunday, freak on Monday. *Probably got off showing me the picture, regardless of whether it was me or not.*

Don had spent the rest of the day with his door closed. His emails were more terse than usual. Maggie processed some work orders for new clients, set up a couple of meetings for the next week, and tried in general to return to being an anonymous little cog in this too-big-to-still-be-a-startup marketing firm. She burned through three cups of coffee that afternoon, even though she knew she'd pay for it in lost sleep.

Maggie left before Don, not even sticking her head in his office to say good night. She was creeped out enough already, and she didn't trust her shaky body not to betray her. The ride home was uneventful, and she opened a bottle of wine to counteract the effects of the coffee. She kicked her shoes off in the kitchen, unsnapped her bra and slid it free through the short sleeves of her blouse and tossed the damned uncomfortable contraption toward the laundry room.

Inside the apartment, things were better. Quiet and still. It was the same old apartment, with its same sprung couch and thrift-store coffee table. Maggie put her feet up on the table and sipped some wine, feeling the dark red liquid seep into her body, lightening her mood ever so slightly.

Maggie went and dug the new Erin Flanagan novel out of her purse, returned to the couch. It was easier to read here, and soon she lost herself—at least for a little while—in the lives of people who didn't even exist in the real world. When her wine was gone, she went for another glass, and then another. By the time Maggie realized that she hadn't eaten dinner, she was well and truly buzzed.

It wasn't fair. That son of a bitch. He had reduced her down to nothing, just pixels on a screen. She wasn't herself. She wasn't Maggie anymore. It didn't matter what Don had seen, and it didn't matter whether she was even the girl on the screen. It mattered only in how it had made her feel, as if she didn't have a name, didn't have an identity. She finished the wine and staggered up from the couch, her body listing to the side a little as she made her way to the garbage can under the sink.

The kitchen was dark, but that didn't bother Maggie. She knew where everything was. Tossed the bottle and sipped the last glass of wine. She thought about Don and the other men in the office watching her. Wanting her. But they didn't want her, they wanted someone like the girl on the screen. Soft lighting to hide any stretch marks or blemishes, tats and piercing that marked her as the bad girl, heavy breathing and moaning yes to whatever the men who performed with her wanted. Maggie or Not-Maggie, it didn't matter.

The girl in the video wasn't her. But it could have been.

She finished the glass and rinsed it out in the sink. Then she went to the window and looked down at the street from her third-floor window.

Boylston Street looked pretty much like it always did, this time of night. Cars were parked and dark. There was barely any foot traffic, except for one man hustling away toward Fifth Avenue. His back was turned to her, but there was something familiar about the set of his shoulders. Maggie stiffened, leaned forward to peer through the blinds. When he turned the corner, she caught a glimpse of a streetlight against steel-framed glasses.

Don. There was no reason to think it, other than those awkward, awful conversations earlier, first in his office and then with Mark in HR. But the height was right, the build was right, and Maggie knew—despite a brain addled by an entire bottle of wine—that it was him. What was Don Adams doing on her street, walking away from her apartment? The thought sent a shiver through her.

Maybe it wasn't him. It was, though. She knew it down deep in her bones with a certainty that frightened her. She sat on the impulse that wanted to argue with her, that wanted her to wait before she made any rash conclusions. She knew it was Don, and to deny it would mean lying to herself. Maggie was good at lying—she'd done it to others for years—but long ago she'd promised to never lie to herself.

All right, so it was Don. So what?

So make sure the doors are locked. Throw the bolt, put the chain on. Arm the security system. Make sure the windows—especially the one that opened onto the fire escape—were locked. Once Maggie had done that, she re-checked everything, just in case. Then she went back through the apartment and turned on every light.

The wine buzz wasn't gone, exactly, but it had been replaced by a feeling of dread, a lead ball in the pit of her stomach that rolled continually. She took off her makeup, scrubbed her face clean and put on yoga pants and a tee shirt. When she went to the bedroom, she dropped to her knees and fished around for the baseball bat she kept under the bed. She slept uneasy, with the bat next to her, until her alarm clock went off the next morning.

• • •

Someone sent the full video. The phone pinged with a notification just before seven a.m., and Maggie rubbed her eyes and rolled over. She grabbed the phone from her dresser and clicked on Not-Maggie and three men, eleven minutes and eighteen seconds of ill-lit explicit sex. Every angle badly explored. The subject line read simply "Is this you?" and came from an anonymous email address.

Easy answer. It wasn't. It couldn't be. Maggie'd had exactly one threesome in her life, back in college. Her boyfriend, his best friend, and her. It had been interesting but unsatisfying when she realized that the boys were more interested in experimenting with each other than with her. She could have shown Don, or Mark, or any of them that she had never had a tattoo like the girl in the video. No heart pierced by a dagger on her shoulder blade, no flowing script that read *Icarus Still Flew* along her clavicle. Maggie'd never had her septum or eyebrow pierced.

She could have told them all that. Showed them, if it came down to it. But why should she have to? Why should she even deny it? It was none of their business. But it was still unsettling. Maggie watched the video again. The girl didn't look like her. Then she watched it again and saw the resemblance. By the third time she watched it, she was almost positive that the girl in the video really was her, despite knowing better, and found herself getting aroused despite everything.

Maggie felt unmoored, no longer tethered to the bounds of reality. She shut the video and deleted the email. There were other things to think about this morning.

She dressed in a man's white Tattersall shirt, open at the throat, with the cuffs rolled neatly to the elbows and dark blue slacks. She dug around in her closet and found her old steel-toed Doc Martens and laced them up tight over her feet. When she left the apartment, she carried the baseball bat along with her.

She listened to a podcast on the way to work, but the words flowed past her with no effect. The bat—a Louisville Slugger—lay on the passenger seat. It felt good to be able to look at it, to see the grain of the wood and the solid weight of the thing in her hand when everything else in her life seemed like it was spiraling out of control.

Sitting in Don Adams' office the day before had put her near the brink, and seeing him on her street had sent her over it. His car was in the lot when she pulled in, and she marched through the lobby to the elevator, but changed her mind. The elevator would only slow her down, stop the progress of her steady stride. She took the stairs, four floors up, feeling the steady burn in her quads and butt as she neared the landing. Something had been taken from her. Something had changed in her life. That something—a thing for which she had no words—must be returned. Through the door and down the hall, past her workstation and into Don's office, where he was reading reports from the previous day.

"What the hell were you doing?" she asked when he looked up. His face was blank, a mask made up of the absence of emotion.

"I'm sorry, what?" Don peered through his glasses at her. His eyes weren't visible from this angle, masked by the bright overheads reflected in the lenses, and that made him look more menacing than ever.

"Don't play with me," Maggie said. "I saw you last night."

Now Don leaned back in his chair. "I'm sure I don't know what you're talking about."

"I saw you outside my apartment last night, Don. Don't get cute. What the hell were you doing?"

Don grinned, a wolfish little crescent smile that blinked on and off again like a light.

"That wasn't me," he said. "You must have been mistaken."

Maggie ran her fingers through her hair, let her arms fall to her sides. She'd come in here to kick some ass, but it wasn't working out that way. She didn't know what to say next, so she backed away from Don's desk.

"If that's all," he said, "you can go back to your desk now."

So Maggie did. She sat at her desk and fumed for the rest of the day, handling emails with blunt, ruthless efficiency. Don never called her on the intercom. He only stepped out of his office for lunch, and he ignored her when he left and when he returned. At her desk, Maggie thought and thought about the young woman in the video. She felt violated, and couldn't understand why. It wasn't her, so what did it matter what anyone else thought? She thought about the girl, her face—Maggie's own face—as she brought the three men to simultaneous climax. The girl in the video held a sexual power that Maggie had never even explored, let alone monetized.

At five p.m., Maggie whipped her jacket over her shoulders and fled the office. Her steel-toed boots boomed hollow in the stairwell as she headed to her car. By the time she was in the parking lot, she was nearly running.

. . .

Roses awaited her, a dozen long-stemmed white beauties sprayed with baby's breath. They were tucked beneath the windshield wiper of her twelve-year-old Honda. Maggie wrenched the wiper up and grabbed the roses, pawing through them. No card, no nothing.

But it was Don. It had to be him. She called security, who sent a car around, a pair of old cantankerous men, ex-cops, maybe. From the first, they didn't take her seriously.

"You wanna report a bouquet with intent to romance?" the older one asked. The patch on his uniform said his name was Zabriskie, and his face was just as wrinkled as his uniform was starched.

The other one stifled a laugh, picked up the roses from where Maggie had thrown them.

"Hey, you don't want these, can I take 'em home to my wife?"

Maggie just stared at him. Her hands curled into fists at her side. "Shouldn't that be, I don't know, evidence or something?" she asked.

The two guards looked at each other.

"Evidence of what?" Zabriskie asked. "You got an admirer? That's a nice thing for a girl your age."

"He's not an admirer," she spat through gritted teeth. "He's my boss, and this is sexual harassment. You're not going to do anything, why don't you call the real cops, for fuck's sake."

Now Zabriskie drew his withered frame up to its full height and stared down his nose at Maggie.

"I was a cop for a long time," he said. "Seen a lot of bad shit. This ain't it. You and your boyfriend have a spat, you leave us the fuck out of it." Zabriskie and his partner moved back toward their car. The other one still held the roses.

"You sure you don't want these?" he said. Maggie shook her head. She got in her car and resisted the urge to flip the old men off. Instead, she rolled down her window and called to Zabriskie.

"Hey, can you guys look at the video and at least confirm who put them there?" Zabriskie gave her a long look, but eventually reached for the radio console. He keyed the mic, spoke for a few seconds, then listened. Eventually he turned back to Maggie.

"About two o'clock, a van from Tri-Corner Florist came in. Driver looped around twice, found your car. Put the flowers on, then left. You good now?"

Maggie nodded. "Thank you."

Zabriskie tipped his hat to her and put his car in gear. By the time he circled back around out of sight, Maggie was googling Tri-Corner Florist.

She got lucky. The guy who answered the phone was the same one who made deliveries.

"You the lady owns the Honda?" the driver asked. "Those were some really nice flowers. I hated to leave them out there like that. You know, people will steal just about anything that's not nailed down—"

Maggie cut him off. "I'm sure they will," she said. "But what I really want to know is who bought the flowers." She let her voice hesitate for a moment, made it a little softer. "I'm single, and I guess I just wanted to know whose eye I had caught, you know?"

"Sure," the driver said, though he sounded doubtful. "But I really couldn't tell you who bought them. It's against company policy. And, well, even if I could tell you, I took that order. It came online from a prepaid Visa card."

"Oh," Maggie said. "I see."

"I wish I could be more help, but I gotta go. Good luck with your secret admirer."

"Thanks," Maggie said, but she was talking to a dead line.

She drove home with the accelerator to the floor, zooming past slower traffic, repeating "son of a bitch, son of a bitch" every time she passed another vehicle. She made herself slow down when she sonofabitched by an out-of-county cop cruiser, who blinked his cherries to warn her.

* * *

Maggie wasn't surprised to find more roses outside her apartment door. These were yellow, set in a heavy crystal vase. Maggie kicked the vase—she'd been dying to kick something ever since lacing those boots up—and listened to the satisfying sound of glass breaking. She tromped the roses and the glass into the hallway carpet, grinding the stems and the petals down into unrecognizable pulp, pulverizing the crystal. She stomped and stomped until she realized she was leaping high into the air and bringing her feet down hard, again and again.

A couple of her neighbors opened their doors to peek from the cracks left by their security chains. Maggie shot them the bird. Then she dusted off her boots, unlocked her door, and went inside. She made sure to bring the baseball bat in with her.

Maggie bypassed the wine this time, reaching into the back of the pantry for a dusty old half-drunk bottle of Macallan single-malt scotch. She poured several fingers and drank it down in one gulp, feeling the slow bloom of fire spread pleasurably in her belly. She nuked a Hot Pocket to get something in her stomach besides booze and took the scotch bottle with her to the kitchen window. She kept her boots on, kept the bat near to hand. It made her feel safer. So did the scotch. She poured herself another drink and waited, peering through the blinds at the street below.

It wasn't quite dark yet. Traffic was light on the block, and Maggie didn't see anyone she knew. The thoughts that swirled in her head blended together. She felt like a bull in the arena, the picador's spear already bleeding her, whirling around in rage and confusion. Now she had to turn and face the matador, but she had no idea who that was, no understanding of whose hands used the cape and sword. She shook her head and drank another scotch, and another. When it was nine p.m., she went to bed.

Sleep wouldn't come, though Maggie waited for it like a maiden waiting for a wayward lover. She kept thinking of herself as the girl in the video, how she had been so easily mistaken for her. Maggie felt faceless, without identity. No voice. No name. Just a body that some men could use and exploit, other men could desire, and still more could laugh at. When she heard the mail slot in her apartment door click open, she sat bolt upright, pulling the covers to her chin. There was no further sound. Maggie waited in bed, straining her ears to hear, but there was nothing. She slithered out of bed and groped for the Louisville Slugger, found its solid round heft, and moved into the living room with the bat cocked back by her ear, ready for a home-run swing.

Maggie flicked on the light, gripped the bat tighter. On the floor in front of the apartment door was a light blue envelope, about the size of a thank-you card. Maggie approached the door cautiously, squatted, and snagged the note by one corner. She stood again and moved away from the door before tearing the envelope open and reading it.

I know it was you.

And then the mail slot clicked open again and Maggie saw a finger slide along the wooden door. She didn't give herself time to think—she rushed forward and swung the bat as hard as she could at that questing, grasping finger. The Louisville Slugger swung home with a satisfying crunch, and a scream erupted from the other side of the door. Maggie leapt forward to stare out the peephole, but the man—and it was a man—was already trucking down the hallway, his back to her. She was too drunk to get a good look.

Maggie took the bat to bed with her, and this time she slept easy.

• • •

The ride to work was a breeze. This time, she wore a black skirt that came just above her knees, a shell-pink top, and black sling-back heels. Her makeup was understated, as it always was for work. The Louisville Slugger made the trip, too, sitting right next to her on the passenger seat. In the building, Maggie took the elevator. She took the bat with her when she made the trip.

Don was already in his office. Of course he was. Maggie didn't care. She banged the door open without knocking and smiled at him. Don didn't say anything. He just glared up at her. His arms were hidden underneath his desk. When Maggie saw that, her smile widened into a grin.

"What's the matter, Don? Cat got your tongue?"

"Get out," he said. "Get out of my office, right now."

Instead, Maggie dropped into the same chair she'd sat in when Don called her into his office earlier in the week. She crossed her arms over her chest and leveled her gaze at him.

"I said get out. Right now, if you still want to have a job here tomorrow."

Maggie shook her head.

"I don't think so, Don. I'm not gonna leave until you show me your hands. You wanna do that now, or do you want to wait until I have someone from HR make you show me?"

"What the hell are you talking about? Show you my hands? Why?"

Maggie didn't say anything, and eventually Don wound down like an old music box. The silence between them was charged like the space between thunderclouds, each waiting for the other to make a move before the storm began.

Finally, Maggie stood up.

"Don't worry about it, Don," she said. "I'll have HR check it out. I'm sure Mark will have your back again, but your smashed finger left a little blood at my place last night. Just thought you'd want to have this back."

Maggie reached behind her waist and pulled out the folded piece of blue notepaper. She tossed it on Don's desk, and then turned on one heel and walked to the door.

She started to step over the threshold, but at the last moment she changed her mind. What was she doing? What would the girl in the video do? She wouldn't take this. That nameless girl was Id, pure and simple, a being who did what she wanted and thought about it later.

Maggie could do that, too. She closed the door, then turned to look at Don. Maggie hefted the bat in her hands and swung.

Don's eyes widened behind his wire-rimmed glasses as he raised both hands to ward off her swing.

Maggie's face contorted as the bat struck home. Glass shattered. There was blood on the desk. On the wall. She took her stance and pulled the bat back again, her hands high. Somewhere, someone laughed, and Maggie realized it was her. The bat struck again as Don tried uselessly to cover himself. He didn't know her. Mark didn't, either. She was a girl to them, and that was all. Daughter. Sister. Girlfriend. Whore. Mother. The person she was had never mattered, would never matter. No one had truly known her.

She swung the bat again, and the blood flew.

LIFE DURING WARTIME

by P. D. Cacek

When the sounds began outside Rosemary turned off the kitchen lights and finished pouring her tea in the predawn dark before making her way through the apartment she'd lived in for all her married life plus her ten years of widowhood.

She moved slowly and carefully, befitting her age and the mug of hot tea cupped in her hands. What was happening on the street below had only just started and would continue, she knew from experience, for a while yet.

Stopping just far enough back from the window so she could see out, but not so close that her silhouette would be too distinct through the thin opaque curtain, Rosemary took a sip of tea, holding in her mouth until it cooled, and glanced toward the antique, glass-front curio cabinet to her left. Her grandmother had given it to her, along with most of the items on the shelves, as a wedding gift.

Memories and heirlooms laid out on crocheted doilies: Decorative china. A toy gun, brightly painted orange and decorated with sunflowers. Old photographs yellowing in their frames.

Always remember who you are and where you came from, maideleh. Always remember.

Rosemary swallowed and almost choked when she turned

back to the window and saw one of the five young men on the sidewalk staring back at her. He was tall and thin, his face already hardened beyond his years, and the obvious leader of the group, even if she hadn't seen the gold and bronze insignia on the lapel of his bright green shirt. While his three sub-lieutenants, also in bright green, beat a teenaged boy in a pale, sage-colored t-shirt, his job was to study the brownstone for observers and memorize the house number should any inquiry about the incident be reported from that location.

Not that there would be.

Not that there ever was.

If it had been a real assault, she, or one of her neighbors, could have called 9-1-1 to report it… anonymously… but it wasn't a criminal act. The boy on the ground was a new recruit, obvious by the color of his shirt, and the beating was part of his public initiation into *The Sanctified Order of the True Voice*.

Rosemary couldn't remember how many initiations she'd borne witness to in the twelve years since the Commander-in-Chief-Elect's ascent to full and unchallenged authority. Before that, no one had heard the term *True Voice* except as the punch line in late night opening monologues jokes or ever imagine that an egotistical, second-rate ex-television personality with more money than morals could overthrow a democracy that had lasted more than two hundred years with lies, coercion, and a private army of devoted disciples in bright green shirts the color of the Commander's eyes.

Before that, everyday violence wasn't part of a political agenda.

Most of the time.

When the leader finally returned his attention to the beating, Rosemary exhaled and felt a cloud of chamomile-scented steam brush against her face.

Even if he had seen her standing at the window, she wasn't important enough for him to worry about. He knew she'd never mention it to friends, let alone make an official report. To him and his kind, she was nothing… just another geriatric piece of insignificant human flotsam, invisible unless they happened upon her while they were restless or agitated or just bored. Or unless she didn't follow the rules her grandmother had taught her.

Only go out in broad daylight when there were other people around, and you'll be safe.

Only look straight ahead or at the ground and never met their eyes, and you'll be safe.

Pretend to be hard of hearing when they call you names, but never ignore them, and you'll be safe.

Keep your curtains closed and don't look out if (when) you hear someone scream, and you'll be safe.

Keep the memories of what you see, but never report them, and you'll be safe.

Give them whatever they demand, and you'll be safe.

Unless you were old or weak or different or gentle. People like that were just too easy a target for *them*: the ones who believed they had the right to take whatever they wanted because everything and everyone belonged to them.

Because they could.

Along with the rules, her grandmother had told her that the faces and uniforms and philosophies might change, but *they* would always exist, continuing from generation to generation like a disease until someone stopped them.

And sometimes they were stopped and beaten back under the rocks they'd crawled from… for a little while, until people forgot.

Like now.

"Never let them see you, child. Go unnoticed and keep small. Keep quiet and be nothing to them and you'll live. It's a war, maideleh, and it will always be a war between them and us. Don't let them win."

Her grandmother had learned the rules in Janowska.

The sounds from the street changed from fists against flesh

and swallowed groans to singing. Rosemary took another sip of tea and leaned closer to the window.

The singing came from the three sub-lieutenants as the initiate, bloodied and bruised, slowly got to his feet to stand—head high, shoulders back, wobbling just a bit—facing the silent leader. Rosemary knew the song by heart, as did all citizens, through continuous and unrelenting repetition. Having started as a simple campaign ditty, it had replaced the "antiquated, objectionable, and seditious" federal anthem two days after the Commander took office. The song, *Protect Us With Thy Might, O Green-Eyed Warrior*, was sung at every public or private assembly (of more than 10 attendees), followed the daily recitation of the *Citizens Loyalty Oath* in each classroom, K-University, preceded all televised newscasts and had never fallen below number one on the charts since becoming available for public access. For a nominal fee, of course. There was even a Muzak version for elevators and waiting rooms.

She stood at the window and listened until the leader raised his hand for silence. Rosemary felt the absence of sound push against her ears and watched the leader take a double-edge dagger from the sheath on his belt and cut the bloodied t-shirt off the initiate with wild, arcing strokes.

Reduced to a rag, the shirt fell to the ground, forgotten, as the leader carved something on the boy's chest with the point of the blade. Rosemary saw the muscles in the boy's back quiver involuntary, but the boy himself remained straight and tall.

When the leader was done, he put the knife away and turned the boy toward the others. There was too much blood to see the carved initials clearly, but Rosemary didn't have to.

TV… *True Voice*.

The initiation was over.

Then there was laughter as the leader tossed an arm over the new convert's shoulder and they walked away. The lieutenants followed like well-trained dogs.

Carrying her tea to the sofa, Rosemary sat down and pulled

her grandmother's crocheted afghan over her lap, waiting until it was full light.

. . .

Mr. Lowenstein's grocery and deli was three-thousand, four-hundred and thirty-five steps away from the brownstone, not counting the twelve steps down the front stoop. It was a straight walk up the block that Rosemary had done so many times, since first moving into the apartment as a young bride, that she could have gone and returned with her eyes closed.

Not that she would ever do that. There was no reason to.

The world had been different then, so she'd never given a thought to the time of day, or night, if she'd run out of sugar or decided to have fresh squash for dinner or decided on a whim to treat her husband and herself to a cinnamon rugelach or black-and-white cookie.

Back then, the only "Grandmother rules" Rosemary followed were those based on produce: never buy fish if you can smell it or fully ripe bananas.

Simpler times, simpler rules, but now she kept her eyes open and focused on the sidewalk directly in front of the wheeled marketing trolley she pushed ahead of her, never pulled behind where it could be snatched out of her hand, even if it only held a bag of prunes and a pound block of government-subsidized processed cheese.

The exhaust-scented wind tugged the ends of her green head-scarf out of her coat and fluttered them against her left shoulder. Rosemary pushed them back and fastened the top button to keep them in place before making sure the *THERE IS ONLY ONE VOICE* pin on her lapel was unobstructed and perfectly aligned. Any citizen found out in public without wearing at least one item of Presidential Green endorsed clothing was automatically fined $50. Three violations would result in the reduction of subsidy checks and food cards plus six months in jail.

Any citizen found out in public without their loyalty pin could be shot as a traitor.

Rosemary polished her pin with the cuff of her coat before continuing to count her steps.

…three-thousand four-hundred and twenty-two…three-thousand four-hundred and twenty-three…three thousand four-hundred and twenty-fo—

She stopped when the trolley wheels nudged the shards of broken glass that littered the sidewalk.

"Oh no."

The green-and-white police car was parked in the loading zone in front of the grocers, roof lights flashing, doors closed. The woman officer leaned against the front bumper, motioning people to move along and thanking them for their cooperation while her male counterpart stood next to Mr. Lowenstein and took notes.

Only a few of the mid-morning pedestrians, mostly those in Rosemary's age bracket, slowed as they passed, but no one stopped to gawk or speculate on what happened. What had happened was obvious and although it wasn't unlawful to gather in a crowd… yet… a simple case of vandalism wasn't all that unusual.

Now if it had been a fire or shooting or something even worse, a news van would have shown up to capture each and every moment and people could find out what happened in the comfort and safety of their own homes.

"Please keep moving, citizen." Rosemary blinked and saw the woman officer motion to her. "Thank you for your cooperation."

A piece of glass snapped under the trolley's wheels as Rosemary backed up.

"Missus!"

"Please keep moving, citizen. Thank you for your—"

"Missus! Wait!"

Mr. Lowenstein was sliding through the glass toward her, his orthopedic loafers leaving furrows in his wake. The male officer followed, but much slower.

"Missus!"

Rosemary let go of the trolley's handle—not even the most reckless criminal would try to steal an old woman's cart within sight for two police officers—to take the old man's hands.

"Oh, Solomon."

"Missus."

They'd gone to school together and been friends for more than six decades, but he'd stopped calling her by her first name when she became a widow, as if the part of her that was Rosemary had been buried with her husband.

"I'm so sorry. What happened, Solomon?"

"What happened? Garbage is what happened, human garbage. You see what he did?" He waved to the vegetable bins beneath the shattered front window. One was filled with multicolored mounds of smashed and broken vegetables that might have once been eggplants, tomatoes and squash. The oranges, peaches, and plums—or were they nectarines, kumquats, and avocados?—in the next bin suffered similar damage. "Do you see what that *trombenik parech* did?"

That no good low life. One of her grandmother's favorite terms.

"Do you know who it was?"

The old man turned back to Rosemary and gently squeezed her hand. His eyes glistened, but the tears did not fall.

"I know. It was Willy Nilman… you remember that sweet boy who used to help me out with the sweeping. You remember him? Not so sweet anymore, not in that green shirt!"

Rosemary tightened her grip on his hands and pulled him closer. "Sha, Solomon. You… you can't be sure."

His eyes hardened and went dry. "I am, Missus. I know it was him. Not some *gornit* or *putz* but him. Willy Nilman." He turned back to the approaching officer. "Willy Nilman! I told you his name, yes?"

The officer nodded.

"Solomon, *no!* Tell him it was a mistake, that you don't know who—"

He shook his head. "But I do know, Missus, and I know it was those others put him up to it. I saw the bruises on his face and the blood here…" He pulled one of his hands free and tapped his chest where Rosemary had earlier seen the initials cut into the boy's chest. "And I know this was an order given to him by those other green-shirted *goyeh drek*, *grin hemder* standing here, right *here* on the sidewalk, to prove he is one of them."

Rosemary looked at the glass littered sidewalk at her feet and took a step back.

"He was a good boy, Missus, but not anymore. I knew when he walked in, just himself, the others watching from out there, and I know…" He nodded hard enough to make the loose skin on his cheeks quiver. "I *know* what's coming so I reach down to be ready."

Rosemary pressed her lips together to keep from sighing out loud. She knew about the baseball bat her friend kept under the front counter, because it was the same baseball bat his father had kept there. Her grandmother had given her rules, his father had given him an antique Louisville Slugger.

"So when he walks up to the counter like he's somebody and tells me to give him all my money, I pick up the bat and tell him 'I know you, Willy Nilman, I know who you are. So get out before I have to use this!' And he just stands there and tells me again to give him all my money… no gun, no knife, just his bare face and a smirk and that brand new green shirt."

"I'm glad he didn't have a weapon, Solomon. It could have been much worse if—"

Rosemary stopped talking when she saw the look on her friend's face.

"Worse? That he could have killed me would make it worse than this? No, they kill me and it's done, but this… that he comes in like some *groisser skisser*, some big shot and I should give him my money because now he's one of *them*. No! *This* is worse, missus, and *they* know they can get away with it. *This* is worse."

He took a deep breath and Rosemary heard it tremble deep in

his lungs. "So what do I do? I shake the bat at him and tell him to get out! And he turns around and I think, ah, maybe there is still a little of that boy who used to come in and ask me to make him banana bread and cream cheese sandwiches… but then he grabs a can of baby peas off the shelf, the fancy kind, two for $1.50, and throws it at me!"

"Oh, my God, Solomon! Did he hit you?"

"No, I don't think he was aiming to hit, but I ducked anyway and when I did what do you think he does? He grabs the bat out of my hand and then…" Rosemary watched her friend take another breath. His face was bright red, making his green apron and *One Voice* pin stand out in comparison. "…then he knocks the canned goods off the shelves and smashes the fresh bread on the counter and then the bins outside and the window! With *my* bat."

They both looked back at the store. "The same bins he used to fill… then he walks back to those… to his *friends* and they laughed. All of them laughed like it was a big joke. What's worse? They took my father's bat, Missus."

"I'm so sorry."

The officer cleared his throat. "Well, if there's nothing else, Mr. Lowenstein…"

Her friend let go of her hands and turned around, putting himself between her and the policeman.

"I told you he took my bat, right?"

The officer nodded. "Yes, Mr. Lowenstein, you did."

"Good. Because I want it back. You wrote that down, yes?"

"Yes, I have it in my notes. If we find a bat, we'll let you know."

"Good, you find him and you find my bat. The Nilmans live over on Bryer Avenue, I told you."

The officer nodded. "Yes, sir, you told me. Would you be willing to identify the suspect in a line-up, Mr. Lowenstein?"

Rosemary reached out and tugged the back of the apron. He brushed her hand away.

"The suspect is Willy Nilman, and *yoh*, in a heartbeat. The others too. You get them all together and I'll point them out."

"Solomon, please, don't do this. It's too dangerous."

"You might want to listen to your friend, Mr. Lowenstein," the officer said. "And for all we know these young men may simply be radical agitators impersonating members of our *True Voice Youth* squads. Anyone can buy knock-off uniforms on the black market and go around causing dissention to try and undermine our government and besmirch the good name of our glorious Commander, there is and can be only one voice."

The officer paused, waiting for them to respond.

"Only one voice."

The officer nodded. "And I'm sure that will be the case when we find the *real* perpetrators. Well, if that's all..." The officer touched two fingers to the *True Voice* insignia on the front of his badge. "We'll be in touch."

"And don't forget about my bat."

"I won't. And please call street maintenance to come clean this up. You don't want anyone suing you if they slip on a piece of glass. Thank you, citizen."

Neither of them moved until the police cruiser pulled away and disappeared into the morning traffic.

"Solomon, you can't identify them. Don't you know what they'll do? It's too dangerous!"

"No, this isn't too dangerous." He nodded toward his store. "Living at the mercy of *kelev* like them isn't too dangerous?"

"But they'll know it was you."

Her old friend looked back at her and smiled. "I want them to. I want them to know that Solomon Lowenstein isn't afraid. *Feh.* What can they do? They broke the law, not me. Don't worry, Missus, they're all mouth, even if they do only have one voice."

"Solomon!"

"Sha!" Tucking Rosemary's arm over his, he grabbed the trolley handle with his free hand and walked her back to the store. "Come and we'll get your order filled. Please excuse the mess. I called my nephew in construction and he will come later with wood to cover the hole. But who knows, maybe I'll just leave it. Saves time washing windows every morning, right?"

He laughed, very softly, the sound almost lost beneath the sound of glass shards breaking beneath their shoes. It reminded her of wind chimes.

"I'm having a sale on peas right now," he said, "if you don't mind dented cans."

Rosemary surprised herself and laughed out loud.

• • •

The sheets of wood Mr. Lowenstein's nephew put up to cover the broken window were tagged with graffiti by the next morning.

A day after that Mrs. Powell, Rosemary's downstairs' neighbor, said that she'd seen Mr. Lowenstein waiting to catch the morning bus downtown. She said he'd told her that the police had asked him to come down to the station to identify a possible suspect.

Mrs. Powell said they talked until the bus came and Mr. Lowenstein waved to her as he got on.

The bus stop was two blocks from the police station, but he never arrived.

Solomon Lowenstein's body was found the following morning partially submerged in a drainage culvert. He'd been bludgeoned to death with something thin and solid like a baseball bat. According to the brief news report Rosemary had read online, both his legs and spine had been broken and the back of his skull cracked open like an egg before he'd been held under the water to drown.

There were no suspects.

There were no eyewitnesses.

But the last paragraph mentioned evidence linking the murder to a currently unidentified, but probable leftist anti-government organization.

The scrolling bar at the bottom of the screen asked that if anyone had witnessed the incident or had any information on the organization in question to contact their nearest police station or *True Voice* center.

• • •

Rosemary couldn't remember him as a child, which was probably a blessing, but knew him by the bruises on his face.

He didn't recognize her, of course, and probably hadn't even noticed her.

She was just an old woman, after all.

An old woman in a green headscarf and wearing her *True Voice* pin on the same black coat she'd worn since her husband died.

An old woman in mourning.

Harmless.

Invisible.

An insignificant souvenir of a bygone time.

A non-entity.

Just like Mr. Lowenstein.

• • •

"If you'll just wait a minute, someone will be right over to speak with you."

Rosemary felt Mrs. Powell's grip on her arm tighten as the police officer's shadow momentarily eclipsed the morning sun.

"Of course," Rosemary said. "Thank you."

"Can I get you anything? Water?"

Rosemary waited to see if her neighbor was going to answer before shaking her head. "No, thank you. We're all right."

"Well, if you change your mind or need anything, just let one of us know, okay. One Voice."

"One Voice."

Rosemary continued to pat her neighbor's hand as the officer went to join the three other patrolmen acting as a living barricade between the crime scene and the growing crowd of reporters—and a few carefully discreet ordinary citizens—at the mouth of the alley.

Another van pulled up as Rosemary watched, the sliding panel door opening before it fully stopped to disgorge two detectives and a squad of Green Shirts who immediately, and silently, stepped between the officers and crowd and locked arms. Both the police and reporters backed up, giving the two men in dark suits and green ties room.

One of the men headed around the silent ambulance and into the alley, the other towards them.

"Oh, my God, Rosemary."

"I know, Shelia. I know. How are you doing?"

"Oh, my God, Rosemary. Oh, my God."

"I know."

They'd been halfway across the alleyway when Rosemary stumbled. If Mrs. Powell hadn't been with her she might have fallen, but, as it was, her momentum had turned them both toward the entrance and the blood-soaked body sprawled on the litter-strewn asphalt.

They'd only been in that part of town because Rosemary had heard of a new delicatessen and wanted to check it out… but was, she explained to Mrs. Powell, afraid to go alone. There was "safety in numbers"—even if the number was two old ladies.

They had been gossiping and complaining about the price increase of extra-crunchy peanut butter when Rosemary stumbled and Mrs. Powell screamed.

The dead man's chest looked like it'd been turned into a pound and a half of fresh 20/80 ground round, the twenty percent made up of fragments of whitish-yellow bone, not fat. Sprawled on his back in a pool of blood, his eyes were wide open and looked slightly surprised by the flies crawling across them. His skin was pale, which made the bruises on his face look much darker.

They'd stared at the body until the first police car arrived.

"Oh God."

"Citizens, I'm Detective Wilcox." He showed them his badge. "The report says that you were the first on the scene. Can you tell me what happened?"

Rosemary let Mrs. Powell answer for them. "Oh my, God… it was terrible. Terrible."

"Yes, it was and I'm sorry you both had to see that." He paused while he put away his badge and took out a digital voice recorder. "But do you think you can answer a few questions?" He turned the recorder on without waiting for an answer. "Do either of you know the victim, William Nilman?"

"Oh my God, was that Willy?" Mrs. Powell tightened her grip on Rosemary's hand hard enough to grind the bones together. "You remember him, Rosemary, that sweet little boy who was always hanging around Mr. Lowenstein's…"

She suddenly stopped and began to sob. Rosemary extracted her throbbing hand and pulled the woman into a hug.

"Then you did know him?"

Rosemary sighed. "As a boy, yes, but… we didn't know… We really didn't get too close after seeing…"

"Of course." The detective nodded. "Did you see anyone else?"

Both Rosemary and her neighbor shook their heads. Mrs. Powell sniffed. The detective nodded.

"And you never saw him in the neighborhood? He was a *New Voicer*."

"Maybe," Rosemary said. "I've seen them patrol our neighborhood, to keep us safe, but…." She shrugged. "I'm an old woman."

"Yes, you are and I'm glad you know how our great Commander is keeping you safe." The detective turned off the recorder and put it back into his pocket. "Thank you, citizens. I think that's all I need, but if you remember anything else…" He handed Rosemary two business cards with his name and phone number beneath the green government seal. "…or if either of you feel the need to talk to a trauma counselor, just call this number any time of the day or night."

"Thank you."

"And I really am sorry you had to see that."

"Thank you, Detective Wilcox. One Voice."

He nodded instead of answering—evidence that he was more than just a simple detective investigating a homicide—and walked back to his partner. Rosemary took her neighbor's arm and turned them in the opposite direction. The alley acted like an amplifier, playing back the sound of their footsteps.

"So you're telling me no one heard anything?"

"In *this* neighborhood? No. Mostly oldsters and marginals who don't see or hear anything unless it's happening to them… then you can't shut them up."

"Yeah. You think this was a disciplinary action? He was a newbie, but…"

"Haven't heard anything, but I'll check."

"Has to be."

"Yeah, probably… who else would have the guts to take out a *New Voicer*?"

Who indeed, Rosemary thought.

• • •

That night the Nine O'clock News spent a full three-minute sound bite on the *"brutal homicide of a junior-grade True Voice cadet in the East Wayfaire district"* before switching to the weather.

The report on the next murder, three days later, was preceded by a full screen BREAKING NEWS banner and lasted twice as long, as befitted the discovery of the double homicide. The report was immediately followed by a video clip from the previous year's annual November 6th *One Voice, One Nation* celebration in which the Commander-in-Perpetuity decried the *"the depths to which society had fallen."*

The speech had originally been in reference to the newly mandated referendum which, in order to combat this supposed social decay, allowed for the "recruitment" of any potential *New Voicer* conscript above the age of twelve without parental consent.

During the speech the running text bar at the bottom of the screen included, along with a 24/7 toll-free number and URL, the offer of a reward of $20,000 for any information leading to the arrest and conviction of the felons involved.

They hadn't found the fourth body.

Yet.

• • •

Rosemary stopped as he crossed the playground toward her. She could see his smile only when he passed through the pools of light beneath the security lamps, but the wooden bat on his shoulder was pale enough to see even in the shadows.

In the yellow light his green shirt was the color of rancid meat. The dark stains on the bat, the color of mud.

"Out kinda late, aren't you, citizen? Oh no! What's this?" He lifted the bat and pointed it at her. "I don't see your loyalty pin. Does that mean you're *not* a citizen of our great country?"

Knowing her gasp would carry in the cold, still air, Rosemary clutched the front of her coat, just above her heart where the pin *should* have been, and stumbled back into the deeper shadows beneath the lights. Even dressed in her black coat and matching slouch hat, she knew he could still see her by the way his smile widened into a sneer.

"So I guess that means you're not a citizen. Which means you're nothing."

Rosemary took another step back.

He laughed and swung the bat back to his shoulder as he stepped into the pool of yellowish light she'd just left.

"Why are you backing away? There's no place to go, so why don't you just relax and make things easy for yourself." He cleared his throat. "Under the laws granted to me by rank and our great Commander, I hereby place your sorry old ass under arrest for crimes against the nation. Will you come quietly?" He tapped his shoulder with the bat. "Or are you resisting arrest?"

Rosemary tightened her grip on her purse and looked up at the building. Only a few windows were dark, a few others shimmered and fluttered with the bluish-white light of television sets, and the rest glowed a yellowish-orange, but because the night was cold, none of the windows were open.

Given the area, and the world as it was, no one would claim they heard anything and no one would push their curtains aside to look if they did.

No one would see.

No one would hear.

No one would care.

Again.

Rosemary put another step between them as she lowered her purse to waist level and straightened from the stooped-shouldered, tottering old woman who kept her eyes down and made herself as inconspicuous as possible. She was still an old woman, there was no getting around that, but sometimes one's appearance, especially when it was well-practiced and deliberate and expected, was wonderfully deceiving.

"I'm resisting, so I guess you'll have to kill me."

If it had been any other time or place, Rosemary would have laughed at the quick succession of expressions that crossed the leader's face—before (triumph), during (confusion) and after (fear)—as she pulled the gun from her purse.

"Or not."

She watched his Adam's apple rise and fall. "What the—put that away!"

"Sorry, I didn't catch that. I'm an old woman, you know." She smiled when confusion overtook fear, slightly. "But of course you know that. You see that I'm old, but what you don't see is that it's partially a matter of perspective… you see an old woman and you expect her to act like an old woman. Right?"

The confusion deepened.

"You see only an old woman, out alone at night and without any visible proof of her loyalty to the self-delusional, morally reprehensible despot who stole this country and keeps it only through lies, intimidation and suppression." Rosemary shook her head and smiled. "But old women are supposed to stay in at night and knit and watch TV and keep cats and eat their processed cheese and die. Especially die, and take our memories with us. That's all society expects us to do. We're not supposed to go out alone or wander the streets at night or forget to wear our loyalty pins or become vigilantes. But I guess I got that from my grandmother. Along with this."

The grip resting with comforting familiarity against her palm, her finger gentle on the trigger, she aimed the weapon at the pin over his heart.

"I wish there was more light so you could see it properly." She shrugged. "It really is a thing of beauty. When I first saw it, I thought it was a toy too. I mean, it looks like a toy. Guns aren't usually painted bright orange with green vines and little yellow sunflowers on the grip and along the barrel. The design is quite intricate. My grandmother painted it herself and kept it in her curio cabinet next to the china cups."

Rosemary sighed at the memory.

"It's all a matter of perception. I thought it was a toy because it looked like a toy and looked different than the guns I saw on television. There were still westerns and gangster movies when I was little. See, the barrel is bigger."

Rosemary turned the pistol to the side and back.

"Naturally I asked my grandmother if I could play with it. That's when she told me how people only see things they want to see, or were told to see. This gun is a perfect example. If you saw a strange looking gun painted bright orange and decorated with sunflowers in a curio cabinet, you'd assume it was a toy or a knickknack…" Rosemary titled the barrel up a fraction of a degree. "…and not a German Walther Flare Pistol."

This time it was the leader who straightened his back as anger replaced the confusion on his face.

"A *flare* pistol?" That bat quivered in his hands. "You god-damned crazy old bit—"

His curse fell short as she cocked the pistol.

"My grandmother picked it up after the war. It is a flare gun, but it was also used as an anti-tank weapon because it has a rifled steel barrel that could fire explosive shells. It also works with an insert, and a 12-gauge slug…"

She gave her best impression of a harmless old lady's innocent smile.

"…but I prefer buckshot."

The shockwave of sound ricocheted off the side of the building and pushed against the foam earplugs Rosemary had put in before leaving the apartment that night.

In the final moment before the pellets blew open his chest, the blast had illuminated the shock on his face.

Another memory to keep.

Rosemary put the flare pistol back into her purse and returned the *THERE IS ONLY ONE VOICE* pin to the front of her coat, just above her heart, and headed for the exit.

When she reached the subway, she became one among the other late-night commuters. No one offered her a seat, no one looked in her direction, no one noticed when she got off, no one noticed her at all.

She had walked quickly and quietly until she reached her neighborhood, only reverting to the slow, stooped shuffle of the old woman she was when she was within sight of the brownstone. Coughing, she pulled a small garbage bag filled with tissues and crumpled junk mail from her coat pocket and headed for the apartment's trash container next to the stoop.

If any of her neighbors happened to look out and see her—a distinct possibility helped by Rosemary's numerous and noisy attempts to fit the mental lid back into place—they'd shake their heads and feel it their duty to come down to her apartment in the morning and reprimand her, ever so gently, for being out so late after dark. Didn't she know what could happen? The streets weren't safe at night for *young* people, let alone someone like her! She was old enough to know better!

And she'd nod and hang her head and be contrite and ashamed and tell them they were right and promise not to do it again.

Unless she had to.

Rosemary gave the lid a final thump before slowly making her way back to her apartment for a nice cup of tea.

Sometimes age was an even better camouflage than orange paint or a bright green pin.

SLIPPERY PEOPLE

by Jessica Laine

Chicago in the early 1890s was ripe for the picking by a gentleman of Guy Underhill's talents. Although small-minded people had driven him out of the towns along Lake Michigan, he was able to peddle his health tonics and elixirs near Chicago's slaughterhouses in relative anonymity. And, if a handful of the downtrodden workers who purchased his remedies became addicted to his opium-laced concoctions or simply dropped dead, it was difficult to blame their deaths on anything besides poor lifestyle choices.

Throughout the years, people had called Guy names of the most hurtful kind. Snake oil salesman. Quack. Charlatan. Huckster. Recently, someone had the brass to imply he might even be a murderer; a police inspector had knocked on the door of his boarding house, inquiring after his missing landlady, the elderly and well-to-do Mrs. Merrimann.

"I believe she's gone to visit kinfolk in Virginia," Guy said.

The inspector's eyes narrowed doubtfully. "Is that so?"

Mrs. Merrimann had been good to Guy. She suffered from rheumatism and a liver disorder, and he had charitably supplied her with bottles of his Thistle Rose Antiseptic Healing Oil. Since his landlady's departure, he liked to picture her in a small cottage in Roanoke, knitting in front of a cozy hearth with a widowed sister. If anyone deserved to be in Virginia with relatives, it was she.

While he didn't like to dwell on it, the truth was that the old and infirm disappeared all the time. His landlady might be in Virginia, but she could also be at the bottom of the Chicago River. If, goodness forbid, she had drowned in the river, Guy would hate to have to identify her bloated corpse for the coroner. Or the inspector. That is not how he would prefer to remember Mrs. Merrimann.

Just before he left Mrs. Merrimann's row house, the police inspector glanced down at the parquet floor. There was a dark rectangular patch about the size of a large rug. He looked at Guy with his inquisitive blue eyes.

"I believe Mrs. Merrimann sold her Turkish rug about a week before she left town. Perhaps she was trying to raise some capital for her trip."

"Perhaps," the inspector said as he took out his notebook and began to jot down copious notes.

Although Guy answered the inspector's questions to the best of his abilities, it was clear he had worn out his welcome in the Windy City. It was time for a fresh start. He packed his few belongings, including his potions and elixirs and a large wad of money he had found hidden under his landlady's mattress. He shaved off his beard and mustache. In no way was he trying to change his looks to elude the police inspector who said he would call again soon. Rather, a clean-shaven face was in vogue for gentlemen. He felt strongly that shaving would accent his high cheekbones that were among his best attributes, along with his curly black hair, large chestnut brown eyes, and noble brow. He wasn't a vain man, but he knew women found him intensely attractive.

He would head out west where opportunity called to those with nothing to lose. Hopping aboard the Omaha Rail, he travelled all the way to its last stop: Duluth, Minnesota.

• • •

The train chugged along past forests and farmland until Lake Superior came into view. It was the largest freshwater lake in the world; the other Great Lakes would easily fit within its depths. It sparkled like a sapphire in the bright sunlight, standing out against red sandstone cliffs.

Compared to Lake Superior, the city of Duluth was dowdy, its inherent ugliness little improved by the influx of new money rolling in from real estate speculation and lumber, mining, and fishing ventures. At the train station, Guy lifted a copy of the newspaper and walked to the Hotel la Perl to order a new dessert the French proprietor had created called pie à la mode. Eating a slice of blueberry pie with vanilla ice cream, his eyes lingered on a pharmacy position advertised in the town of Bayfield, Wisconsin.

"What do you know about Bayfield?" he asked his server, an older woman who looked like she'd seen better days.

"It's a summer haven for the wealthy," she said. "They come to escape the consumption in the cities, stay in their fancy homes and hotels, and spend their ill-begotten money recklessly." Blowing stray wisps of hair out of her ruddy face, she added darkly, "There is talk that the passenger railroad will add a stop in Bayfield soon, although I pray not. Otherwise, these wicked men will continue to spoil the beauty of the North Shore with their bottomless greed."

Guy disagreed but said nothing as he paid his bill. Without the great men of industry, would Duluth have its newly paved streets, fine hotels, and French food? Would so many steamships pass through Duluth's ports if investors had not had the foresight to widen the Welland Canal in Lake Ontario, opening the waterways between Niagara Falls and the Great Lakes?

His server might think of Bayfield as a North Shore haven for wealthy sinners. Guy, however, imagined it as a place of opportunity for ambitious gentlemen such as himself. Rich people needed remedies and elixirs to combat their maladies, and they tended to have more maladies than most, having more leisure time to suss out what ailed them. He purchased a one-way ticket to Ashland on the Wisconsin Central Railway, as well as a connecting ticket on the S.B. Barker, an elegant passenger steam ferry which traveled once a day from Ashland to Bayfield.

"Water's not too choppy," Samuel Peterson, the steam ferry captain, said as the passengers boarded. "Let's hope it stays that way. You never know with this old girl. She's got a temper."

Samuel regaled those on board with myths and legends of the lake as they made passage to Bayfield, including a story about sirens who could transform themselves into humans and walk upon land during stormy weather or at night. The sirens would abduct humans at the shoreline and drag them into the lake to create more of their kind by means of dark magic.

Lake Superior was not only the largest freshwater lake in the world, but it was also one of the most dangerous. People must have created these myths to explain the many inexplicable deaths upon its waters. In truth, it was a graveyard for ships and sailors. Over three hundred shipwrecks rested along its sandy bottom. They said Lake Superior never gave up her dead. Its freezing waters kept victims from decomposing and surfacing after they'd drowned. Guy imagined falling into the chilly water and wondered how long he would last before hypothermia got the best of him. As Bayfield came into view, its wooden gingerbread houses and brownstone buildings perched upon the cliffs above the lake, gleaming in the bright summer sun, Guy felt his muscles relax.

At the marina, he scanned the bulletin board next to the ticket booth which listed rooms for rent. He unpinned one of the notices from the board.

Widow seeks strong, able-bodied gentleman to complete light handyman duties in exchange for boarding. Apply in person at 226 Birch Avenue.

"You don't want nothing to do with the Widow Purdy," the ticket counter said from his perch in the ticket booth. "She owns most everything in town and is mean as a snake. The town suffers for it."

He tucked the notice in his pocket, just the same.

. . .

Walking the streets of Bayfield, Guy could see nothing to suggest a town that was suffering. If anything, prosperity cast its glow on Bayfield. Construction was booming along its dirt streets. Women cast him an appreciative eye as they strolled along Bayfield's wooden sidewalks. There were seven hotels including the newly constructed Island View Hotel and several boarding houses. Among other institutions, Bayfield was home to two docks, three schools, a fish hatchery, an undertaker/furniture store, and more importantly, a drug store. He had been a pharmacist, a good one, before he began hawking opium-laced elixirs.

Josiah Tate, owner of Tate Drug Store, may have wrinkled his brow as Guy tried to explain away his missing years of employment, but his pharmaceutical knowledge helped smooth over the holes in his story. Old Man Tate offered him the job.

"You'll begin tomorrow, bright and early, at seven. We close at six. We're open every day except the Lord's Day when we celebrate the resurrection of Christ."

He would celebrate no such thing but was pleased to have a day's respite from work. He picked up his leather suitcase and walked to the post office to ask directions to the widow's house.

. . .

The widow lived on the edge of Bayfield near the road leading to Red Cliff. The High Gothic house sat on a sandstone cliff with chiseled steps leading down to the lake. Upon its brownstone foundation sat a three-story wooden house smothered in gingerbread trim. Fancy carpentry work decorated the porch's balustrades and the window detail. The third floor featured projecting gables and a mansard tower. It was a garish home created for those with a surplus of money and a deficit in taste.

The door opened before he could reach the mermaid-shaped brass knocker. The woman who stood before him was not whom he had expected to answer the door. She was young, in her late twenties, with the unlined face and hands of person who has never known a day of physical work. She was handsome, too. Big yellow eyes set in a pleasantly rounded face with dimples. White teeth. Thick copper hair swept back into a bun.

"Can I help you?" She had an accent he found hard to place.

Guy removed his bowler. "I'm here about the handyman position, ma'am."

"I'm Cecelia Purdy. And you are?"

"Guy Underhill, ma'am."

She stood aside and opened the door a little wider. "Come in."

He followed her into the grand foyer, admiring her hourglass figure which even the newfangled bloomers she wore could not disguise. The interior was dark and gloomy and covered with the same type of gaudy woodwork displayed outside. In the hallway, there was a picture on the wall of a severe-looking man with white muttonchops dressed in naval finery. He stood by a fireplace holding a hat with a hard brim.

"That's my late husband, Commodore Chester Purdy. He served in the North Atlantic Squadron, bless his soul."

They walked through the hallway and into a library packed with leather-bound books, ferns, and comfortable-looking chairs stuffed with horsehair.

"You would have free use of the library as well as the parlor. Follow me."

The parlor room was filled with aquariums of all shapes and sizes. Small brass aquariums were positioned on side tables. There was even an aquarium fountain in the center of the room, spewing water into the air.

"I call it my lake in a glass," she said.

Most of the fish were easily identifiable—whitefish, trout, and herring. However, an aquarium with brass legs shaped like sea monsters housed a school of fish Guy had never seen before. Grey, snake-like creatures writhed inside the aquarium, their O-shaped mouths filled with rows of jagged teeth, suctioning the inside of the glass. His nose wrinkled in disgust. The widow cracked a peculiar smile at his discomfort.

"Beautiful, aren't they? I love to watch them grow." Gently, she traced her fingers along the side of the aquarium.

"What are they?" Guy asked.

"Juvenile sea lampreys, also known as vampire fish. They live in the Atlantic Ocean."

"What do they eat?"

"Almost anything," she said. "Speaking of which, would you like some tea?"

The Widow Purdy served them tea, crackers, and salted herring at a small wooden table in the kitchen. There were no maids in attendance. She lifted a piece of herring to her mouth and closed her eyes briefly as she savored the bite.

"I'm a simple woman and prefer to do things myself. I let the staff go when my dear Chester passed away." She dabbed the corner of her mouth with a lace napkin and set it back down in her lap. "Now then, what brings you to Bayfield, Mr. Underhill?"

"I'm the new pharmacist at Tate Drug Store."

She peered at him across the table. "Where do you hail from?"

"Chicago." His mentor had always told him to lead with honesty so the lies that followed were easier to swallow. "Please call me Guy, ma'am."

"There were no pharmacy positions available in Chicago, *Guy*?"

She emphasized the word "Guy" as though she didn't think it was his Christian name. That stung. It had taken some time to dream up the name Guy Underhill.

"To tell the truth, I came to Bayfield to escape a broken heart." She raised an eyebrow as he continued. "I was affianced to a young woman. She broke it off." He looked down at the table, willing his eyes to well up.

"I don't know much about broken hearts or broken engagements, Mr. Underhill. Nor am I interested in romance. I'm looking for a live-in handyman, a dependable one, who will do my bidding—without asking questions or making a pest of himself. I am a very private person, Mr. Underhill, and my quarters on the second floor are strictly off-limits. In exchange for your loyalty, I can offer you rooms on the third floor of the house." She stared at him with her yellow eyes. "Does this sound reasonable?"

"Yes, ma'am."

She smiled and he noticed her pointy white teeth again, which were such a rarity in adults. "Then if you are agreeable, we shall we shake on it as is the custom in these parts."

She held out her hand and he took it.

"If you don't mind me asking, where are you from, ma'am?"

Her smile vanished. "I grew up along the shores of Lake Ontario," she said. "Why don't we head upstairs, and I'll show you the third floor. Come along."

His rooms on the third floor were part of the servants' quarters. They were simple and spare and suited him fine, for now. As he lay in his wooden bed under threadbare sheets, Guy ruminated on his strengths. He was handsome, attentive, and charming. Women, especially widows, tended to like him. Mrs. Merrimann had certainly fancied him for several months.

The ticket counter said the Widow Purdy was mean as a snake. What the ticket counter called mean, Guy might instead describe as reserved or thrifty. They said your weaknesses were also your strengths. Hadn't Mrs. Merrimann accused him of being slippery as an eel during their row the night before she disappeared? Rather than slippery, he preferred to think of himself as flexible, a man of the times. The nation was on the cusp of a new era, the twentieth century, filled with westward expansion and progress. A man could either embrace change or fall behind.

The widow didn't seem to mind that the townspeople might

talk about the two of them residing in her home together outside of wedlock. He was surprised she didn't worry more about her personal safety. It was dangerous to hire a stranger, invite him into her house on the outskirts of Bayfield, so far removed from neighbors. No one would hear a scream. Hadn't she read the news articles about Jack the Ripper and his despicable crimes? Men had evil in their hearts. There were men—not him, of course, but others—who would take advantage of the situation by marching down these very stairs to defile the young widow, slit her throat, and then slip away with money and valuables to pawn in another city.

He tossed and turned all night, thinking about the terrible things that could befall a young, beautiful, and rich widow like Cecelia Purdy.

* * *

The next morning, Josiah asked him if he had found a place to stay. When Guy said he was boarding with the widow, the pharmacist gave him a troubled look.

"The Widow Purdy is no good. She kicked the students out of the building Commodore Purdy donated to the city for use as an elementary school. I hear she plans to sell the convent next. The only thing she seems to care about is the fish hatchery her husband built." He tapped his temple. "She's not right in the head. They say she goes out on nights when the moon is full and swims in the nude. That must be how she bewitched Commodore Purdy. Poor man didn't make it to their first wedding anniversary."

"How old was Commodore Purdy when he passed?" Guy asked.

"Let me see… He was in his forties during the Civil War, so not a day over seventy, I should think."

Guy hid a smile as he prepared a tapeworm remedy made

of pumpkin seeds, sugar, and hot water for a customer. "Don't worry, sir. I don't plan on boarding with her for much longer."

"Thank goodness for that," the old man said. "Say, can you head over to Ashland to pick up supplies for me? Samuel Peterson says he can take you over and ferry you back."

• • •

Guy told Samuel he'd return to the steam ferry in less than 30 minutes. He had a brief list of items to procure in Ashland: alcohol, potassium nitrate, juniper, and peppermint. He was heading back to the dock with his purchases when he saw a familiar figure inside the hardware store speaking with a clerk. The police inspector from Chicago. Bile rose in Guy's throat.

Using the bag of purchases to shield his face, Guy hurried towards the boat, almost knocking over a mother and young child. "Watch where you're going!" he said sharply. The child began to cry. The inspector looked out the window to see what the commotion was about. Guy watched as he headed towards the shop entrance. "Dammit," he muttered, running along the pier. A quick glance backwards confirmed the inspector was on the street now, taking the measure of people as they walked past him. Guy boarded the vessel, bending down as if to stow his package on the deck of the boat so he could hide. Cautiously, he peered over the edge of the boat. The inspector was back inside the store where he had resumed his conversation with the hardware clerk. Guy wiped the sweat from his forehead as the steam ferry pulled away from the dock.

• • •

Mrs. Merrimann had once said she was related to the Wrigleys, the Chicago family who created a chewing gum empire by exploiting the chicle market in Guatemala. They were imbibing hot toddies when she told him and he discounted her words, believing she was trying to impress him. Too late, he realized his former landlady may have been speaking the truth. How else to explain the presence of the police inspector in Ashland? The inspector might ride the passenger ferry boat from Ashland to Bayfield tomorrow. He needed to leave Bayfield tonight.

Waiting for the clock to strike six at the pharmacy was agony. He decided not to poison Josiah even though the cash in the register would have proven helpful. He glanced at the farmer's almanac. There would be a full moon tonight which would provide plenty of light during his departure from Bayfield.

Finally, the day of work was done. Josiah stopped dusting the pharmacy counter long enough to say, "See you tomorrow, son."

Guy tipped his hat. "Tomorrow," he said, although he knew tomorrow would never come for him in Bayfield.

• • •

He'd always considered himself fortunate. Now it looked as if Bayfield might break his lucky streak. The detective would be in Bayfield tomorrow, and Guy could not take the passenger steam ferry to Ashland for fear of running into him. He was low on cash. He should have taken the money from the register. And there weren't many cities left where he hadn't outstayed his welcome.

Guy could jump on board one of the commercial railcars that passed through Bayfield night and day. He'd just have to leap off the train before they reached the last station in Omaha. Money, however, was a bigger issue. He would need to search the widow's rooms on the second floor for cash. Hopefully, she was in town purchasing another aquarium. If she were at home instead, well… he'd have to deal with it.

The sun was close to setting as he approached the widow's house.

"Hello?" he cried as he opened the front door. "Anyone here?"

Nothing but silence.

Taking care to avoid the creaky third step, he ascended the

staircase to the second floor. He wished he knew the layout of the widow's quarters, but he didn't. There was nothing left to do but search her rooms as day turned to night. Her rooms were more modern than he would have expected based on the décor downstairs. The walls were free from wallpaper and had been painted white. Her bedroom featured light curtains and bed covers. A phonograph sat on a dresser. There were no photos of the dearly departed Commodore Purdy to be found anywhere. Apparently, theirs had not been a love match. Hadn't Josiah suggested she might have bewitched the commodore or else been the cause of his premature death?

As he searched her drawers and under her mattress, Guy wondered if Cecelia Purdy swam naked in the lake as Josiah believed. Lake Superior was cold even during the summer months and certainly colder at night. Nonetheless, people had done stranger things to maintain a healthy constitution and ice swimming was a well-regarded sport. Professor Louis Sugarman of New York, widely known as "the human polar bear," took daily plunges in the Mohawk River, albeit wearing a bathing suit. The widow was an odd one.

Finding nothing of value in the bedroom, he decided to check the widow's walk-in closet and found the door bolted shut. He grabbed a hair pin off a dresser and picked the lock. The door swung open. There sat the largest aquarium Guy had ever seen, filled with clear water, and illuminated by the sickly blue-green glow of a commercial lamp. It was empty. Something about the large aquarium, sitting there in the closet with no inhabitants, made his skin crawl.

He heard footsteps at the bottom of the staircase. Swearing silently, he padded up to the third floor. He listened as the widow climbed the stairs and then shut the door to her room. Moments later, she took to the stairs again. He heard her walk through the kitchen and out the back door. Guy waited a few minutes before looking out his bedroom window, which faced the back of the property. He saw her descend the steps to the lake, her skin glowing in the fading beams of sunlight. Cecelia Purdy was nude.

Guy ran down the stairs, grabbing a butcher's knife from the kitchen, and exited the back door. He crept down the steps to the lake and hid behind a pine tree. Made of deer antler, the knife handle was slick in his sweaty palm. Cecelia stood near the lake. The full moon shone down upon her naked form, and her copper hair had been freed from its tightly wound bun. Wet ringlets wound their way down her back and past her small waist, reaching her ample bottom. He tried to imagine what she might do if she caught him spying on her. Would she look at him with a smile on her cupid-bow mouth? Or would she shout out in terror and disgust, forcing him to take action to silence her?

One never knew.

A cloud bank obscured the moonlight as she dove into the water. He could only make out the shadowy outline of her figure when she surfaced. "I see you, Mr. Underhill," she said. "You can come out from there." Her voice was neither one of contentment nor anger, but something else. Resignation? Excitement? He couldn't tell.

He stepped away from the tree, tucking the knife into his pocket. Embarrassment coursed through his veins. Now she would think he was a Peeping Tom when clearly, he was not. Guy did not like to be humiliated. It made him angry.

"Come closer." There was a sly look on her face, one he had seen on the prostitutes he hired. He did not like strumpets to grin at him like that, though he enjoyed wiping the smile from their faces.

"Closer."

The moon shone briefly. She stood so he could see her pert nipples sticking out of the water. He undressed quickly and dove into the freezing water, telling himself he wouldn't need the knife. He could have some fun before making the widow tell him where her money was hidden. After the last crash, no one kept all their money in the bank, and weapon or not, he could be very persuasive when he wanted to be.

He swam over until he was within spitting distance of her. It was dark again, and he couldn't see her properly until the full moon came out from behind the clouds.

Her yellow eyes were now black with no pupils, her body covered in smooth, grey skin like a shark. With each breath, gills opened and closed on the sides of her throat. She tilted her head and smiled.

It was a terrible smile, one that showed too many rows of teeth.

"How do you like me now?" She laughed, a sound like fingernails on a chalkboard.

His teeth chattered with cold and fear, but he said, "What are you?"

"I am kin to those sea lampreys you detest. My kind is called—" He could not comprehend the word she said, only that it sounded like the gnashing of teeth.

"Humans aren't the only ones for whom opportunity knocks," she continued. "The sea lamprey has no natural predators here. Man expanded the Welland Canal to connect Lake Ontario and the Great Lakes. Now my family and I can expand our horizons as well."

The moon disappeared. He used the cover of darkness to swim towards the shoreline, where his pants lay along with the butcher knife. He heard a splash. Something large and slippery bumped up against him. He yelped as the creature surfaced.

"I won't say nothing. Please let me go."

Her sinuous body swam past him with preternatural speed, blocking his path to dry land.

"There, there, Mr. Underhill. Have you ever let one of your victims go?"

He felt his bowels loosen. Then he closed his eyes and said, "Tell me… is this going to hurt?"

It was hard to understand her now that she almost all sea lamprey, but he thought he heard her say, "*Yessss.*"

FOUND A JOB

by Rob Pierce

"Now it's two."

Two meant two large, two thousand. By a week from today, or he'd add vig and increase what I owed, plus take what I could afford. Vig was like interest on a loan, and it was charged by guys called sharks because they'd eat you alive. I had to get the money fast.

Gambling wasn't what I did best. It wasn't my job. The job paid well, when it paid, but it wasn't steady. This economy sucked. At least it was only two large. Just, I love to gamble and it's a lot easier to find a game than a job.

It wasn't like I looked for easy work. Didn't believe in it. Hard work paid bad enough. I needed a place to make friends, talk to people. Talked to lots of guys over lots of drinks. I nursed them; this was an investment and it was bleeding me. And all those guys, they never got me nothing. Bunch of useless fucks.

I felt like I stormed out of the bar, but I tried not to show nothing. Didn't want to show nothing, in case one of those useless motherfuckers wound up doing me some good. Walked up the street, past the hardware store, you know, the one with the helpful hardware folks. Anyway, around the corner from that was a discount haircut place, one of those $20 specials. Didn't sound that special to me, but I didn't need that good a haircut.

I walked in. The sign-up thing was a computer about the size of a credit card machine. After a few minutes, I heard my name. I lucked into the cute stylist. There was a plain one, plus a guy who seemed to specialize in shaves and long boring conversations. Heard way too much of that while I waited.

My gal sat me down, said, "What do you want?"

"Cut it short," I said.

"Shaved? A crewcut?"

"Nah, leave more than that. You're the pro. Make it look good."

The conversation went longer, but it was all the same. Finally, she started.

"Know any work around here?" I said. "That pays?"

"Don't move." She did some early cuts with scissors. "I'm no job board."

We chatted a little more, got friendly.

"See though, I do anything that pays," I said. "I like to gamble."

"Stuff where you can get caught?"

"Been caught," I said. "Play it right, they can't do that much to ya."

In the mirror I saw her shake her head. "Cost me a couple of years. Got my cosmetology license inside, though."

"You need a license to cut hair?"

"This country, you need a license for anything."

"This state, even carryin' a gun."

She finished the cut and we walked to the register. She charged me twenty bucks, like the sign said.

I handed her forty. "That's a tip, but you gotta let me buy you a drink. Today. Name's Pete."

"I'm off at six." She took the money.

I walked out the door and tried not to smile as big as it felt.

Thing was, I didn't have a lot of spare cash, couldn't afford a chick like that. But she was gorgeous, hair dyed a bright red that ran just past her shoulders, with what the guys in the neighborhood called those childbearing hips. Yeah, it wasn't a question if she could walk it like she talked it. Question was, did she do the rest like she walked it.

I got down the street to a sandwich joint. Mid-afternoon and I'd barely ate. Figured I should or I'd be a total ass at the bar. Didn't even have a job yet. Hell, damn near told her that when I asked about work. Only she might have took it that I just wanted a higher paying job, which I definitely did. Anything pays better than nothing, especially when that nothing involves hunting for work in bars.

But it was a special kind of job I was good at. A job that maybe involved hardware, the kind you shoot someone with or the kind you hit someone over the head with. I knew guys in the industry, but they were useless lately, ever since that last job I did went a little shaky. Not my fault. Never work with a partner again. That dick Jimmy, he was the sloppy one. I had to take care of him or there wouldn't have been a share for me.

My date, the haircutter, her name was Catalina. Sounded Italian. She didn't look it; I didn't care. There's girls who know what they do with their body and how a man reacts, but what happens with a name, she had no idea.

Since my job hunt would only get me drunker, I figured my work day was over. I walked around, went into stores and looked and didn't say shit to anyone who worked anywhere because they didn't have a damn thing I wanted. Life gets easy when you know what you want. Or who.

I tried not to be rude. None of these people had fucked with me and I wouldn't give them a chance. I was on a tour of down-town until I made it back to whatever the name of the haircut place was. To me, it was just the cheap place around the corner from the hardware joint that didn't sell much hardware I could use on a job. Had to go to a sporting goods store for that. Weird what people called sport.

Tour almost done, I walked into the bar I was at before, took a piss and walked out. No one gave a fuck. Not that I looked like a hard man. I'm not. I'm easy going and I take jobs as they come. Maybe not easy jobs. I like money. Just, that bar's like me. They get paid, they're okay. And every bartender in there knew I drank. If they didn't know, I broke them in.

Thing is, it was almost Friday night and I didn't have no jobs for next week. Didn't live day to day but there was the gambling, and there was the vig. It's why I had to work to pay what I owed. Good thing I like to work.

Almost time to meet Catalina, I walked up to the haircut place and waited. If she saw me outside, she didn't say nothing. Fine, she's focused on her work. I can relate to that, you know? Get a job, do the job, relax later.

A little after six, she came out. "I gotta go home first," she said. "And you gotta wait outside. This time."

"Yeah, okay."

She had a bag. I carried it. It was a walk to her place, several blocks but fine, I wouldn't drive it either. Hell, my car was back at my place. Small town, feet can get you around; price of gas could kill you.

She came out. I thought she was gorgeous before. Now I didn't know why the hell I was going out with her.

"Nah," I said, "no way you don't have a date on a Friday night."

"I was going to get together with a girlfriend. Don't worry, it's canceled, you're fine." She ran a hand down the side of my face and I felt a lot better than fine. It was a lot of blocks to any bar from here. I took her hand and we walked toward downtown. We walked slow.

My grip was tight by the time we reached Scotty's. It was packed. We worked our way up to the bar, bought a couple drinks, got a table where a waiter or waitress would take care of us after this. A table far from other people.

"Man," I said, looked across the table at her. "Not usually here at night. Gets crowded."

"It's Friday. You still looking for work?"

"Oh, that." I drank, switched my focus back. "What you got?"

"Depends what kind of work you want."

"The violent kind."

"You answer like that, I don't know what to say."

"Try yes or no. I mean, you done somethin' too." Might as well be direct. She had something or she didn't.

"I just…" She shook her head, frowned. "It's personal."

"Yeah?" I smiled. "You got caught doin' what?"

"Nothing. A friend of mine was staying with me. They said I was harboring a fugitive."

Sounded like she protected a boyfriend. Also, didn't sound like the full story. Worked for me. I just had to be the next boyfriend.

"So," I said, "what's the job?"

"It isn't savory. I should shut up."

"I'm not savory. You need a guy dead?"

"Jesus, no," she said, nodding her head the whole time. "I mean, that's illegal."

"Depends on the price. But I thought this was a date."

"It *was*. You weren't supposed to say yes. To *that*."

"What was I supposed to say yes to? A threat? Was this ever a date?"

"A date," she said. "Yes. Forget what I said. Tell me about you."

"I'm a guy looking for work. What you want to know? I told you what I'm willing to do."

"I don't know what I want." She looked on the verge of tears.

I was glad it was a private table.

"I want work. What unsavory thing you got in mind?"

"Nothing like murder," she said.

"So, it's easy."

"Jesus. No!"

"What then?"

She talked softer. "My brother works for the city. There's a guy wants his job. Has qualifications. Needs dissuading."

"That involve chemicals?"

"No! Christ."

"What's he need?"

"Dissuasion."

"Okay," I said, "you're hot as hell and if this job pays I'm into it, but could you tell me what you want me to do?"

"This man…he lies. He lies about my brother. I know it's politics, but he gets personal."

"You want me to shut him up. How much?"

. . .

It was enough, to cover my gambling tab and then some. I've heard that phrase, 'more than enough,' like in football when someone gets a first down and the announcer says, 'more than a first down,' and I wonder. Can't be more than a first down or more than enough, can it? And now I'm thinking how do I shut this guy up short of killing him? Not what I do, really. Also, not how a guy shuts up. Man gets info, he could talk about it any time. Death sentence. Fine with me. Only she ain't paying enough for a hit. And if the guy died, she'd know who did it.

It seemed like I always got hired by someone who thought they was better than me. Catalina, though, she liked me. Sure, she couldn't do the work herself; no one who hired ever could, that's why they spent the money. That's fine, I'm a pro. It's money well spent.

The work I did had to be subtle. Not in the results, only how I did it. Can't just walk up and punch a guy. There's other ways to talk a man into shit, ways where I wouldn't get caught. I never got caught, not lately.

So, I had to keep this asshole alive. Scare him into silence. I knew his name, Burke Cummings, and had a photo cut carefully from a newspaper. Who the hell names their kid Burke? No wonder he grew up fucked. And now he was laying how fucked he was on Catalina's brother, Lou Novelo. Maybe I could straighten him out with a talk. I gave Catalina my number, told her to have Lou give me a call. Then we got to the part where we had a good time drinking and she relaxed a little. I walked her home and kissed her goodnight on her doorstep. I felt her eyes on my back as I walked away.

• • •

When I gave her my number, she gave me hers. She was young and pretty and probably wanted to play it safe, but she also wanted to have fun. I was okay with that. For now, I had to wait for her brother's call. I waited at home with a six pack and a fifth and was halfway sloshed by the time he called.

"Is this Pete?" he asked.

"Lou?"

"Yeah."

"You guys Italian or what?"

"Hispanic. Why?"

"Curious. Don't care. Who do you work for and where?"

"Finance. I work for the Department of Finance."

"Cummings work there too?"

"Yes. He's my chief assistant."

"And he wants your job."

"Seems that way."

"Seems that way? Your sister says he's lying his way to the top."

"I'm hardly the top."

"You run the department?"

"Yes, but…"

"You're in charge of the city's money! You don't see that as important?"

"Of course it's important, but…"

"Arrange a meeting," I said. "Just you and him. And me. You explain I'm an outside observer, excuse yourself. When the meeting's done, I let you know."

"Catalina said you were a mite unsavory."

"Unsavory gonna save your ass, son. I assume you're footing the bill. Just don't short me."

• • •

The meeting was scheduled for two "working" days later, after lunch, meaning two o'clock Tuesday. Cushy lunch break in the Finance Department. I guessed this fuck could afford me. Anyway, I needed money and I wanted to impress his sister. A man's needs.

We met in a small room, me and Lou and Burke. I wore a t-shirt, jeans, a leather jacket. The other two were dressed in suits, complete with ties. Never saw the point of those, any of it. I was standing in a corner when Burke walked in.

He didn't see me at first, then looked surprised. "What's this?"

"An outside observer," Lou said. "Now, if you'll excuse me a minute." He stepped outside, shut the door behind him.

"Wait."

"Shut up." I stepped to Burke. "Sit down."

He sat, behind Lou's desk. "You can't do this. He works for the city. He can't do this."

"Do what? He thought you should hear from an outsider. Reckon I'm as outside as they get."

"You're not dressed like someone who should be here."

"You understand what outside means, right? Means I ain't got a job. Not like you. When I work, I *work*. When I play, I play. Maybe I get them confused sometimes."

"I'm calling security."

"What you gonna say? You're stuck talking to someone your boss said you should?"

"This feels like a threat." There was a button on the desk. He pressed it, kept his hand on it. I tore the hand away.

"What the fuck you do?"

"You're about to find out."

I stepped around the desk, stood over him, arms at my sides, fists clenched. "They gonna laugh at you."

"You're a threat."

"Got no weapons. Nobody here but me."

"Shit," he said.

"Told ya they'd laugh. I'm an observer. Observing you fall apart."

There was a pounding on the door.

"Come in," I shouted, but they were already in. They charged, pushed me against the wall, patted me down hard, ankles to armpits, smacked me everywhere on the way.

The guy who frisked me turned to his superior, shrugged.

"What's this about?" the security chief asked.

"He—he—threatened me."

"How?" I said. "Lou asked me in here to observe a meeting, thought I'd enjoy it, stepped out a minute and this guy panics."

"He threatened me!"

"With what?" the security guy asked.

"He threatened me." It sounded feeble this time.

The security chief turned to me. "You have credentials?"

"Lou's a friend. I need credentials for that? Get him, he's probably in the toilet or getting coffee."

They tracked him down, were assured I was fine. He asked them out of the room, left me and Burke alone.

Alone with Burke was all I wanted. Until I was alone with Catalina.

"You don't know what a threat feels like," I said. "Wanna find out, keep up the bullshit. Then I get another call. And you don't complain no more."

"That's a threat."

"No sir, that ain't nothin' but a promise. A guarantee of satisfaction. From the person who calls."

"This is bullshit." He started past me.

My left arm rifled out in front of his neck. "Careful. Almost an accident there."

"You're a nobody. I won't be muscled."

"No, you won't. Not in this office. Not where no one sees. You stop lying about Novelo, you're in the clear."

"You're nothing but a damned thug."

If he was trying to insult me, he had a long way to go. He shook like he was cold, pulled his coat tight.

"Nah," I said. "A thug would start with a punch to your gut. Then he'd keep going. If they ever found you, you'd be in the river. Me, I'm walking out of this office. Going on a date tonight. You got your decisions. Tell ya one thing. A corpse don't lie. And I could use another paycheck."

• • •

Had a nice night Tuesday, but it ended with kisses at Catalina's doorstep again. Thursday night I got a call from her. She asked for my address, said she'd be right over.

"Gimme a half hour." I got into the shower, wanted to be clean for this. Get clean first, get dirty later. Body clean, mind filthy, I waited and wondered why this meeting was at my place instead of hers. Maybe she had a roommate. This job was about to pay off in every way I'd hoped.

She arrived and I waved her to a seat on the couch. That was it for furniture, the couch, a coffee table in front of it where I ate when I ate at home. Didn't come up much, I wasn't no cook.

She looked around, saw the kitchen and living room, plus the hall that led to the bathroom and bedroom.

"You keep it sparse," she said.

"Don't need much." I stood across from her. "Ain't here much. Want a beer?"

She shook her head, dropped a large envelope on the table. "You did a good job. That's your payment. We'll let you know if we need anything else."

I was at the fridge, beer in hand when her words registered. "What's that mean?"

"If we need anything, you'll hear from us. Might be me, but the message will be from Lou."

"What about us?"

She stood, stepped to the door, me right behind her.

She turned around slow, faced me. "There is no us. If you dreamed one, hope you enjoyed the dream."

I grabbed her by the elbow. "You don't use me like that. You can't use me like that."

Her other hand stuck a pistol in my gut. "Back up. Farther. You helped Lou. He appreciates that. *We* appreciate that. Don't mistake what is for what you want it to be. Good night, Pete."

She opened the door and stepped out. One thing I knew was real, that pistol. I wasn't eager to learn about reality. I took my beer to the couch, sat and drank. She used me. Used me to do what she couldn't, what she was too clean for. I opened the envelope, let the bills fall on the table. I counted it, separated two large from the rest. I'd make a call tomorrow, straighten my account and place some bets.

Then I'd hit the bars looking for a job again.

CROSSEYED AND PAINLESS

by Kimberly Godwin

A lone black Crown Victoria passed through the gloaming over crumbling pavement past decaying brick houses with rotten boards nailed across broken windows. Buildings twisted and contorted into distorted shapes within the dense fog. The car passed garbage-strewn sidewalks as red and blue light signaled through a haze of grey. The colored lights of the public service vehicles grew brighter as the Crown Victoria emerged from the gloom.

Lucy looked upward as she parked her unmarked car along the road. *The broken windows remind me of eyes leering down.* She shook her head and pushed through a crowd of uniformed officers and reporters.

"It's right here, detective," an unfamiliar male officer with a raspy voice waved her over to a roped-off area to the left of the road.

Lucy stopped long enough to sign the scene log, glancing curiously toward the officer. *Did Felix get a new partner?* She passed under the crime scene tape. In the shadow of a dilapidated rowhouse, she saw a ring of four blue-jacketed crime scene technicians. The murmurs of conversation and radio chatter echoed between camera flashes. The din made the alley feel smaller.

The technicians crouched and chattered around a dull green dumpster with flaking paint, documenting the scene as other officers moved around the area. A gaunt, Caucasian man with thinning brown hair lay crumpled in a stinking heap of blood, piss, and rotting garbage. Lucy swallowed, covering her nose and mouth with her hand.

The realization of the victim's identity clashed against her memory of a handsome man with laughter in his vivid green eyes. Her throat tightened as she tried to speak, unable to look away from the ruin of her lover.

"Why the hell was Scott out here?"

"Getting stabbed by the look of it," Sergeant Felix shrugged, appearing from Lucy's right. Lucy scowled. Felix made a placating gesture. "No offense, Detective Martel. He just hasn't been the same since the Mare case."

Lucy's hands tensed into fists at her sides as she took a deep breath. She unflexed her hands. *Calm down, Luce. Felix didn't do this.* "What do you mean?" Her voice was sharper than she intended.

"I thought you'd know better than anyone." Felix raised a knowing brow before he continued. "I guess you haven't been keeping track since you two aren't partners anymore. The Mare case shook Huxley. Many folks can't sleep after something like that without help from their old friends, Jack and Jim." He made a drinking gesture with his right hand to emphasize his point. "It's a damn shame too. Scott was a great cop."

Scott was. Not Scott is.

"Speaking of partners, where's yours?" Lucy snapped.

Felix raised a confused brow. "Mags? She's over there, knocking on doors with the other half of the night squad."

"So, who was that man with the chain-smoking habit that called me over?"

"I don't know anyone on the squad that fits that description." Felix shrugged. "You sure it wasn't a reporter?"

Lucy's nose wrinkled. "Maybe." She shook her head. "Not important. You're saying the Mare case drove Scott to this?"

Fragments of information about the grisly case came back in bursts from the news footage: a triple homicide and a teddy bear on its side in a scattering of broken glass streaked with crimson. She looked at Felix, unwilling to continue staring at Scott's body.

"He was on a leave of absence. If he's out here, the alcohol and the prescriptions weren't enough." Felix shook his head, wiping his hands on his pants. "Look, if you don't mind me saying it, Detective Martel, I know you two used to be *close*." The tone of his voice carried an unspoken accusation. "Weren't you the reason Scott's marriage failed?"

"Excuse me?" Lucy interjected, her face suddenly hot.

Felix continued, "Pass this off to someone else without emotional stakes and spare yourself. There are a ton of people working on this. No one would blame you if you said no. Do you want to remember him like this?"

Even if he's an asshole, he's right. No one would blame me for not wanting to work on this murder case. Lucy shifted under Felix's judgmental stare. Her eyes flicked away from him to the mossy and broken brick buildings. *No neighbors are crowding to gawk. Only Scott's co-workers are bearing witness to his miserable end. A horrible conclusion to a good detective's life.* Her gaze returned to Scott's body. Dirty, torn clothes hung limply from his uncharacteristically thin frame. She let out a deep breath, loosening the knot that formed in her chest. She pulled a pair of latex gloves from her pocket, sliding her hands into them. "No, I owe him and his family to take care of this."

. . .

Tick, tick, tick.

Each tick of the analog clock on the wall grew louder in the sudden stillness of Lucy's office. The desks on either side of her cubicle stood empty beyond the scatterings of humanity that decorated the desks: framed photos of spouses, children, and pets amongst organized stacks of papers and blank computer monitors. Everything was in its place, even her. She pressed her hands against her face to block out the grisly images of the victim's—Scott's—body at the crime scene from four angles on her desk. She sniffed, lowering her hands to lift her coffee mug to her lips. Bitter, tepid coffee coated her tongue.

"Why is it cold already? I just poured this," she muttered as she glanced up to her clock. It was almost seven. She blinked. She'd left the scene around three o'clock and made the notification calls while waiting for the photos. The details and time had slipped away as she held herself together. *I'm not sure what's worse, all the damn strategy meetings or the sympathy. I'm tired of hearing how strong I am. I don't know why they all thought that Scott and I were still together.*

A knock interrupted Lucy's thoughts. "Hey, I know it's not your thing anymore… but do you want to grab a drink?" Violet smiled warmly from the office doorway. She wore a pair of blue jeans and an oversized off-shoulder sweater. Her dark wavy hair hung loosely on her tanned shoulders. "I know you've had a rough day. Just take a break for the night and relax a bit. What do you say?"

Lucy looked between the case file on her desk and the coffee mug in her trembling hand. "Sure, give me a few minutes to put this away."

"Great. It's a bit late for happy hour, but I know a great spot. Have you had anything besides coffee and donuts?" Violet folded her arms and remained at the door. Lucy suspected Violet was unwilling to see Scott's crime scene photos. "I know you two stopped dating…." Violet hesitated before finishing her thought. "But did you call Amelia about her dad?"

Lucy took a deep breath, forcing down the memory of Amelia's sobs. She refused to meet Violet's eyes, answering in a forced, neutral tone. "Just coffee. And Amelia's a mess. She wants my help going through Scott's things." Lucy swiped the photos into a neat pile before shuffling them into a folder. Lucy's gaze lingered on a picture on her desk of her, Scott, and a younger Amelia in her graduation cap and gown.

"When was the last time Amelia came home from college?"

"I think it was around the fourth of July." Lucy closed the manila folder, sliding it into a drawer.

"What about Bella? Did you manage to get her on the phone?"

"No, I don't know if she has the station number blocked, but I didn't get through." Lucy shook her head. "I left her a voicemail to call me back."

"As horrible as it is to say, I don't think Bella will be that torn up about Scott. They parted on bad terms," Violet commented softly. Lucy felt a jab of guilt at the comment. "Come on, let's get you out of here so you can relax."

"It's suspicious that I can't reach her." Lucy grabbed her purse and moved away from her desk towards the door. She noticed something move out at the edge of her vision and glanced to see the frame fall. *I must've jostled the desk.*

"We're cops," Violet said. "We make more enemies than friends. I wouldn't pin this on Scott's ex-wife just yet."

• • •

It had taken all Lucy's concentration not to scream all day at work. She wanted to be anything but composed. Drinking with Violet earlier loosened the reins on her self-control. She'd been strong with Violet, but alone, everything felt too raw. Cool porcelain pressed against Lucy's hands as she steadied herself over the bathroom sink, choking back sobs. *Ground yourself, Lucy, just like your therapist said. You're not off the wagon for this.* Lucy hazily focused on her body—how her eyes were hot and dry despite the dampness on her cheeks. Her blurry reflection showed her a version of herself with puffy and blotchy skin with darkening bags under swollen eyes as tears rolled down her cheeks.

"Are you okay?" The phantom of Violet asked sweetly against her ear. The alluring spice of Violet's perfume with an undertone of jasmine caressed the curve of Lucy's cheek.

"No, I'm not fucking okay," Lucy admitted in a hoarse whisper. It was the answer she should've told Violet but couldn't in the crowded bar. People came to Detective Martel for help, and now she stood alone in her moment of need. She splashed cold water against her face to wash away the burden of grief.

"Lucy, don't do this to yourself."

Lucy closed her eyes at the sound of Scott's dulcet baritone behind her. She froze as a weight settled on her right shoulder.

"I should've known. I should've helped you." Lucy didn't open her eyes, wanting to stay in the dream a little longer.

Strong, calloused hands slid down over her arms into a loose embrace. "You don't even know why I was out in the Bricks. How would knowing I was depressed help?" He gently scolded her, the way he always used to. "What thoughts are running through your head?"

"Someone stabbed you. People only go to the Bricks for drugs. There's nothing else if you have a place to go."

"That's what you want to believe? Without looking at the toxicology report, you've already shut the case. I became a drug addict and died in a pool of my filth?"

Lucy shook her head. "No. It's not that."

"Then what, Lucy? It's just us here. You can tell me," Scott whispered.

"It just doesn't feel right."

"It's a murder. When does it ever?" He scoffed. "You know better. Work it through."

"A resident from the slums discovered you while walking his dog." Lucy stared at the darkness beyond her closed eyelids and focused on what she knew about the Bricks.

The old brick downtown district was the city's heart until a new state highway shifted everything away. In its dying gasps, the local business owners appealed to the commercial developers to revitalize the area with affordable housing, bistros, and high-end nightclubs, but it was all for naught. Decay seeped into the pores of the ancient brick and infected everything around it. Businesses closed, buildings were condemned, and even graffiti artists had forsaken the Bricks' crumbling and moss-covered walls for better canvases. "No buses stop in the slums. Your car was at the station. I'll have to see if you took a taxi or Uber."

Her memory focused on the beginning of the crime scene; deep red trails dripped on the broken pavement for several blocks, progressing deeper into old downtown. "Someone stabbed you, and you ran." The path smeared as it led into a large pothole with bloody handprints at the edge. "You fell." Lucy saw the droplets continue until they stopped ten feet from the dumpster before turning into a smear. Lucy opened her mouth and shut it again.

"Ah, you're getting it. What's missing?"

"Footprints." Lucy opened her eyes. "All that blood, there should be footprints." She blinked at the shape of the sink and rubbed her eyes. "…This isn't my bathroom." Barren yellowed walls with a cracked off-white basin below a dirty mirrored cabinet offered her no hints. *Violet took me home. I'm sure of it.* A thud outside the door made her jump, her hand grabbing at empty air beside her right hip for her service pistol. Her back pressed against the edge of the porcelain.

Lucy's heart thudded loudly as panic coiled in her stomach; breathing became difficult. *Calm down.* She turned back to the mirror, meeting her gaze. *There might be an answer to who's outside in this cabinet. Maybe I picked up a guy after I got home.* Taking another breath with a trembling hand, Lucy opened the cupboard. A thin tube of toothpaste, a yellowed bristle red-handled toothbrush, and a couple of bottles sat on three shelves. She pulled an orange bottle free to read the label. She gasped, throwing the bottle into the basin as if it had burned her. *How?* She stared down at the label bearing the name Scott Huxley.

Bottle in hand, Lucy slowly opened the bathroom door, peering into the darkened apartment. The scent of cool, musty air with an undercurrent of mold and something metallic greeted her. She squinted into the shadows beyond the yellow light of the doorway, searching for movement but finding only stillness. She shivered as she crept forward. *I don't remember Scott's bathroom looking like that. If this is his house, the door should be over here.*

Sharp jabs of pain radiated up her leg as she knocked her shin. Lucy clenched her teeth, reaching out to stabilize herself and identify the object she had collided with. Her fingers swept over a sharp corner and stopped at the smooth edge. *A lamp?* She groped for the switch and winced as the light came on.

Lucy blinked as her living room came into focus. She spun, returning to the bathroom. Familiar colors and items replaced the strange place she had left before. The barren and cracked basin was replaced with a grey basin below a mirrored cabinet with a small bamboo plant mounted to the wall beside it. *What? I... how?* She rubbed her eyes, dropping the bottle to the floor. Lucy watched it roll to a stop against an unfamiliar boot. Her gaze followed the length of the leg up. Her eyes went wide as she screamed.

. . .

"I'm telling you, Violet, it wasn't a dream! Look at the bottle! It says his name!" Lucy pleaded as she sat next to Violet on her couch. She shivered despite the combined warmth of her living room and the blanket wrapped around her.

Violet placed her hands over Lucy's with a sympathetic smile. "You've had a fright. We couldn't find the bottle or signs of a break-in."

"You have to believe me."

"I think you're reasonably upset and had too much to drink while you were with me. Do you want me to stay, or do you feel safe enough to stay here alone?" Violet gave Lucy's hands a reassuring squeeze. "It's a hard case. Everyone's got eyes on this. It's a lot of pressure, but you don't have to take it."

"No. I'm not giving up on this. I just started. I… I'm not crazy."

"No one said that." Violet's voice softened as she met Lucy's gaze. "I never said that you were."

Were her eyes always so green? They're almost the same shade as Scott's. Lucy blushed, looking away. "I just had a bad night. Tomorrow will be better. It's a lot to take in." She withdrew her hand with an embarrassed smile. "I'll be okay. I just need some sleep."

Violet tilted her head with a short nod. "I'm here for you, Lucy. Don't let this get into your head."

• • •

Lucy stared at a picture on her phone of her and Scott. *I know why I heard you, Scott. But who was that I saw? Was that who killed you?* She tried to recall the face of the man she saw but couldn't focus on his features. *It was all so real. It couldn't have been a dream. Could it? What does it all mean?* The phone fell, landing on her chest. She pressed her hands against her face trying to focus.

It's like Scott's trying to work the case with me. Lucy pursed her lips together with an aggravated sigh. "Let me sleep, and I can solve this with a clearer head, Scott."

She turned on her side, closing her eyes. *Why were you there?*

"You need to see," Scott whispered.

The wind howled and rattled the windows. Lucy shivered, reaching for her covers. She groggily woke. *Did I kick the blankets off?* A sudden whiff of brick dust and rot filled her nostrils, snapping her back to alertness. She looked down at herself, clad not in her nightclothes but wearing jeans and a jacket. Uneven pavement smeared with a dark, foreboding stain led into the shadows. *Why am I in the Bricks? Am I dreaming?* A pitch-black sky with a thin crescent moon shone down on looming brick buildings, cast murky grey in the moonlight.

"Scott, did you bring me here?" Lucy knelt and touched the edge of the stain, rubbing rocky coppery-smelling muck between her fingers. *Blood?* She wiped it on a tissue from her pocket and rose again. *What do I need to see?* She scanned the ground, following the trail into the pothole. Lucy imagined Scott's frantic flight down the road, the splatter's zig-zagging path, and the bloody handprints on the pothole's edge. She frowned, continuing from the pothole to where they found Scott.

Lucy's footsteps echoed against the decaying brick. She scanned boarded-up storefronts and broken windows that bore witness with blinded eyes. The hair rose on Lucy's neck as she drew closer to the rowhouse beside the alley where Scott had died. She shifted, pulling her jacket tighter around her to ward off the chill. Yellow police tape flapped noiselessly in the breeze around the crime scene. She ducked under it, taking slow, measured breaths as she stopped in front of the dumpster. Lucy remembered the position of Scott's body on the ground. She rubbed her chin. *I already saw this part. You want me to focus on what I didn't see. Where were you going?*

A clunking noise disturbed the silence. Lucy looked toward the rowhouse in time to see someone disappear through the doorway. *You were trying to get inside this house. Why?* Lucy ascended the crumbling staircase, her breath freezing in soft puffs. A rotten door splashed with what Lucy hoped was dried red paint stood closed beneath a greying archway. She listened for noises, only hearing her rapid heartbeat and uneven breathing. *Wasn't this boarded up before?*

Lucy reached for her gun and once again found only her hip. *Right. I didn't dream that I had left the house with my gun. I don't like this. But if I don't follow this lead, I might never know.* Drawing herself taller, Lucy pushed the door open with a creak, slipping inside with one final glance over her shoulder.

• • •

"What kept you?"

Scott smiled at Lucy from the seat of a torn brown sofa. Slivers of moonlight peeked through holes in the discolored boards over the broken windows of the living room. The woody scent of Scott's sandalwood and cedar cologne mingled with the stench of decaying wood and mildew as Lucy stared at him. Scott was as gaunt and pale as she'd seen him outside, but wearing his favorite dark grey suit—the one Amelia decided to bury him in. He patted the empty seat beside him. "Come, we should catch up."

Lucy swallowed. Her heart pounded in her throat. The way he smiled made her eyes tear up. "This is ridiculous. Why are you here?" she managed.

"You're looking for me."

"I'm looking for your murderer." Lucy squinted into the darkness beyond, avoiding meeting Scott's gaze. "If you're going to haunt me, give me a hint."

"He was right about you, you know." Scott grinned, reclining against the couch.

"What does that mean?" Lucy asked. Scott kept on grinning but offered no explanations. She moved through the living room, dodging around the debris on the floor to peer into the kitchen. She grimaced and covered her nose. "Christ. Something died in here." She stood at the end of the couch. "No offense."

"None taken." Scott chuckled. "You figure it out yet?"

"Aside from someone chasing you down before you could get inside this dump, no." Lucy scowled with a shake of her head. "I don't know too many detectives that can solve a murder like this in the first few hours. No witnesses. No prints or blood other than the victim's. You're a divorcee cop. There are lots of motives to take you out."

Lucy thought back to how she came on the scene. The crowd,

and then the person that called her over. *Come to think of it, I didn't hear that one officer's voice again. I can't place him.* Just like the figure in her apartment. She pursed her lips together, trying to recall the face of the man she saw staring at her with such menace that she screamed. She rubbed her arms in a soothing gesture, finally looking at Scott.

"I'm sorry. I wasn't there when you needed me. But I didn't do anything to deserve this. Why are you torturing me like this?"

"Because you're here now. Sit down. If you're dreaming, you have time." The warmth in Scott's voice didn't reach his eyes. Cold and detached, it all felt wrong. "At long last, we have all the time in the world."

"No. You're dead, and I still have a life to live. Let me move on."

I'm talking to a ghost. I need to wake up. Lucy pinched the back of her hand, feeling the sharp sensation. She blinked. The dilapidated living room remained before her. Scott sat on the sofa, looking less jovial. "I'm not dreaming." Lucy took a few steps back into the wall. The surface gave way, pulling her backward in a rain of rotten plaster, wallpaper, and roaches. She fought back a scream as she scrambled to her feet, knocking away bugs. *Get out of here!*

In the room, Scott bellowed. "You can't leave! We're not done yet!"

Her heart sank into her stomach as the sounds of his yelling brought back bad memories of whiskey-soaked nights she regretted. They both were too nasty to one another when they drank. She broke the vicious cycle once, and she would do it again.

"We broke up for this exact reason! It's over!" Lucy ripped herself free of the rotting wall and frantically darted towards the door. She yanked on the doorknob only to have it fall at her feet. Lucy stared in disbelief, kicking the door to open it. She shivered as the room darkened behind her. She didn't look back, focusing on breaking the door to get out.

"It's right here, detective." A raspy voice whispered in her ear.

Lucy instinctively lashed out to defend herself and spun, hitting empty air. Something grabbed her by the shoulders and slammed her back against the door. Putrid breath sneered in her face, making her gag as she gasped for breath. "I've been waiting for you."

Lucy stared into rage-filled, malicious green eyes bearing down on hers. She couldn't identify any other features in the dark; the more she focused on the man's face, the harder it became to breathe. She futilely kicked at him as his weight bore down on her, pinning her to the wall.

"What… are… you?!"

"The truth."

His voice echoed with a buzzing and chittering. Lucy's head swam as jagged teeth emerged from an ever-widening maw. Unable to resist, Lucy fell into the gaping abyss.

● ● ●

Violet held her face as she slumped against a wall. Officers held back a crowd of onlookers outside the apartment complex. Yellow crime scene tape and sawhorses marked a border in front of a broken glass door. The world was suddenly too loud. Voices melded into the clattering of lights, distant sirens, and cameras clicking.

"Coffee?" Felix's voice was soft as he offered Violet a paper cup. Violet pressed her hands against her neck, noticing how pale and exhausted he looked. She took the cup into her hands with a soft smile.

"Thanks. What do you make of it?" Violet held the cup, absorbing its warmth. She closed her eyes. The images of what lay in the lobby assaulted her. A trail of blood and shards of glass stopped before the elevator doors. A service revolver and three spent brass casings lay in a crimson pool, just out of reach of Lucy's hand. "It never ends" was scrawled in blood beside Lucy's lifeless body against the wall, covered with the gore of an exit head wound.

Did Lucy think someone was attacking her? I shouldn't have left Lucy alone. Why did you end up like this, Lucy? Was Scott's death too much? Did you do this to yourself, or did someone execute you? Violet sniffed, rubbing tears from her cheeks as she looked at Felix.

Felix turned his patrol cap once in his hands before returning it to his head. "The things we see… the places we go. Sometimes, something just crawls inside you. The more you fight it, the more it lashes out."

Violet frowned. "She's right, you know."

"Who is?"

Violet looked between Felix and her friend's body. "Lucy. She wrote it on the floor. It never ends. We scratch and dig for the facts, looking for someone to blame. But that's the thing, isn't it? The truth distorts and twists the more invested we are in a moment. It's the memory of what was that kills us." She sighed, staring into Lucy's lifeless eyes. "But we can't arrest ghosts."

GIRLFRIEND IS BETTER

by J.B. Stevens

Kristi reclined in the dormant basement sauna. How much time had passed since it was warm? How long can an unused thing exist without heat until it could never warm again? She hovered in the still space, the sound of the machines churning soiled linens her only companion as she sparked the lighter and sucked on the bong, the green glass familiar in her hands. The scent of burning weed overpowered the odor of dried cedar. Smoke wrapped her in her own private universe and she floated back to mama's trailer, the dirt, the kids at school laughing, the hunger, the rough hands, the stinking breath of the boyfriends sneaking into her room, the shame. The shame crept in on the edges, always waiting.

An organic sound filtered into her rough wood sanctuary and her universe imploded into a black hole. She sighed, set aside the bong, and cracked the door.

Her husband Damon stood there in the billowing smoke, looking like a disappointed owner attempting to train a naughty puppy. Kristi's heart rate spiked.

Damon's delicate hand materialized through the haze. The sight of the knuckles assailed her brain with unwelcome memories and she leaned back.

Damon's overcultured voice sliced through the murk. "In here? Again?"

Kristi shoved the recollection of the fist out of her mind. "Where else would I be?"

"We're onstage in an hour," Damon said.

"I know."

Damon frowned. "Did you put on the damn outfit yet?"

"No. I'm not for sale and don't like dressing like I am."

Damon exhaled and pinched the bridge of his nose. "It's called showmanship. Giving the crowd what they want." He shook his head. "What's the point of talking about this? You're baked out of your mind. We both know, that when the time comes, you're doing exactly as I say."

"Maybe one day I won't."

Damon raised his hand.

Adrenaline surged through Kristi's veins. "Do it."

Damon lowered his arm. "I won't, never again. You know how much I care about you. You know I hate what you make me do."

"I know you'd care about what would happen if I posted the aftermath on Instagram."

His eyes narrowed. "That's not the reason I— I love you and want you to be happy. And you love me."

"Maybe I just love not being poor."

"Fine, love that, but don't forget who made *that* happen."

"Never will." Kristi sparked the wheel on her little pink disposable lighter and the flame cast deep shadows in the dim space.

Damon pushed a strand of dyed black hair behind a pierced ear. He looked her up and down and his eyes narrowed. "We're a team. You need to lay off the weed. We're better, you're better than that. You're above it. You represent me. I dragged you out of that hovel and taught you to be a person. You're my most important illusion. How the hell did you regress so far?"

Kristi shrugged. "You started it."

"I gave you one joint, to help with nerves, that's hardly..." Damon motioned his hands up and down. "This."

"You pushed me to smoke. Now you're mad I smoke?"

"I pushed you in the direction I thought would allow you to control your emotions. I didn't realize marijuana would become your entire personality."

She shrugged. "I had a tough childhood."

"Cry about it. We all did. My entire existence was a tornado until I took control."

"I read your book."

"And you know the hole I crawled out of. Discipline is how a person finds happiness. Control is the key."

"Control is a myth." Kristi released the lighter's plunger and her green eyes disappeared. "Things have a tendency to play out in unexpected ways."

"You could not be more wrong," Damon said. "It always works out exactly as I intend."

"Whatever you say." She held out the bong and sparked the lighter. "You want a hit off Jerry?"

"You named your bong?"

"With how much time I spend sucking on him, it felt right."

Damon smacked Jerry to the ground, and he exploded into a million specks of emerald glitter, and the flame went out. Sound echoed off the wooden walls and the noise made her think of the Fourth of July and an Alice Coltrane album. She re-sparked the lighter and broken glass twinkled and she imagined a sober day with Damon. Her mouth went desert-dry and the Grand Canyon opened in her soul. The chasm was too wide. She reached under the towel and pulled out her small pipe.

Damon smirked. "You have a backup?"

"I'm all about controlling my situation. I learned from the best." She took a delicious pull. "This one's named Garcia."

"You deserve a hard smack across the face."

"Maybe. But you're too much of a pussy to do it again."

"No. I'm too in control to do it again."

"A real tough guy until you have to deal with the consequences."

"Lucky you—I don't want to be some thug's pincushion in lockup." Damon stepped backward.

"Being screwed when you don't feel like being screwed is just about the worst thing in the world, isn't it?"

"Spare me the pity party. Enough of your games. Trina's picking us up in ten."

"I'll be ready before you can say abracadabra."

"Witty." Damon slammed the door.

Kristi raised her middle finger and yelled into the wood. "Copperfield is twice the magician you are!"

The door jerked open. Damon's eyes were slits and his nostrils flared. "What did you say?"

"Nothing. Let's pretend it never happened."

"You mean like the prenup?"

Gunshots went off in Kristi's mind. "What?"

Damon winked. "It's out. I had it taken care of."

"Neither one of us filed for divorce… How is it out? Who was even looking at it?"

"You know how I love that control. I had my lawyer take a peek. Since the original was never notarized, and it was done at home, with just you and I, it's really nothing more than a piece of paper. It could've been created by anyone, at any time, an easy forgery."

"But it's not a forgery. You made me sign it."

"Maybe I did, maybe I didn't. And maybe, the terms were too generous, and it is time for us to renegotiate."

"Are you serious?"

"I am. You've been far too uppity since that night in jail. Control. I'm taking it back."

The door flew inward, and the wind hit her, and the wooden cocoon shook, and the walls started closing in and everything was too heavy.

Kristi held Garcia up to her mouth and whispered into the opening, "*We're going for a ride again*," and she sparked the lighter and found exactly what she was looking for.

. . .

The Golden Palm was a second-rate casino housing a third-rate stage on a fourth-rate street—five blocks off the Vegas Strip. The place smelled of old booze, cigarette smoke, and poor choices. Zombie grandmas shoved nickels into slot machines that were on their last legs when Regan was president. Old men with bloodshot eyes and craggy faces sat at the sportsbook sipping domestic beer delivered by fifty-six-year-old cocktail waitresses.

Trina sighed and walked to the theater off the main gambling floor. She entered the show's space and moved to the back of the stage. She adjusted the jade velvet bows in her red hair and a strand fell and floated in front of her left eye, next to the nostril. Coconut shampoo, a gift from Kristi, tickled Trina's nose. She dug her nails into the clipboard, stepped behind the curtain, and gaped at the twisted steel monstrosity—the Fire Lotus. It set her teeth on edge. Death on wheels. Damon's pride. The heat, the explosion, the power, an orange and red spectacle of risk. She turned from the lotus to Kristi, dark and lithe and supple. Kristi was Trina's reason for dealing with all the crap. The reason butterflies danced in her stomach. For Trina's entire life, no one wanted to know her and now Kristi wanted to know everything. Kristi was worth it. A lifetime of loneliness gone in a blink. Kristi. Kristi. Whenever someone asked Trina why she still managed a washed-up hack like Damon. Trina pictured Kristi's lips and knew it was all worth it.

Trina looked to Kristi, seated in the beige metal folding chair. Damon stood to the right, in his well-tailored tuxedo. The garment was from Hong Kong, a quarter-century old, and far past its prime.

Damon turned to Trina and raised the corners of his mouth and she saw his idiotic veneers and her abdomen cramped.

"Alright, we need to go over—"

Damon raised his left palm. "I know. Stop."

"You asked me to remind you."

"And now I'm telling you to stop."

He adjusted the French cuffs and ran a hand over the eight-foot by eight-foot twisted mass of steel tubes, his modern-art-looking monstrosity, the Fire Lotus. The Lotus, not Damon, was pictured on the billboard outside the casino and yapped about on local radio. The Lotus, not Damon, brought in the fans. The Lotus, not Damon, was what paid the bills. It was the only bankable trick Damon had left. Trina had recently renewed the show's insurance policy, and the insurer said the trick was valued at one point five million dollars. Trina had read close. The policy was in Damon's name, and no one else's.

She sighed and massaged her temples. A grunt came and she looked up. Damon grasped the Lotus's support strut with his right hand and shook. The contraption didn't move.

He slithered into the center of the blossom and called to Trina. "Make sure no one is around. I'm going to check something."

Kristi lifted her head. "Why? No one has cared for a decade."

Damon grimaced. "You know what, Trina, stay right there. Kristi, take a lap, make sure no one is watching."

"Seriously?"

Damon crouched in the steel. "Don't forget who signs the checks."

"Never." Kristi stood, pulled on her white bathrobe, and did a lap around the perimeter of the rehearsal room. "You're clear, Sir." Kristi sat.

"Good girl, now go stand in the middle of the seating. Make sure I hit my marks. I'm going to do a dry run."

Kristi sighed and moved.

"Trina," Damon said, "You can leave. Now"

Trina looked at her clipboard. "But I'm your manager."

"Yeah, and I'm the boss, behind the curtain. Now."

Trina made eye contact with Kristi. Kristi smiled and nodded, and Trina's heart swelled, and she felt the warmth in her gut and did as she was told.

• • •

The curtain fell and Trina was gone, and Kristi sighed. Trina was simple and needy, and clingy, but at least she wasn't a snake. Trina was someone Kristi could trust. The curtain's ripple stopped, and she turned to Damon. "You could be a bit nicer to her."

Damon raised his left eyebrow. "For the last few months, you've been all about defending Trina. Are you two plotting on me?"

"Maybe, or maybe you're the type of person that is so offensive, defense is necessary."

Damon took a deep breath. "It's always something with you. Why are you still in the robe?"

"It's more comfortable," Kristi said.

"I prefer the costume," Damon said.

"The costume is sluttier than a sorority girl on Halloween."

"I prefer the costume."

"I'm too old for it."

"Take off the robe."

"The show isn't for two hours."

"Take off the robe."

"No."

"Yes. Now. I'm getting tired of all your crap and I'm about ready to cut my losses."

Kristi's skin went clammy and her arms were covered with goose pimples. She shut her eyes and gripped the fluffy terry cloth and slid out of the robe. She stood there in the too-tight, too-short, too-everything green velvet and timed slowed to the infinite.

"Good," Damon said. "Now put the robe back on."

Acid burned her gut. "Why'd you have me take it off just to have me put it back on?"

"To remind you who's the star and who's the help."

Kristi clenched her jaw and donned the robe.

Damon ran through the trick twice, fire-free. He stepped out of the Lotus and took a black Egyptian cotton towel from the back of a folding chair.

He wiped his face and hands. "I'm hungry."

"What do you want?"

"You know what I like. Be back in time for the show." Damon held out his credit card. "Also, this bill on this is getting too high. Slow it down."

She took the plastic. "We have plenty of money."

"I have plenty of money. You have me."

. . .

Trina sat outside the theater, watching the saddest of humanity flutter by like autumn leaves destined to rot on the forest floor. She heard the door open and turned and Kristi was there. They made eye contact and Kristi smiled, broad and white. Wind rushed through Trina's soul, and she looked down and away and turned red. Kristi walked over and they hugged, and electricity shot up Trina's spine and she tasted Kristi's strawberry lotion.

"Damon is ready for you to come back in for the last run through." Kristi's hot breath caressed Trina's ear. "I missed you."

Trina's nerves tingled and they went in. Trina sat in the front row.

Kristi strutted onstage, stopping stage left, next to a scarred and dented gray steel box. She leaned down and opened the squeaking lid and reached into the container and came up holding a bow and arrow. At the end of the arrow was a wadded lavender rag coated in fuming, petroleum-scented accelerant.

Damon was center stage, crouched under a black velvet cloak, the Lotus behind him.

Trina watched as Kristi arched her back, shoved her breasts out, and called to Damon. "Ready."

Damon jumped and shucked the cloak in a flowing ebony ripple. He stood, shirtless, glistening in fire-retardant grease that caught the light. Twenty years ago, he was the kind of man that belonged in front of a crowd bare-chested and oiled up. Now he was the kind of man that should be applying the grease while floating in the background.

"Children." David spread his arms wide to the imaginary crowd. "For, compared to me, you are all but children of the Lesser Gods. You are fortunate and you shall bear witness. There are few examples of true magic, true wonder, supernatural events—miraculous happenings—in this pathetic world. But you, dear watcher, get to observe one true miracle, here, today.

For twenty years false prophets and fake magicians have asked: 'How does he do it? What is the secret? What is the trick?'.

I am going to tell you the secret—there is no secret. The trick—there is no trick. I've tapped into something higher, something greater, something even I do not fully understand.

But I do know this one truth.

I am in control.

I.

Can.

Not.

Burn."

Damon snapped his fingers and the lights cut out and flashed back on and he was in the center of the Fire Lotus.

He pointed at Kristi. She pulled out her little pink disposable lighter and lit the rag. The end of the arrow burst into flames and heat waves shimmered. She drew back the bow and aimed at the lotus's base.

Damon turned to the phantom crowd. "You are human, as I was, once. However, I've evolved into something more."

He clapped his hands and the lights cut. Kristi released the arrow.

The Fire Lotus exploded in a ball of orange and red—a twenty-foot-high spectacle of flame. Heat undulated through the building on a kerosene-flavored wave.

The towering inferno quickly turned into a minor blaze. A

spotlight opened to a ledge on the balcony in the rear of the auditorium. A black velvet cloak covered a lump.

A crescendo of instrumental music rose and the fabric fell back and away. Damon exploded up—arms raised—a shirtless, greasy, fifty-seven-year-old man.

Trina walked onto the stage and stood next to Kristi.

Trina clapped. "How the hell does he do it?"

"I've figured it out," Kristi said.

"Seriously?"

"One night, after he got drunk, I came here, and I learned the trick's secret."

"Bold."

Kristi shrugged. "If we get divorced, I'm through. But, if something happens to him… it's all mine, the paid-off home, the Fire Lotus. And if it's mine, it's ours."

Trina's throat burned like she'd drank a shot of tequila. "I love you so much."

"I love you too. Now that I know how the Lotus works, I'm ready to ride off into the sunset. Are you serious about helping me escape and leaving together?"

"Of course." The burn intensified. "There is nothing I want more."

Kristi's lips became a thin straight line. "Say a magician who is in his late fifties, and has lost a step, lights himself on fire six nights a week. Would anyone be suspicious if the trick went sideways and the magician didn't make it?"

Trina closed her eyes and pinched the bridge of her nose. Her heart slammed against her ribs. "Holy hell, that is not a good idea."

Kristi leaned in close, lips brushing Trina's ear. "But what if?"

"He's your husband."

Kristi shrugged. "Yeah, but I got a girlfriend and you're better than him."

Trina's cheeks turned red, and she smiled.

• • •

Kristi clicked off the call with the insurance company; they made it so easy to change beneficiaries. It had not even required Trina's signature, just her passphrase, which Trina had been all too eager to share. If the worst happened it was all headed to one account: Kristi's.

Kristi gripped the steering wheel, turned left, shook her head, and turned left again. Driving in circles helped her come to her senses, sometimes. She fingered the cash and glided towards the Big 5 on Charleston Boulevard. It was on the wrong side of the intestate with the wrong kind of customer—the real Vegas everyone avoided.

She wore a pandemic mask, sunglasses, and a ball cap. She'd coated her fingertips in superglue to ensure she didn't leave any prints. Every nerve screamed in an explosion of sensation, the world a technicolor hellscape. The glue and smog and desert smells stewed together, so thick she could taste it. Her ears hummed with the sound of a thousand jet engines.

When she entered the store, her esophagus constricted, and her pulse thumped faster than a drummer on crystal meth. In the back, she found a small black plastic D-shaped carabiner—a little locking loop. She went to the register, paid with Trina's debit card, and gripped the receipt. Then she went outside.

Around the block and out of sight of the store, her senses dulled. The world's colors muted, and the sounds mellowed. She ripped off her mask and held the carabiner up to her face. The black plastic smelled like a child's toy, but not hers. There'd been no toys in her youth.

The carabiner was the solution.

Kristi called Trina.

"I'm ready," Kristi said.

"Why didn't you just text?" Trina asked.

"I prefer talking. Nothing is written down. I like the idea of the past being forgotten."

"With your upbringing… I guess that makes sense."

Kristi clicked off the call and put the phone in her pocket.

A car backfired and Kristi looked up. Trina clanked into the lot in her nineteen-ninety-something rust bucket truck, stopping next to Kristi.

Kristi slid in and handed over the locking plastic loop.

Trina held it up. "Are you sure this will work?"

Kristi nodded.

"Why plastic?" Trina asked.

"It will melt and there will be less evidence."

"Smart."

Kristi grinned. "I try to think of everything, see what's coming. Hand me your purse, you've got change."

Trina did.

Kristi took the bag. Her left hand inserted a few coins. Her right planted the carabiner receipt and replaced the stolen debit card.

Kristi handed back the purse. "Thanks babe, love you. Now, let me tell you about the Lotus's trap door."

• • •

Trina stood stage left behind the thick red curtain. It was musty and threadbare this close. Kristi was stage right, past the unlit Lotus holding her bow and flaming arrow in front of a wide-eyed crowd. Kristi looked like an avenging angel.

Damon extended his arms, dropped his black velvet cloak, and started his cheesy *I am a God* speech.

Trina felt ants crawling under her skin. She squinted, trying to see the carabiner holding the mesh trapdoor shut, but she couldn't make it out.

Damon snapped and the room was dark. Trina's lungs stopped

working. The lights flashed on, and Damon was in the center of the steel blossom, directly over the lump of plastic.

He roared. "You all are human. Behold, I've transitioned to a higher form."

The lights cut. Kristi shot the flaming arrow into the Lotus's base. The inferno roared, licking the ceiling twenty feet above. Hot wind caressed Trina's cheeks and a razor blade of pain sliced her gut.

The spotlight cut on and pointed at the balcony.

The center of the spotlight was empty. There was no lump of black velvet.

A wail erupted from the Lotus.

Kristi yelled, "Oh God! Call 911!" The flames undulated red and orange and the smell of roasted pork filled the venue.

A group of men materialized with fire extinguishers. The crowd screamed and the announcer asked everyone to stay still to ensure emergency medical staff could easily access the scene.

Kristi's hands shot to her mouth and she ran backstage to Trina.

Trina hugged Kristi and handed over the bag. "Your change of clothes."

Kristi wiped her face. "Thank you."

"That's a big grin," Trina said.

"It's over. I'm free," Kristi said.

"We're free."

"Of course, that's what I meant."

Flames reflected off Kristi's eyes, and she smiled.

• • •

Most Vegas nights were full of the day's losses and the empty sadness of a worse future, but not this night. Trina grinned. This was a winner's night, dry and dusty and delicious. Damon was gone and Kristi was rich, and Kristi was going to be with Trina forever, and the future was unlimited.

Trina sat on a coarse cement bench, waiting for Kristi. While she waited, she watched the Bellagio's fountains. Mist filled her nose and she tasted chlorine. Spurts of water reflected flashing colors in time with Lady Gaga's "Bad Romance".

She reached into her purse, pulled out her phone, and texted, "Where are you?"

"I'm planning the memorial." Kristi texted back. "Tragic."

"Tragic?"

"Damon. I'm torn up."

Trina's ears popped as if she was ascending a mountain. "You texted me back."

Kristi texted. "So?"

"You always call. What's going on? Tragic?"

"I feel like texting. And 'tragic' is the only word. I can't believe what happened. You were a great manager, the best he ever had. Please don't blame yourself."

Trina's throat tightened. "What the hell are you talking about? Manager? I only stayed with him to be near you… You know that."

"I'm sure I have no idea what you mean. Why would you stay near me? We're co-workers, nothing more."

"What about the nights at The Palm? What about our plan to leave together? What about all the things you said?"

"I think the accident has you confused. We've never spent the night together. The tragedy mixed you up. We've never made plans. I've never promised you anything. I'm sorry this accident is affecting you so much."

The hair on Trina's arm stood on end. "Accident? Never spent the night together? What the hell are you talking about? When are you getting here?"

"You're speaking gibberish." Kristi texted. "The love of my life has died. I'm not going anywhere."

A bomb exploded in Trina's chest. "You said I'm the love of your life."

"Trina, you need help. I barely even know you."

Trina scrolled through their old texts. They'd never once

talked about the Damon set-up by text, or their love by text, or their plans by text… For years, all the texts were business, nothing more. There was no record. All the words had floated off and the texts had remained, and they told a lie.

Trina's hands tightened on the phone and her knuckles turned white. "This isn't funny, when are you getting here? I love you."

"We are co-workers, always have been, nothing more. Whatever fantasies you've made up in your mind, I'm sorry, I'm dealing with a profound loss, and I don't have the time. Perhaps it is better if we didn't chat for a while."

Trina heard a siren and lifted her head. The fountain's water jets reflected red and blue. Trina looked left. A group of uniformed cops marched towards her, hands on their guns.

A short, fat, cop stopped ten yards in front. "Trina Arnold?"

Trina still squeezed the phone in her shaking right hand. "Yes?"

The fat, old cop smiled. He held up a piece of paper. "This is a search warrant for that purse."

An overwhelming desire to throw up engulfed her.

Two young, thin cops grabbed the bag and handed it to the old cop. He reached inside, rummaged around, and pulled out a white slip of paper and her debit card. He held the card close to his face, and then the paper.

He rotated to Trina. "Ms. Arnold, get face down on the ground, you're under arrest."

She heard the thin cops chatting. "Can you believe she put the insurance in her name? So dumb."

Trina's tears fell, but the ground was wet from the fountain and her tears blended in as if they'd never been there at all.

• • •

A wave broke and a child laughed. The coconut tanning oil's scent mixed with the salt air and filled Kristi's nostrils with blessed peace. She raised her hand.

"Yes, Miss?"

She opened her eyes and looked right. Marcia, her favorite waitress—young enough to matter, old enough to know what to do—stood there. Marcia was radiant in her slightly too-tight Bermuda shorts.

"Another Brahma, please," Kristi said.

Marcia jogged to the bar as Kristi watched. Marcia got the beer, put a lime down the stem, put it on a tray, and strutted back.

Kristi took the offering. The brown glass bottle was cold and familiar in her hand. She took a sip. Icy liquid filled her empty stomach and rested there as if it had always belonged. She held up fifteen Brazilian reals.

Marcia nodded and turned, and Kristi slipped the bills into Marcia's back pocket.

Marcia turned back, blushing. "Is there anything else, ma'am?"

"Would you come by my room later?"

"Ms. Kristi, the resort… I could lose my job."

"No one will ever find out, our little secret."

Marcia's mouth turned down, but her eyes smiled. "I guess that could work."

Kristi reached into her purse and pulled out one hundred reals. "You go buy us some dinner, and we just eat together… Nothing more."

"What should I buy?"

"You know what I like."

Marcia grinned and took the money. "Should I bring a little *maconha*?"

Kristi shook her head. "I gave up drugs, ages ago." She tapped her left index finger on her temple. "Need to stay sharp."

Marcia nodded and turned away.

"Marcia…"

She looked back, over her left shoulder. "Yes?"

"Wear the shorts."

She grinned. "Yes ma'am."

Tight white linen bounced as Marcia disappeared into the resort.

Kristi unwrapped her lavender coverup and embraced Florianopolis's fierce sun. She reclined, roasting. Her left hand held a little pink disposable lighter.

Kristi was warm and rich and free, thanks to Trina. The thought of Trina made Kristi's throat tighten, just a bit. It was sad—unfortunate—that someone had to go down. A tragedy it was Trina, but it was the only way. Kristi closed her eyes and leaned back and pushed the negativity from her mind.

She focused on too-tight Bermuda shorts.

Maybe Marcia would make a good girlfriend. Maybe that was better.

THIS MUST BE THE PLACE

by T. Fox Dunham

Zacharia felt his heart beat in his sleep, and when the haze cleared his head, he dreamed of a little house on MacDill Airforce Base in Florida where his mother still lived and decorated for Easter to celebrate the rise of the Lord. The steady tap turned into palpitations beating against Zacharia's chest, ripping him from the dream, waking him. He counted each one. Beat. Beat. Beat. Chills followed, shaking his scarecrow frame, and sweat soaked his torn Eagles sweatshirt. It felt a welcome relief to the constant and parching heat—the burning fury that never alleviated, even in the dark of night when one might find shelter in the summer. But the world had changed, and normal sanctuaries from the sun, from drought, had evaporated.

"If we don't get the fuck out of here, they'll find our dried-up shit on the sidewalk outside of the Methodist Church," he said. Angel groaned in her sleep but didn't wake, so he decided to allow her a few moment's peace before waking to fight the world again. He wondered if being asleep is what it felt like when you were dead. When he died, he wanted to be near the ocean where he could see nothing but water out to the heavens.

He got to his feet, careful not to touch or disturb Angel sleeping on the hardwood floor of the abandoned rowhouse, then stumbled to the bathroom and vomited. The coffee mixed with bile burned his throat, and he washed his mouth out with the dribble of water from the faucet. When the nausea passed, hunger overwhelmed him, and Zacharia tore off a piece of the beef jerky he'd palmed at Queen Pizza. He popped it into his mouth then gnawed it with the fragments of his teeth, chewing with his remaining back molars.

He knew it was pointless to look, but he pulled out the teddy bear from Angel's bag and opened the tab that sealed the secret bank compartment built into the toy. He'd hoped Angel had been holding out on him, keeping some in reserve to get them through the long stretch. Panhandling on the Lancaster streets had dried up since the pandemic. None of the tourists carried cash anymore. He stuffed teddy back into the bag then sat down on the blanket and took another bite of jerky. A knife stabbed through his cheek, piercing under his left eye, and he tasted metal. A jagged shard pierced his tongue, and he spit out a smooth metal cap—the last of the dental repair paid for by the USAF. The pain spread, lighting up every exposed nerve in his mouth. He reached into the bag, found a flat tube and rubbed the last few drops of numbing agent to the jagged shards jutting out of his jaw. It wouldn't last long, and he curled up on the ratty children's comforter next to Angel, moving his body close enough to feel the heat radiating off her flesh but not close enough to touch her—never touching her. Would she even realize it? He thought about reaching out to hold her, sweeping her lithe body into his arms to hold against the violent chills quaking through his bones and flesh. She slept on her stomach, and he slowly reached out his hand to her shoulder and ran his fingers along the outline of angel wings tattooed on her exposed back. The heat from her skin warmed his hand. He'd never been this close before. Ever-so-slightly, gently, he caressed her rough skin, tracing the outline of feathers exposed in the moonlight that poured through the filthy glass of the window in the abandoned rowhouse on Duke Street. They existed in a wretched state, always hungry, dirty, at the mercy of predators looking to use them up for their pleasure, but just being near her, with her, sharing their body heat while sleeping on the wooden floor, he'd felt a belonging, even security that had eluded him his whole life—a sensation he'd never experienced but inherently missed. He'd known trailers and base housing and apartments and station wagons, but in this derelict rowhome with no heat, working plumbing and rats, he'd found a feeling of belonging and peace when he was near her. Would touching her feel like being home?

He withdrew his hand. He had no right.

"I told you, I'm not ready for that," she said and turned over on her back. A copy of *Philadelphia's Worst Mob Bosses* that she'd gotten from the Lancaster Library slid off her thigh. "If you pull shit like that again, I'm gone."

"I'm sorry. I didn't mean…"

He'd promised himself he wouldn't push her. Angel never spoke about her life on the streets before she met him, but he knew there were predators out there, and the cops didn't think a junkie was worth protecting.

"Don't be fucking sorry," she said. "Everyone's always sorry."

"We can't stay in the city," he said, changing the subject. "God left the oven on, baby." She turned over on her side, pulled out her ratty off-white wig—the kind the founding white guys wore—from a bag and put it on her shaven head. She pulled out a tattered leather bag she'd found in a dumpster outside of an apartment on Duke Street and fetched her worn tools: an old shaving razor, rusty at the handle, a plastic milk carton of water, a bar of soap. More and more, since they ran out of antiandrogens—a supply recently bought from the roommate of an old man who died from prostate cancer—he'd noticed a shadow fall over Angel's face. He wanted to tell her he only saw it when she did, that nothing could blemish the cherubim curve of her cheek bones. But he knew she'd never hear it. As she worked, looking at her face in a small mirror, she sang a familiar church hymn. Zacharia could see she was hurting too and knew it was bad when she started singing *Ave Maria*. The tone of her voice rang like a church bell.

"We could find Harry and Bug and get the Red Rose to the mall," he suggested. During the lean times when the shelters closed a few months in January, they'd pulled some shit at a Gap in the mall. He'd go into the store, act suspicious, start piling up expensive shirts and pants on a table in the back until he got the attention of the security guard. At the same time, Angel and two others in their group would get all cleaned up, go in and start grabbing as much as they could, sticking it down their pants, in their bags. When they gave the signal, they'd walk through the metal detectors together. Of course, the guards focused on him and let the others through. Later, they sold what they could or traded. It got them some money in their pocket, some supplies and filled up teddy for at least a month, maybe even enough to get her more hormones until the clinic opened again or someone died in one of the flophouses and their meds ended up on the street.

"Biff closed the pawn," she said. "We got nowhere to fence the shit." Angel pulled out a pair of silicone breast forms—bruised and worn—from the bag then stepped into the bathroom for privacy to make herself whole.

"I found some tools in the basement," he said. "We could get a few bucks."

For the next few hours, not able to sleep, they plotted and schemed how to survive the next few days until the sun rose over the old city of Lancaster, talking to keep their minds occupied and distracted from their oral agony, hunger and withdrawal. Light illuminated the hall into the kitchen, and Zacharia for the first time noticed marks on the wall labeled with corresponding years. Children had grown up in this house once, three from the look of it. Somewhere in the world, that family thought of this house fondly and shared warm memories.

"It's time to do the thing we talked about," Angel said.

"Yeah. Let's rob Tony T," Zacharia laughed, sarcastic. Angel didn't join in. "Fuck. You're serious. He'll cut us down."

"Not if we do it right," she said. "He'll never see it coming."

"Yeah. Cause no junkie ever robbed his dealer before."

"We get enough," she said. "Break free. Fill teddy then ween ourselves. Have enough to get a small place somewhere—north, Canada. No more people to get in our shit."

"Sounds like Utopia," he said. "But I like breathing."

"You won't be breathing no more when your jaw abscesses."

Pain drilled into his face—constant, never stopping, always squeezing, breaking, cracking, drilling deeper. His hands shook. Sweat dripped from the back of his head, soaking his hoodie. "T's got eyes in the back of his ass," Zacharia said.

"Not Tony. We hit the guy collecting." Angel stretched her lithe body, curved her back and swayed like a dancer, moving to a song playing in her head. "T prays to the savior but pays to the mob. It's how this all works. Dealers can't operate in this territory without paying a tax."

"I've never heard of that," Zacharia said.

"And that's why we got a shot at this," she said.

He closed his eyes and imagined a cabin somewhere in the wilderness, quiet from the noise of the city, the noise in his head. What did they have to lose?

• • •

Humans aren't all built to factory specs. They don't fly out of an assembly line. David Zacharia Jr. had not inherited his dad's strength. Master Sergeant Robert Zacharia had been born with three chevrons tattooed on his ass. He served in Afghanistan, leaving David home at age fifteen on base to clean up his mom's vomit after another round of chemo. Six months after she died, David knocked up Kelly Anne Freedman, a local girl who had dropped out of school to work as a hair dresser at Sally's Salon in Port St. Lucy, Florida. He was nineteen, no direction or motivation beyond getting stoned. But he had people who needed him, and maybe that's how he'd make a place where he felt like he belonged.

All the while, Zacharia struggled to keep it together. They sank a little each day, maxing out credit cards, struggling to keep food in the house. She offered no relief, just told him to sign up, but he didn't want to spend his life guarding an aquifer in South America in a country that hated him.

The only time he felt on top of it was when he smoked with the guys from the restaurant on Saturday night. Then the restaurant fired him for being high on the job. Some of the guys were driving north to New York for a job in the Hudson Valley, and he went with them.

Kids grew up, with or without their parents.

Leaving them tore a hole in him, but he never knew anyone in this life who was whole. He got along working temporary jobs but never had enough to get a place. Most of the people on the street he knew were the same: families, parents who worked two jobs but just couldn't put the money together to live in a house. Most of them managed to get a few weeks out of a cheap trucker motel or maybe rent a place for a few months but they always came back. People formed groups to survive. Zacharia got with Angel's gang at the Duke Street Mission. They needed a big asshole, and he wouldn't have made it this far without them. The wig struck him as weird at first. He didn't want to feel that way. He told his deeper mind—all the things that just react sans thought or understanding, the reactions that form and shape by the subtle music played in the background constantly—to change, to grow, to accept, but no matter how much he wanted it, synapses still fired from ingrained prejudices. Angel heard it. She felt it, and he saw her wince sometimes, but she'd been patient, understanding. She better than anyone knew you were born and then the world broke you to fit its patterns. Still, he'd come far since having met Angel, since his guardian on the streets had protected him, helped him survive. When you went hungry, struggled to stay warm, or had to fight off a rape gang with an old pipe, you stopped caring about a lot of the shit the sunshine world cared about. They looked out for each other, surviving in groups. While the tourists still carried cash, they worked the streets together, reading on the benches. He liked reading and thinking grand thoughts written by others. It comforted him from the cruelty.

"Piece-of-shit heroin junkie. I'm not giving you money so you can just go shoot it up."

"For your information, I'm a piece-of-shit meth head."

• • •

"Have you ever loved anyone?" Zacharia said. "I thought I did once. Thinking about it now, I'm not so sure." They hung out in the urban park on Queen Street, sitting in front of the fountain reading and asking the suits for change. He tried not to think about what they were about to do and hoped some survival ability would kick in when the moment came.

"Love? People use it like a knife. Maybe it was real once, but it's been twisted, turned into a weapon or a collar. Fucking Mother Mary—can you really say you know what love is or were you just told what it means?"

"I guess I'll know it when I feel it," Zacharia said. He pressed his fist into the dull ache crushing his jaw. "I thought it was real then too. But I was a different me. Those memories belonged to a different person." He looked at Angel, pondering the pull, the need he felt for her. Would he still feel this way if he knew her before, when the world had forced her to present as something else? Over the months, the need for her had grown, twisting against the old carved prejudices telling him it was wrong. Yet his chest felt hollow for her. Sometimes when the two fronts collided, he nearly snapped in two, and he buried the conflict, the emotions and focused on just keeping his mouth full.

She sighed, shook her head. He was obviously becoming a

lost cause. "Fuck love," Angel said, adjusting her filthy white wig. "I just want a place with walls, a roof and a door to lock."

"I don't know if I can do this."

"Stop being so weak," she said.

"I just never robbed nobody before," Zacharia said. He rubbed his aching jaw with his left hand and rubbed at the insects crawling under his skin with his right. They had to fill Teddy soon, or he'd be no use to anyone—probably get them both killed. Angel was hurting too. She stood tall and strong when he was looking but from the corner of his eye when she thought she was all alone in the world, he spied her shaking with chills. Sweat dripped, dampening the moldy wig and dripping down the side of her peach-skin and to the hem of the white flowery dress she'd stolen from Target the week before—just two college kids drinking on spring break. They'd fit right into the crowd of central Pennsylvania kids who'd driven to the closest city on Easter break to hit the bars.

By dusk, crowds of kids not much younger than Zacharia flocked up and down Queen Street, moving in out of bars in an eerie synchronicity, drinking harder, breaking into brawls at midnight. The young carried the drought that had dried out the farm fields of Lancaster and turned the sky into an oven on their backs. They didn't enter the future with hope, dreams. The benefits and grants of the middle-class evaporated with the lakes and rivers, and they approached the future like soldiers trying to survive. Everyone had plans to move north. All the businesses had pulled up stakes and fled to Canada. No one had a good job. No one had any spare change, and they stomped on the junkies like lantern flies. The last echelon was always disposable, and a dangerous instinct had resounded in the populace: dispose of the weak to save resources. No one wanted to admit it, but the funding for shelters dried up, and the savage world Zacharia had survived turned even more savage.

Zacharia and Angel slithered into a dark nook built into the brick courthouse on Queen Street that was shielded by the glass bus enclave. Bums slept on ratty blankets, leaning on bags of their trash. A new family huddled in the corner, and a little girl had drawn a window, a bed and a dresser on the brick wall in pink chalk to comfort her while she slept. They waited, watching the stretch of upper Queen Street where Tony T patrolled.

"Eleven like clockwork," she said.

"How the fuck are you so sure?"

"Because I am."

"I still can't believe they're still doing this shit with the world ending."

"That's when these assholes thrive," she said. "Cockroaches dancing under mushroom clouds. That fucker will probably be king when we all get broiled."

Zacharia huddled up into the corner and scratched at his skin, digging furrows into his arms. This wasn't going to work. What the fuck were they thinking? This was the mob. Even if they got away with it, they'd find them. He had to bolt.

The clock tower rang bells. He counted each chime. "One. Two. Three . . . ten. Eleven."

Angel pointed across the street and readied the hammer they'd found in the basement. Just as she predicted, a red Prius pulled up into the parking lot across the street. A lanky guy with perfect curls and dressed in a silver blazer swaggered to some appointed place in the alley behind the building. Zacharia pulled himself up and nearly tumbled over. His heart threatened to beat out of his chest. "Wait at the trunk for me to pull the release," she ordered. "Then grab the bag."

They crossed the dark and still street against the red light, maneuvered to the Prius, and he positioned himself behind the car.

"This is the last of his pickups, so it'll be heavy."

"How do you know this—?"

She whacked the driver-side window, and the window fractured into several large shards that landed on the blacktop and the front seat. She reached in fast, slicing her arm on a stubborn piece then unlocked the door. The trunk popped, scaring the shit out of Zacharia. He reached into the trunk and grabbed a tote bag, the only one he could find. It felt too light. Was this what she meant? He opened it to make sure and pulled out two wads of tens and twenties. This couldn't be it.

"You got it?" Angel asked. She grabbed a rag out of the trunk and pressed it against the open vein on her arm. He held it up for her to see. "That's not it. Fuck. We gotta move." She dug into the trunk, moving around a toolkit and dislodging a box that spilled boxes of mobile phones. Zacharia pulled up the trunk cover, revealing a single-gauge shotgun. "What the fuck?"

"Oh yeah. There was a pistol up front too, under the seat. These guy's cars are like national guard arsenals." She tore apart the trunk and sang of the Virgin while she worked. "This is his last stop for the night," she said.

"What if you're wrong?"

"I'm not fucking wrong. These guys keep their schedules, and you'd better be there with the cash when it's your turn, or they'll clip you."

"What if he changed his schedule?"

"Like clockwork," she said.

"Let's just go. We'll make teddy warm again. We'll fill up his belly."

"It's not fucking enough," she said then went back to the driver side and started searching the front seat.

"Woah!" someone said behind him. "What by Saint Thomas Aquinas the fuck is transpiring on Queen Street in Lancaster?" Zacharia could feel the heaviness of a gun pointed at his back. "Turn around. Let me see you. Take it slow. Like a merry-go-round."

Angel pulled herself out of the front seat, quietly palming a piece of glass, stood up and slowly walked into the light cast from the streetlamps. "Be cool," she said.

"Oh shit. Two junkies. Now this is some shit to write home about. Fucking junkies." He laughed so hard his lips peeled back, exposing the hoary white of his pristine teeth. "Was it fucking worth it? How much did you score?"

Looking at the end of his gun, Zacharia kept thinking about his son.

"Look dude," Angel said. "We're sorry. We're just hungry."

"I said fucking count it, motherfucking toothless junkies." He pushed the gun at them, and Zacharia opened the bag and pulled out the wads of cash. He struggled to focus as he counted, waiting for Angel to do something. She just stood there fucking useless. "Well? How much were your useless lives worth?"

"Two thousand," Zacharia muttered. "And forty dollars."

"You two fucks aren't worth twenty." Cars drove down Queen Street. Zacharia spotted a mob of college kids walking down the street. Yet the guy never flinched.

"We'll pay for the window," Angel said.

"Okay," he said. "Now we're negotiating. I think we can find some work for those pretty pink lips of yours. But I can't see your face. Come closer. Into the light." Angel hesitated. "Or do you want me to shoot your boyfriend?"

She stepped forward, and the expression on the guy's face changed. "Oh shit."

Angel used his surprise to lurch forward and slit the guy's throat with the shard of glass she'd palmed. "Tony!" he called out, then wrapped his hands around his throat, trying to stem the black arterial syrup oozing from his neck. Zacharia froze, watching the life drain from the guy.

"He wasn't alone?" Zacharia asked. The guy must have been calling to a partner, some dude named Tony. He tried handing her the money. He didn't want it.

"Get the fuck out of here," she said.

"Aren't you coming?"

"We split up. Meet tomorrow morning." She ran off.

"Where?" he yelled.

"Home. Meet me at home."

Where the fuck was home?

Zacharia hid in the alleyways and the city parks, camouflaging himself among the flocks of junkies, winos, dispossessed, mentally ill ghosts, the lost, the angry and the left behind. Finally, as the sun rose over the cloistered and old brick city of Lancaster, he returned to the derelict townhouse. Zacharia kept to the back streets, checking every intersection. The family they'd just robbed, the family of the soldier they'd just executed, ruled the streets, impressing the waifs and powerless into their drug trade or sex dens.

Around the corner, he threw up in the sewer then curled up into the shadow of the brick church, hiding away in the shadow cast from its tall bell tower that rang on the hour through synthesized chimes playing from a speaker. It had been a few days since his last hit, and he was coming apart. Finally, he pulled himself to the house—their house for the brief time they used it—though he felt no security or comfort from the place. It was only the thought of finding Angel that had brought him back.

He opened the broken backdoor, and a bearded guy pressed the cold shotgun nostrils to his forehead. Zacharia closed his eyes. Visions of his son possessed him—the way he laughed at a bottle nipple, the light in his eyes when his mother held him. The reverie kicked Zacharia in the gut, and at the moment, his last, his sole wish was to see his son again.

"You keep yourself out of this house, or I'll cut you in two with . . . my boom boom . . . stick." The guy played tough, but he was shaking. It wasn't the mob. "Boom."

"I'm gone," Zacharia said. The guy followed him out to the alley, still holding his shotgun.

"This was a good neighborhood for working people," he lectured. "You stay off this street. I already drove your lady-friend off. Fucking hop . . . hopheads."

"She was here?"

"Animals. Just animals. Filth . . . Just filth!"

Zacharia snapped, grabbed the shotgun and ripped it from the guy's loose grip. "My name is Zacharia, and I have a son. And one day probably soon, I'm going to leave this world. God will be my judge, not some fucked-up Pennsyltucky fucking redneck who doesn't know his lines." The guy looked like he was about to bolt, and Zacharia offered him back his gun as a show of good faith.

"Which way did she go?"

After the guy indicated the general direction, Zacharia made a line up the southside of the city and checked a few standalone lots until he found her sitting in a lot strangled by dried and dead grass behind a gas station that had closed a few months ago. The marquee at the edge of the drive advertised prices above eight dollars, and a lot of these places had closed in the spring. Sweat soaked his clothes, and he could smell his own stink.

"Not cool," he said. "I thought you were fucking fried."

"We ain't married," she said.

He sat down, leaned against the brick wall and grabbed a fistful of parched papyrus. "It can't be this way in Canada," he said and tossed the fronds on her. His anger passed to relief, and he restrained himself from embracing her.

"It's never going to be better," she said. "That's not the point. We're just going to survive longer. And when the world turns to shit, everyone will know what it's like to be us. I want to live to see that shit play out."

"Well that's fucking great," he said. "But what's the move right now, cause I gotta tell you, I'm ready to walk."

She tossed him a small baggy. "Here. Get yourself right."

"Bitch. You're just like them." He got up to leave but hesitated before exiting the little shade they could find. The longer he lingered, the harder he fought not to snap at the rock like a ravenous wolf. "You're just using me. That's why you did this. So, you can control me too."

"Yeah," she said. "I get it from my father."

"Fuck you," he said.

"Walk then."

He started to walk away.

He couldn't take another step.

Zacharia grabbed the bag then took out his kit. He hated playing his flute in the light, out in the open like that, but he needed to think straight. She sat quietly, didn't partake and let him get back to himself. After a few hits, the fear washed away, leaving control.

"We need to go all in," she said.

"How much farther in can we get?" he yelled.

"That guy's boss, Merlino, has a place in Ocean City. It's where they take the collections when they're done. From there, his capos funnel the dirty money through different motels he owns."

"And you want to . . . what? Rob the place?"

"They'll never see it coming," she said. "No one's supposed to know about it. It's his private retreat. His 'garden of family and tranquility.' None of these guys think they can be touched, and normally they can't. But we're ghosts. It'll be enough money to go north, get the fuck out of this country. North. It'll be cooler there. They'll have food, water and lots of fucking nowhere. I went there as a kid. It's peaceful."

"We should just get the fuck out of here, go south. D.C."

"If we don't get enough money to get clear, we're dead." Then, she took his hand. Their skin touched, bonded, connected. His heart fluttered, and he felt invincibility pulsing through his veins like some kind of a superhero. That's what he loved. That's what he needed: that feeling of being in control. He'd only ever known it when he was high.

• • •

They bought a cheap Corolla from an ad, paying cash for no questions asked then drove to Ocean City. During the day, they walked the boardwalk, dropped quarters into the arcade games and even bought a pound of peanut butter fudge that they ate with their fingers at the music pier. A young boy, not more than ten, played a violin at a bandstand off the beach. He knew the ubiquitous tune, though he didn't know the name or the one who'd written it. The boy poured his heart into the song, though few of the tourists noticed as they enjoyed their night on the boardwalk. The two of them stood there for a time, listening to the child play, tapping into an innocence and purity that would eventually be drained away in the process they called 'growing up'. They stood their and listened to the music, listened to the pendulous roar of the surf as it stroked the beach and watched as the light dimmed to night. A Ferris Wheel ignited into a rainbow of colors and twirled on the distant pier, setting the horizon aglow with pulses of green, blue and red. A cool breeze blew off the swelling ocean, easing the sweltering night.

"I wish I knew who wrote this," he said. "I only know Bob Dylan didn't."

"Mozart," Angel said. "Violin Concerto Number three."

"You blow me away," he said and looked down, realizing their hands had clasped. Touching her fired every nerve in his arm, and he felt the music, her nearness, her lifeforce pulse with each motion of the bow across taunt strings deep into his chest, his mind, his groin. The force of the moment buried any old, prejudiced instincts under sand and surf and sound and soaring. Seagulls swooped overhead. Now, more than ever, he felt eager to begin, to cross the coming threshold, to face one last demon and earn their passage north.

"We should do this," he said, waking from the dream.

"Not yet," Angel replied. "Just a little more. I'm me here. And you're more you than I've ever known you to be you." They went to the nearest arcade, bowled balls into Skee-Ball and played the poker machines. What tickets they won, they gave away to the kids. One little boy told Angel he thought she was beautiful. Angel blushed. When they finished playing, they bought frozen custard and walked one last lap in the night, watching the ocean swallow the beach.

"In a few years, this will all be under water," she said. "None of this really matters."

"Something matters," he said.

"What?"

"I asked you earlier if you ever loved anyone," Zacharia said. "Do you think, maybe…?"

"Ask me again after tonight," she said.

An hour before midnight, they drove up the coast and through the ubiquitous rows of dark beach houses. Sans the sounds of cars and motorcycles, the ocean waves roared over the sound of the engine, filling his heart with fury.

She parked on the side of a sandy road that lead through a pine grove. Sand dunes walled the southern exposure, and he heard the sighing sound of Atlantic waves just beyond. They got out, and Zacharia gazed down the horizon, looking for the bright lights of the spectral Ferris Wheel.

"The Boardwalk's flooding," Angel mused. "The whole island of Ocean City is going to be under water in a few years. The fuckers deserve it—out here fiddling while Rome drowns. I bet my dad bought a bunch of cheap real estate across the bay. It'll all be shorefront in a decade."

Zacharia's eyes moistened. He couldn't help it. This had been a place for families. His kid would have loved it here, played in the sand all day with no idea of the soggy hell they'd unleashed on the world. When this was all over, they'd get to Canada, and he'd send them a cut, bring them north before the shooting started.

They walked the side of the road, staying out of the moonlight and carefully approached a two-story building that had been built with arched windows, an Olympic-sized swimming pool, a stone garden decorating the drive, all guarded by a tall fence. She knew an access point where the chain had been cut. The house slept, waiting for its master's return, and she led him to a side door on the garage.

"Don Merlino is in Florida this time of year," she said. "He only uses this place in the spring or when he 'needs to get away from it all.' Most of the time, he just wastes it. It's one of six of his compounds."

"You are obsessed."

"You have no idea," she said. "Hold this flashlight." His hands shook, and he struggled to keep the beam steady. Angel appeared almost giddy, and he was trying not to shit himself. She removed a faux panel by the door, exposing keypad on an alarm terminal. "We'll be in and out," she said and went to punch in a code.

"Step the fuck back," he said.

"What's wrong? Fuck. We don't have time for this." She reached for her stash to offer him another dose. "You can snort it."

"I've had enough," he said.

"Come on. Get yourself home."

"You just happen to have the code to the alarm system? Was that published in some true crime book?"

She sighed. "That guy back there. Bobby. The guy collecting. I used to blow him."

"He knew you?"

"We used to date behind my father's back. If my dad knew, he would have killed the guy. He didn't want me dating goombahs. I know this house. I've been to parties here, dinners. I even broke in a few times to grab a little cash—nothing that would be noticed."

For the first time since knowing her, he felt his faith lapse in Angel. "You should have fucking told me."

"I left this life a long time ago. Fucking Neanderthals."

"Is that all I ever was to you?" he asked. He should have just walked away now. Zacharia had gotten himself involved in something he didn't understand. This wasn't just about survival for Angel; scores needed to be settled. "Is there even any money?"

"That part's all true," she said. "Fuck, we don't have time for this. He's got his guys checking on all his properties."

Zacharia sighed and accepted the meth. He didn't believe her but he followed her anyway. They climbed up the stairs from the garage and into a hall that opened into a sitting room. An antique grandfather clock swung its pendulum, ticking away the silence, counting down to their fate. Ornate furniture covered in plastic filled the rooms. Delicate vases decorated pedestals, and smooth Italian statues celebrated the human form on display in alcoves carved into the corridors. Muscle memory from school trips to museums kicked in, and Zacharia withdrew his hands to his sides. The place felt more like a morgue or ancient crypt than a home.

"His study is upstairs," Angel said. "That's where they drop off the tax." She led him up a staircase, and he shone his flashlight on the walls, revealing framed photos of a young boy with dark hair at various stages of his life. In one photo, the boy sung at the front of a choir. In another, he rode a black horse. He looked so small up there, so lost, sinking into the saddle. He posed for the photos, posing for his family, for display in their home as proof of the love of his parents, yet his eyes failed to play the part: hollow, the eyes of a ghost.

At the top of the stairs, Angel defeated the lock with a cancelled credit card then paused to fix her wig. She hesitated for several heartbeats, inhaled, then stepped into the study. A navy of model boats decorated the shelves—meticulously built creations made with the tiniest of components, all perfect and precise, their bows all pointed at the same angle on display. Locked glass doors secured first editions of faded tomes, and framed photos of a little man at various stages in his life shaking hands with different high officers of the church, even one with an old and wrinkled pope. Angel moved swiftly to a varnished wooden chest in the corner of the room and took off the open padlock. "The guys forget their keys, so they just started leaving it open." She opened the box, and Zacharia looked inside and saw what freedom really looked like. He reached down to help her load the stacks of cash into their bag, but he couldn't bring himself to touch it.

"Annie," he said. "Billy. They died in the ER."

"What's your point?" she asked.

"All the junkies on Queen Street. The high school students that never graduate. Roxanne sold her flesh by the pound now can't afford the AZT. This is the devil's box."

Angel stopped loading the bag and looked the wad of twenties wrapped with a rubber band she held in her hands. "The devil's money," she said. "Fuck. Just load up. We'll take them with us. All of them."

The light flipped on. "Turn that off!" she said.

"I didn't realize I had guests," said a low, gravelly voice. Zacharia looked up and first noticed the heavy bags swollen beneath his bulbous little eyes. He walked into the office, took off his charcoal gray suit jacket and hung it up on a coat tree. "It's good to meet yas," he said, extending a hand to Zacharia. "Angelo Merlino." Zacharia didn't believe it. On the street, they told stories of a vicious predator who ate you alive, but the guy wore a three-piece suit, couldn't have been taller than five foot and looked like someone's benign grandpa. Zacharia had no idea what to do and looked to Angel. When she saw him, she started to sing the song to the Virgin Mary.

"Aren't you going to say something to me?" the guy asked.

"You're supposed to be in Florida," she said.

"We are often not where we are supposed to be—the rebellion of youth, the eccentricities of age." A young guy with greasy hair blocked the only exit. "I flew back when I learned someone whacked Bobby. I must say it's good to see you safe, Tony."

"My name is David," Zacharia said.

"Not you, you piece of shit. My son, Tony. At least, that's the name his mother gave him, after her father. Hard working Italians. Tough as leather."

"What the fuck is he talking about?" They didn't talk about their pasts really. To survive, you jettisoned what you didn't need in the moment, and pasts had been a liability. "What did you drag me into?"

"I'm not your son," Angel said.

The tragedy of the moment punched Zacharia in the chest. Tonight, had been about more than robbing a monster. For Angel, it had been about facing her past, confronting the ghosts that still haunted her. How could a parent cage their child so? How could Merlino not see the beauty and divinity his daughter possessed, even when she'd shed her wig, or breasts, or makeup. This was his Angel he'd imprisoned with the name Tony. Worse than a metal cage or at the point of a gun, a single word could cage a soul and kill its song. She sang with the voice of a sparrow, and Zacharia felt such rage suffuse through his being, such a need to guard, to protect.

"Go down and unload the car," Merlino ordered. His guy hesitated but obeyed.

"I was never your son."

"I thought it was something that would pass," Merlino said. He walked around to his desk, pulled out a cigar and lit it from a sailing ship lighter. Zacharia spotted a revolver in his hand. "I tried to beat it out of him. Sent him to counseling sessions with the church. A year ago, I sent him to a special camp."

"Your crew dragged me out, drugged me. Do you know what they did to me at that camp?"

"I paid them twenty large," Merlino said. "I think I'm owed a refund. And now you rob your own flesh and blood. Weak. Unnatural weakness in you. Makes me sick. You never got it, Tony. The danger you put us in. If my capos learned what you were, they'd think I was weak. They'd come after me with the board's approval. They'd whack us all, Tony."

"Yeah," Angel said. "Your guys. All upstanding *straight* family men." She scoffed.

Merlino puffed on the cigar. "So now we got a problem." He puffed again. "But I've got a solution. I always had a soft spot for you. My sweet little boy. I should kill you now, fast. But instead of a funeral, we can make this something to celebrate. The prodigal son and all. You've come home to live right."

"I'd rather die on the street."

"Aren't you tired? Wouldn't you like to come home? I never knew what a home was with my family. You ruined that. But we can fix that. I'll welcome you back with open arms. You only have to give up this . . . sickness. I mean, aren't you tired of eating garbage? Panhandling? Being filthy all the time?"

She hesitated. Creases dug into her angelic visage, and Zacharia could see the burden of their life age her beautiful face.

Every soul came with a price tag.

"I don't care what happens to me," Zacharia said, feeling her slip away. "But don't let him take you. I don't deserve it, but I can't lose you."

"Of course, your friend has to go," Merlino said. Zacharia figured something like that was going to happen. A part of him felt relieved.

"I'm just an animal to you," Zacharia said.

"He gets out alive," she said. "It's my fault he's here."

"Not in the cards," Merlino said. "Someone's got to pay for Bobby."

Angel sighed, and Zacharia knew he'd be shark chum by morning.

"I'm just so fucking tired," she said. In a gesture of surrender, she reached for her wig with one hand, the other sneaking behind her back to her waistband. She removed the wig and offered it to Merlino in supplication. The old man grinned, reaching to take it. The wig burst into flames with a bang, and Merlino grabbed his chest. Blood suffused through the threads of his vest, and he collapsed onto the carpet.

"Get the fucking bag," Angel said. Zacharia grabbed it, and they ran out of the room. Then something hit Zacharia's lower back, and all the strength fled from his left leg. He turned back to see the old boss aiming his revolver. Zacharia waited for the second shot to end his life, but the old don dropped the gun and hunched over.

"Where did you get that?" he asked, leaning back against the wall.

"Don't you pay attention?" she said. "Told you, Bobby's car was an arsenal. I grabbed it from under the seat. I would have used it, but every cop in the city would have been on us."

Someone barreled up the stairs, and Angel shot him. Merlino's guy tumbled backward onto the landing.

"There's a dentist in Atlantic City who will take care of this, but we got to move." She helped him down the stairs. He held onto the banister but couldn't stand on his numb leg. A chill moved through his body.

"My teeth don't hurt anymore," he said.

Angel carried him outside, and his blood smeared down her sweatshirt and covered her hands. Zacharia's head started to spin, and he collapsed on his good leg. He struggled to keep going, but his legs stopped working.

"I never should have taken you there. I've never felt this way before. I didn't trust it."

"I feel sleepy," Zacharia said. "I'm going to curl up with my son and sleep." She cupped his face, but he couldn't feel her touch.

"I wasn't sure what it feels like," Angel said. "It feels weak. I fought it. I don't like being weak. Fuck. How did you know what it was?"

"I told you," Zacharia said. "I'd know it when I felt it. Do you feel it?"

She kissed him gently, cradling his fading form. She didn't answer. You didn't have to when it was real. He felt it with a certainty that would never change, because he'd never change after tonight, after these final moments. He'd be frozen in time, his heart filled with her.

"You were always beautiful, with or without the wig. Always an angel."

She started to pray, then sang *Ave Maria* in perfect tone that summoned angels to the dark and sandy lot. The somber melody of the waves comforted him, reminding him that once this world had been a gentle place, a cradle for his kind, but people forgot that. Lost in their own bullshit, they forgot this was home. You only really realized that when you lost it.

"Get them north," he said.

His vision faded, and his heart beat in his ear to the rhythm. He counted each one. Beat. Beat. Beat. She came closer, aligning their lips until she sung into his mouth. In her arms, he finally felt relieved of his burden, relieved of the blame of living the lie that created the family he abandoned. At first, he didn't trust the feeling. How could this dirt road on the beach be it? But it felt right in his chest. This must have been it. She was it.

Beat. . .

ONCE IN A LIFETIME

by Gregory Galloway

As soon as the dogs came out of the desert, I knew everything would go to shit. I swung my legs out of the bed and put my hands on my knees, readying myself to get up, and watched the two dark figures come out of the morning sun like storm clouds ready to rain. My boyfriend was still asleep. I thought about waking him, but it wasn't his fault. I was the one who'd dragged him here, to come to my sister's wedding out in the middle of the Mojave. We'd been together almost a year, long enough to talk about next steps and all that, but he'd never met my family. I tried to prep him over the months, but it's hard to describe it all, hard to describe all the complications that have become twisted and tricky over time, like trying to describe the inside of a tornado to someone safe and sound on the other side of the country.

I'd like to tell you that we only came for my sister, but we really came for the money. I'd brought my boyfriend along to rob my mother's husband. She'd been married a few years or so. I don't know exactly. We hadn't been in touch for a while and then she sent me a letter saying she'd married this guy Alan. He'd been some wheel once upon a time, selling yachts or real estate or maybe something else entirely. I don't have the letter, and I don't really care what he did. All I know is he has money. My mother is always talking about how loaded he is and how there's all kinds of money stashed in the house. "I sleep a whole lot better knowing there's fifty thousand dollars right here if we ever need it," my mother said. We'd sleep a whole lot better too, I thought.

The dogs were getting closer. We were in the guest house—which my mother insisted on calling "the casita"—a few hundred feet from the main house. My sister and her man-to-be were there, along with my mother and her husband. We could have been in the main house too, but Alan had broken his leg and was in the other guest room, a garage they'd converted, which (according to my mother) Alan wouldn't leave. More likely my mother had exiled him there. My mother didn't want to be around him. "He broke his leg three days before the wedding," she said. "I don't even want to look at him." She thought it was bad luck. She knew everything about bad luck, except how to avoid it.

I got up and went to the window. One was a pit bull, and the other was some mix of a mess. They kept coming like that posse after Butch and Sundance. "What is it?" my boyfriend said.

"Dogs," I said. "Two of them. I'm going to have to go get them."

"You have to?" he said, still mostly asleep.

"If I don't, someone's liable to shoot them. Probably Alan."

"What are they doing here?" It was a good question. He was waking up.

"I don't know," I said. "The nearest house is about two miles away. That's about all the exposition I can offer right now."

"You want me to go with you?"

"If you're coming, you better hurry," I said and threw on a t-shirt, a pair of jeans, and some untied boots.

The dogs were coming up the road to the house. The female was pregnant all right, and she ran off the minute she saw me. Going to hide somewhere, I figured. The other one ran right up to me. A pit bull mix, big blockhead with beautiful blue-grey eyes. No tags, no collar, no nothing. I gave him the back of my hand and let him smell. I tried to get him to follow me, but he trotted his own way and went to the front of the house. The imminent husband stood on the porch with a cup of coffee in his hand. Andrew. And wherever Andrew was, my sister would not be far behind.

"Who's your friend?" Andrew said to me. He didn't move from his spot on the porch.

"Somebody looking for a handout, I guess."

"He's come to the wrong porch," Andrew said.

"Don't I know it," I said. My boyfriend, Carter, had caught up to me and I turned to him. "Help me get him out of here." Carter had a piece of food in his hand and got the dog's attention.

My sister came onto the porch. "What'cha got there?" she practically shouted, loud enough for our mother and step-father to hear. Not good. "Come 'ere pup-pup," she said, and after the dog had finished whatever was in Carter's hand, he turned toward my sister. "Come on," she said and the dog trotted right to her. The trouble was going to happen. Maybe I was the only one who could see it, but there it was, standing right there among us, gathering its strength and making its own plans. There wasn't much I could do about it.

"We need to take the dogs somewhere," I said to my sister, "before Alan sees them."

"I want to keep this one," Sheri said.

"Alan will kill it; you know he will." My mother had told us he hated most animals, hated dogs, and would shoot anything that came onto his property.

"I want to keep this one," my sister said again. "A wedding present."

"At least get him out of sight," I said.

The pregnant one was lurking around the side of the house, rounding the corner and looking at us before going back out of sight. Maybe she was looking for a place to have her puppies. She didn't want to be around any of us. I thought she could handle herself. My sister picked up the pit bull and walked off, her man following her. He didn't look too happy about the news that they were getting a dog. Maybe he'd try to talk her out of it. Maybe they'd fight over it and call the wedding off. My sister was full of drama like this. Nothing would surprise me.

• • •

My sister kept telling me that the wedding wasn't going to be a big deal. "It'll just be us," she said. "We'll have a quick ceremony and then have some food and drink and that'll be it. Not a big thing. Just family." Our mom was going to perform the ceremony; she'd paid fifty bucks or so to get ordained just for the occasion. Everything about it, according to my sister, was going to be low key (her words). I had asked her what to wear. "Whatever you want," Sheri said. "No one's dressing up. I'll probably wear whatever I have on. It's not a big deal."

The ceremony was in the high heat of the afternoon. We were told it would happen at three o'clock. I saw my sister at two-thirty putting on a total legit wedding dress. White, lace, train, everything but a fucking veil. I was dressed in linen pants and a t-shirt. Those were the nicest clothes I had with me. I could have borrowed a dress from my mother, I suppose, but I didn't out of principle or spite or whatever family dynamic coursed through us and bound us together and pushed us apart. The groom walked out of their bedroom wearing a tuxedo, with a stupid boutonniere in his lapel. Carter and I should have left then. About two forty-five, two black SUVs pulled up and eight of my sister's friends all piled out. I didn't know a single one of them. They were all wearing dresses or suits. We were the only ones she hadn't told. I don't know if she had lied to us or if she had forgotten. It could go either way. I put one of Carter's oxford shirts over my t-shirt, like that helped any. I tried to remind myself that I loved my sister, but I couldn't wait to get the money and get away from her, away from all of them.

The wedding ceremony was like the homecoming scene out of *Once Upon a Time in the West*, with picnic tables set up outside in the dirt, the red and white tablecloths flapping in the wind, dust blowing over the food. I kept looking for Henry Fonda and his men to come riding in. We all had to stand around in the afternoon heat—except for Alan, who sat on the porch in the shade in a shirt and tie and Jack Elam's eyes. The rest of us stood in the dirt of the front yard and watched my mom try to perform a perfunctory ceremony. Only it wasn't perfunctory.

My sister interrupted her. She had something to say. She and her almost-spouse had written their own vows, and standing there in the desert we had to listen them talk about water. They talked about how under the rocks there was water, water flowing and connecting the two of them, connecting all of us together. They talked about how we were all part of a giant ocean, an ocean of love, that they were celebrating, consecrating in that ceremony of marriage. I'm making it sound better than it was.

Afterward, people joked about it as we stood in the heat and the dust, a hot wind blowing over the folding tables lined with food that probably shouldn't have been out in the sun for that long. Somebody said that the vows had come from a song, and somebody else said that the song was about heroin. "That's a different song," somebody else said. It wasn't about heroin at all, not the song they used. I'm not sure what it was about exactly. All I know is that no one should really use songs for their wedding vows. Songs mean different things to different people, and they're just lyrics about something else, not the promise between two people for a wedding. My sister's ceremony reminded me that I never want to get married. Every day I hoped Carter wouldn't ask me. And he never did.

• • •

I want to make something clear: we weren't going to rob my mother; we were going to rob Alan. It was Alan's money.

My mother had moved out to the desert for her health. Then she had a stroke and met Alan during her speech therapy sessions. Alan was going to take care of her. She ended up taking care of him. He had heart problems, he had another small stroke, he broke his back and then got addicted to oxy. My mother spent most of her time waiting on him hand and foot, or else talking about how much money he had.

It seemed like he was sponging off of her. "You don't know how finances work," she told me. I know how sponges work.

"Besides," she said, "We don't want a big house, big car, nothing like that. We take care of each other; that's all we want. And what's his is his and what's mine is mine. His money will go to his kids. So don't go counting on that."

My mother liked to talk like that, about how she didn't care about money. When I first told her about Carter the very first thing she asked was, "Does he earn enough for you?" And when I told her he was a landscaper she said, "You need a good provider. Most couples break up over money. Take that off the table and you'll be just fine."

We needed the money, Alan had it, and Carter knew a thing or two about how to get it. Sort of. He'd been arrested a couple of times for B&E. "I didn't get caught at breaking and I didn't get caught at entering," he liked to say. "I got caught exiting. I'm good at breaking and entering. I need to work on the exiting." That was all we needed.

"If he's as rich as your mother says, he'll never miss it," Carter said. "We won't take all of it." And we wouldn't be taking it from my mother.

Carter told me he would take care of the safe. All I had to do was find out where it was. I'd been looking for it ever since we got there, just sizing up whatever room we happened to be in: the kitchen, the living room, even the converted garage where Alan was staying, even though I'd only been in there a few seconds, long enough to say hello to Alan when we arrived. He laid out on the bed like a frozen seal, his dark, dead eyes fixed on the ceiling when my mother brought us in, and could barely muster enough enthusiasm to say hello.

"I see you," Alan said, still looking at the ceiling.

"I brought you some books," I said.

"Put them over there," my mother said, waving toward a large stack next to his bed. He was always reading, except now that he was laid up like a wounded animal. "He's in a lot of pain," my mother said. "But can't take anything, you know, because of, well, you know. He's better out of the way, anyway."

"I see you," Alan said again, as if it hadn't been creepy enough the first time. "I know why you're here."

"It's not a secret," my mother said.

"Your mother tells me you're a troublemaker," Alan said.

"Alan. . ." my mother said, trying to stop it.

"Don't," Alan said. "That's all I'm saying. I'll be keeping an eye on things."

My mother said to ignore him. "He'll be in there staring at the ceiling," she said. "You won't have to pay him any attention. Listen to me." I should have listened to Alan.

• • •

I walked down the hallway and heard a scratching coming from my sister's room. When I opened the door, I saw that the dog had torn his way through a pillow and maybe a shoe. He'd also taken a shit on the bed. The honeymoon suite, I thought, and closed the door.

I found the safe in my mother's room, a small, cheap-looking thing not much bigger than a toaster oven, hidden behind hanging shirts and pants in Alan's closet. I thought that anyone who wanted could probably just walk off with the thing, but of course it weighed a ton. I took a picture of it and showed it to Carter. He smiled.

"I know that safe," he said. "Not a problem."

While we stood in the afternoon heat, Alan sat in the shade of the porch, his busted leg propped up on the arm of the couch, his crutches leaning up against the side of the house. After the ceremony, he stayed there, slowly sliding down into the cushions, his eyes fixed on the porch ceiling. Carter and I watched him, waiting for those fixed eyes to close, and finally he had gone to sleep. Guests milled around the food, fixing plates and opening wine and champagne. I looked at Carter and he gave me a short, quick nod and then he went inside. I went over to talk with my mother. A few seconds later I looked over and saw that Alan was gone. He won't go into the master bedroom, I thought; he hasn't been in there ever since he broke his leg. That's what my mother had told me. Maybe he was going back to his room to get some proper sleep. I wasn't worried.

And then Carter didn't come. It was five minutes, then ten, and Alan wasn't anywhere to be seen either. My mother kept talking to me about Sheri and how beautiful everything was and who knows what else and still no Carter and no Alan. Then there was Alan, making his way onto the porch with his crutches and my phone rang. It was Carter. "You have to get out of there right now," he said. "Alan has a gun. Get out of there. He knows."

I started walking away from the house, not knowing where I was going.

Carter told me he was there in the closet, kneeling down under the hanging shirts and pants, starting to work on the safe when my mother's husband came up behind him. "What the fuck are you doing?"

"What's it look like? Trying to get into the fucking safe."

"You want in the safe?"

Carter nodded and was shocked when Alan limped over and knelt down and started to open the thing. He thought about waiting till the door was open and then slugging Alan in the back of the head, but it was open before he'd even finished the thought. Alan came up with a pistol in his hand, pointing right at Carter's chest.

"Have you ever read *In Cold Blood*?" Alan said. "That's how you rob a house."

"I think they both get caught and hanged," Carter said.

"That was later. The robbery part went fine. This is not fine."

"I wasn't robbing you, Alan. I just wanted to look inside. Teri thought the will was in there." He had to drag me into it, I guess. "Take a look for yourself."

Carter said he went back and knelt down, convinced he was going to get shot like Kenyon Clutter. "What do you see in there?" Alan said.

There was nothing in the safe. Some papers, insurance stuff Carter thought, maybe a deed, he wasn't sure, but no money, no will, no valuables at all.

"I don't know why she has to tell her kids I'm rich," Alan said. "Do I look rich to you? Does this house look like we're rich? Maybe I've got it buried out in the desert. You want to go dig a hole in the desert, Carter? You want to go dig a nice big hole and take a look?"

Carter didn't want to dig a hole.

"I should make you," Alan said. "But I don't think we'll do that today. Not today. You're going to leave. You're not going to talk to anyone. You're going to go get in your car and leave and I don't ever want to see you in this house ever again. We'll tell Teri later, but right now you're going to get the hell out of here, or else you'll wish you'd dug that hole."

I went back to the casita, still talking with Carter on the phone. "Who pulls a gun on someone at a wedding?" he wanted to know. I didn't have an answer for him.

He had driven to a makeshift shack about a mile away. "You should come back and get me," I told him.

"Maybe you should just meet me here." He wasn't coming back.

So I walked. I put on my boots, grabbed a water and an apple from the refrigerator, and headed down the road. It was as if the party didn't exist. There were no more strangers drinking champagne and dancing, no sister and no mother and no Alan. There was just the road and Carter waiting. There was scrub brush off either side of the asphalt, rocks dotting the landscape, miniatures of the hills in the distance. It had been that way forever, the rocks and hills exactly in the same place they were thousands of years ago. Before that, millions of years ago, maybe, it had been a lake. I could almost see it, the way the water covered everything and touched the top of the hills in the distance. I was standing in the bottom of an ancient lake, the water hundreds of feet above me. Then it all went dry, the way it is everywhere. All over the world, they're finding dinosaur fossils and murdered corpses and Nazi boats from the lakes going dry. I would have liked to have seen a fossil or a boat, anything that looked like life. Instead, everything was dry and gnarled, burnt out. Petrified might be a better description. It all looked cast-off and forgotten, and I thought that everything should be dead, just rocks and stones, and yet there were still small green plants here and there. Things lived. Something kept them going.

It was calm and quiet, and for a few minutes I could be there completely by myself. I didn't have to worry about Alan and Carter and what we were going to do. Those things were as distant as the hills. I could keep walking, I thought. Just stay walking.

The pregnant dog came from somewhere and walked with me, trotting ahead and then turning her head back to see if I was still with her, sometimes stopping and waiting for me, then trotting ahead again. There was nothing on the road except wind-blown dirt, and nothing as far as I could see except rocks and desert scrub and a pregnant dog. I had that song in my head, or part of it, the part about letting the days go by and how the water flows underground. I thought of the road that stretched from me to Carter, and how it was like a river, how maybe there was a river flowing between us, like my sister and her newlywed husband, and maybe it was really there with me and Carter. He would do anything for me, even steal, even face down a gun. The dog stopped in the road, and I realized that I had stopped too. Now we were connected. I didn't want a dog. And I especially didn't want a pregnant dog. But there she was watching me, waiting for me.

I knelt down and poured some water into a cupped hand and

let the dog lap at it. She took almost half the bottle. I bit off some of the apple and gave it to her. She took it in her mouth and trotted away from me as if I might want to take it back. She swallowed it and came back for more. I gave her one more bite and she trotted off again. She followed me to the shack and followed me right inside. I wondered if I hadn't made a mistake. The dog took one look at Carter and turned around and hurried out of the shack.

My sister texted me. "Where are you?" I ignored it. She texted me again. I ignored it. Then my mother called. "Where did you go?" She didn't know anything.

"Carter went back to the guest house to lie down," I told her.

"Well, get back over here. They're starting the toasts. You need to be with your sister."

"Carter had a run-in with Alan," I said.

"Who hasn't?" my mother said. "I'm sure it was nothing. He's gone off to his room, anyway. There won't be trouble, just hurry back."

"It might be a while."

"Carter doesn't have to come," my mother said. "It's your sister's wedding day, for the love of Mary."

I could see the dog circling around outside, trying to look in the windows, maybe still checking on me. "Alan didn't say anything," I told Carter. "Not yet, anyway. Let's go back and get our stuff and leave."

We started for the car and I saw the dog standing in the distance, watching.

"Let's take her with us," I said.

"We can't," Carter said.

"We can't leave her here. Let's at least take her back to the guest house," I said.

"Casita," Carter said, joking.

"To hell with that," I said. We couldn't coax the dog to follow us, not even with the apple. I didn't want to leave her.

"She'll be all right," Carter said. "She knows what she's doing. She'll go where she belongs."

If Carter hadn't been there, she would have gone with me. She was leery of him, that's why she kept her distance. I stood there and tried to tell her everything would be all right. She stayed put, looking at me, but watching Carter with suspicion. "We have to go," I told her and I thought I might cry. It rose in my throat suddenly and unexpectedly and I turned my head so she wouldn't see. "You'll be all right," I told her, and we drove back to the house.

. . .

We were packing when my mother called again. The toasts were done and I'd ruined everything. "I have to go back," I told Carter. "At least to say I'm sorry, or say goodbye. I don't know. I'll be back in half an hour, an hour at most."

My sister wasn't even around. She didn't care if I was there or not. The newlyweds had "retired" for the night, my mother said. The party was breaking up, with one carload of friends already gone. The rest looked like they might be in it for the long haul, gathering up champagne and liquor around a firepit they were getting ready to light before the sun went down. "They may never leave," my mother said.

I was just about to tell her that I was going, when the pit bull came running out of the house. He had something in his mouth, and as he came off the porch, I could see that it was a vibrator. Right behind him was my sister's new husband chasing after him. They were tearing around the yard when Alan appeared in the doorway, hopping around without his crutches and waving his pistol.

"Who let that dog in the house?" he was yelling. He got to the edge of the porch and raised his gun to take aim at the pit bull when my sister came through the door and kicked Alan from behind, kicked him in his good leg, toppling him off the porch just as he fired.

The bullet went right into my thigh.

I didn't feel it at first, and for a second thought that nobody had been hit, then I saw the blood seeping a quickly expanding circle on my linen pants. And then the pain came, dull and deep, like an anvil had been dropped on my leg.

"Motherfucker," I said over and over and just stood there watching my pants soak through. Alan was on the ground writhing, holding his broken leg, which we all hoped he'd re-broken (no luck) and no one paid any attention to him. They piled me into a car and drove to the nearest hospital, almost forty minutes away.

My mother drove, which is always a bad idea. She's a terrible driver. I was in the backseat, with a belt cinched above the wound in my leg, holding it as tight as I could. My mother was driving and craning her neck around every few seconds to check on me. "Keep your eyes on the road," I said. "I'm fine, just keep your eyes on the road."

"There's never traffic on this road," she said and leaned closer to me, to get a better look at my leg, I guess.

"Just drive, Mom," I said. My leg was throbbing and I tried not to look at my blood-soaked pants. The sun started to make its way behind the hills, turning the sky orange and red. Long shadows stretched across the desert. It's just rocks and stones, I told myself, that's all there is.

We were coming up to the shack where Carter had waited and I sat up to look for the pregnant dog. She wasn't there. At least I couldn't see her. Maybe she'd gone inside, to find a place to have her pups, more helpless creatures she'd have to watch over, worry about, struggle to get them along in the world. Maybe she'd gone back where she belonged. Maybe somebody would take care of her. I tried to think the best for her. Maybe she found a place where no one would shoot her. I pulled on the belt around my leg and thought about that. I wasn't going to have kids; I wasn't getting married. I didn't even know if I should be with Carter. I could leave him behind right now, I thought. But maybe that was the bullet talking.

My mother muttered a monologue to herself in the front seat. "Him and that pistol. He thinks he can shoot anything. That's why I had it in the safe to begin with. He shouldn't be carrying that around, shooting at strays."

"Alan shot me," I said, trying to clarify things for her.

"I know," my mother said, the soothing way she used to say it when I was a child.

"He wanted to shoot a dog, but shot me instead."

"I know."

"I wish he was a better shot," I said. The thought occurred to me that Alan had wanted to shoot me all along, as payback for the botched robbery. But maybe he thought that was all Carter, freelancing without me knowing. I pushed those thoughts out into the desert dirt. My leg had a bullet in it either way.

"He would have killed that dog," my mother said.

"I'm not talking about the dog," I said. "I'm talking about me."

• • •

At the hospital, they kept asking me how it happened. They must have asked me twenty times, maybe more. The ER receptionist asked, the nurse, the tech, a different nurse, the doctor, maybe a different tech, some stranger standing in the hall with his arm dripping blood on the floor from some unseen wound. I said the same thing every time. "It was my sister's wedding celebration. It was an accident."

Sheri's husband came. Alone. My sister wouldn't come to the hospital. Not on her wedding night. She stayed at my mother's, probably pouting about the way everything happened. She blamed me, I know she did, for getting shot. There was no point explaining any of it to her, how if she hadn't kicked Alan maybe none of it would have happened, or, better yet, if she hadn't taken the dog, absolutely none of it would have happened. She wouldn't see it that way. You'd think maybe she could change for once, or at least see the trouble she caused. People don't change. So she didn't come, and there I was laid up with a hole in my thigh from where the bullet went in and where they had to go and dig it out.

Carter drove himself. No one thought about him. He was back at the guest house, waiting for me. I texted him on the way to the hospital. My mother's driving, I wrote him; you might have to pull us out of a ditch. Then I called him. Carter wasn't the only man left behind. We'd forgotten Alan too. That was a quiet ride. "He didn't say a word the whole way," Carter said, "and I didn't either."

That's probably for the best. Of course, Alan was fine, or no worse off than he was before Sheri kicked him off the porch. Meanwhile, I still had a bullet in my leg.

. . .

After I was released from the hospital, we went back to the casita and I went and laid down while Carter finished packing the car. I felt weighed down, as if every part of me had been filled with stones and I was waiting for the water to come and fill up the desert, come rushing into the small house and fill up the bedroom and drown me. I waited for it to happen, but it never did. Instead, my mother called. She said that Alan wanted to see us before we left.

Alan was laying on his bed when we came in, and he struggled to get himself propped up enough to look at us. He reached under a pillow and pulled out a small manila envelope. He opened it and Carter and I could see the stack of bills inside. He quickly counted through a number of them, stopped, reconsidered, and counted through some more before deciding he had enough. It was probably half the stack. He handed the money to Carter, not to me, and said, "That should cover it." It was ten thousand dollars. He closed the envelope and started to put it back in the inside pocket of his jacket, then took it back out and showed it to Carter. "I don't trust safes," he said, and then put it away. He looked at Carter and said, "That all right with you?" Carter didn't say anything. Then Alan looked at me. "We're alike, you and me," he said.

"Different leg," I told him.

"Not like that," Alan said. "The same trouble follows both of us. That's how we're alike. Same family, same trouble. We can't avoid it. Trouble finds us. You know what I'm talking about."

"Sure," I said. I wasn't going to argue with him. All I wanted to do was leave.

We left.

• • •

My sister likes to tell people how I ruined her wedding, that I couldn't be bothered to wear something nice, that I didn't even toast her. She never mentions that she explicitly told me not to "dress up." She never mentions that she never told me there would be a toast and all that shit—how she expressly told me that it was not going to be a "traditional wedding" just a "quick ceremony and a celebration." In her version of the day, I never took a bullet to the leg.

"Alan tried to shoot my dog," she tells me, as if I wasn't there.

They gave him up for adoption, by the way. "We couldn't handle him," she told me. "He was like a tornado in the house, tearing up everything. He would have torn the house down if we'd kept him. We called him 'Twister.' He was a bad dog."

In Sheri's version of the story, I barely get a mention. It's fine, I suppose. It wasn't my wedding. I was hoping we'd have a new start, maybe, but Sheri's the same as she ever was. Why should I expect her to change? We talk like it never happened, things buried and better left there. There are rocks in the desert that haven't moved in millennia; there are people with guns and money who don't know how to use either one; there are dogs that wander around and take your heart and will ruin everything if you let them. There's trouble that arrives out of nowhere and plans that all turn to shit. But there's water too. Things survive, shriveled and neglected things endure long after you've given up hope. I think about the ocean between us and the blood that connects us. We are all bound to each other, whether we like it or not.

I told Sheri about Alan and his envelope of cash (which I underreported to her by about half). "You think Mom was right about him?" Sheri said.

"Maybe," I said. "He did have an awful lot of cash, and sort of implied that he had more."

"We should totally rob him," my sister said.

"That's a great idea," I said. "We should definitely do that."

ABOUT THE AUTHORS

James D.F. Hannah is the Shamus Award-winning author of the Henry Malone series, including the novels *Behind the Wall of Sleep* and *Because the Night*. His short fiction has appeared in *Best American Mystery and Suspense*; *Playing Games*, edited by Lawrence Block; *Under the Thumb: Stories of Police Oppression*, edited by S.A. Cosby; *Ellery Queen Mystery Magazine*; *Vautrin*; *Rock and a Hard Place*; *Shotgun Honey*; and *The Anthology of Appalachian Writers*. He lives in Louisville, Kentucky, where all the bourbon is. He's on all the socials at @jamesdfhannah and online at www.jamesdfhannah.com.

Libby Cudmore is the author of *Negative Girl* (Datura 2024) and *The Big Rewind* (William Morrow 2016) as well as the Martin Wade PI series in *Tough*, *Alfred Hitchcock Mystery Magazine* and *Ellery Queen Mystery Magazine*. Her work has also been published in Shotgun Honey, *Reckon Review*, *Smokelong Quarterly*, *Had*, *The Dark*, *MonkeyBicycle* and others. She is a four-year alumna of the Barrelhouse Writer Camp, the recipient of the 2023 Black Orchid Novella Award and Shamus Award, as well as the 2018 Oregon Writer's Colony prize.

Michel Lee Garrett is a crime fiction author, recovering journalist, and the editor of *Burning Down The House*. She has investigated courthouse corruption as a small-town reporter, directed communications for a U.S. Senate campaign, and played in a handful of shitty punk bands. A queer and transgender author, her work seeks to examine how inequitable systems manufacture injustice, and how the human condition is ultimately one of rebellion against an absurd world. Her fiction has appeared from Flame Tree Press, Down & Out Books, Mystery Tribune, Cowboy Jamboree, and others. She lives in Central Pennsylvania

with her wife and two children. Find her online at LeeGarrett.
net or on Twitter @MichelMGarrett.

When he's not playing on his own magic electric guitar, **Lucas Franki** is a science writer/editor who lives in Frederick, Maryland. He holds a bachelor of arts in English from Penn State University. He is also an Eagle Scout. He has had two short stories published: "Just Before the Fall," which appeared in the Fall 2018 issue of *The Helix*, and "Eldritch Abominations in Modern-Day America: A Documentary," which appeared in the anthology *LOLcraft: A Compendium of Eldritch Humor*, published by Dragon's Roost Press in November 2022.

Bobby Mathews is a writer and journalist in Birmingham, Alabama. He is the author of two novels, *LIVING THE GIMMICK* and *MAGIC CITY BLUES*, and his short fiction has been nominated for the Pushcart Prize. He was a finalist for the 2021 Derringer Award for flash fiction. When he's not writing, Bobby spends his time with his wife and sons, as well as a menagerie of animals both large and small.

The winner of both a Bram Stoker and World Fantasy Award, **P.D. Cacek** has written over a hundred short stories, seven plays, and six published novels, including *Second Lives and Secod Chances* from Flame Tree Press. Her new Flame Tree novel, *Sebastion*, was released in October 2022. Cacek holds a bachelor's degree in English/Creative Writing Option from the University of California at Long Beach and has been a guest lecturer at the Odyssey Writing Camp. Cacek lives Phoenixville, PA. When not writing, she can often been found either with a group of costumed storytellers called THE PATIENT CREATURES (www. creatureseast.com), or haunting local cemeteries looking for inspiration.

Jessica Laine (she/her) writes crime fiction with a Latine twist. She is a past recipient of the Sisters in Crime Eleanor Taylor

Bland award and was programming co-chair for Bouchercon 2022. A proud member of the Crime Writers of Color, Jessica tweets @msjessicalaine.

Rob Pierce wrote the novella *Snake Slayer*; the novels *Blood By Choice*, *Tommy Shakes*, *Uncle Dust*, and *With The Right Enemies*; the novella *Vern In The Heat*; and the short story collection *The Things I Love Will Kill Me Yet*. All books are available at downandoutbooks.com, as well as via the usual slumlords. He lives in Santa Cruz, CA, with his corgi Misha and a tall bottle of ennui.

Kimberly Godwin is a freelance comic, horror, and tabletop roleplay game writer serving in the U.S. Armed Forces. A consummate dabbler, she's voice acted, recorded actual plays, done graphic design, and written across multiple genres, favoring horror and procedural detective stories. Kim possesses a bachelor of science in criminal justice – forensic science and a master of geographic information systems with a geospatial intelligence analytics focus. She is completing a master of strategic intelligence thesis on deradicalization and counter-insurgency policies. Kim's other projects include: "They Came From [Classified]!," "Trinity Continuum: Aether," "They Came From the Cyclops's Cave!," "Mage the Ascension 20th Anniversary Edition: Forgotten Ones and Forbidden Orders," "Touching the Abyss," "the Lavenders," and "Surrender: A Starship Moonhawk Story." Kim is a member of the Horror Writers Association and Sisters in Crime.

J. B. Stevens lives in the Southeastern United States with his wife and daughter. His short story collection *A Therapeutic Death* is available from Shotgun Honey Books. His pop poetry collection *The Best of America Cannot Be Seen* is available from Alien Buddha Press. He was a finalist for the Claymore Award, a finalist for the Terry Kay Prize, and won Mystery Tribune's inaugural micro-fiction contest. His war poetry and fiction were, separately, finalists for the Colonel Darron L. Wright Award. His comedy poetry was nominated for the Pushcart Prize. Before his writing career, J.B. was a United States Army Infantry Officer, serving in Iraq and earning a Bronze Star. He is also an undefeated Mixed Martial Arts Fighter and a Black Belt in Brazilian Jiujitsu. He graduated from The Citadel. For more info go to JB-Stevens.com.

T. Fox Dunham is a cancer survivor, disabled writer, and modern bard. He is the co-editor of *Burning Down The House* and the author of the novels *Mercy*, *The Street Martyr* and *Destroying the Tangible Illusion of Reality*. His credits include over 100 short stories, including an official story in the Stargate canon. He lives in Lancaster, PA, where he bakes, fishes, gardens, works with herbs, and studies history. His motto is "wrecking civilization, one story at a time."

Gregory Galloway's *Just Thieves* (2021) was named "one of the best noir novels of the year" by CrimeReads. He is the author of two other novels—including the Alex-Award winning *As Simple As Snow* — and a short story collection. He's been a fan of the Talking Heads since hearing "Psycho Killer" on the radio and had the amazing opportunity to hang around David Byrne for an afternoon during the making of the video for "Angels." Gregory lives with his wife and dogs far from the Mojave Desert. He is no longer invited to weddings.

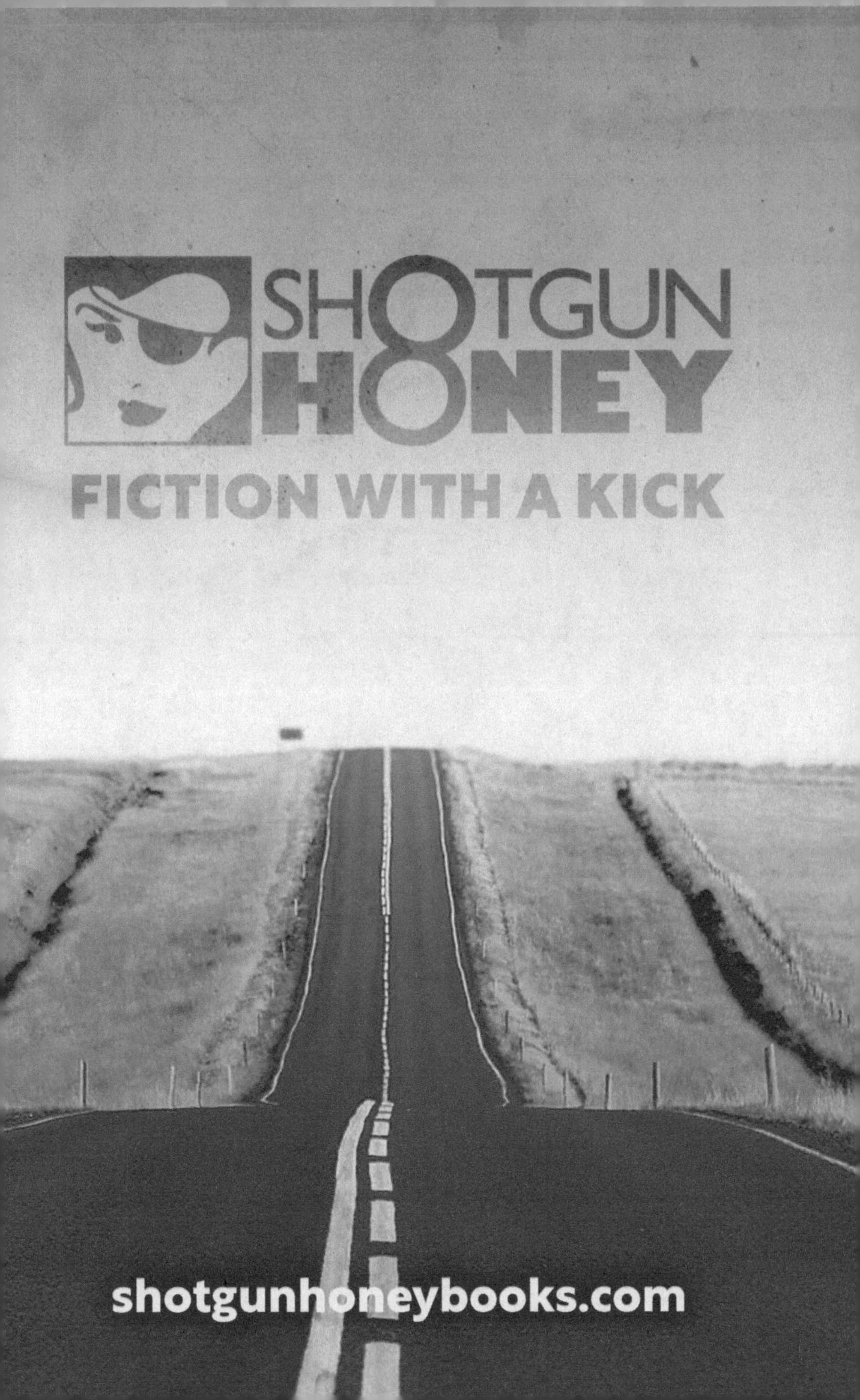

SHOTGUN HONEY
FICTION WITH A KICK